Dear Mouse Friends,
Welcome to the world of

Geronimo
Stilton

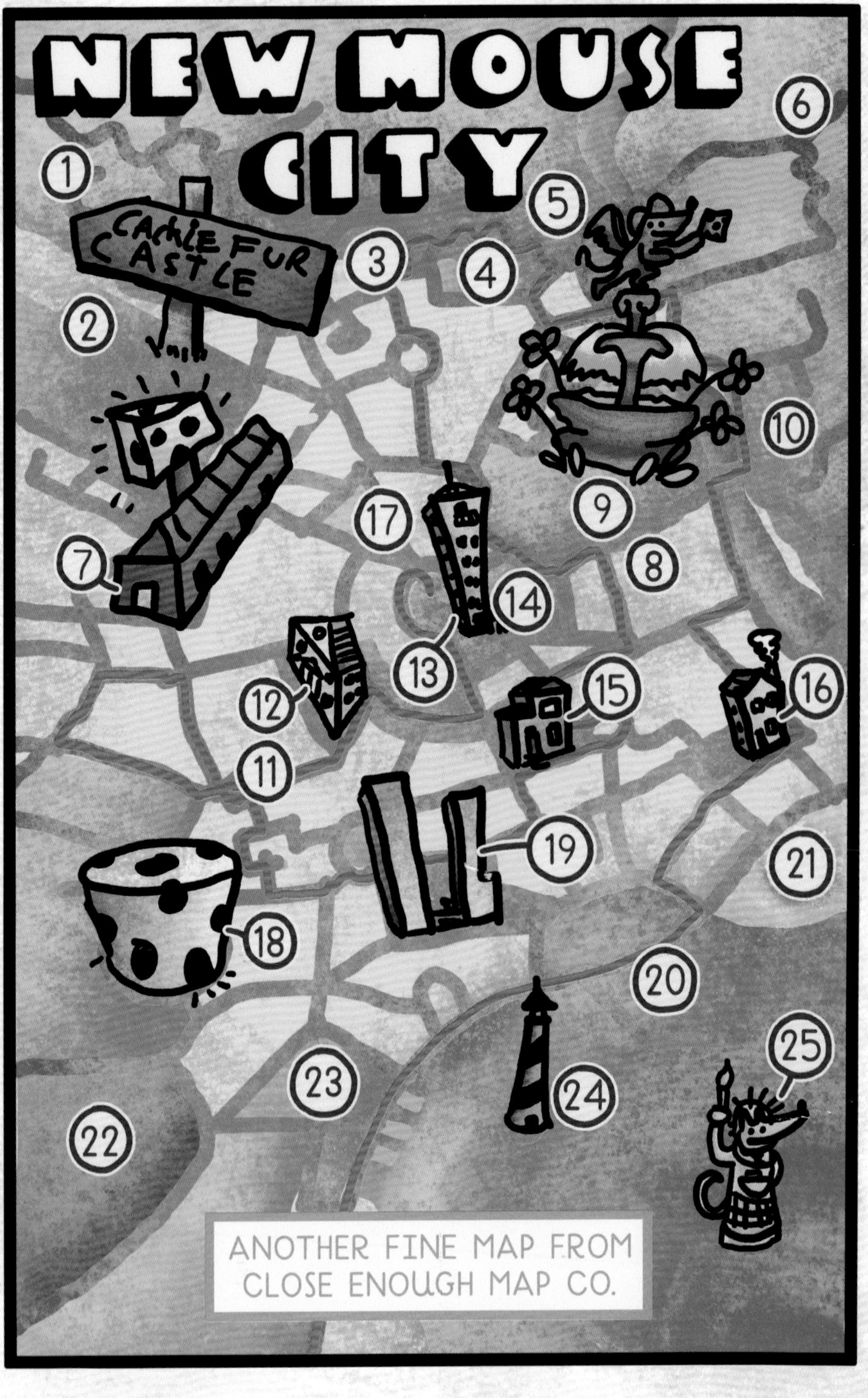
NEW MOUSE CITY
CATTLEFUR CASTLE
1
2
3
4
5
6
7
8
9
10
11
12
13
14
15
16
17
18
19
20
21
22
23
24
25
ANOTHER FINE MAP FROM CLOSE ENOUGH MAP CO.

1. Cheese Factories
2. Angorat International Airport
3. Comic Book Store
4. Mouse General Hospital
5. WRAT Radio & Television Station
6. Snotnose Castle
7. Cheese Market
8. Grand Hotel
9. Botanical Gardens
10. Petunia Pretty Paws's House
11. *The Daily Rat*
12. *The Rodent's Gazette*
13. Thea's House
14. Cheap Junk for Less
15. Geronimo's House
16. Benjamin's House
17. Public Library
18. Mousidon Square Garden
19. Hercule Poirat's Office
20. New Mouse Harbor
21. Beach
22. Curlyfur Island Amousement Park
23. Shipyard
24. Luna Light House
25. The Statue of Liberty

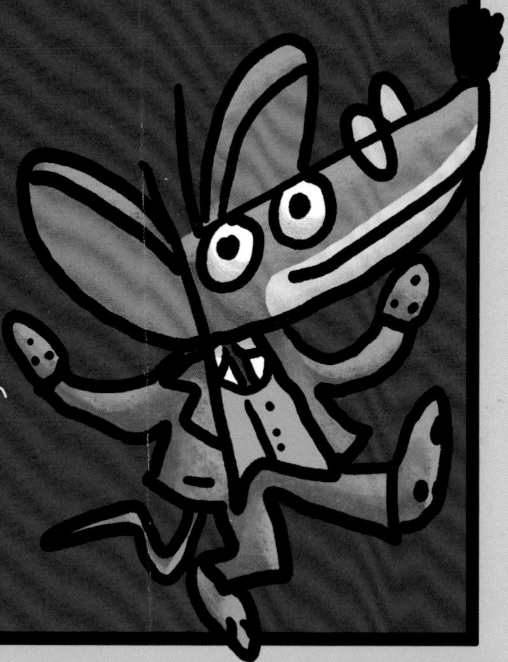

Geronimo Stilton

THE GRAPHIC NOVEL

THE GREAT RAT RALLY

with **Tom Angleberger**   story by **Elisabetta Dami**

color by **Corey Barba**

graphix

An Imprint of

SCHOLASTIC

Published by Scholastic Inc., *Publishers since 1920,* 557 Broadway, New York, NY 10012. SCHOLASTIC and associated logos are trademarks and/or registered trademarks of Scholastic Inc.

"National Anthem of the Sewers" adapted and composed by Oscar Angleberger

ISBN 978-1-338-72938-2

Text by Geronimo Stilton
Story by Elisabetta Dami
Original title *Metti Il Turbo, Stilton!*
Cover and Illustrations by Tom Angleberger
Edited by Abigail McAden and Tiffany Colón
Translated by Emily Clement
Color by Corey Barba
Lettering by Kristin Kemper
Book design by Phil Falco and Shivana Sookdeo
Creative Director: Phil Falco
Publisher: David Saylor

10 9 8 7 6 5 4 3 2 1 21 22 23 24 25

Printed in China 127
First edition, November 2021

TABLE OF

CONTENTS

CHAPTER ONE
Gorgonzola DONUTS

Ah! What a BEAUTIFUL day for my VACATION!

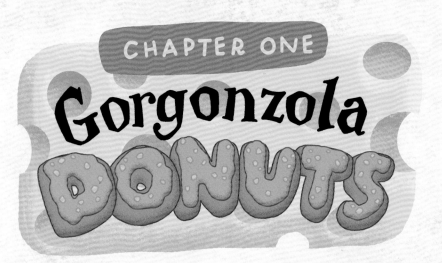

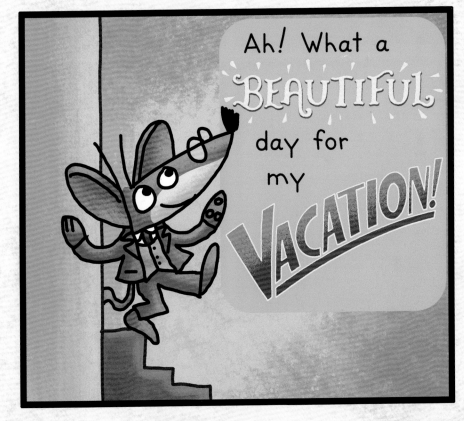

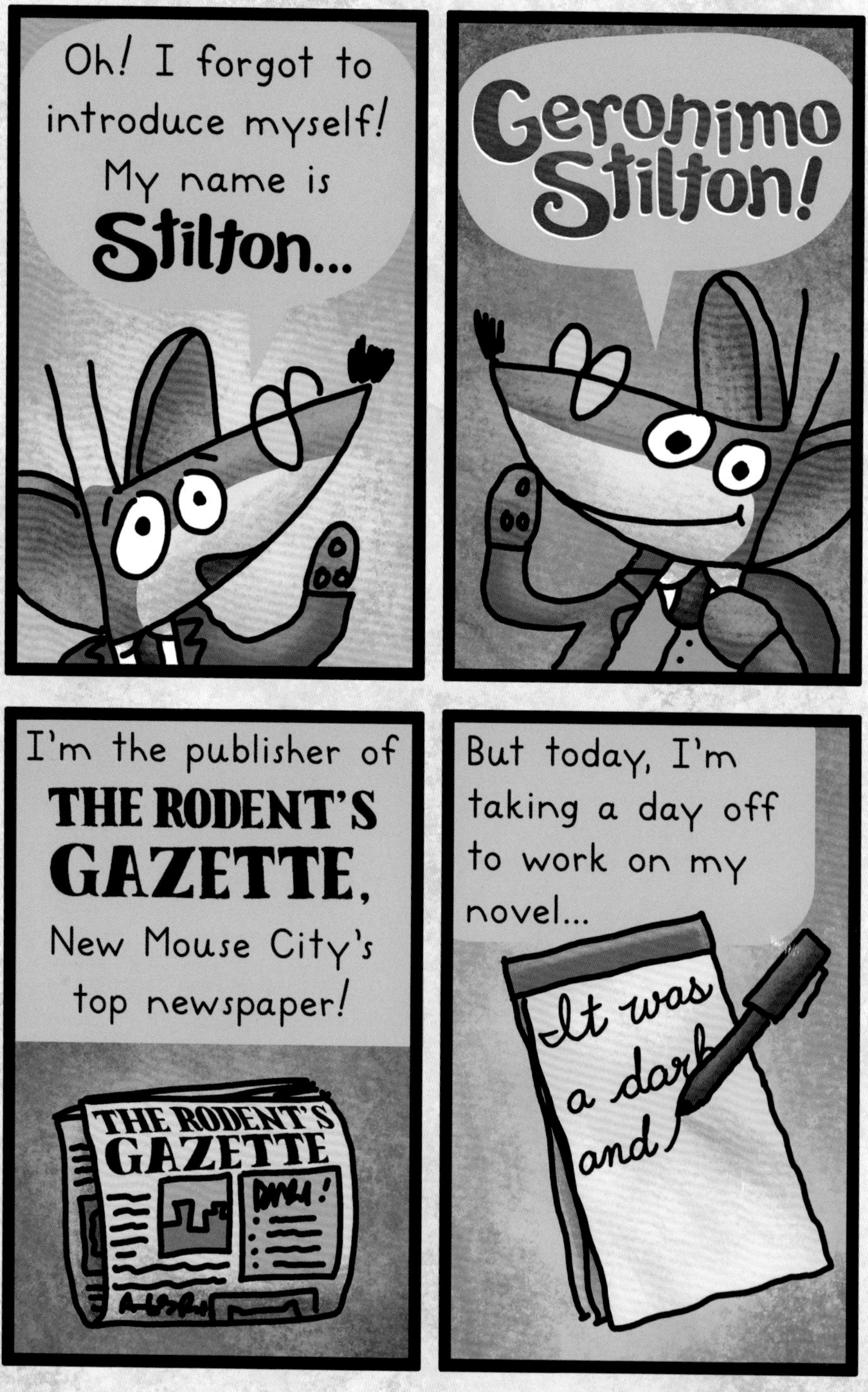
Oh! I forgot to introduce myself! My name is Stilton...
Geronimo Stilton!
I'm the publisher of THE RODENT'S GAZETTE, New Mouse City's top newspaper!
THE RODENT'S GAZETTE
But today, I'm taking a day off to work on my novel...
It was a dark and

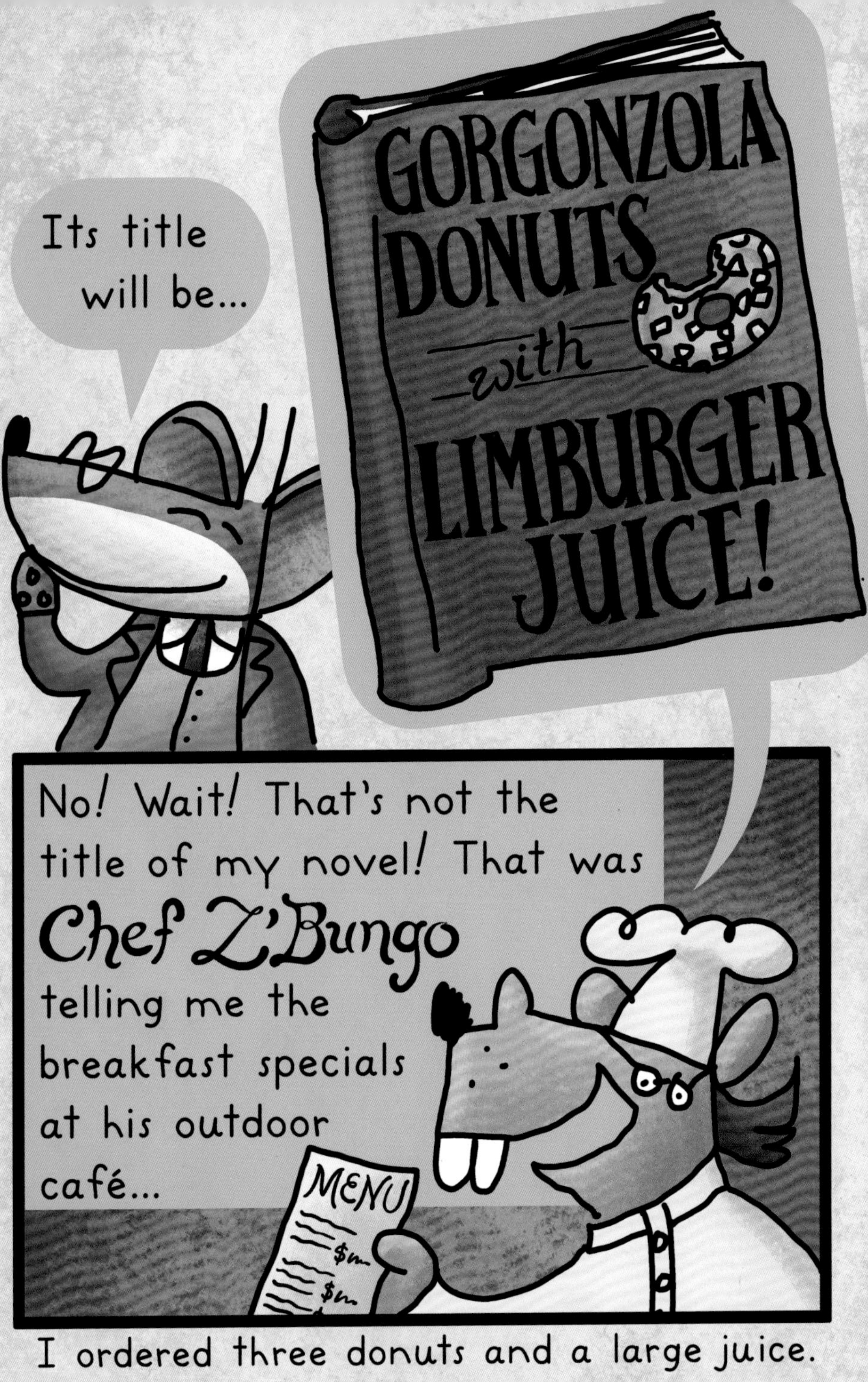
Its title will be...
GORGONZOLA DONUTS with LIMBURGER JUICE!
No! Wait! That's not the title of my novel! That was Chef Z'Bungo telling me the breakfast specials at his outdoor café...
MENU

I ordered three donuts and a large juice.

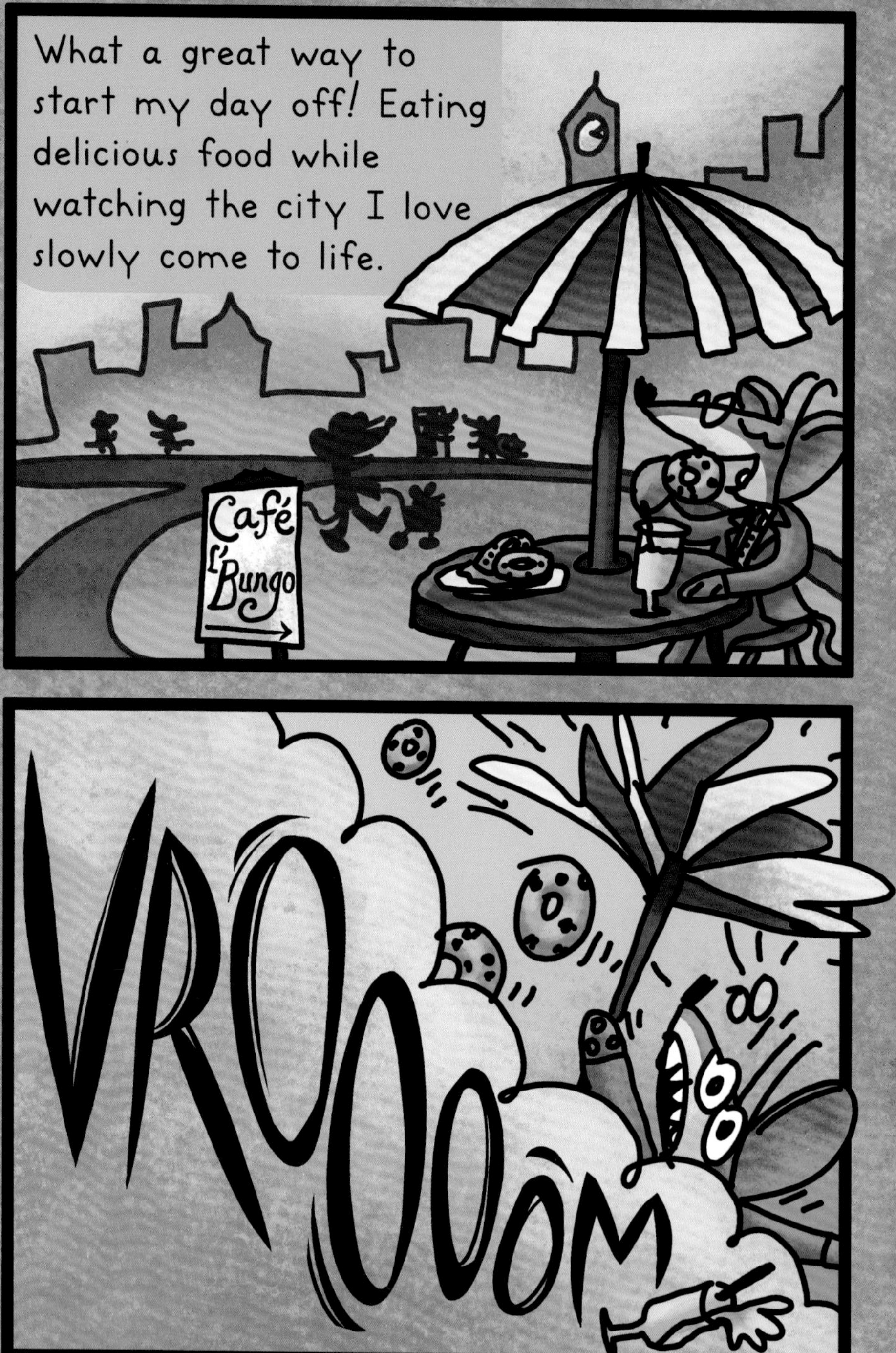
What a great way to start my day off! Eating delicious food while watching the city I love slowly come to life.
Café L'Bungo
VROOOOOM

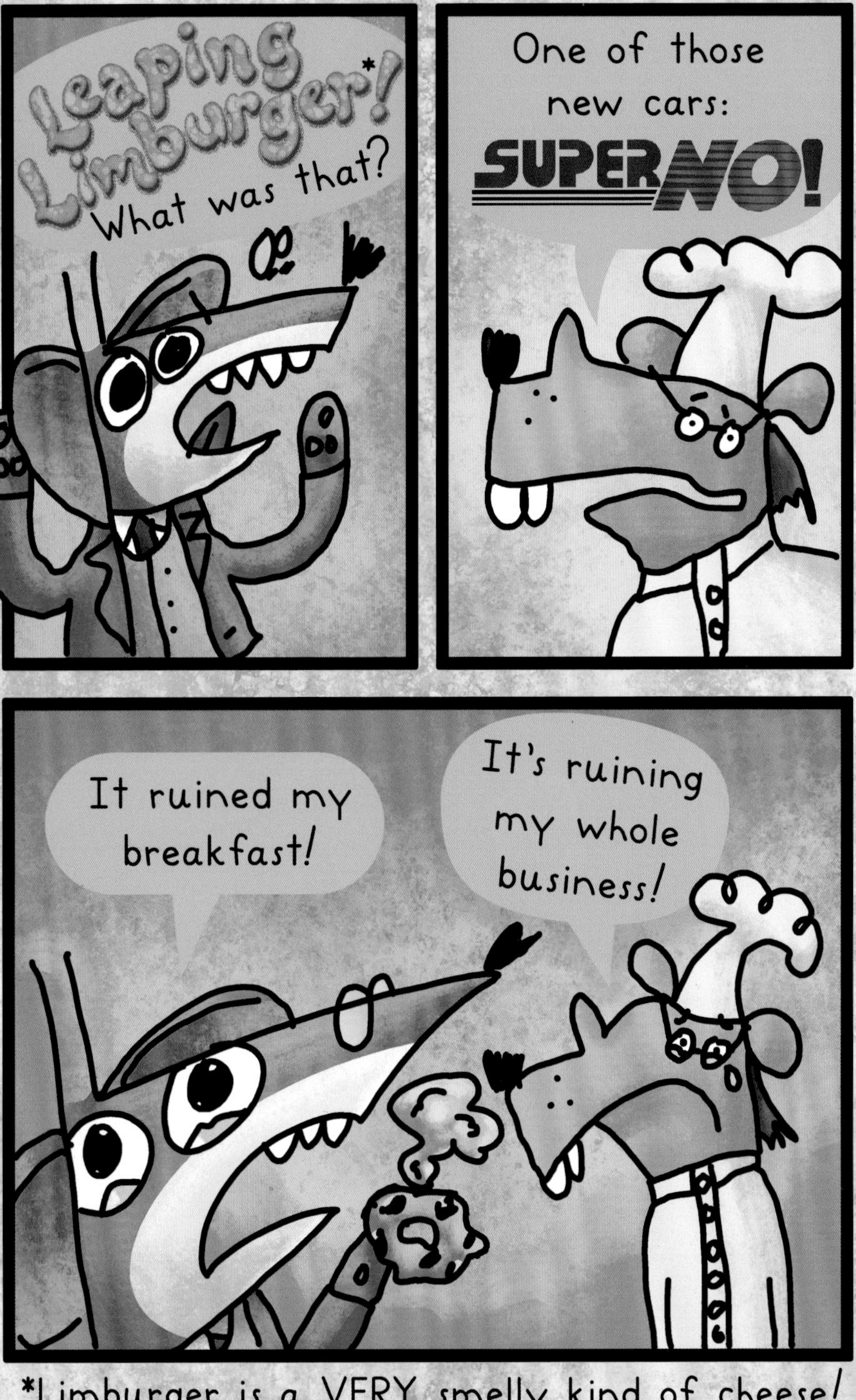
Leaping Limburger*! What was that?
One of those new cars: SUPERNO!
It ruined my breakfast!
It's ruining my whole business!

*Limburger is a VERY smelly kind of cheese!

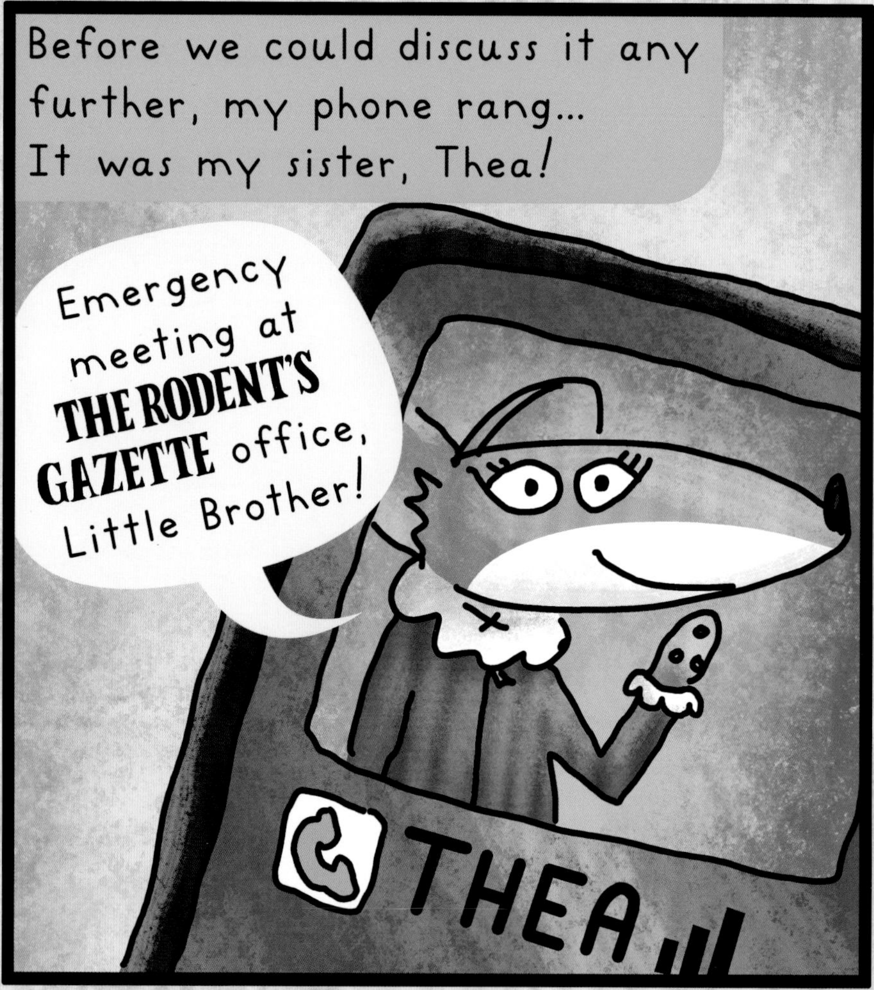
Before we could discuss it any further, my phone rang...
It was my sister, Thea!
Emergency meeting at THE RODENT'S GAZETTE office, Little Brother!
THEA

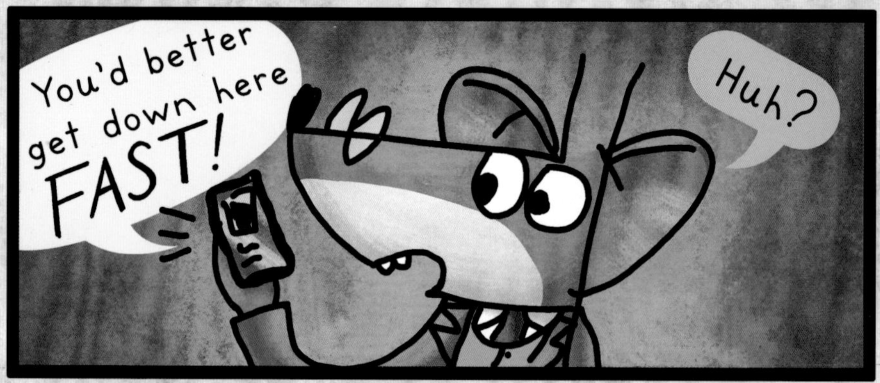
You'd better get down here FAST!
Huh?

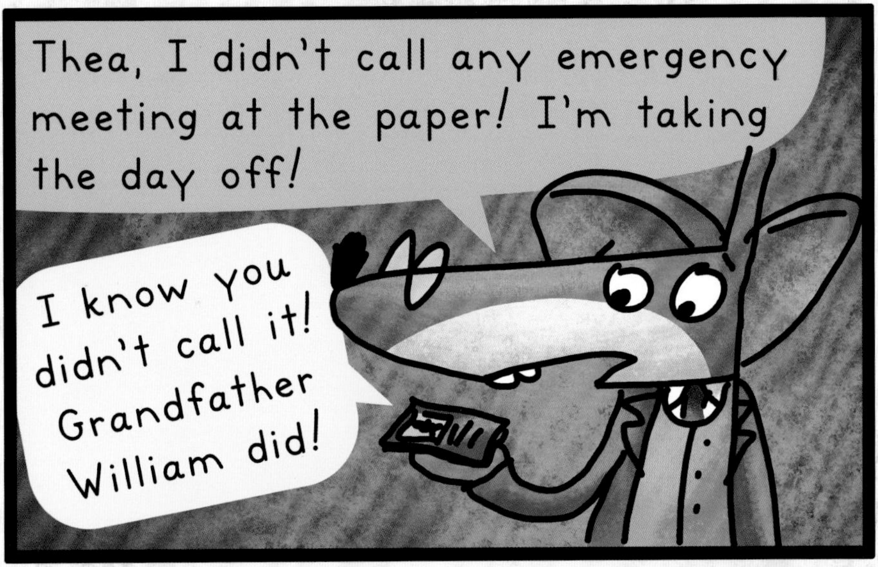
Thea, I didn't call any emergency meeting at the paper! I'm taking the day off!
I know you didn't call it! Grandfather William did!

Grandfather William is the owner of *The Rodent's Gazette!* We don't call him "Grandpa," but sometimes we call him "SIR"! The only thing he hates more than someone taking a day off is someone being late to a meeting!

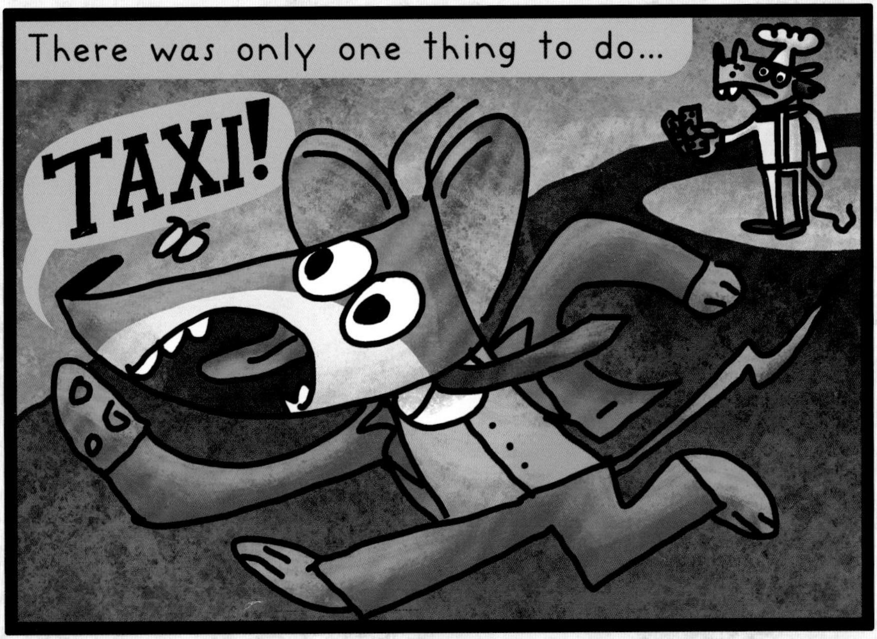
There was only one thing to do...
TAXI!

CHAPTER TWO

SUPER NO!

I found an empty taxi and jumped in.

QUICK!

To the office of *The Rodent's Gazette*, New Mouse City's top newspaper!

I thought **The Daily Rodent** was New Mouse City's top paper.

JUST GO!!!

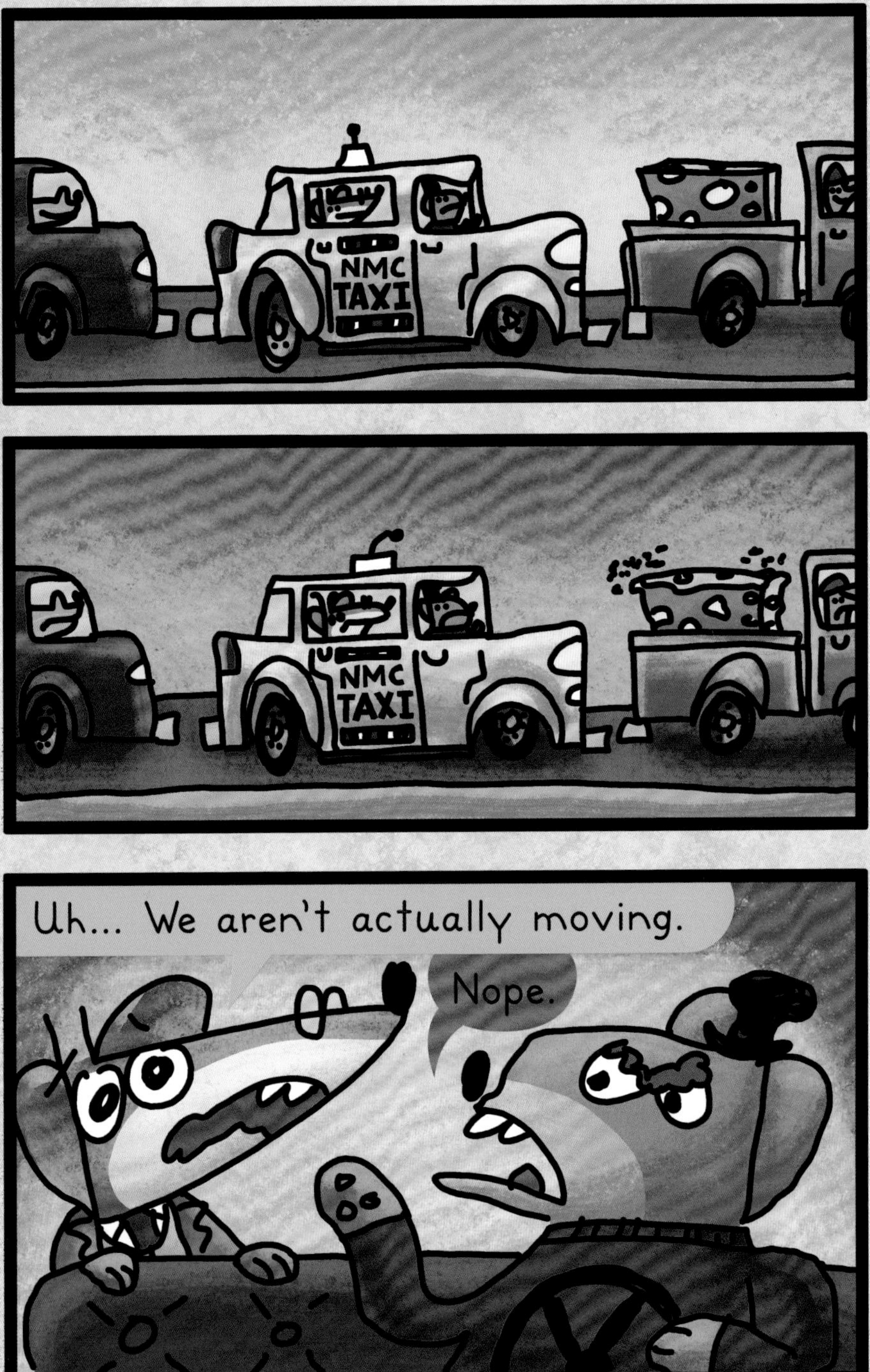
NMC
TAXI
NMC
TAXI
Uh... We aren't actually moving.
Nope.

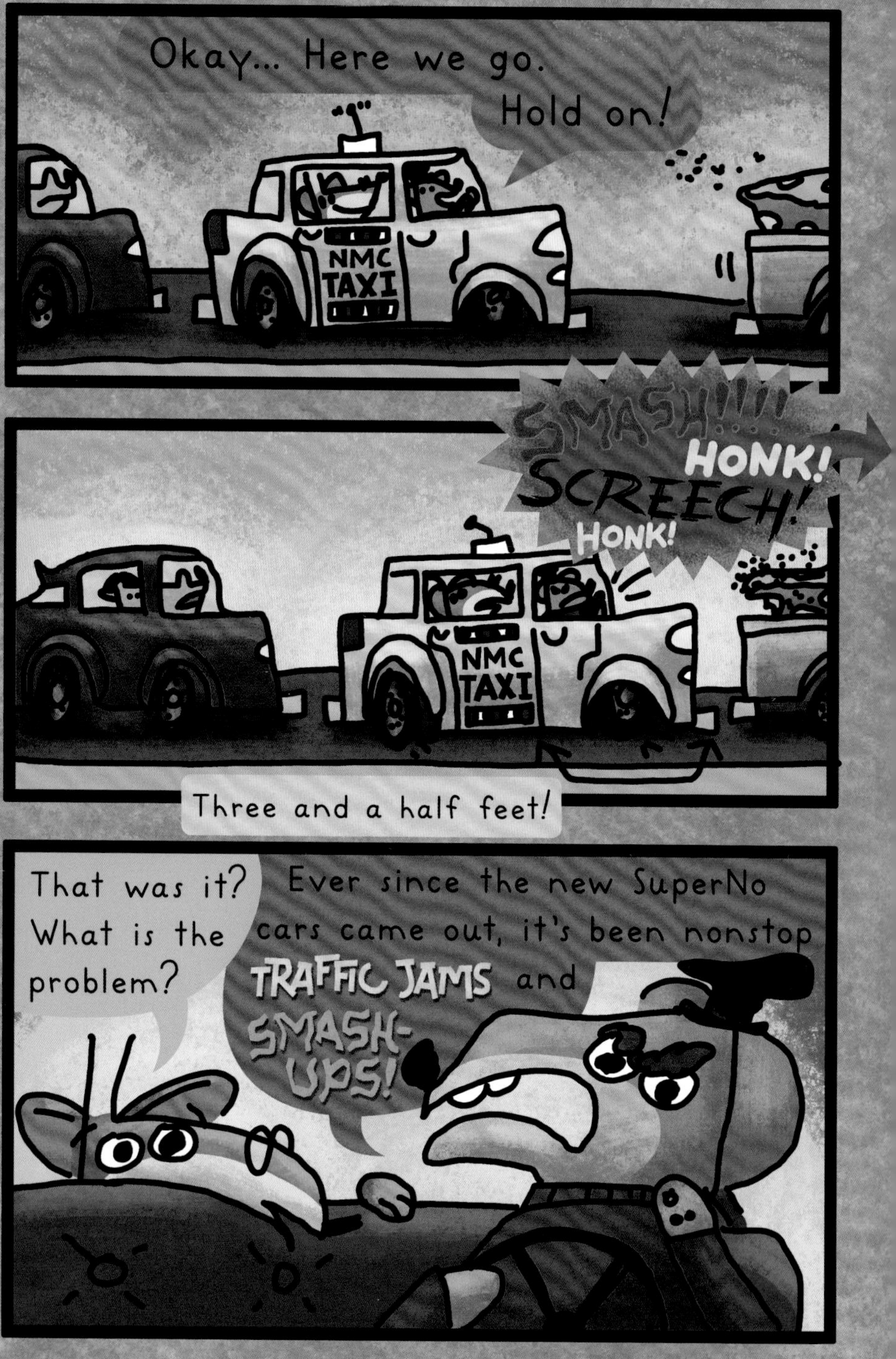

Okay... Here we go. Hold on!
SMASH!!!!
HONK!
SCREECH!
HONK!
Three and a half feet!
That was it? What is the problem?
Ever since the new SuperNo cars came out, it's been nonstop TRAFFIC JAMS and SMASH-UPS!

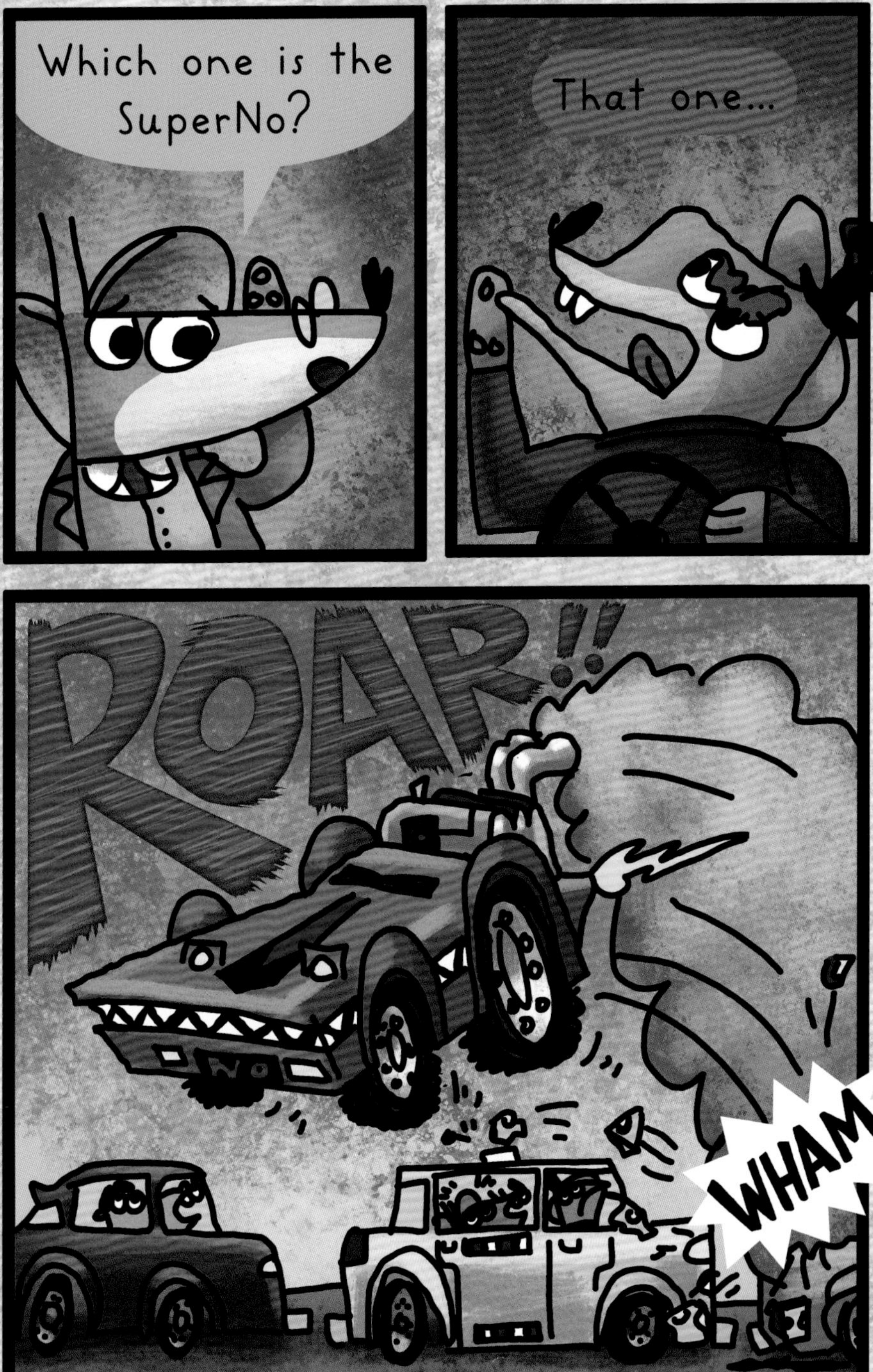
Which one is the SuperNo?
That one...
ROAR!!
WHAM

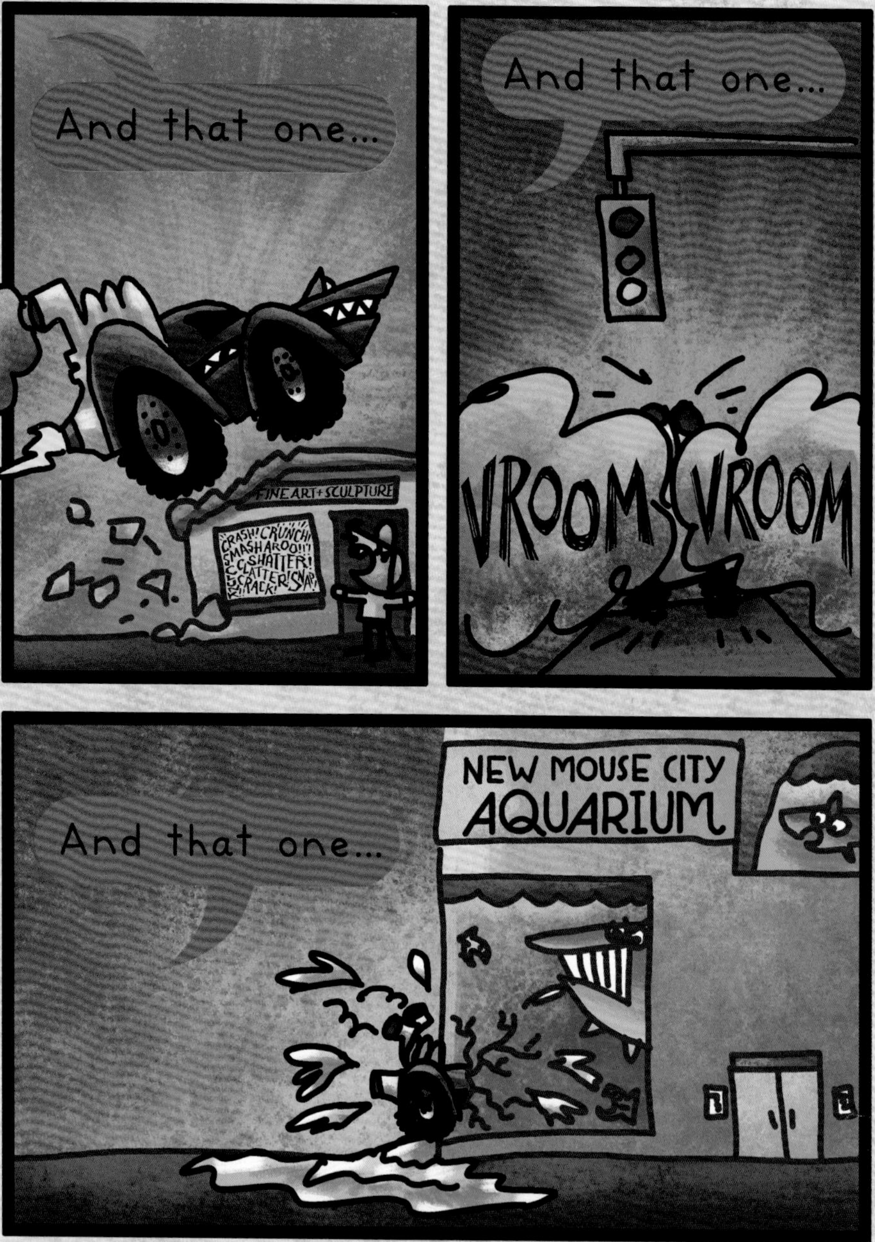
And that one...
FINE ART + SCULPTURE
CRASH! CRUNCH! SMASHAROO!!! SHATTER! CLATTER! CRACK! SNAP!
And that one...
VROOM VROOM
And that one...
NEW MOUSE CITY AQUARIUM

I was already sick of the SUPERNO cars! There were LOUD! They were DANGEROUS! And they were making me even later for the meeting I was late for!

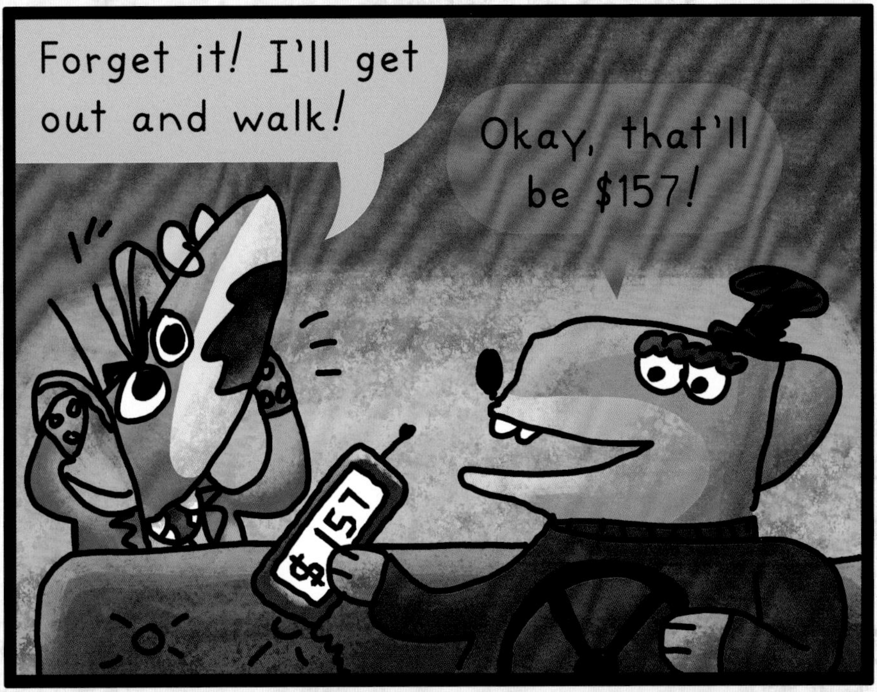
Forget it! I'll get out and walk!
Okay, that'll be $157!
$157

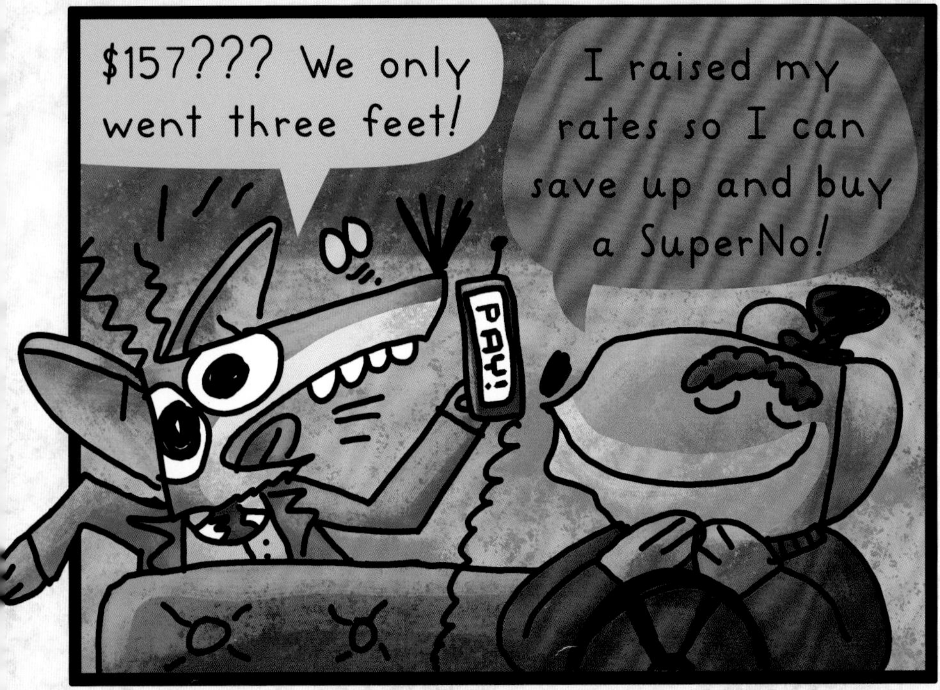
$157??? We only went three feet!
I raised my rates so I can save up and buy a SuperNo!
PAY!

CHAPTER THREE

SUPERNO, SUPERNO, AND MORE SUPERNO!

I ran the rest of the way to the office, rushed through the door, and finally got some good news...

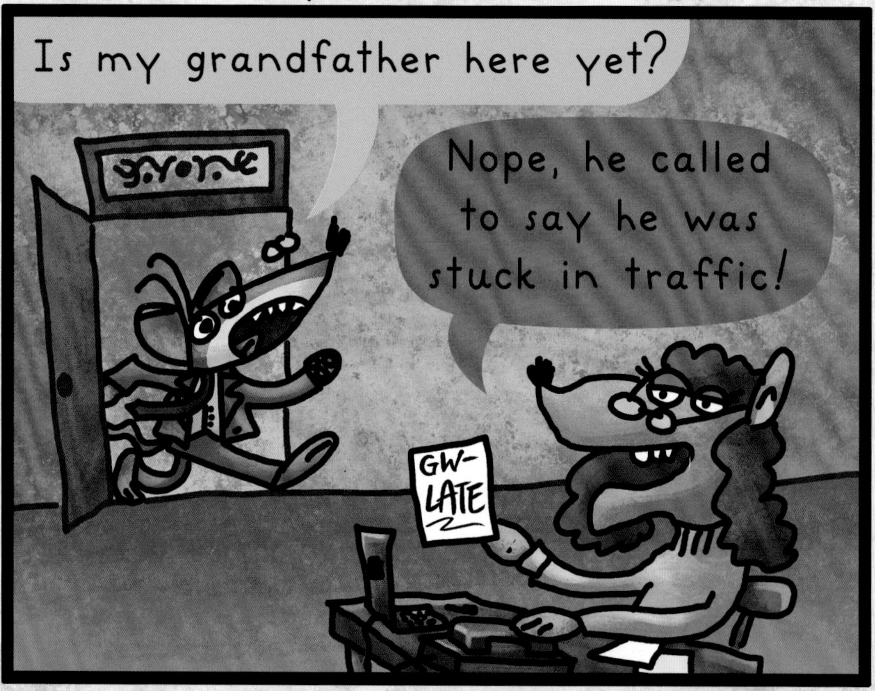
Is my grandfather here yet?
Nope, he called to say he was stuck in traffic!
GW-LATE

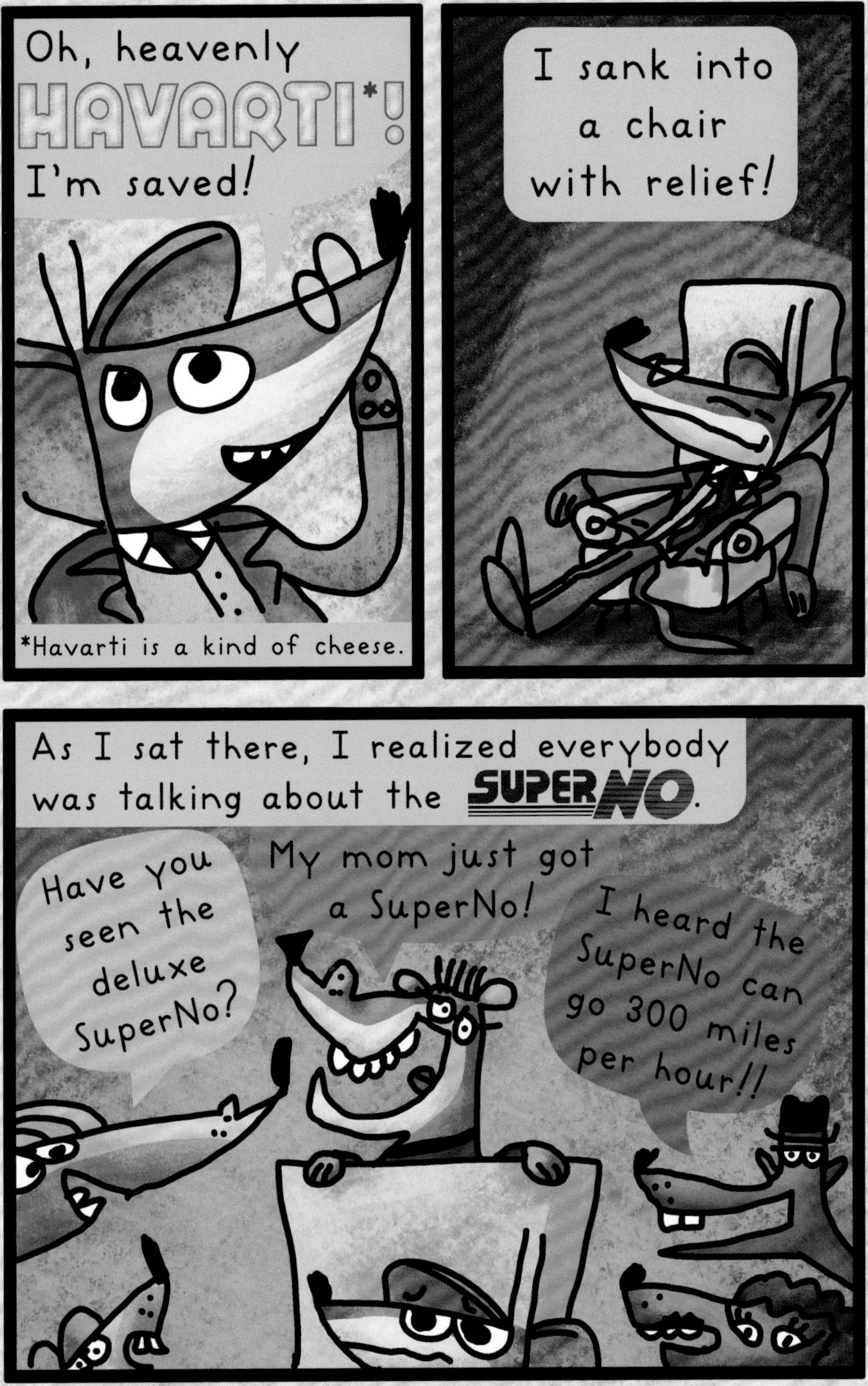
Oh, heavenly HAVARTI*! I'm saved!
*Havarti is a kind of cheese.
I sank into a chair with relief!
As I sat there, I realized everybody was talking about the SUPER NO.
Have you seen the deluxe SuperNo?
My mom just got a SuperNo!
I heard the SuperNo can go 300 miles per hour!!

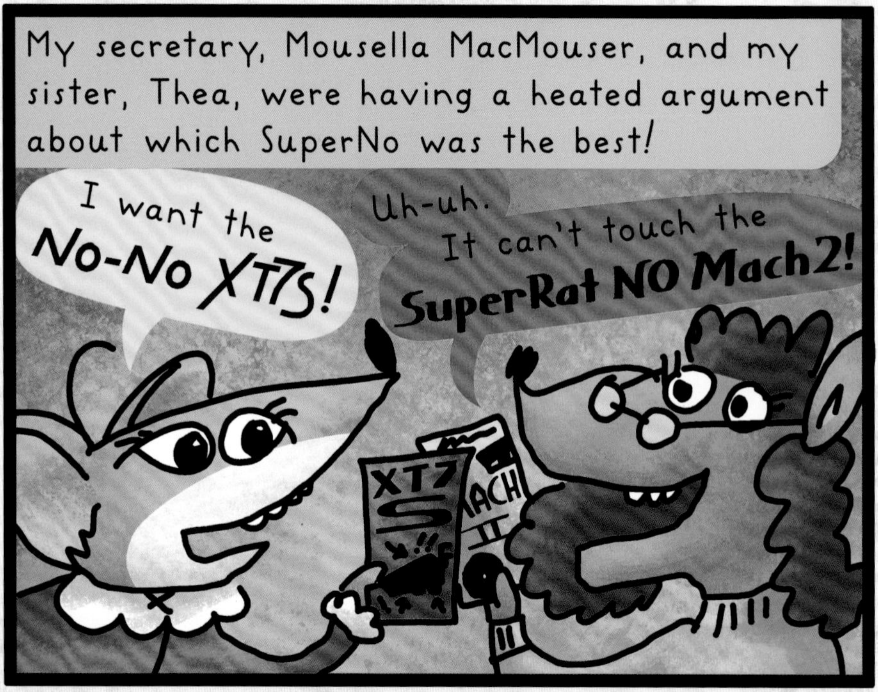
My secretary, Mousella MacMouser, and my sister, Thea, were having a heated argument about which SuperNo was the best!
I want the No-No XT7S!
Uh-uh. It can't touch the SuperRat NO Mach2!
XT7 S
MACH II

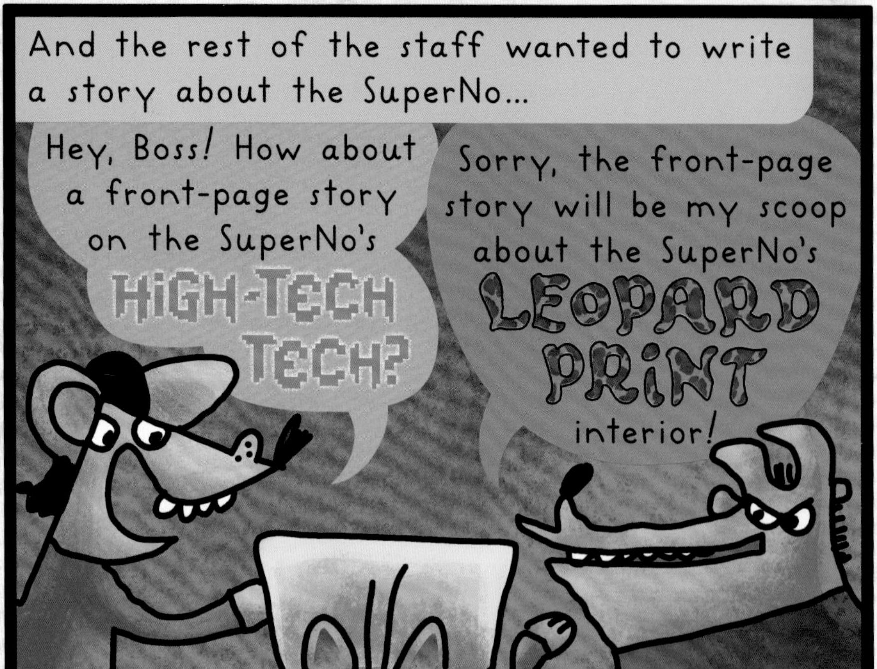
And the rest of the staff wanted to write a story about the SuperNo...
Hey, Boss! How about a front-page story on the SuperNo's HIGH-TECH TECH?
Sorry, the front-page story will be my scoop about the SuperNo's LEOPARD PRINT interior!

Even my assistant, Pinky Pick, was fired up about the SUPER NO!

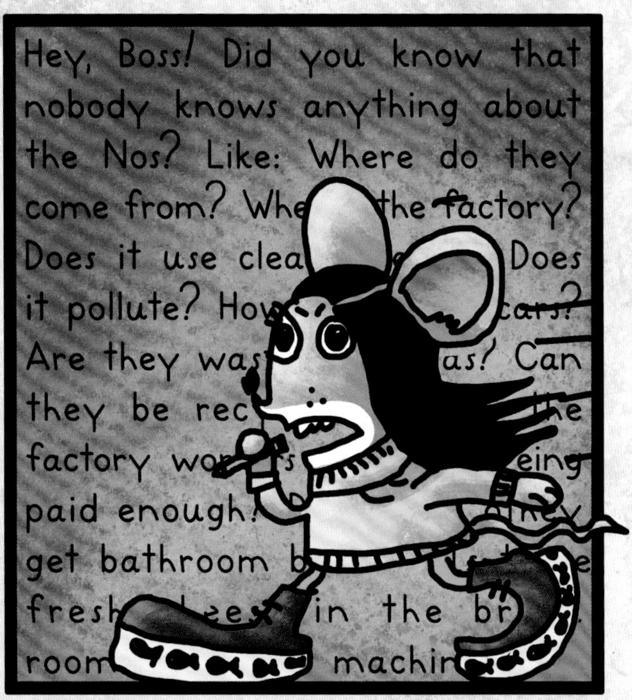

Hey, Boss! Did you know that nobody knows anything about the Nos? Like: Where do they come from? Whe the factory? Does it use clea Does it pollute? How cars? Are they was as? Can they be rec factory wo eing paid enough? get bathroom b fresh in the br room machin

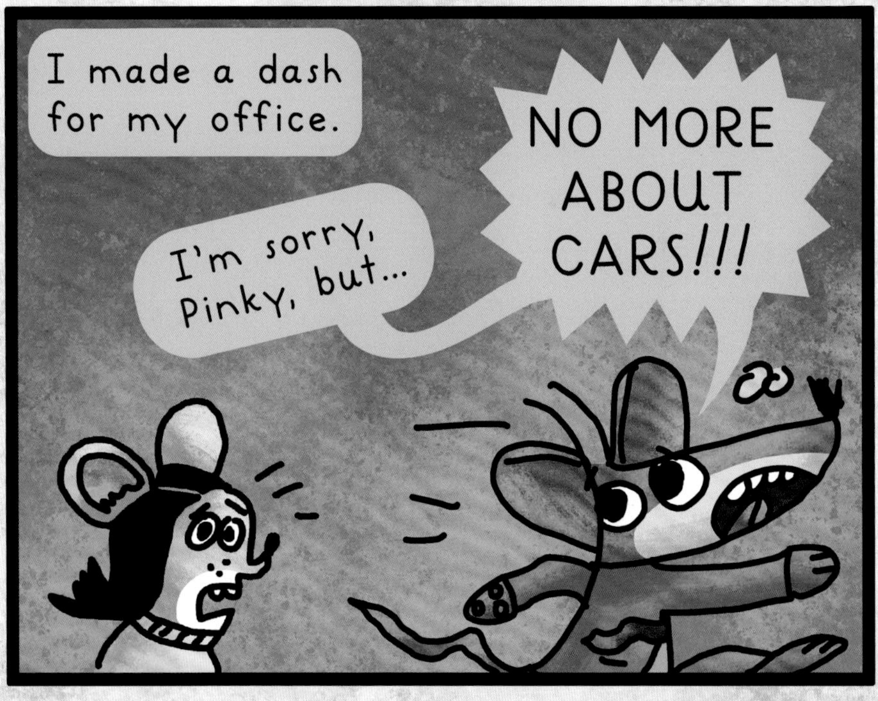

I made a dash for my office.
NO MORE ABOUT CARS!!!
I'm sorry, Pinky, but...

CHAPTER FOUR

MORE ABOUT CARS!

My cousin Trap was already in my office, with his feet on my desk, eating my cheese and picking his teeth with my Pawlitzer Prize reporting award!

Hey, Cuz! Let's talk about cars!

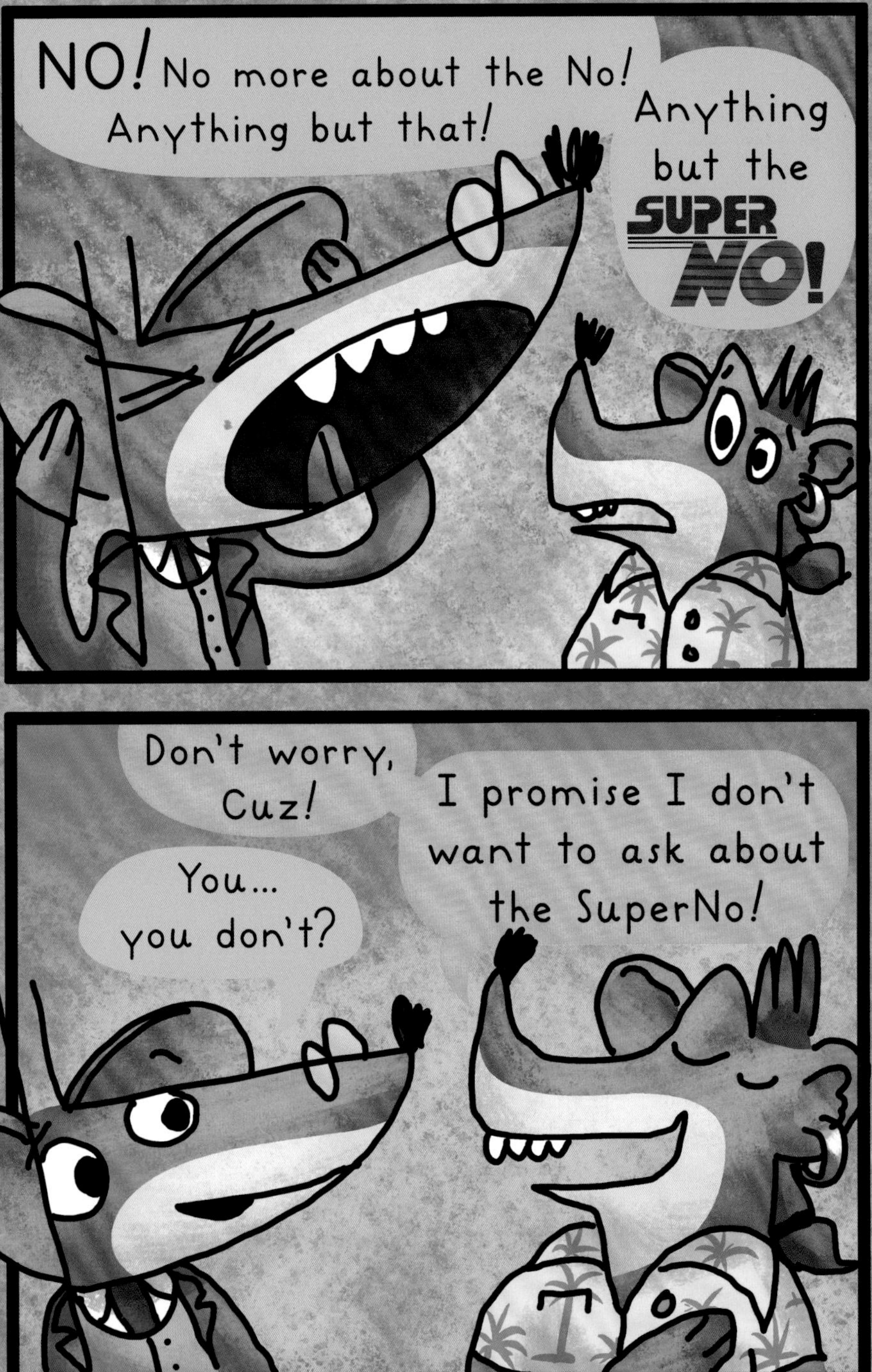
NO! No more about the No! Anything but that!
Anything but the SUPER NO!
Don't worry, Cuz!
I promise I don't want to ask about the SuperNo!
You... you don't?

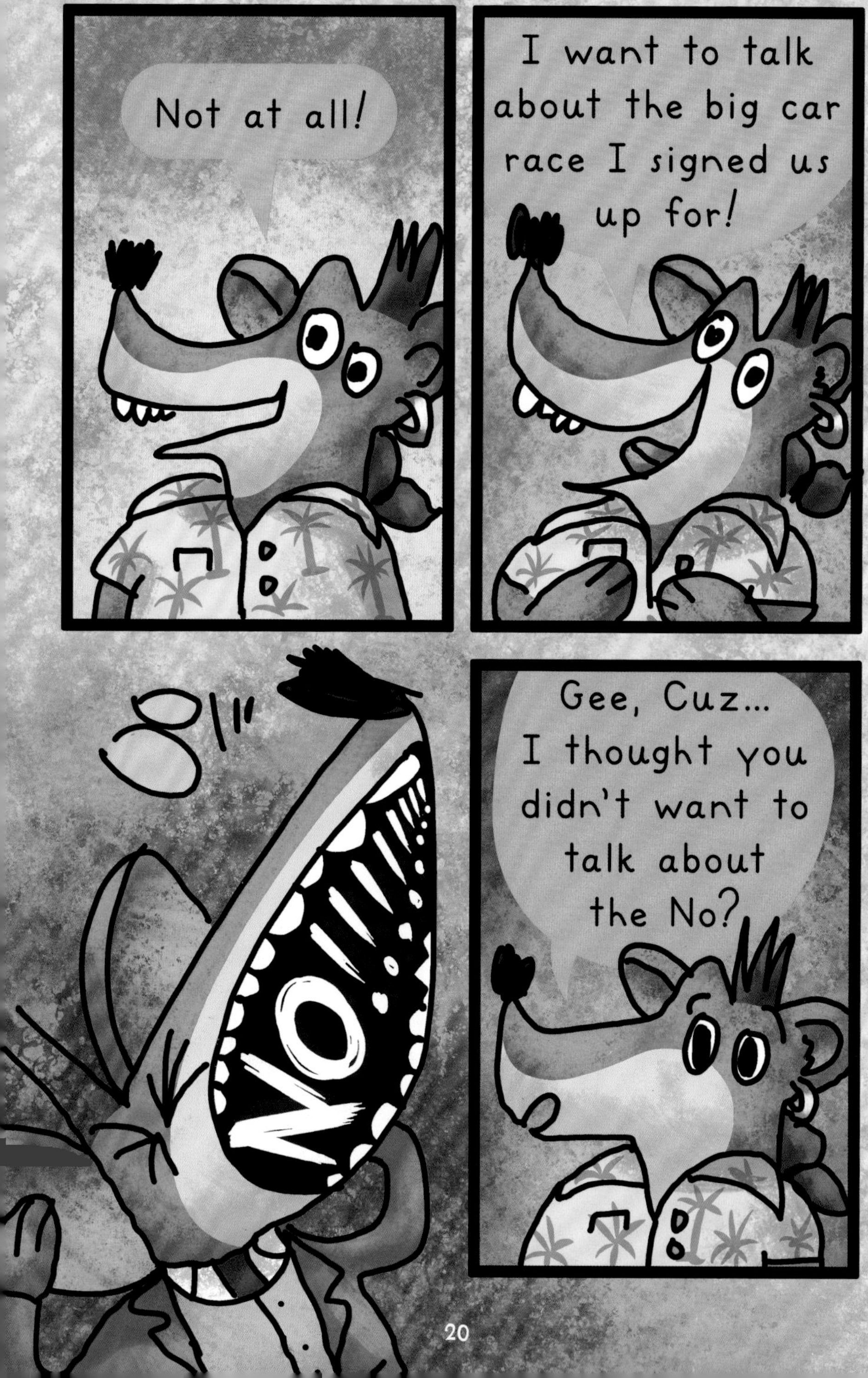
Not at all!
I want to talk about the big car race I signed us up for!
NO!!!!!
Gee, Cuz... I thought you didn't want to talk about the No?

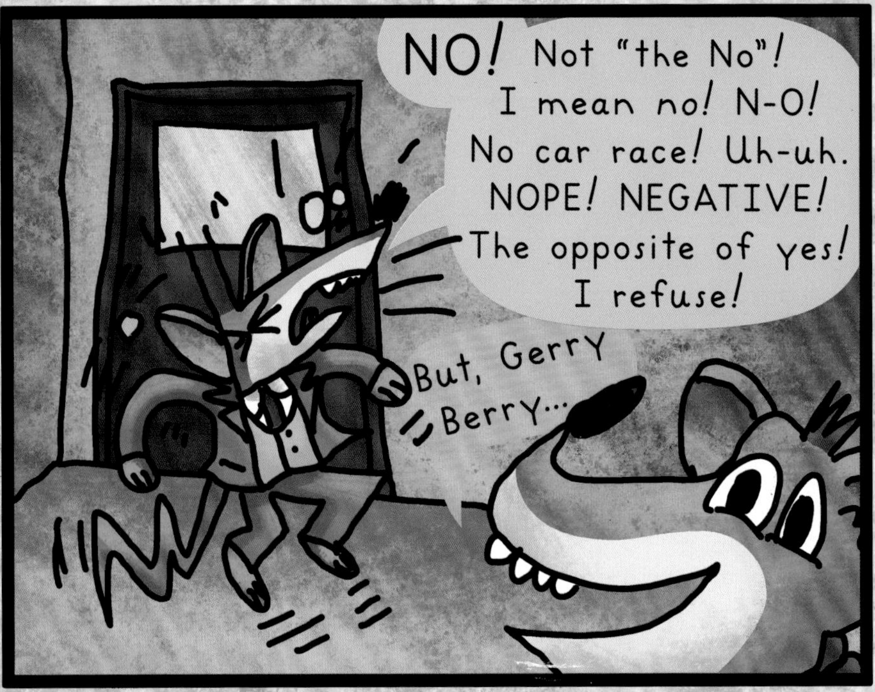
NO! Not "the No"! I mean no! N-O! No car race! Uh-uh. NOPE! NEGATIVE! The opposite of yes! I refuse!
But, Gerry Berry...

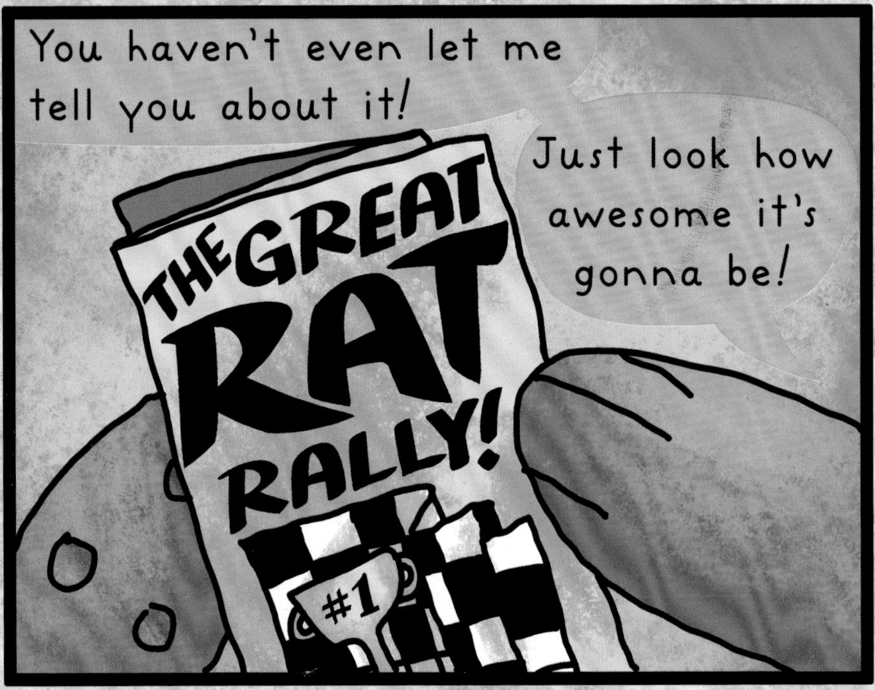
You haven't even let me tell you about it!
Just look how awesome it's gonna be!
THE GREAT RAT RALLY!
#1

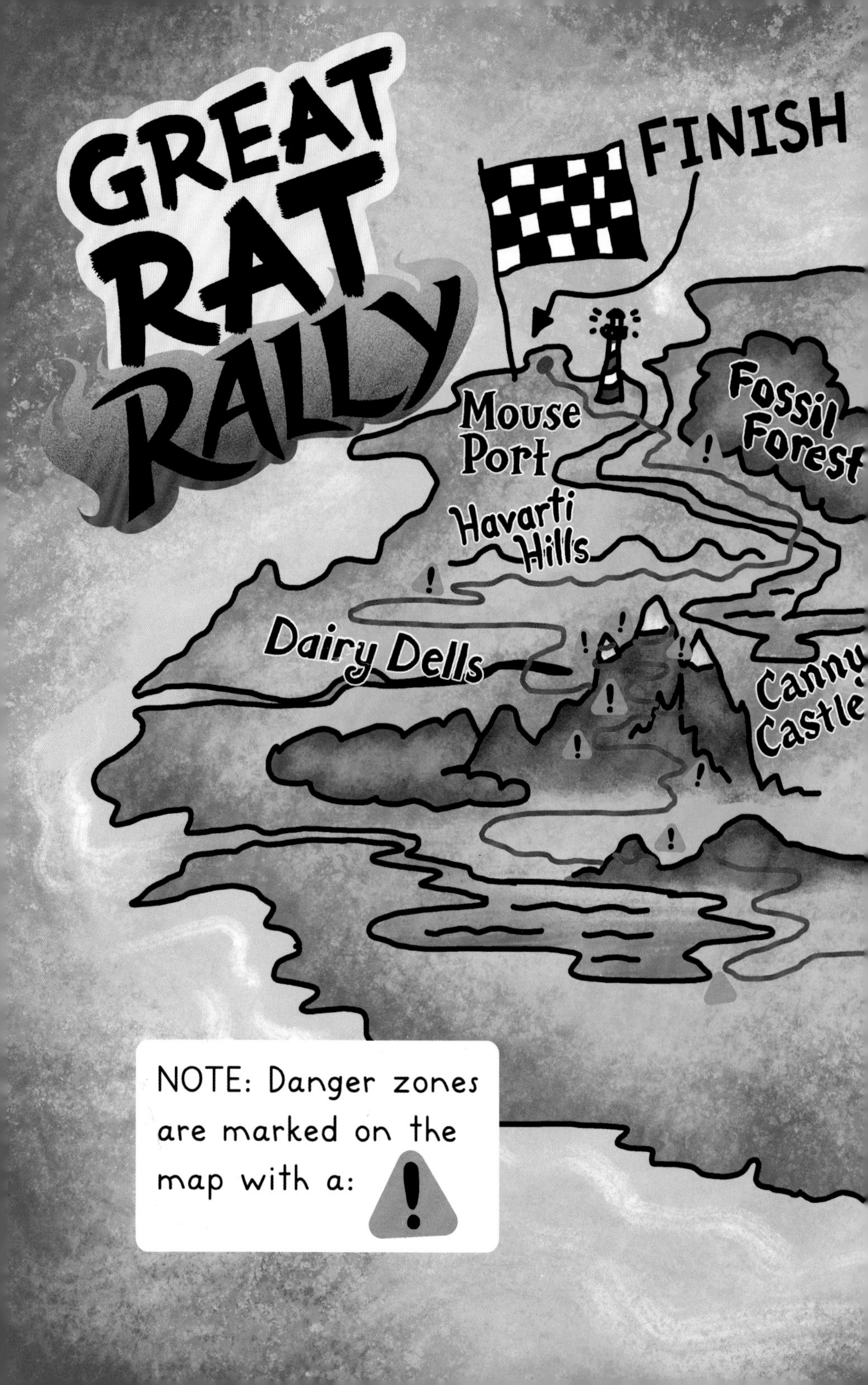
GREAT RAT RALLY
FINISH
Mouse Port
Fossil Forest
Havarti Hills
Dairy Dells
Canny Castle
NOTE: Danger zones are marked on the map with a:

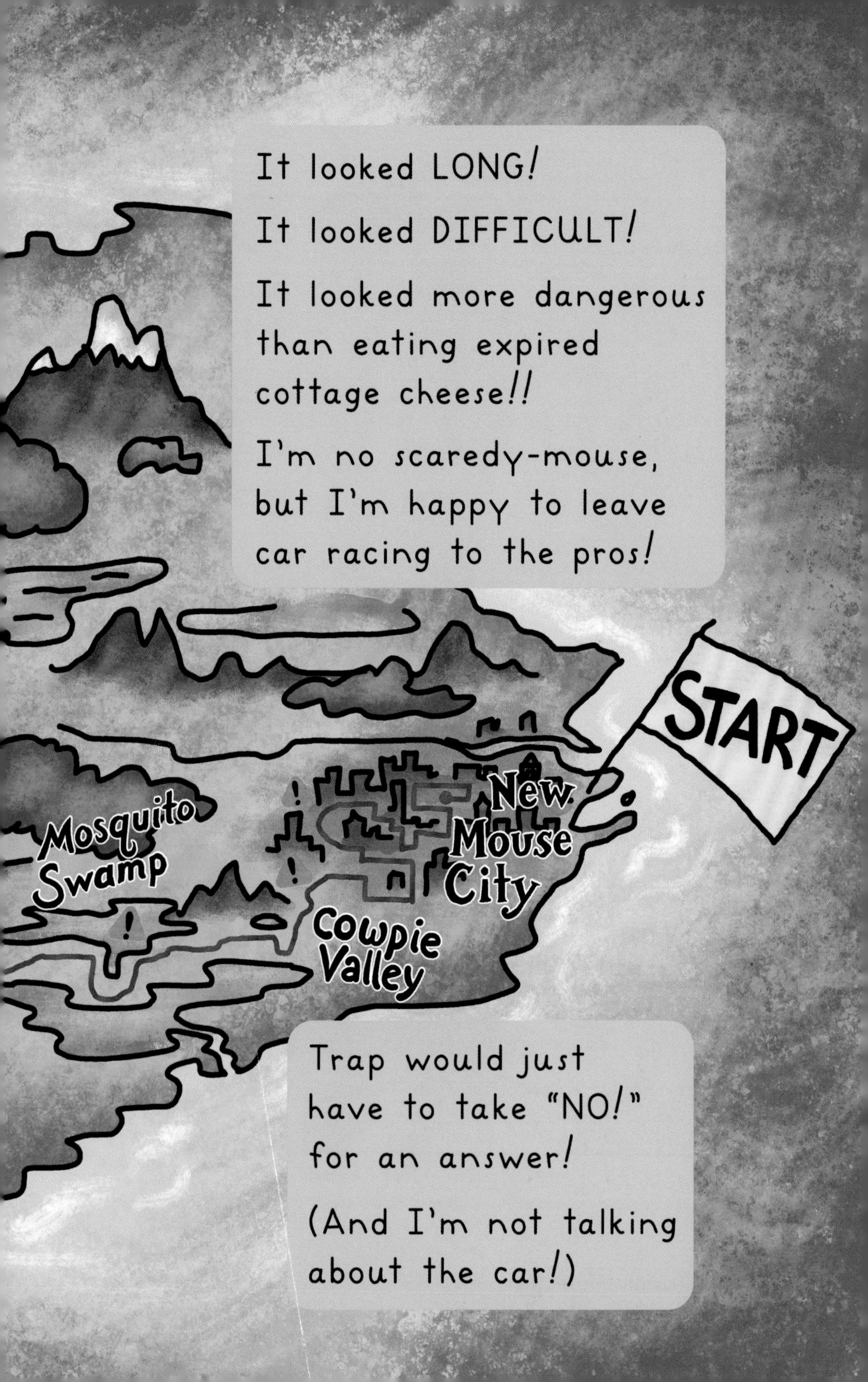
It looked LONG!
It looked DIFFICULT!
It looked more dangerous than eating expired cottage cheese!!
I'm no scaredy-mouse, but I'm happy to leave car racing to the pros!
START
New Mouse City
Mosquito Swamp
Cowpie Valley
Trap would just have to take "NO!" for an answer!
(And I'm not talking about the car!)

CHAPTER FIVE

You're not ⟨⟨SCARED⟩⟩, are you, Cuz?

I told Trap that he was welcome to race, and I would even watch the race on TV and cheer for him. But that's not what he wanted...

Gee, Cuz, don't you know anything? Rally races have two people per car. One to drive and one to read the map.

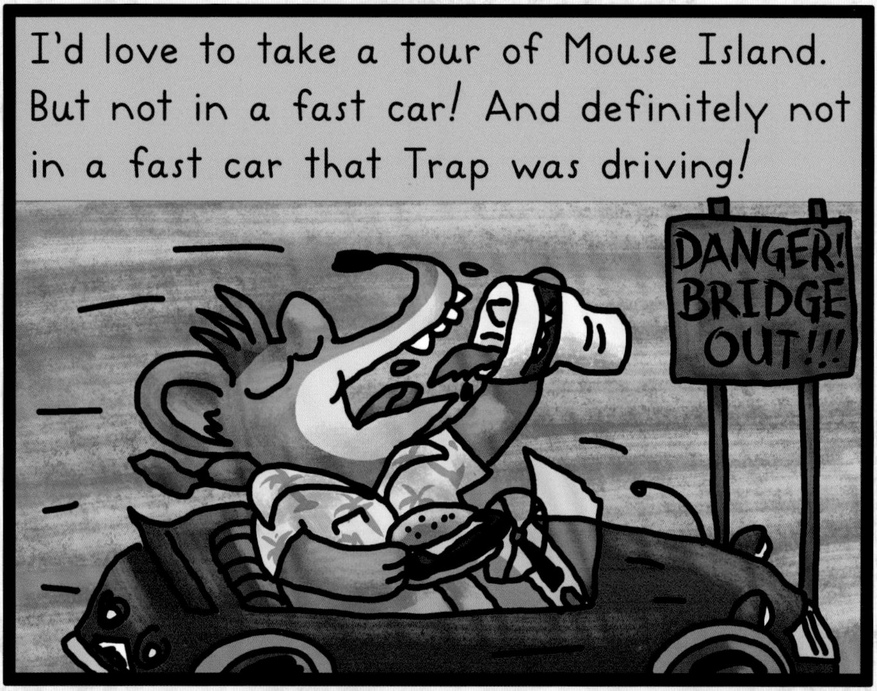
I'd love to take a tour of Mouse Island. But not in a fast car! And definitely not in a fast car that Trap was driving!
DANGER! BRIDGE OUT!!!

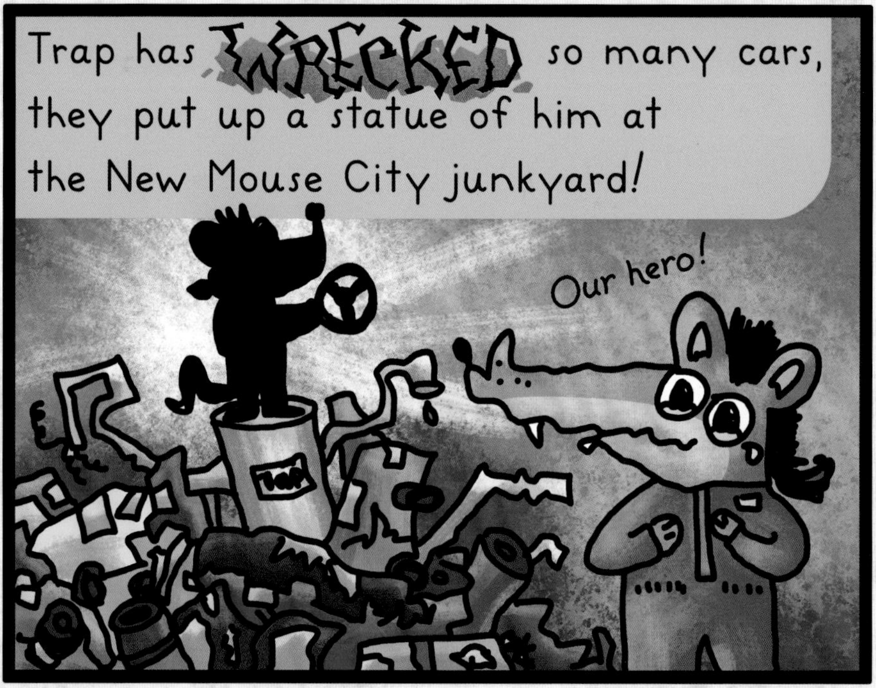
Trap has WRECKED so many cars, they put up a statue of him at the New Mouse City junkyard!
Our hero!

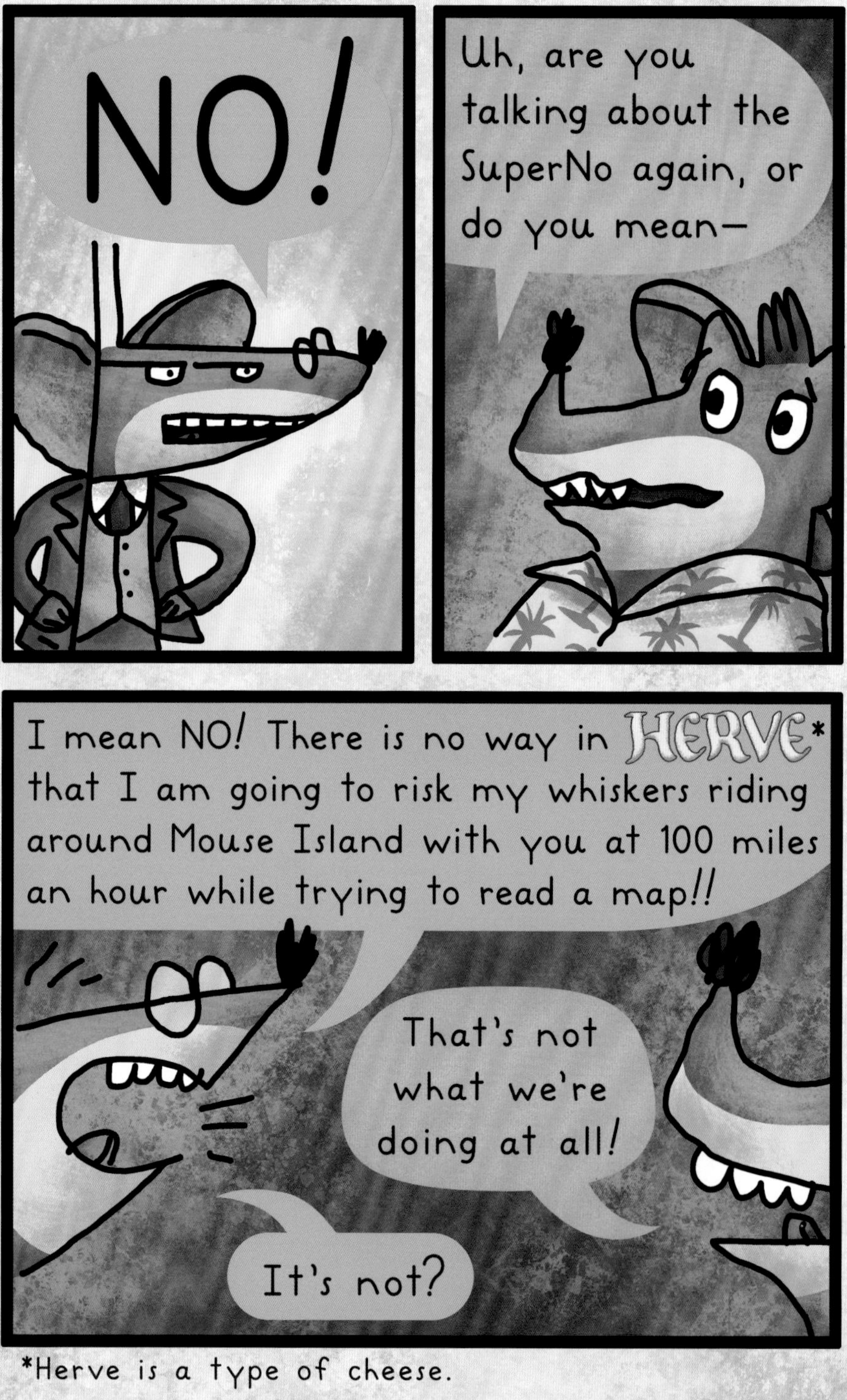
NO!
Uh, are you talking about the SuperNo again, or do you mean—
I mean NO! There is no way in HERVE* that I am going to risk my whiskers riding around Mouse Island with you at 100 miles an hour while trying to read a map!!
That's not what we're doing at all!
It's not?

*Herve is a type of cheese.

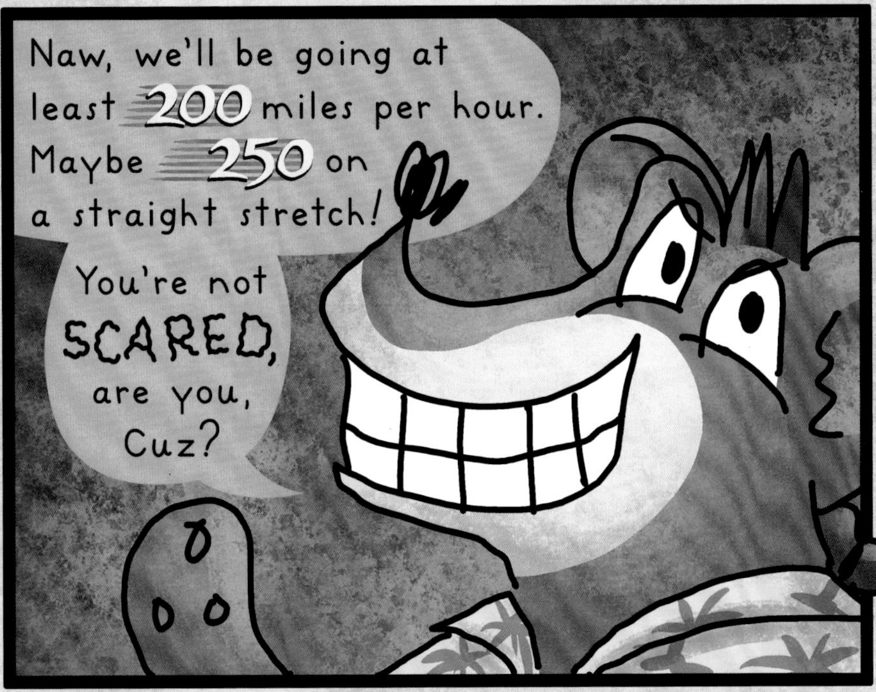
Naw, we'll be going at least 200 miles per hour. Maybe 250 on a straight stretch!
You're not SCARED, are you, Cuz?

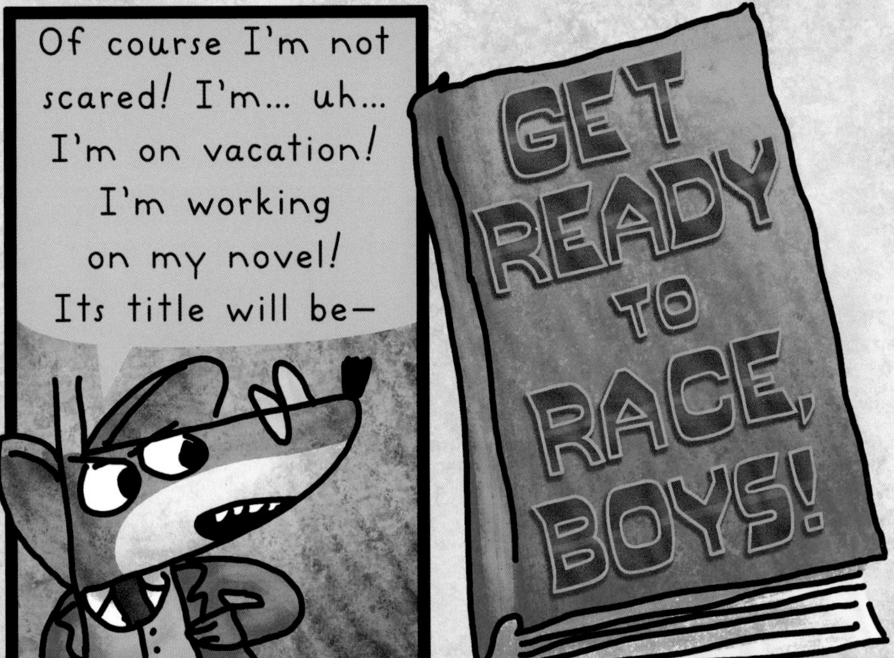
Of course I'm not scared! I'm... uh... I'm on vacation! I'm working on my novel! Its title will be—
GET READY TO RACE, BOYS!

CHAPTER SIX

A GLORIOUS FAMILY TRADITION!

No, that's not the name of my novel. It's what someone was yelling from the doorway! And that someone was...

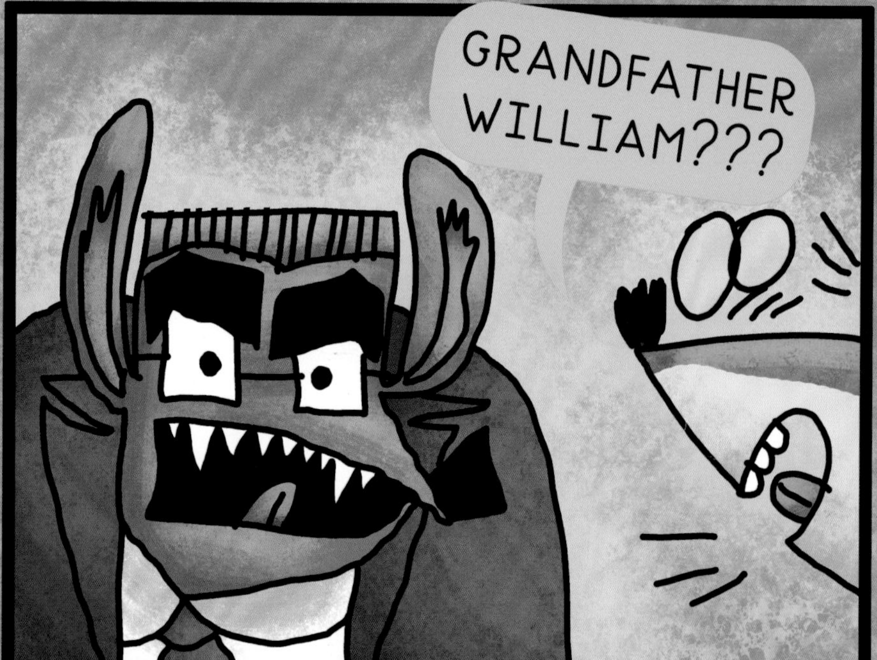
GRANDFATHER WILLIAM???

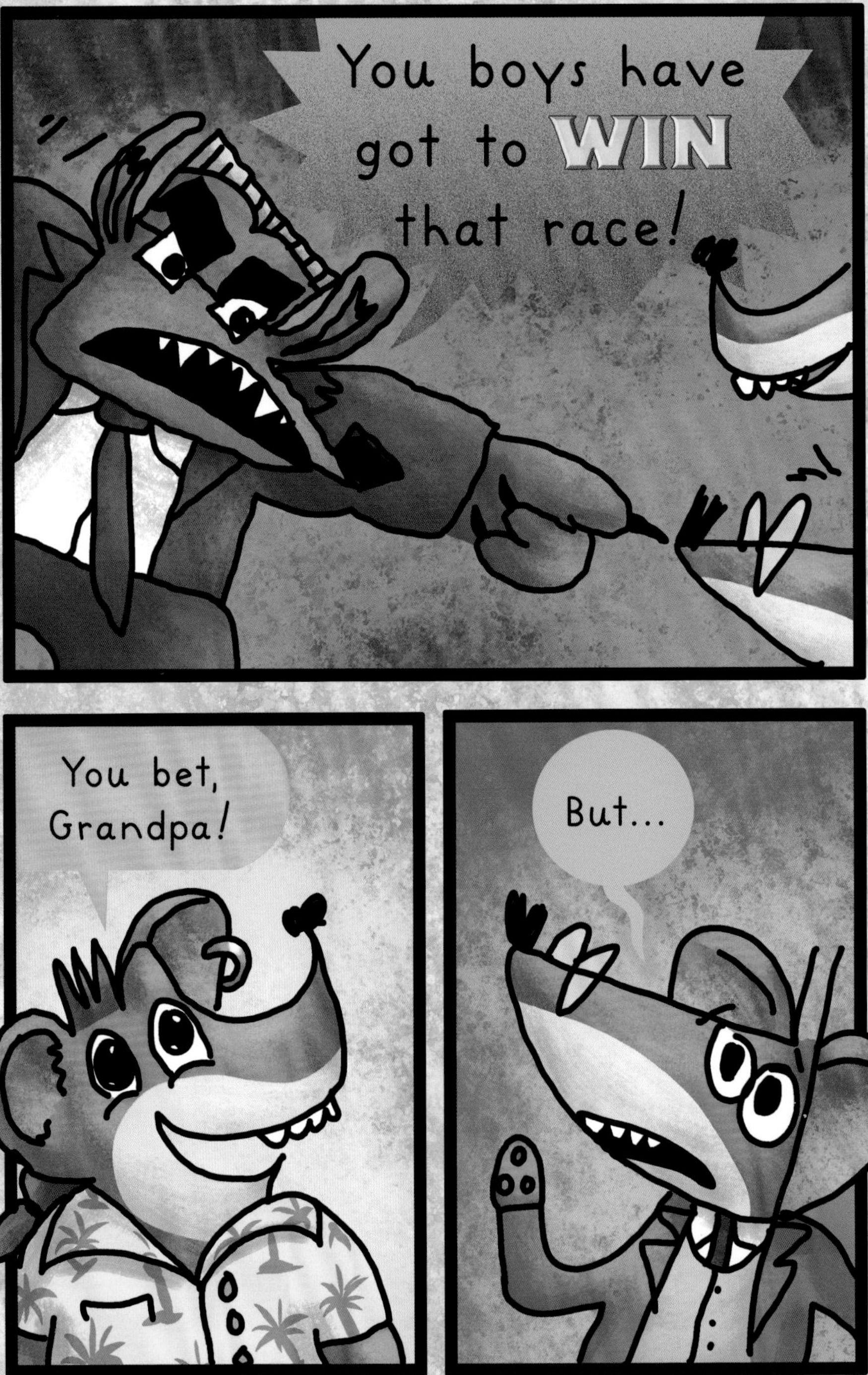
You boys have got to WIN that race!
You bet, Grandpa!
But...

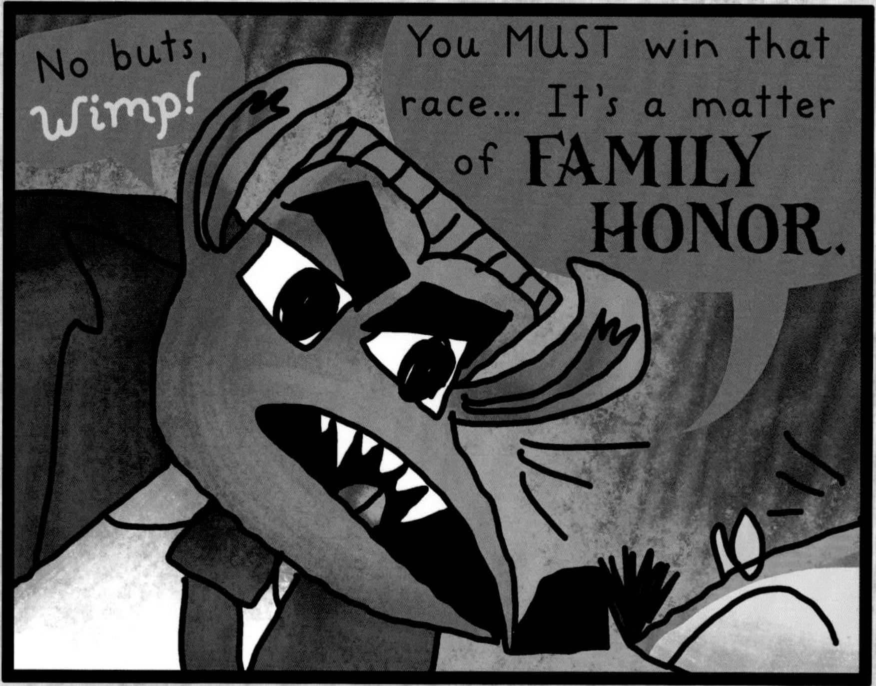
No buts, Wimp!
You MUST win that race... It's a matter of FAMILY HONOR.

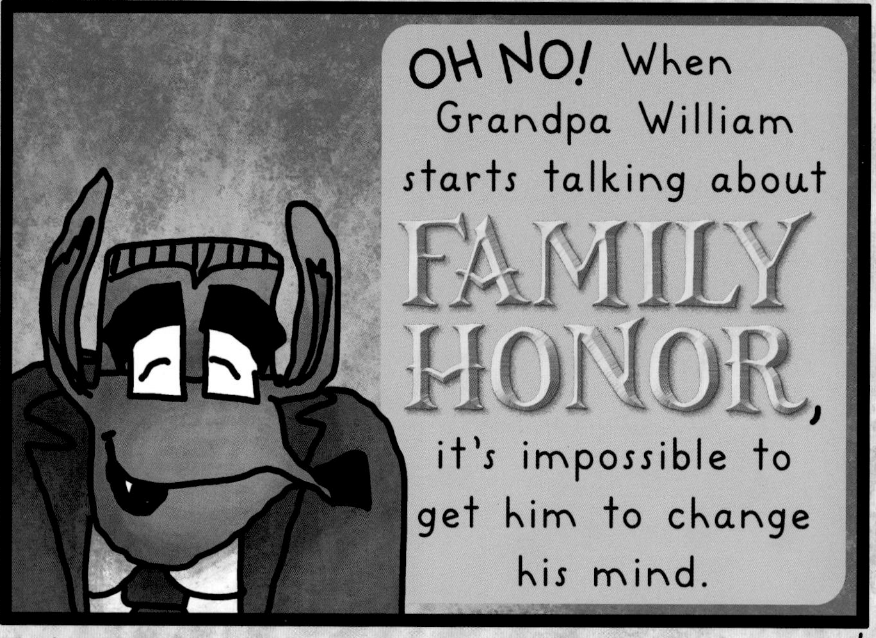
OH NO! When Grandpa William starts talking about FAMILY HONOR, it's impossible to get him to change his mind.

It's also impossible to get him to STOP!

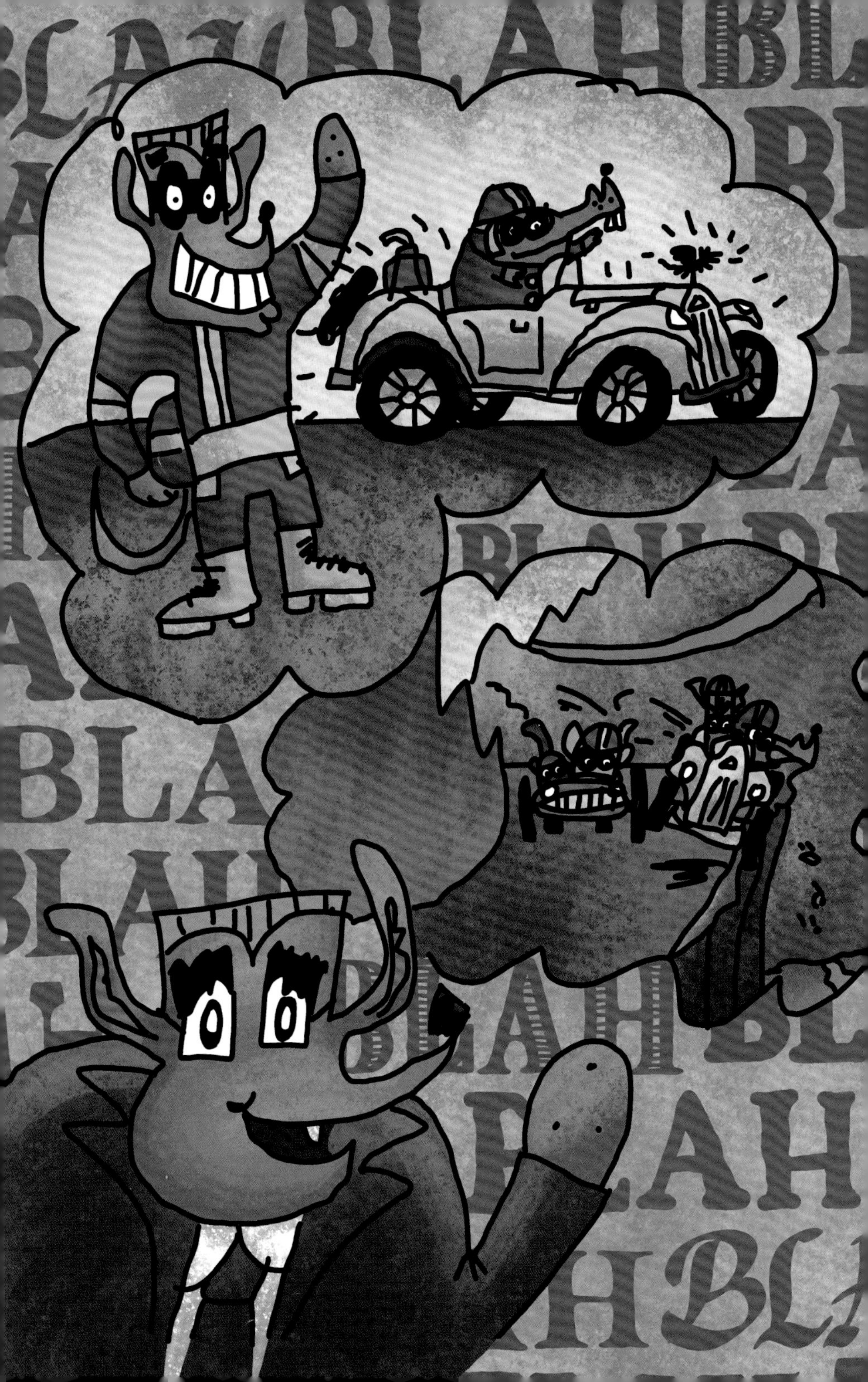
BLAH
BLAH
BLAH

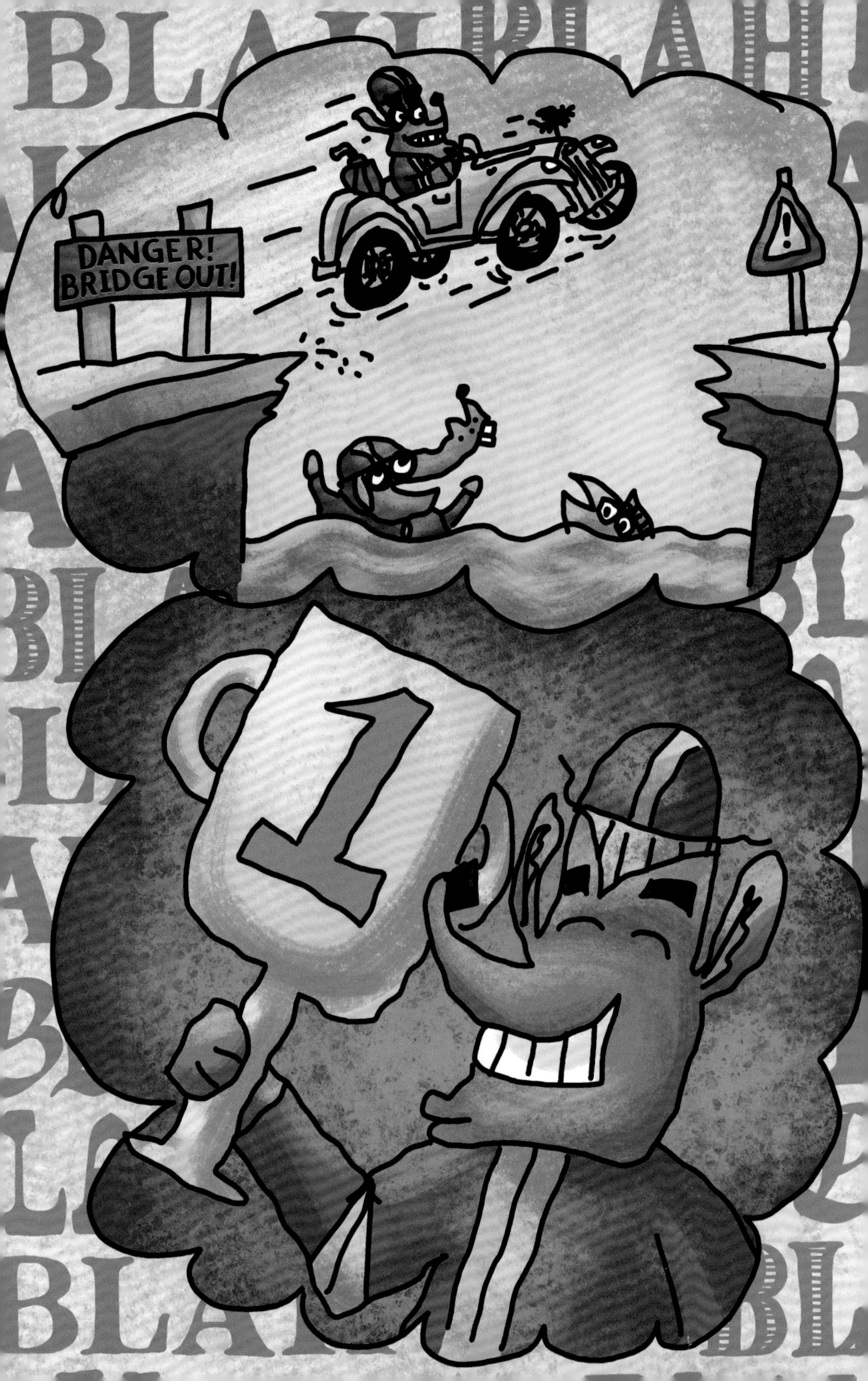
DANGER! BRIDGE OUT!

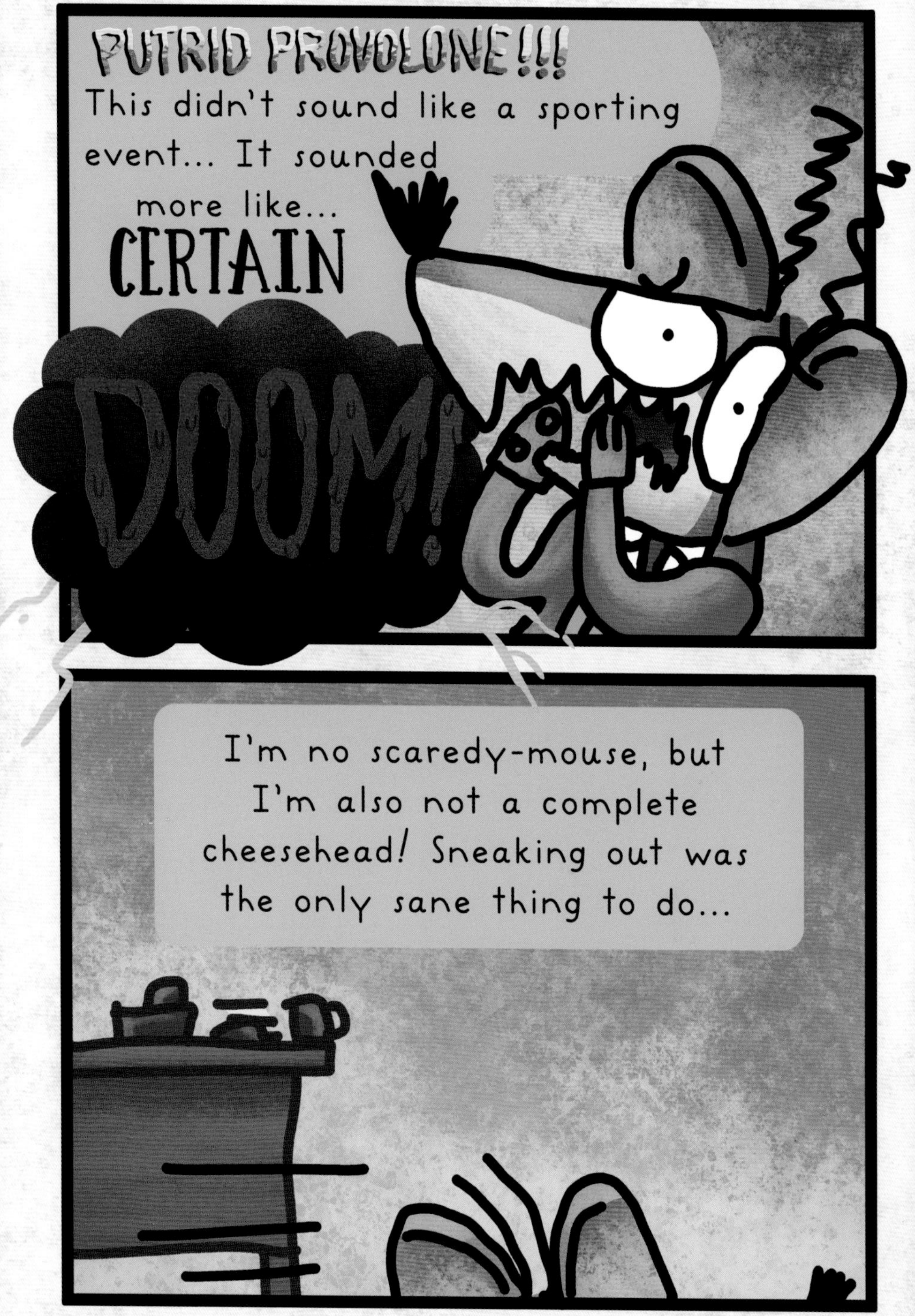
PUTRID PROVOLONE!!!
This didn't sound like a sporting event... It sounded
more like...
CERTAIN
DOOM!
I'm no scaredy-mouse, but I'm also not a complete cheesehead! Sneaking out was the only sane thing to do...

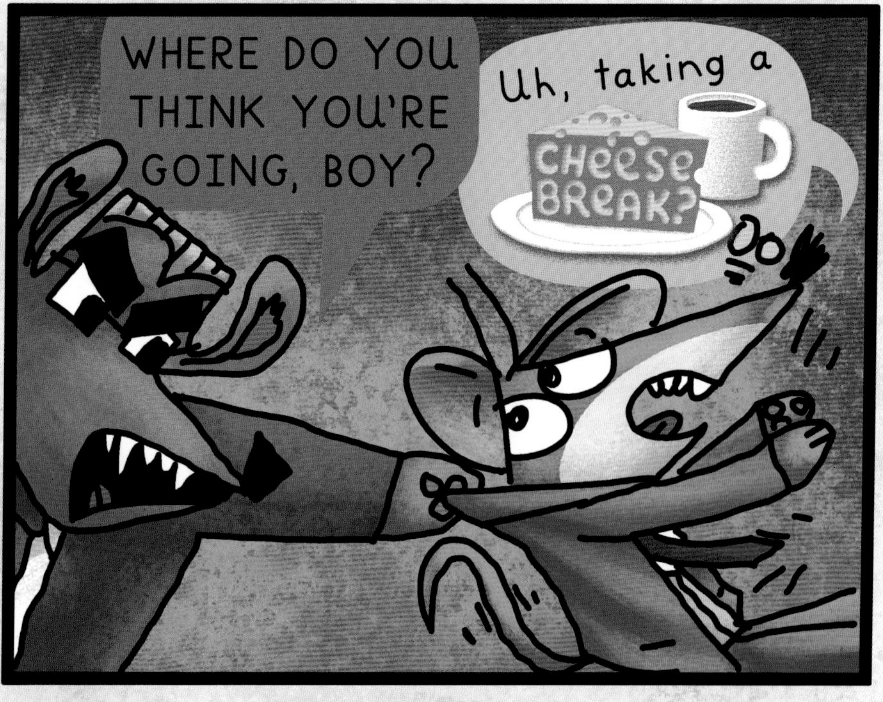
WHERE DO YOU THINK YOU'RE GOING, BOY?
Uh, taking a
CHEESE BREAK?

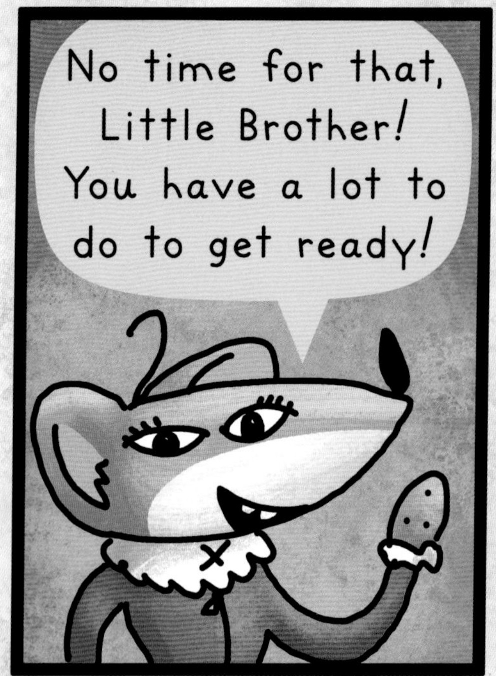
No time for that, Little Brother! You have a lot to do to get ready!

I hadn't seen Thea come in, but for once I was happy that my sister had barged into my office uninvited!

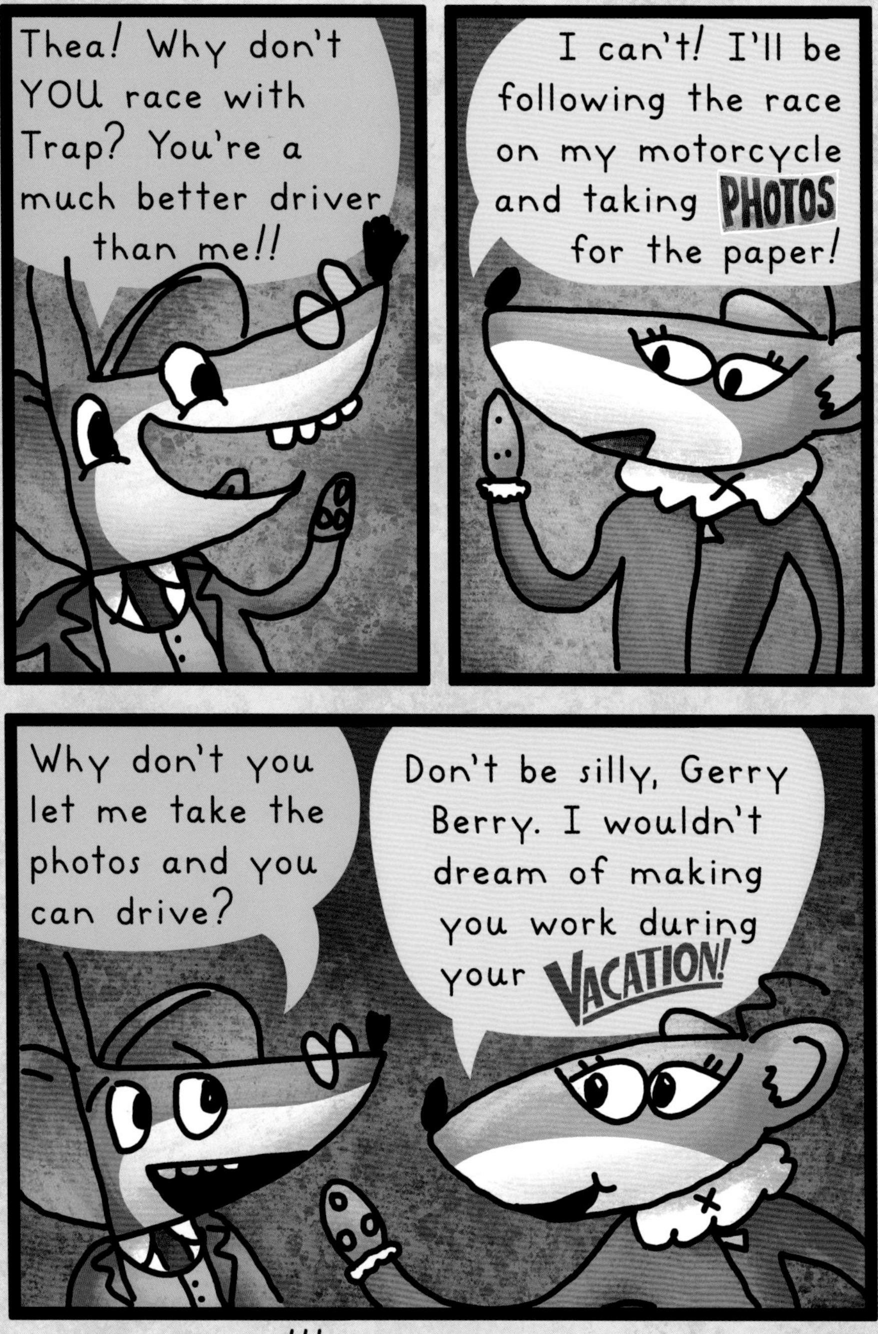
Thea! Why don't YOU race with Trap? You're a much better driver than me!!
I can't! I'll be following the race on my motorcycle and taking PHOTOS for the paper!
Why don't you let me take the photos and you can drive?
Don't be silly, Gerry Berry. I wouldn't dream of making you work during your VACATION!

Some vacation!!! I started wishing I'd booked a cruise to CAT ISLAND instead!

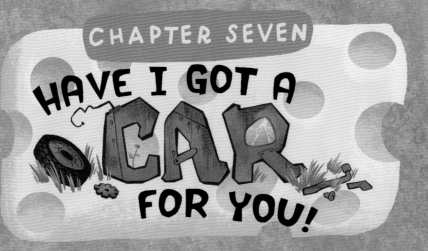

CHAPTER SEVEN
HAVE I GOT A CAR FOR YOU!

My "vacation" began with a trip to a used car lot with Trap...

SQUEAKY ¢ARS
"SPEND A LITTLE AND YOU WON'T GO FAR!"
KEEP OUT!

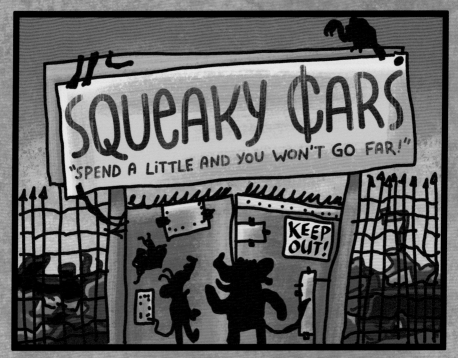

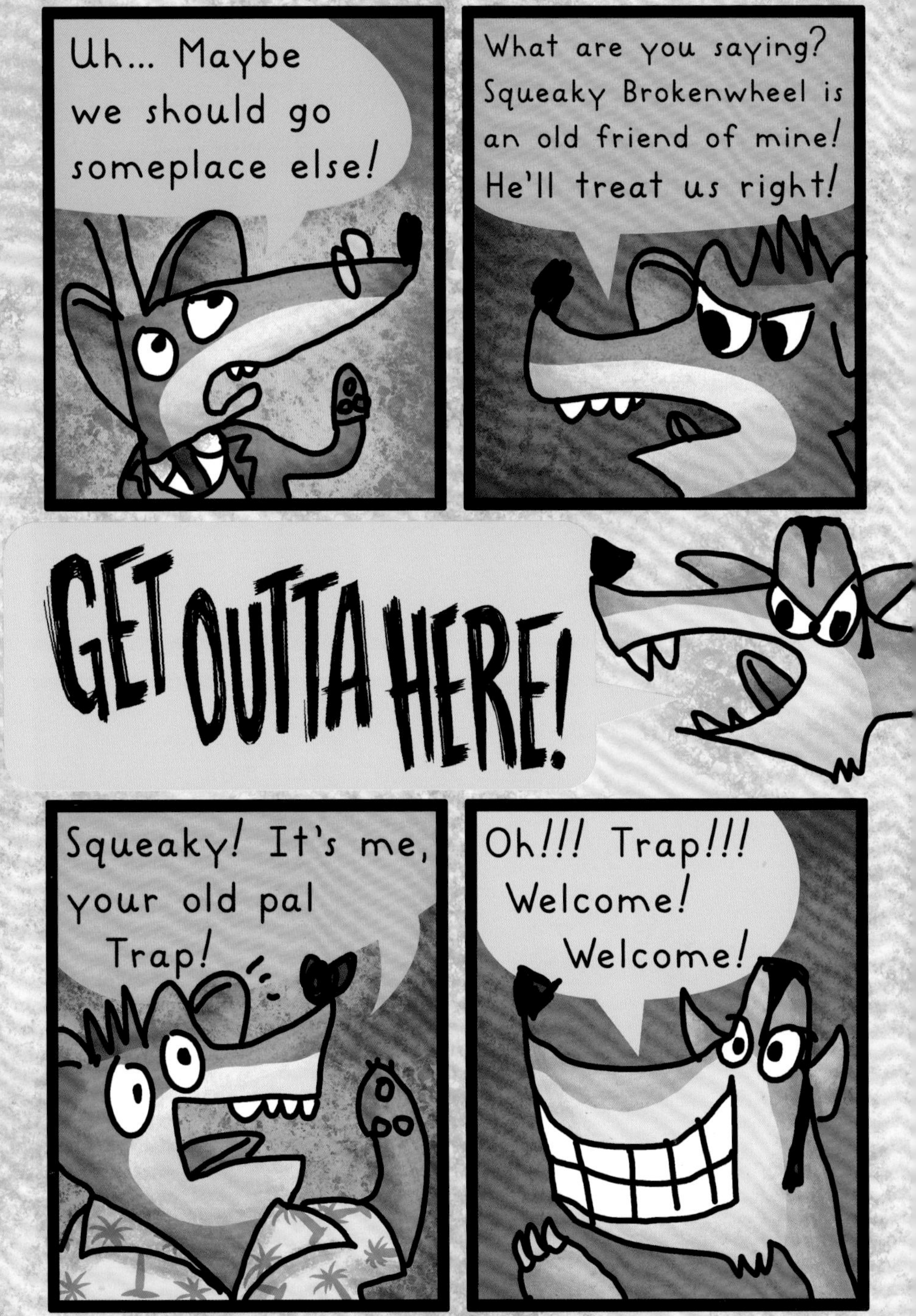

Uh... Maybe we should go someplace else!
What are you saying? Squeaky Brokenwheel is an old friend of mine! He'll treat us right!
GET OUTTA HERE!
Squeaky! It's me, your old pal Trap!
Oh!!! Trap!!! Welcome! Welcome!

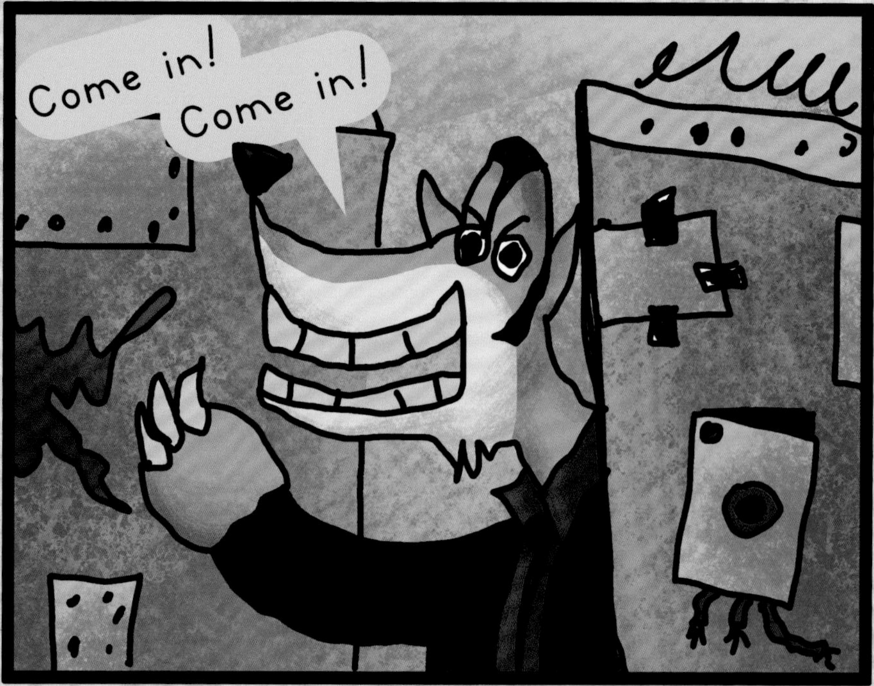
Come in!
Come in!

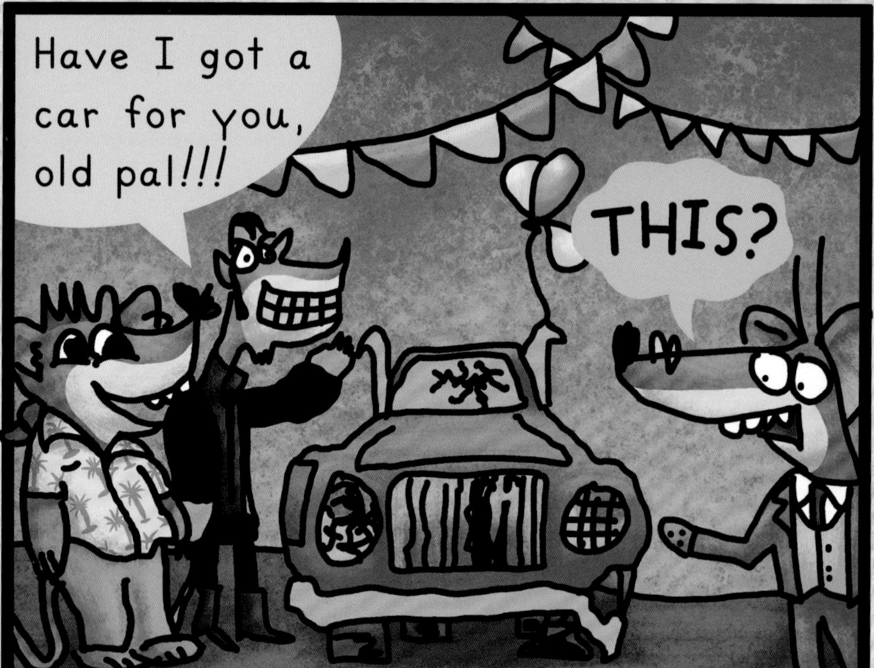
Have I got a car for you, old pal!!!
THIS?

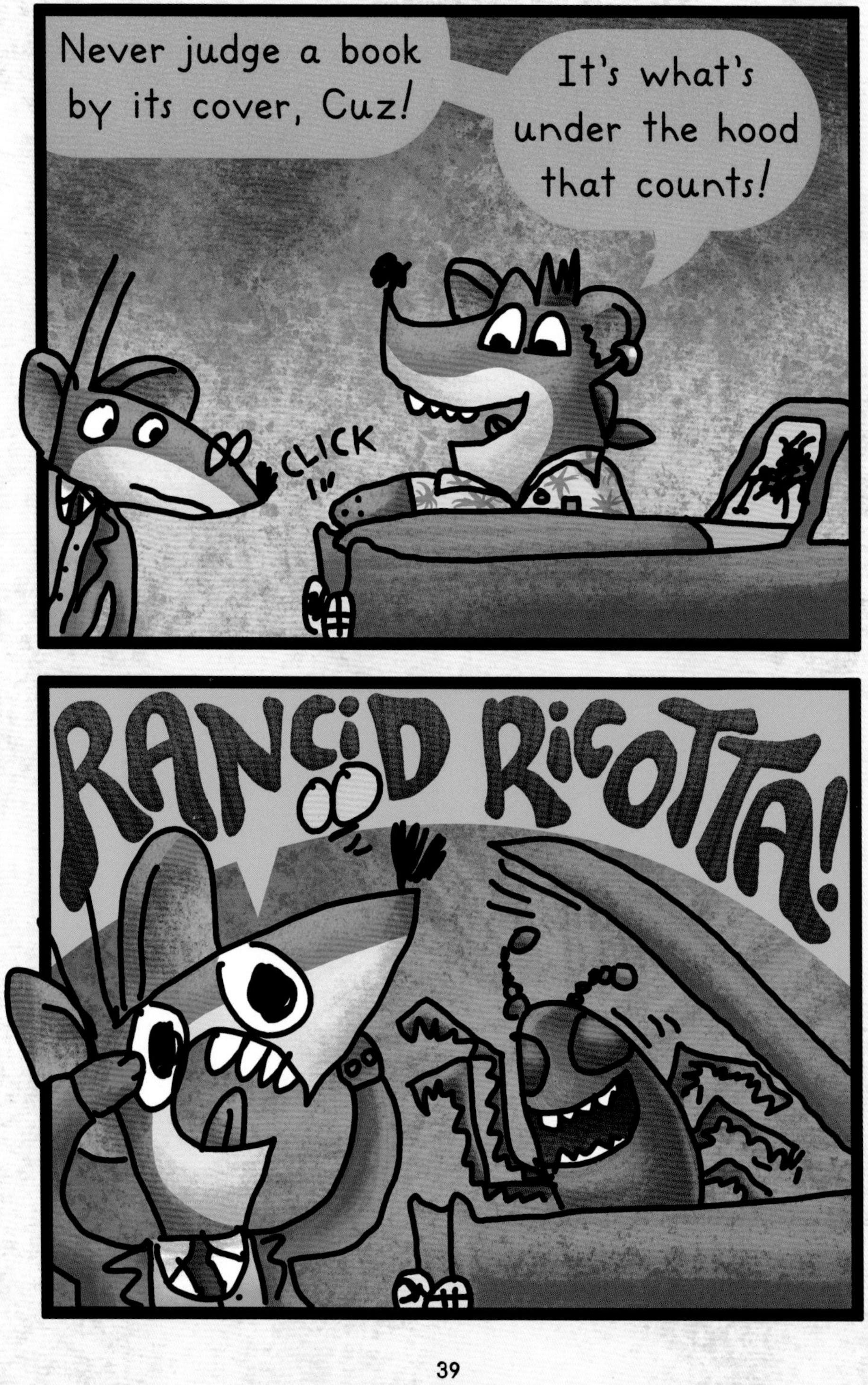
Never judge a book by its cover, Cuz!
It's what's under the hood that counts!
CLICK
RANCID RICOTTA!

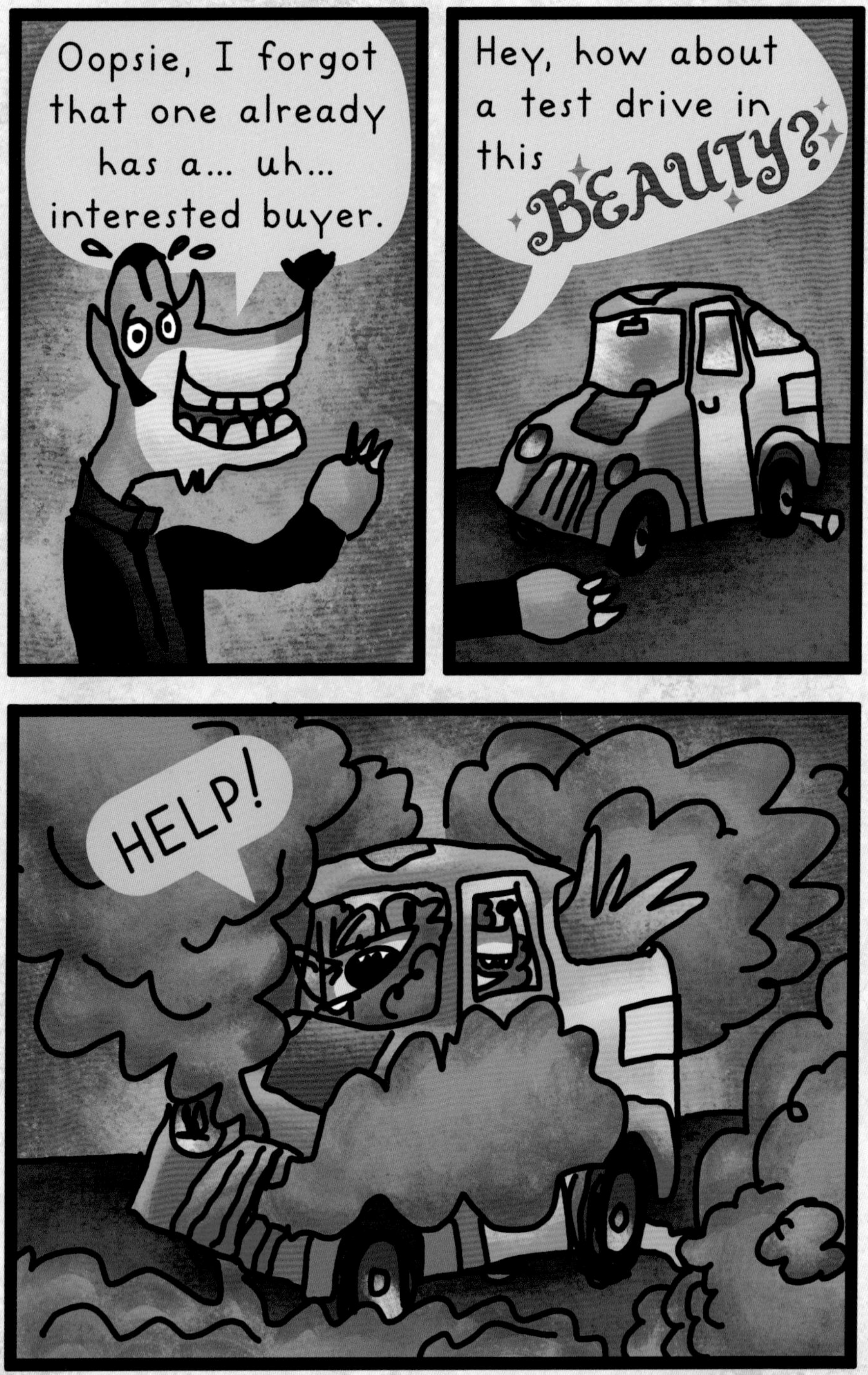

Oopsie, I forgot that one already has a... uh... interested buyer.
Hey, how about a test drive in this BEAUTY?
HELP!

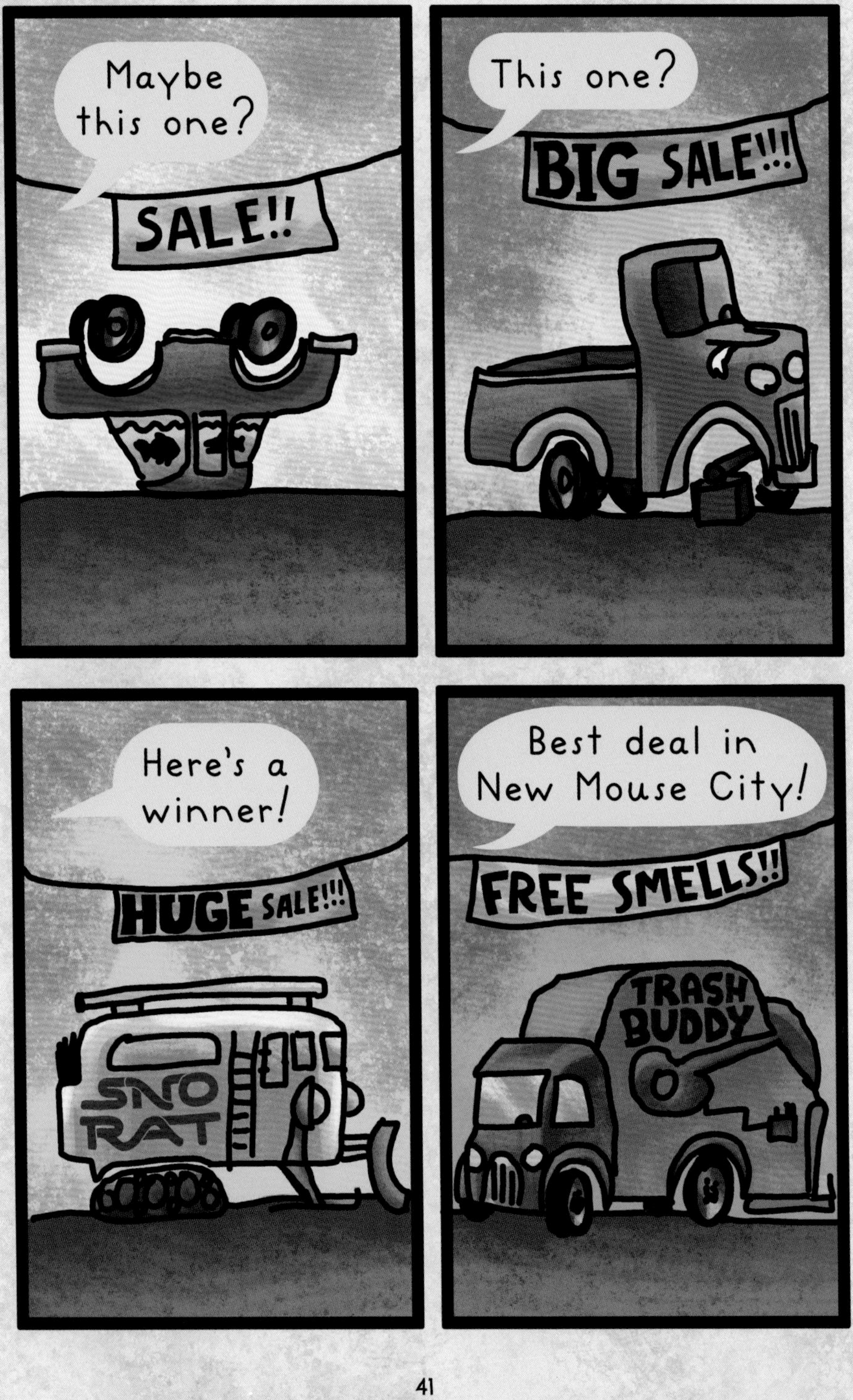
Maybe this one?
SALE!!
This one?
BIG SALE!!!
Here's a winner!
HUGE SALE!!!
SNO RAT
Best deal in New Mouse City!
FREE SMELLS!!
TRASH BUDDY

Okay, okay, I saved the best for last! Believe it or not, this car won the Great Rat Rally just a... uh... FEW years ago. Then it was used by Speedy Cheese™ Delivery... but... uh... they only delivered cheese on Mondays, to their closest neighbors. The rest of the week, they kept it in the garage and family of mice to handwash with silk

We'll take it!!!!

WHAT???

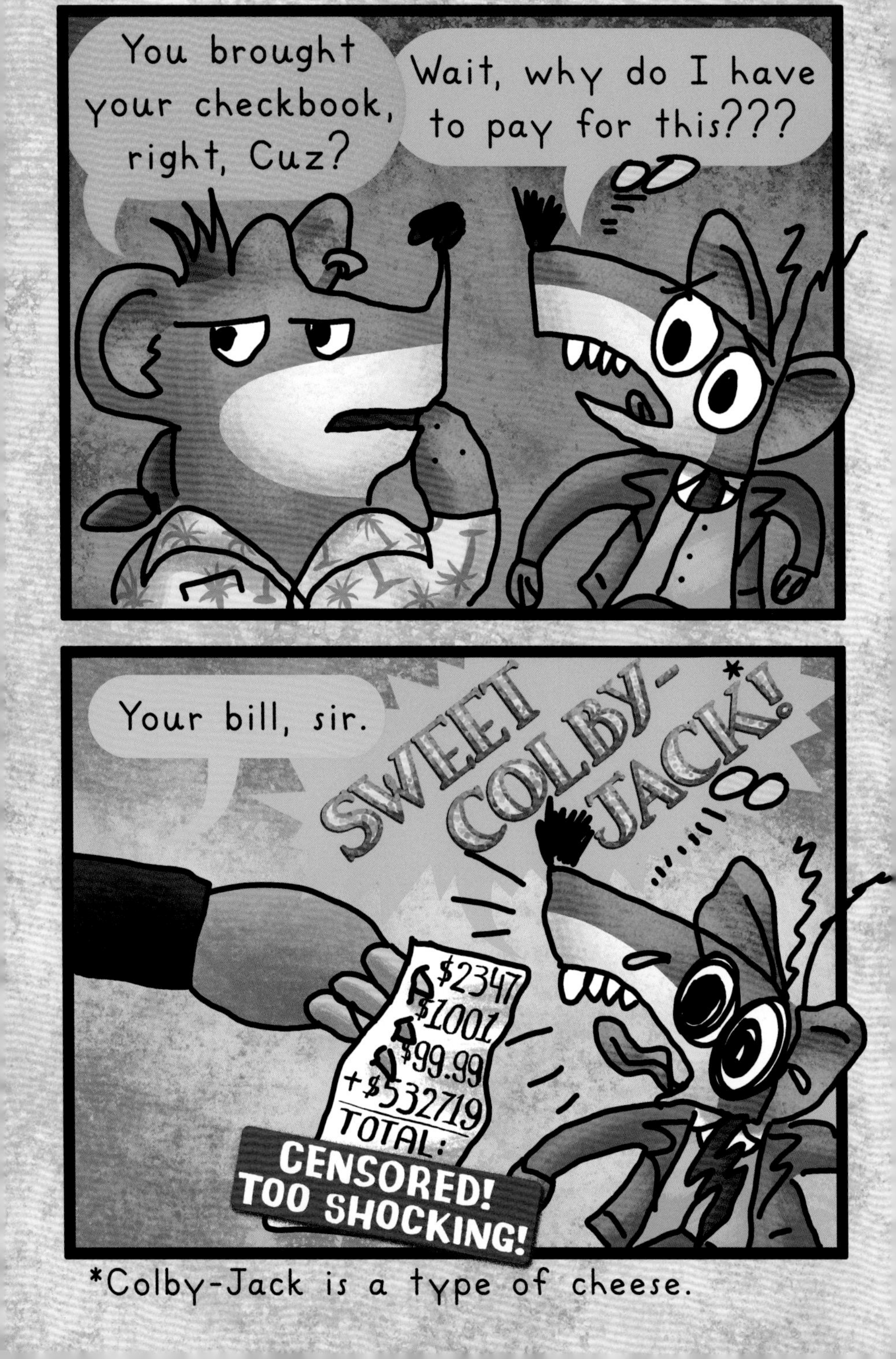
You brought your checkbook, right, Cuz?
Wait, why do I have to pay for this???
Your bill, sir.
SWEET COLBY-JACK!*
$2347
$1001
$99.99
+$532719
TOTAL:
CENSORED! TOO SHOCKING!

*Colby-Jack is a type of cheese.

CHAPTER EIGHT

AN XTREME MAKEOVER!

Somehow, Trap and Squeaky
got the car started!
We lurched and *swerved* out of Squeaky's
junkyard, and Trap headed downtown.

Okay, Cuz, I'll drop you off to meet
Thea. Then I'm going to take this car
back to my garage and tinker with it.

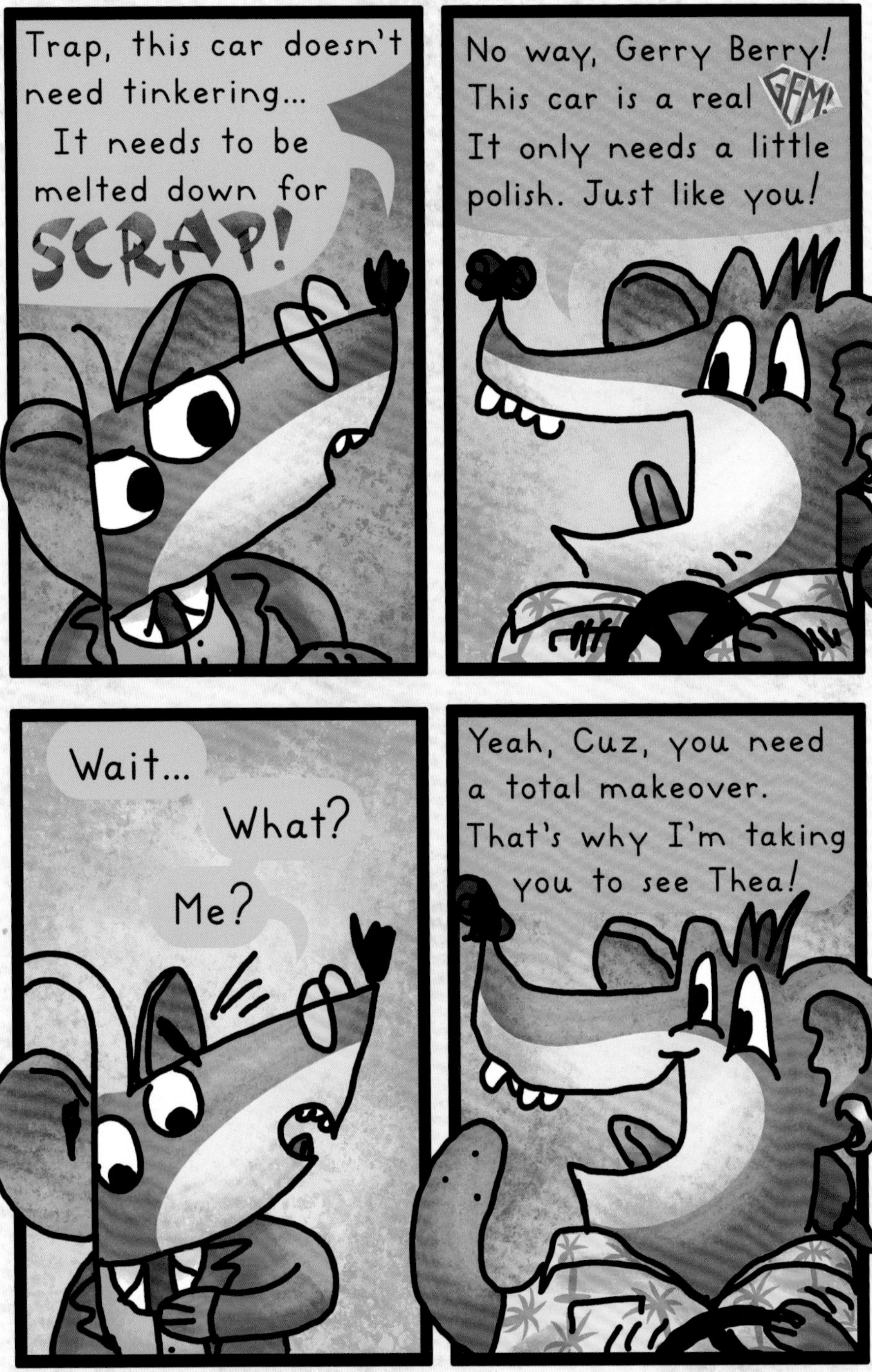
Trap, this car doesn't need tinkering... It needs to be melted down for SCRAP!
No way, Gerry Berry! This car is a real GEM! It only needs a little polish. Just like you!
Wait...
What?
Me?
Yeah, Cuz, you need a total makeover. That's why I'm taking you to see Thea!

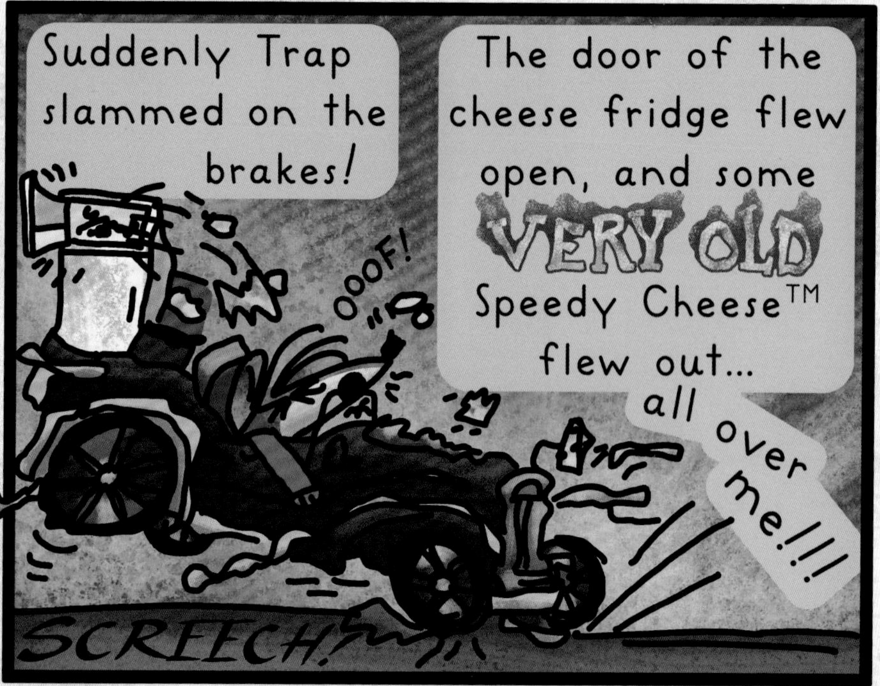
Suddenly Trap slammed on the brakes!
The door of the cheese fridge flew open, and some VERY OLD Speedy Cheese™ flew out...
all over me!!!!
OOOF!
SCREECH!

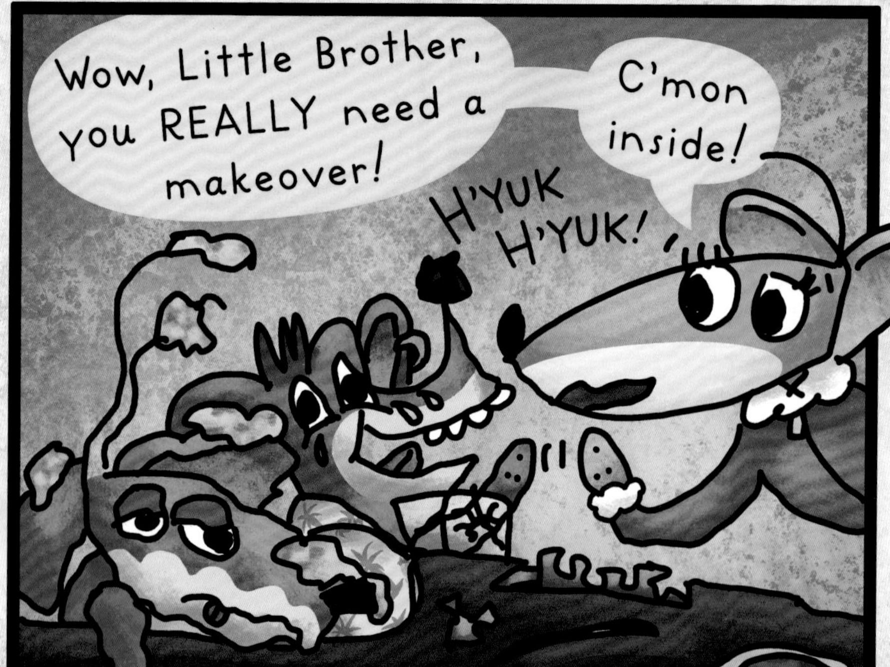
Wow, Little Brother, you REALLY need a makeover!
C'mon inside!
H'YUK H'YUK!

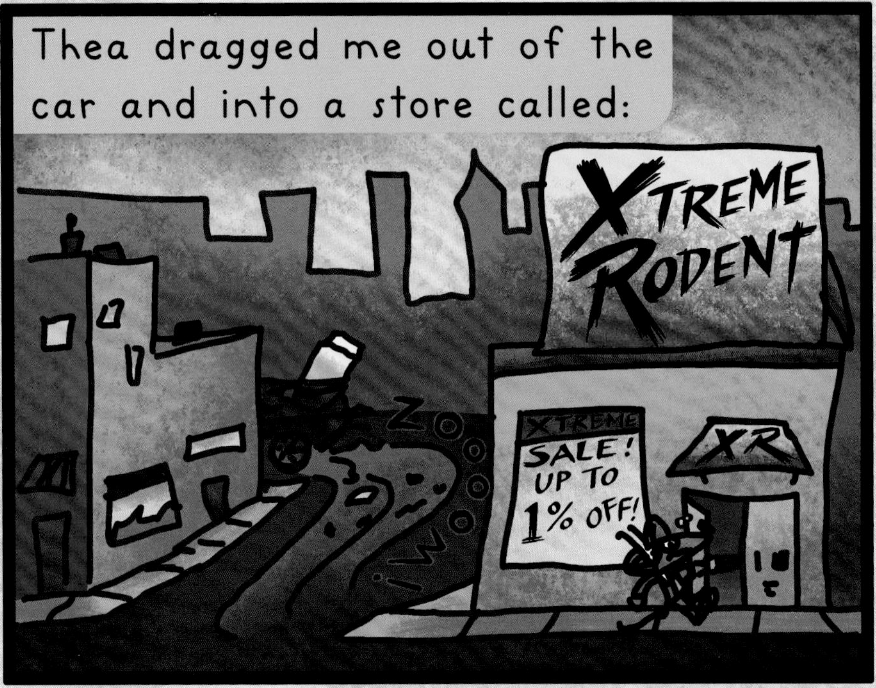
Thea dragged me out of the car and into a store called:
XTREME RODENT
XTREME
SALE! UP TO 1% OFF!
XR

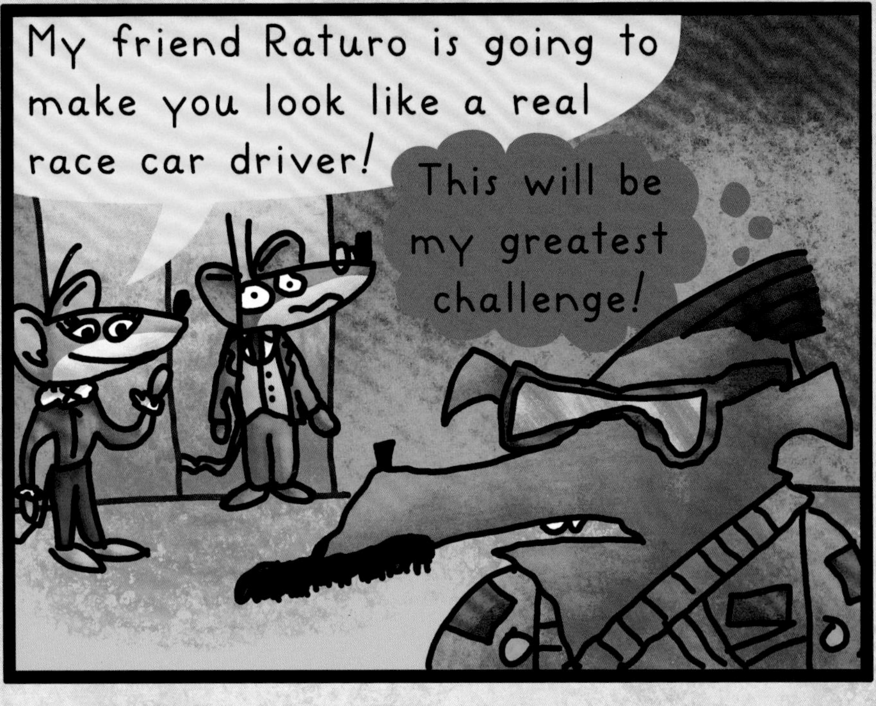
My friend Raturo is going to make you look like a real race car driver!
This will be my greatest challenge!

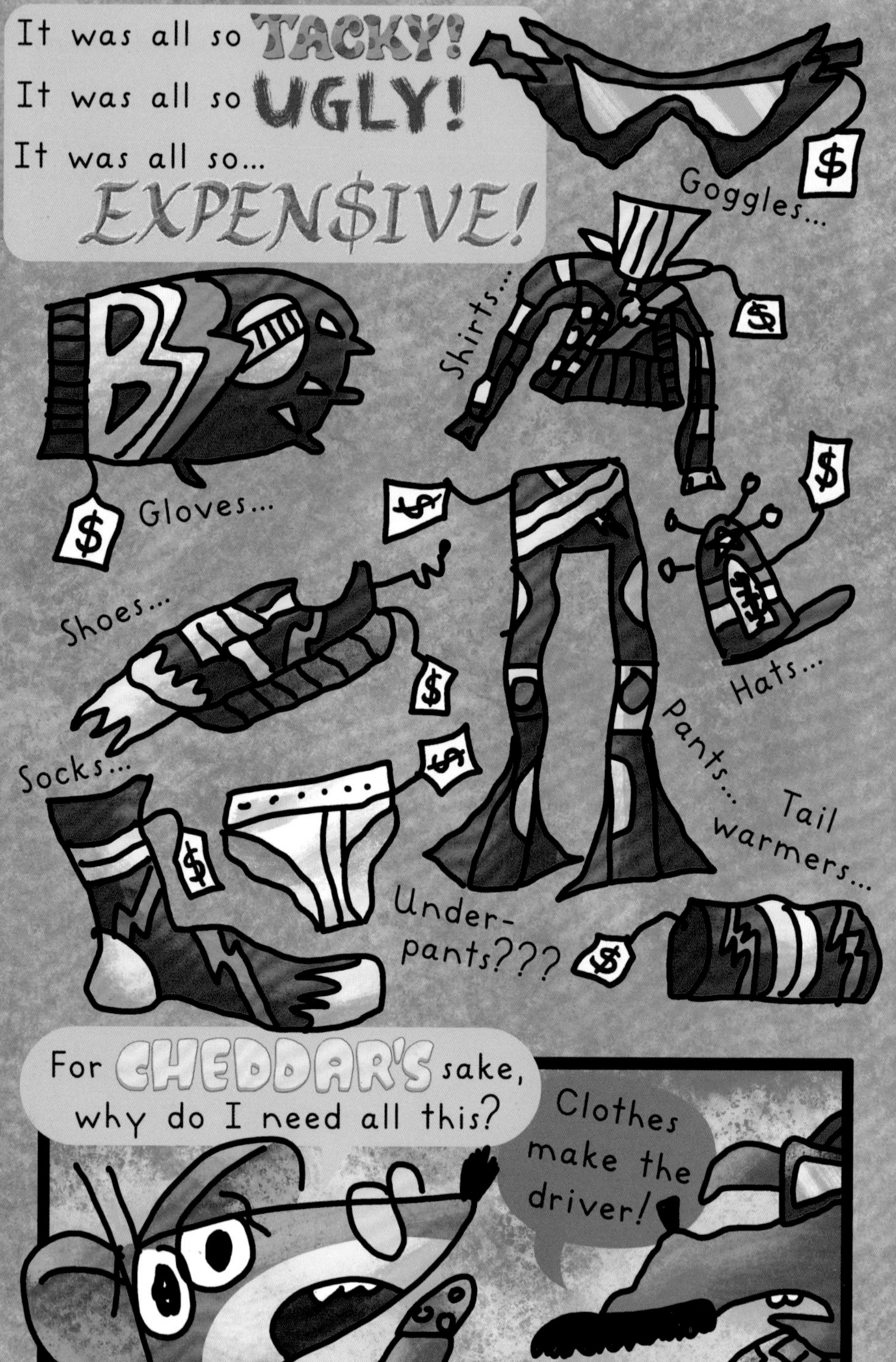

It was all so TACKY!
It was all so UGLY!
It was all so...
EXPEN$IVE!
Goggles...
Shirts...
Gloves...
Hats...
Shoes...
Pants...
Tail warmers...
Socks...
Under-pants???
For CHEDDAR'S sake, why do I need all this?
Clothes make the driver!

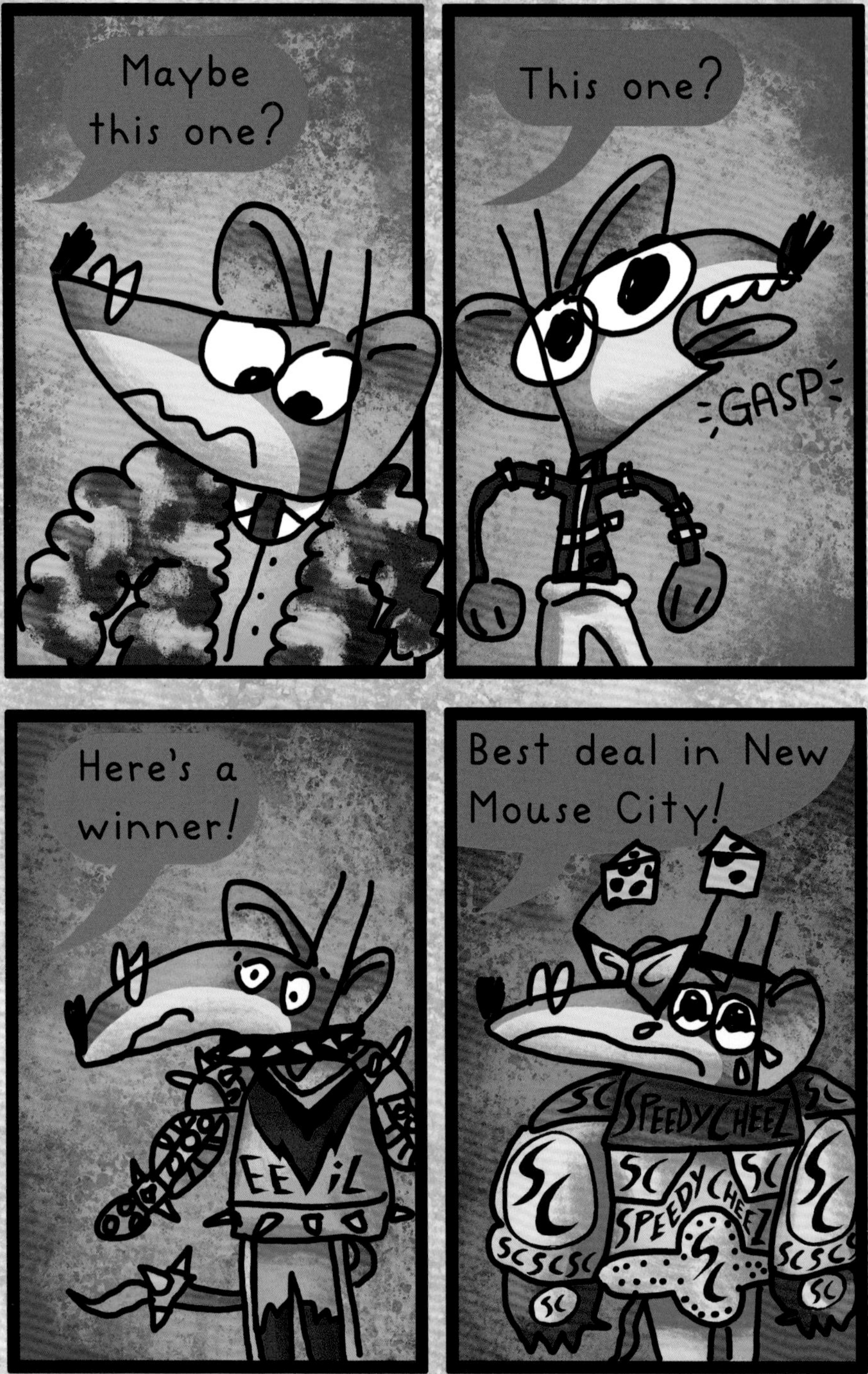
Maybe this one?
This one?
GASP
Here's a winner!
EEViL
Best deal in New Mouse City!
SPEEDYCHEEZ
SC
SPEEDYCHEEZ

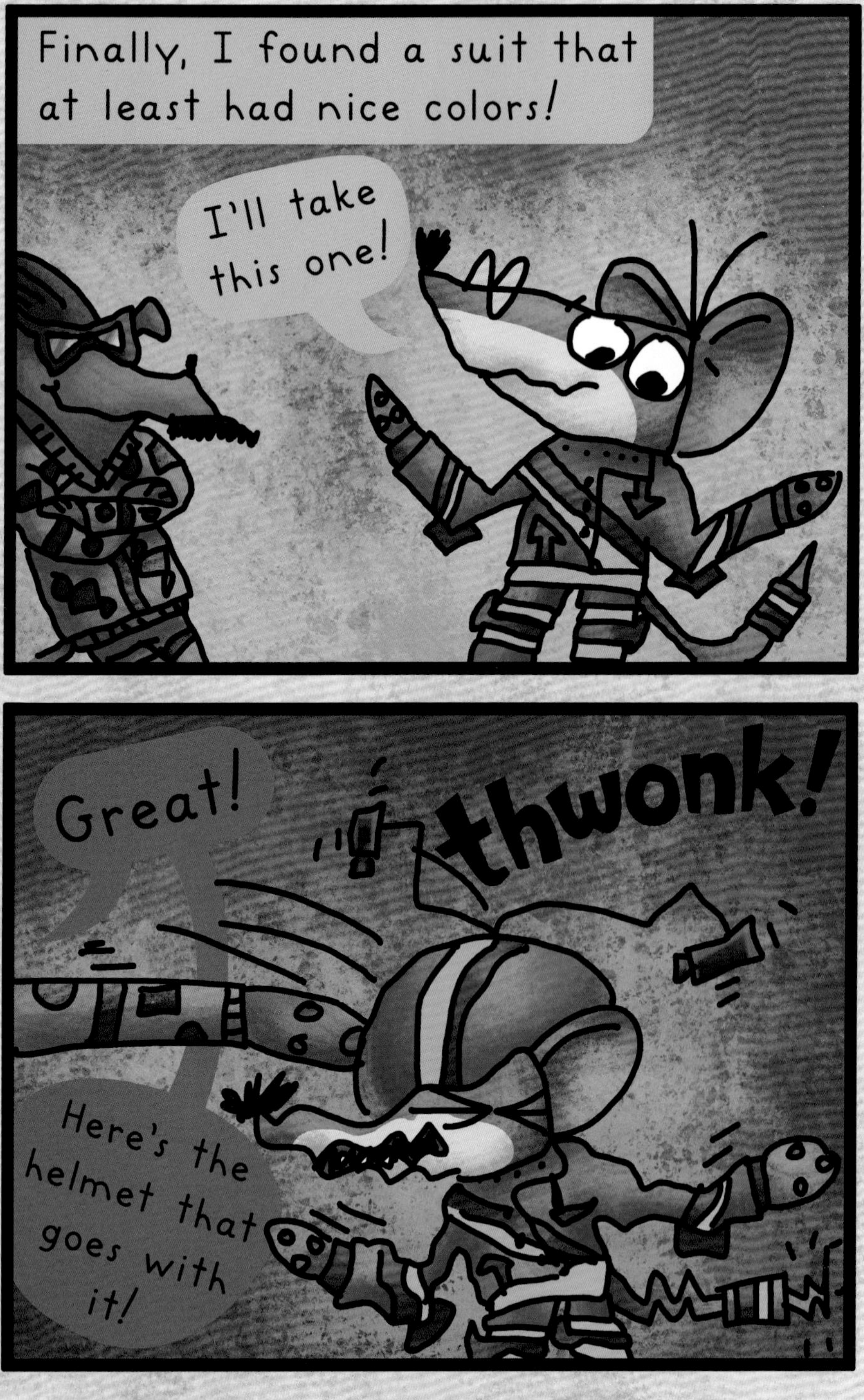
Finally, I found a suit that at least had nice colors!
I'll take this one!
Great!
thwonk!
Here's the helmet that goes with it!

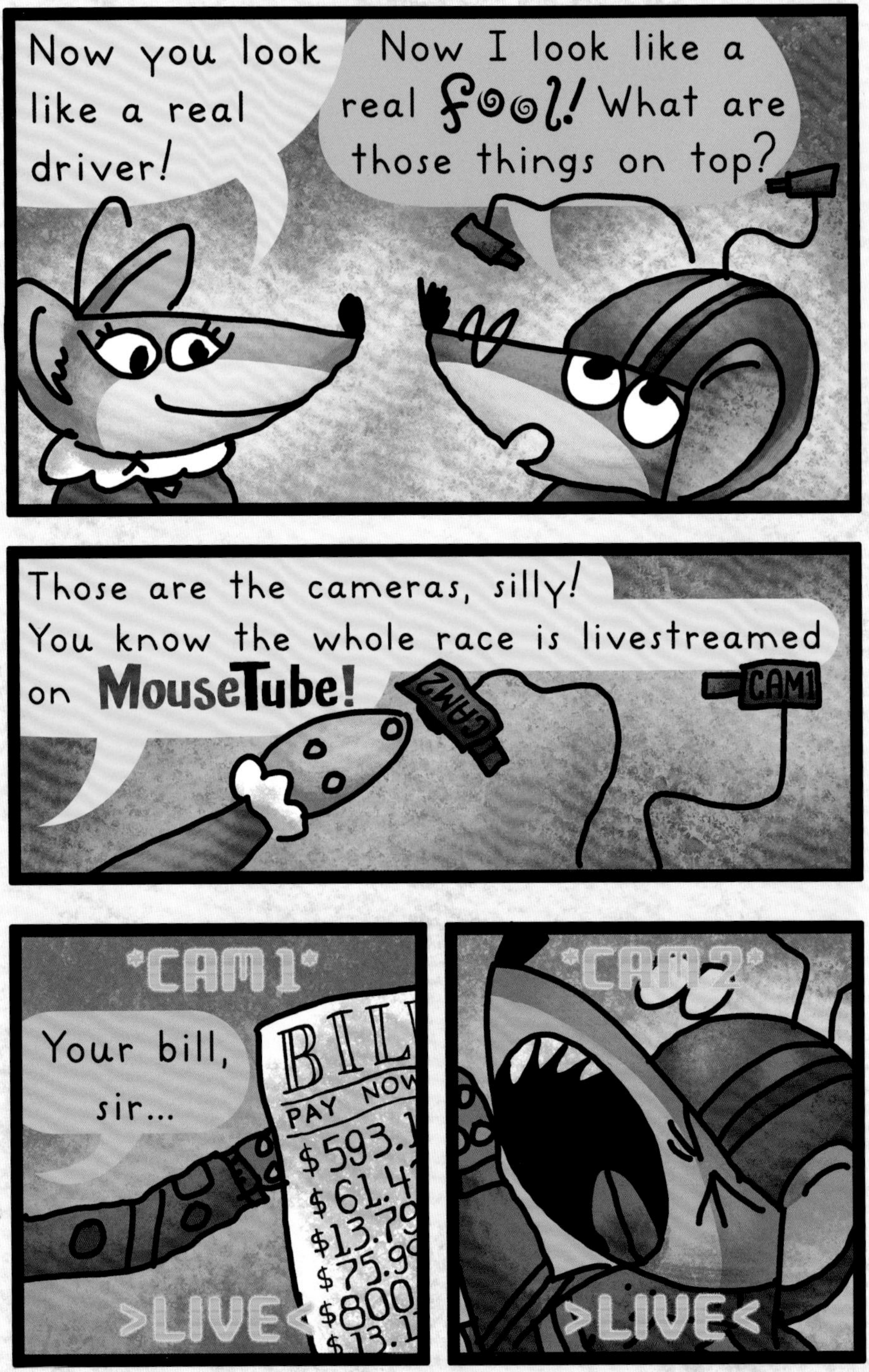
Now you look like a real driver!
Now I look like a real fool! What are those things on top?
Those are the cameras, silly! You know the whole race is livestreamed on MouseTube!
CAM2
CAM1
CAM1
Your bill, sir...
BIL
PAY NOW
$593.1
$61.4
$13.79
$75.9
$800
$13.1
>LIVE<
CAM2
>LIVE<

CHAPTER NINE

Now, That Is REAL NEWS!

When we finally got out of the store, we were swarmed by sports reporters!

Mr. Stinkton!
Mr. Spilton!
Mr. Stilting!
Mr. Spittoon!
Mr. Stiltine!

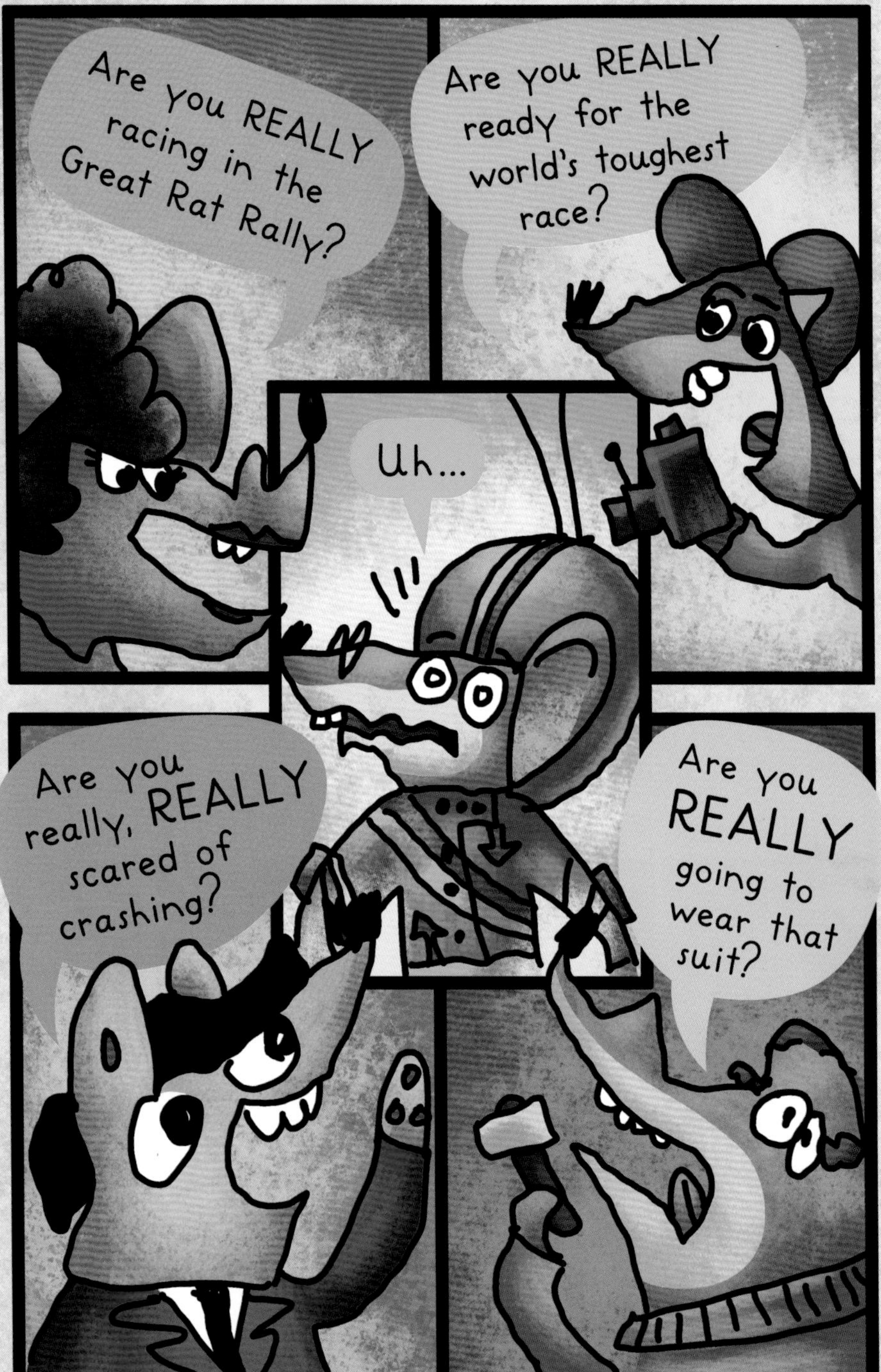
Are you REALLY racing in the Great Rat Rally?
Are you REALLY ready for the world's toughest race?
Uh...
Are you really, REALLY scared of crashing?
Are you REALLY going to wear that suit?

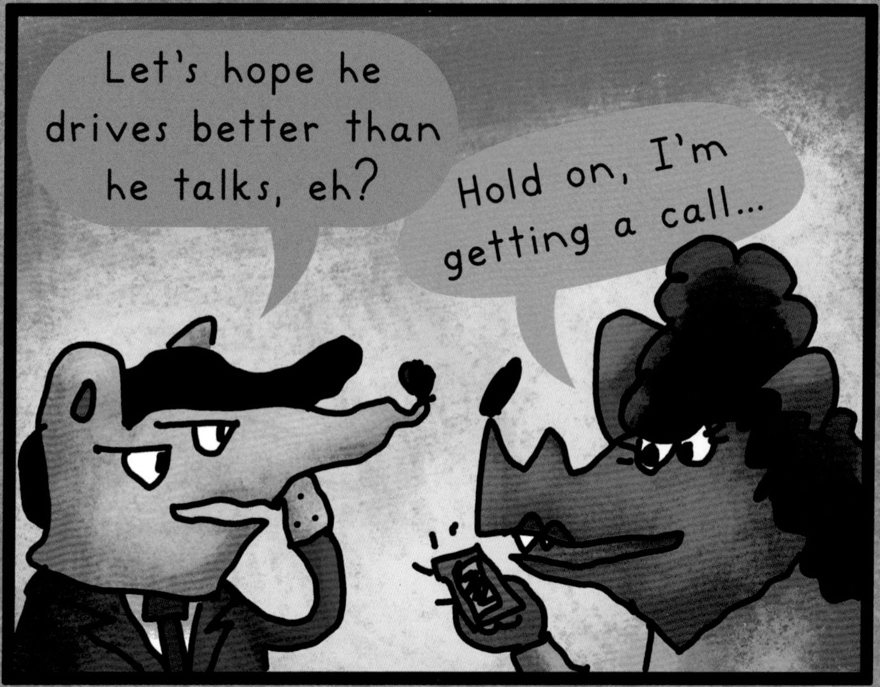
Let's hope he drives better than he talks, eh?
Hold on, I'm getting a call...

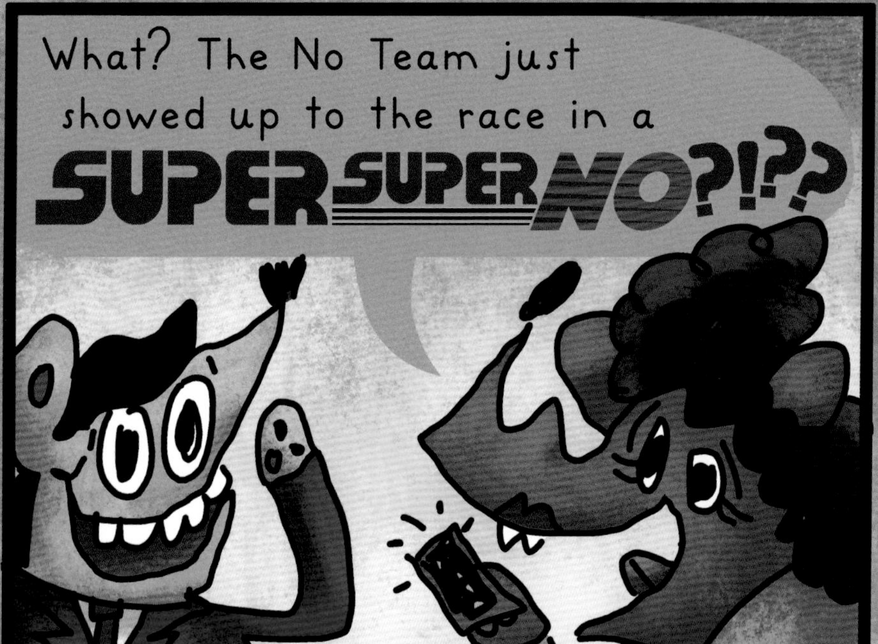
What? The No Team just showed up to the race in a SUPER SUPER NO?!??

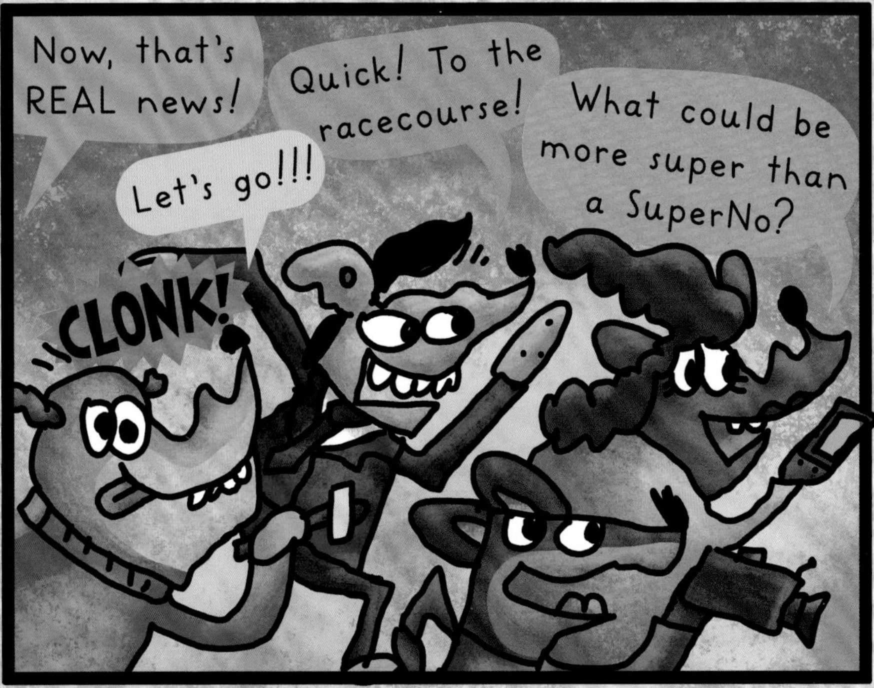
Now, that's REAL news!
Let's go!!!
Quick! To the racecourse!
What could be more super than a SuperNo?
CLONK!

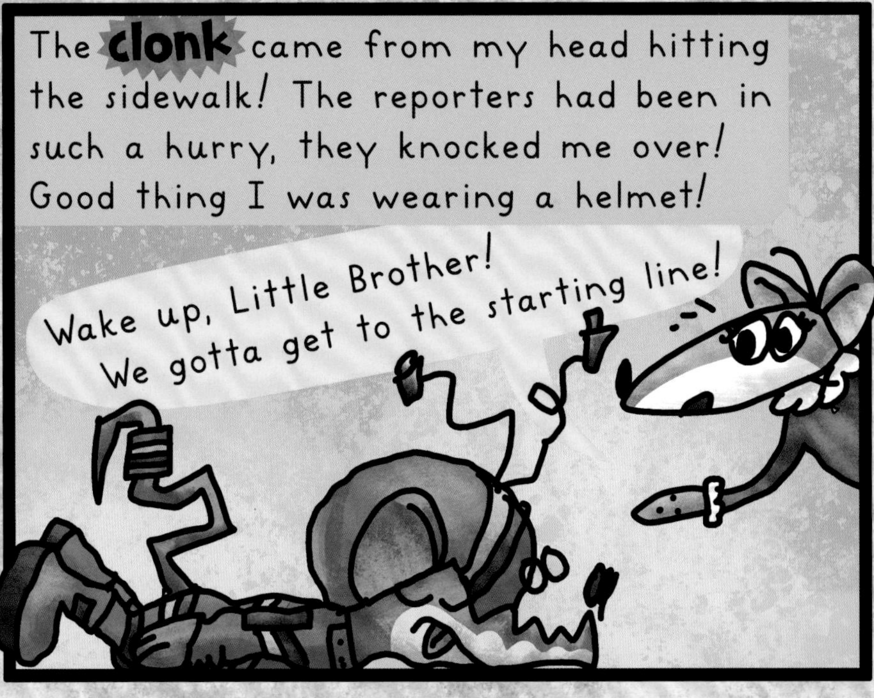
The clonk came from my head hitting the sidewalk! The reporters had been in such a hurry, they knocked me over! Good thing I was wearing a helmet!
Wake up, Little Brother! We gotta get to the starting line!

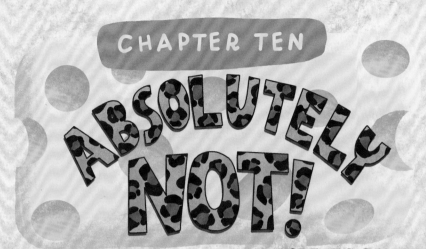

CHAPTER TEN

ABSOLUTELY NOT!

Thea reminded me that, as **THE RODENT'S GAZETTE** photographer, she had to get to the starting line to take a picture of the start of the race! And, of course, I was supposed to be there, too.

Hop in the sidecar, Gerry!

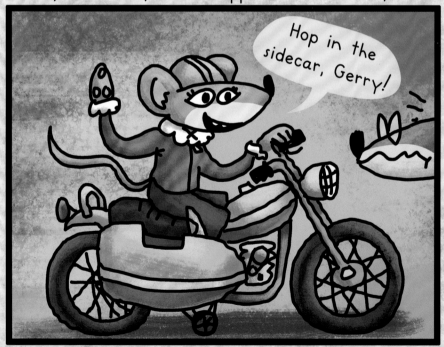

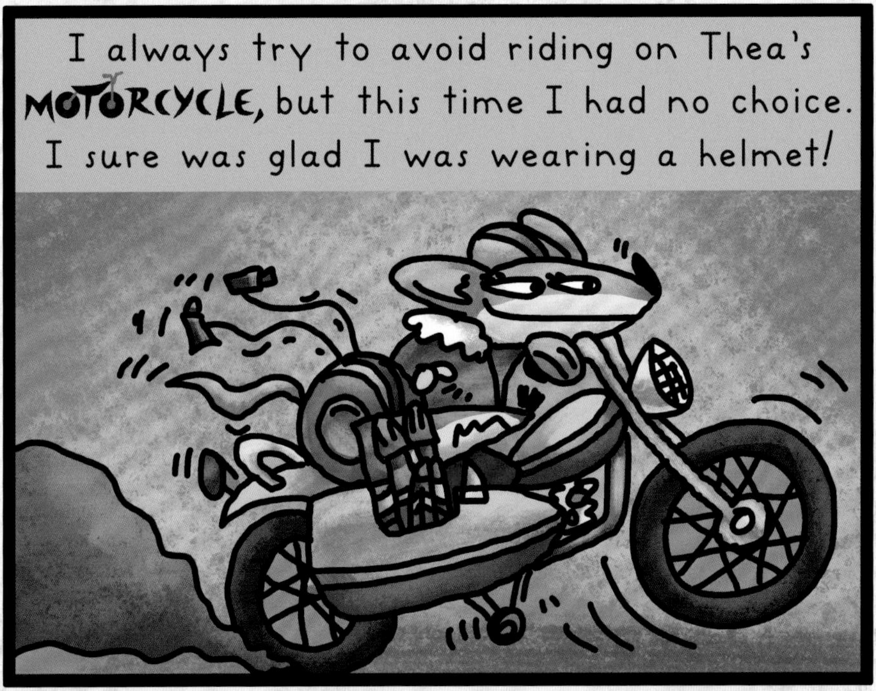
I always try to avoid riding on Thea's MOTORCYCLE, but this time I had no choice. I sure was glad I was wearing a helmet!

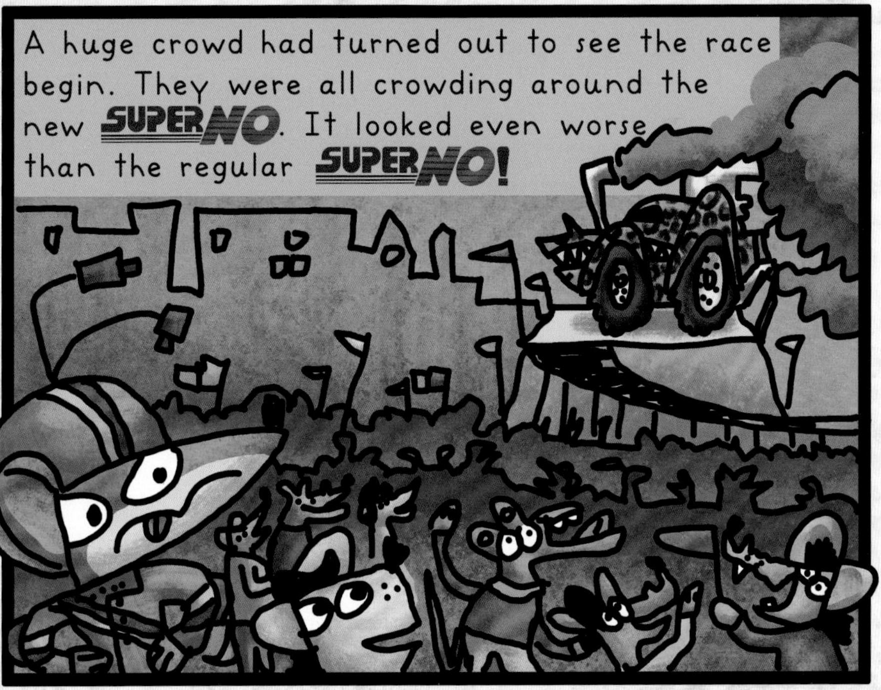
A huge crowd had turned out to see the race begin. They were all crowding around the new SUPERNO. It looked even worse than the regular SUPERNO!

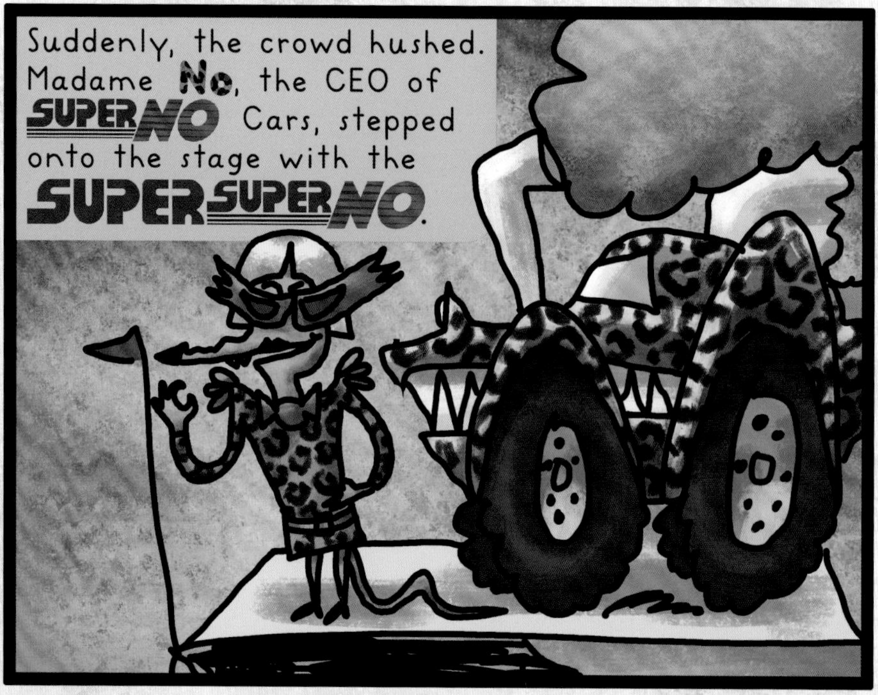
Suddenly, the crowd hushed. Madame No, the CEO of SUPERNO Cars, stepped onto the stage with the SUPERSUPERNO.

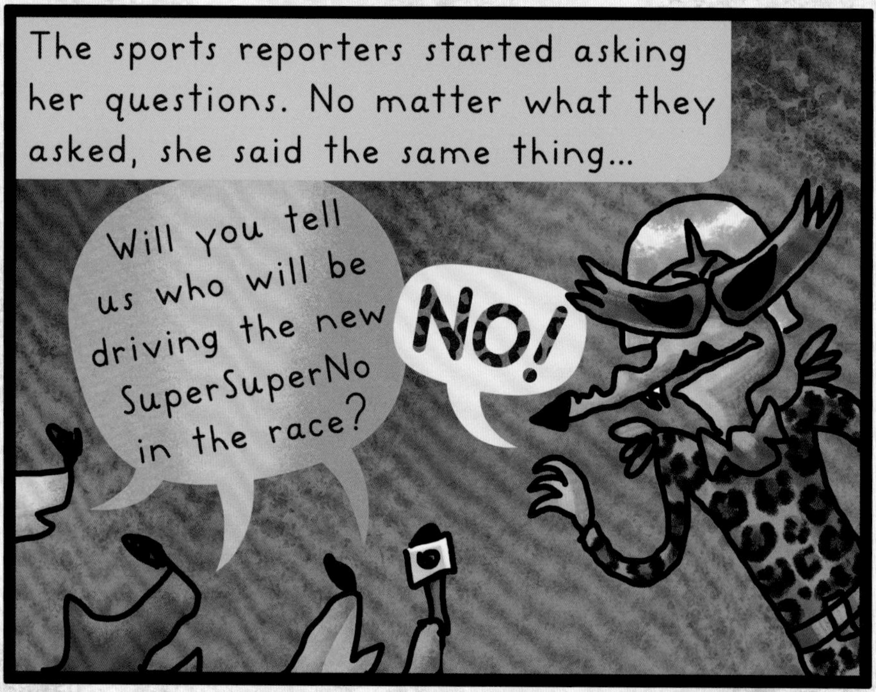
The sports reporters started asking her questions. No matter what they asked, she said the same thing...
Will you tell us who will be driving the new SuperSuperNo in the race?
NO!

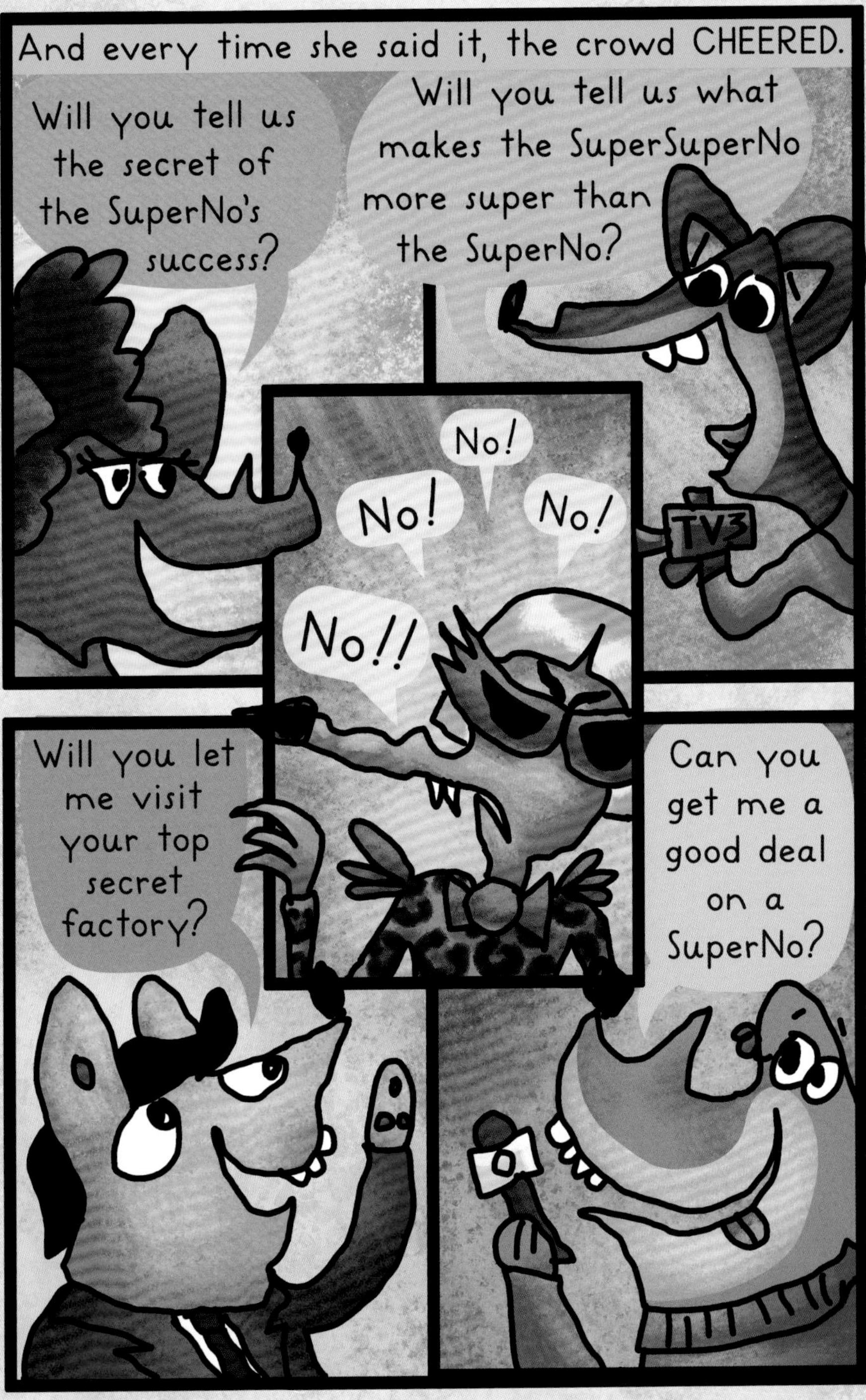
And every time she said it, the crowd CHEERED.
Will you tell us the secret of the SuperNo's success?
Will you tell us what makes the SuperSuperNo more super than the SuperNo?
TV3
No!
No!
No!
No!!
Will you let me visit your top secret factory?
Can you get me a good deal on a SuperNo?

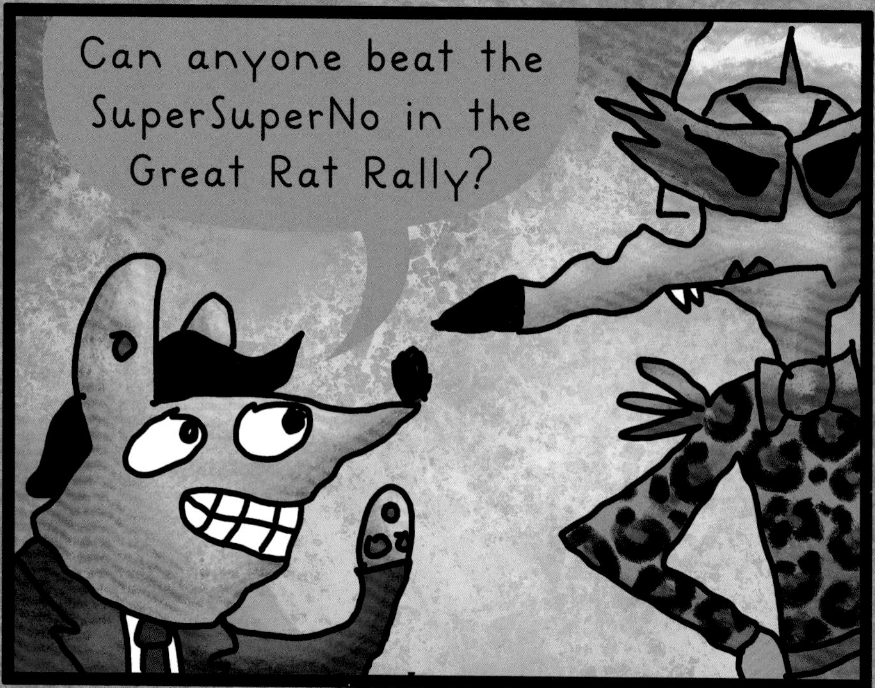
Can anyone beat the SuperSuperNo in the Great Rat Rally?

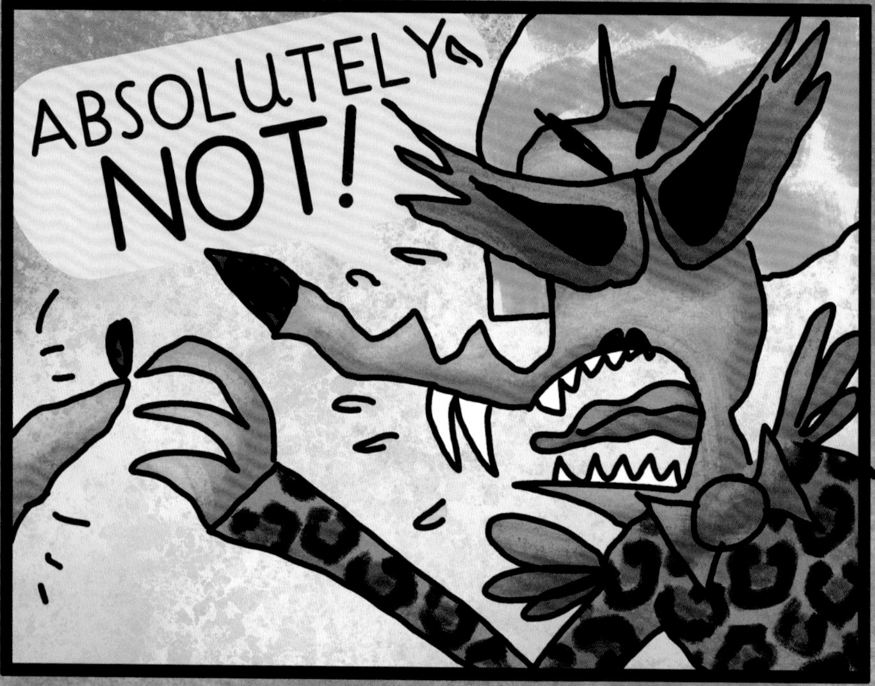
ABSOLUTELY NOT!

CHAPTER ELEVEN

READY...

SET...

The SuperSuperNo roared off to the starting line. Then the other cars began to parade past...

Molinda Clawpaw and Wes "The Wonder" Weasel!

START

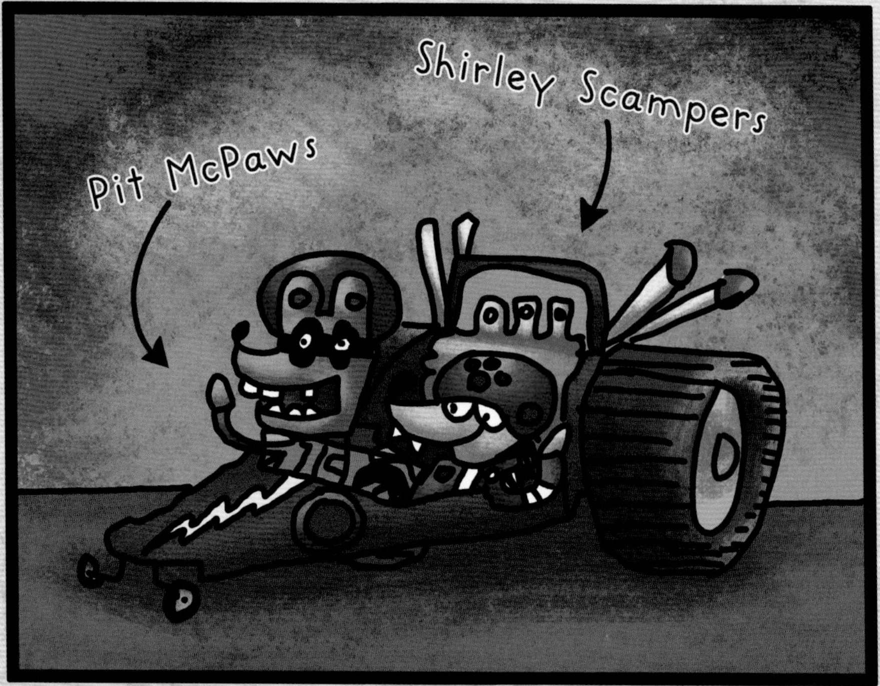

Shirley Scampers
Pit McPaws

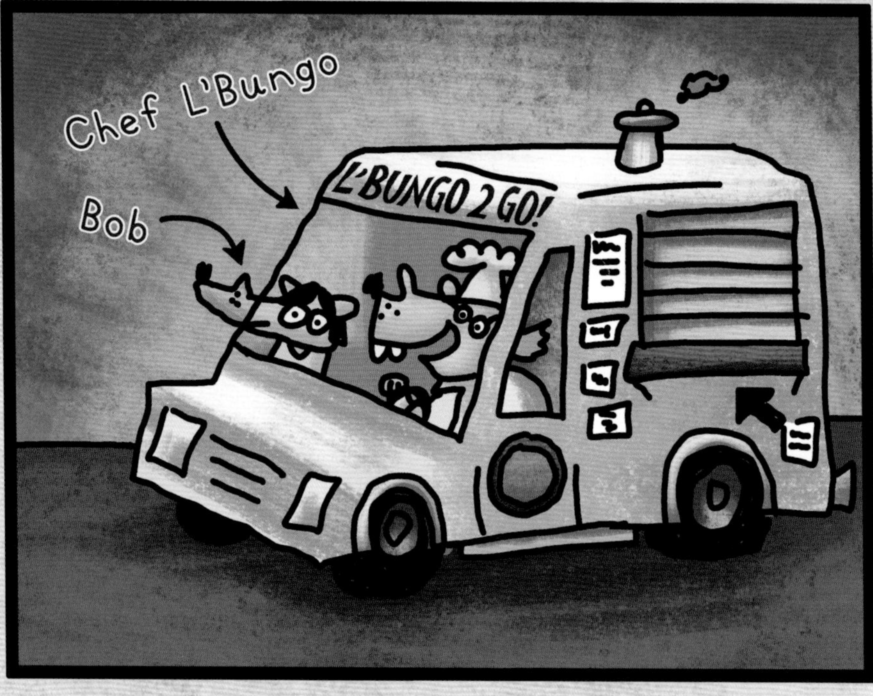

Chef L'Bungo
Bob
L'BUNGO 2 GO!

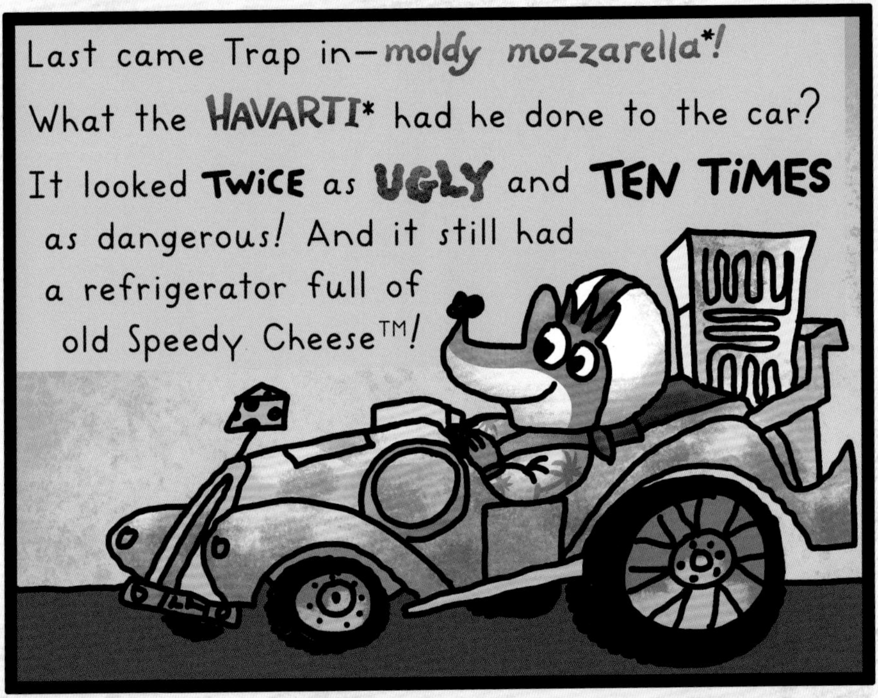
Last came Trap in—moldy mozzarella*!
What the HAVARTI* had he done to the car?
It looked TWICE as UGLY and TEN TIMES as dangerous! And it still had a refrigerator full of old Speedy Cheese™!

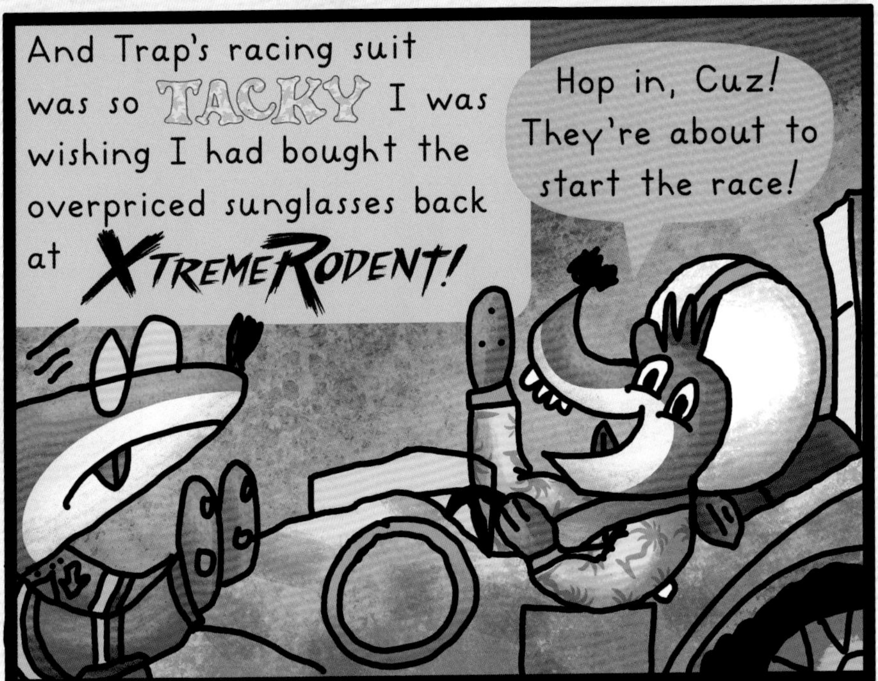
And Trap's racing suit was so TACKY I was wishing I had bought the overpriced sunglasses back at XTREMERODENT!
Hop in, Cuz! They're about to start the race!

*Mozzarella and Havarti are types of cheese.

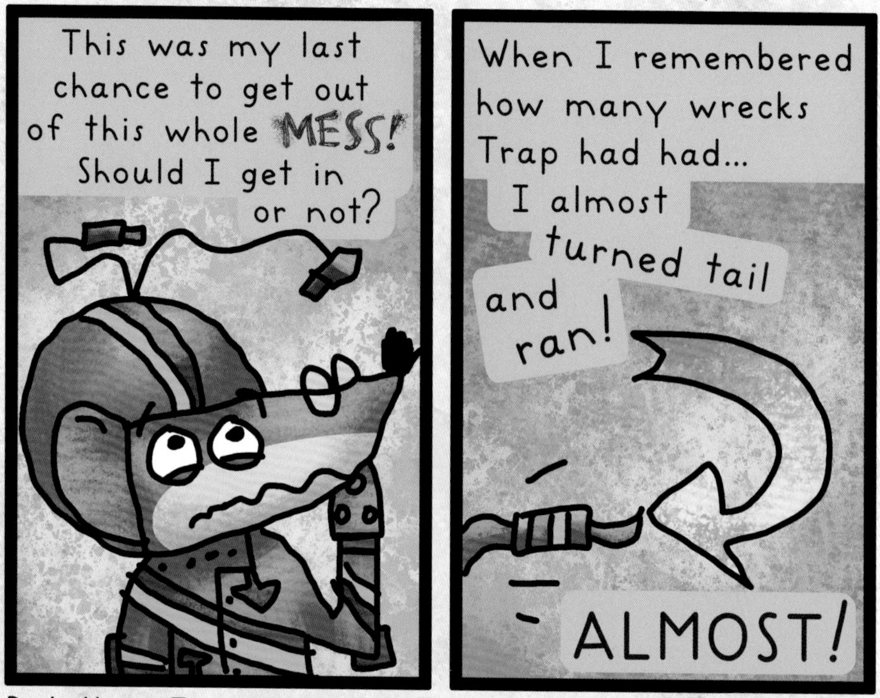
This was my last chance to get out of this whole MESS! Should I get in or not?
When I remembered how many wrecks Trap had had...
I almost turned tail
and ran!
ALMOST!

But then I remembered what Grandfather William had said:

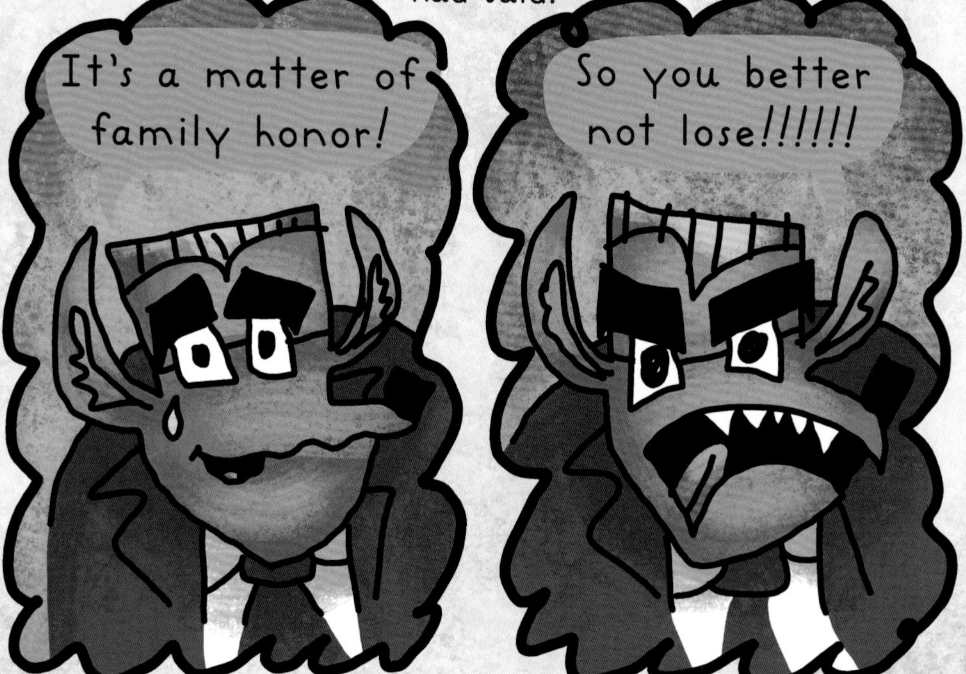
It's a matter of family honor!
So you better not lose!!!!!!

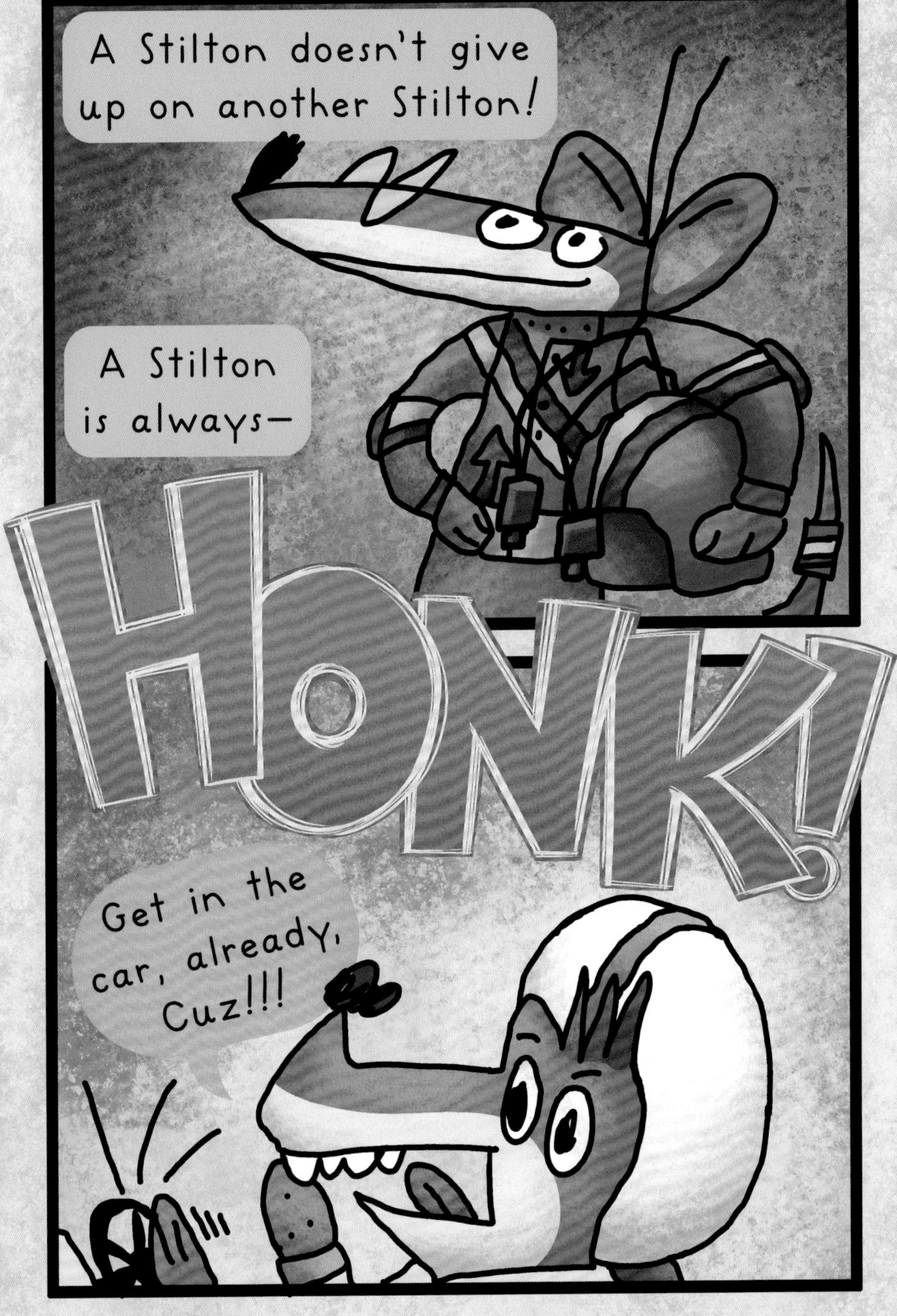
A Stilton doesn't give up on another Stilton!
A Stilton is always—
HONK!
Get in the car, already, Cuz!!!

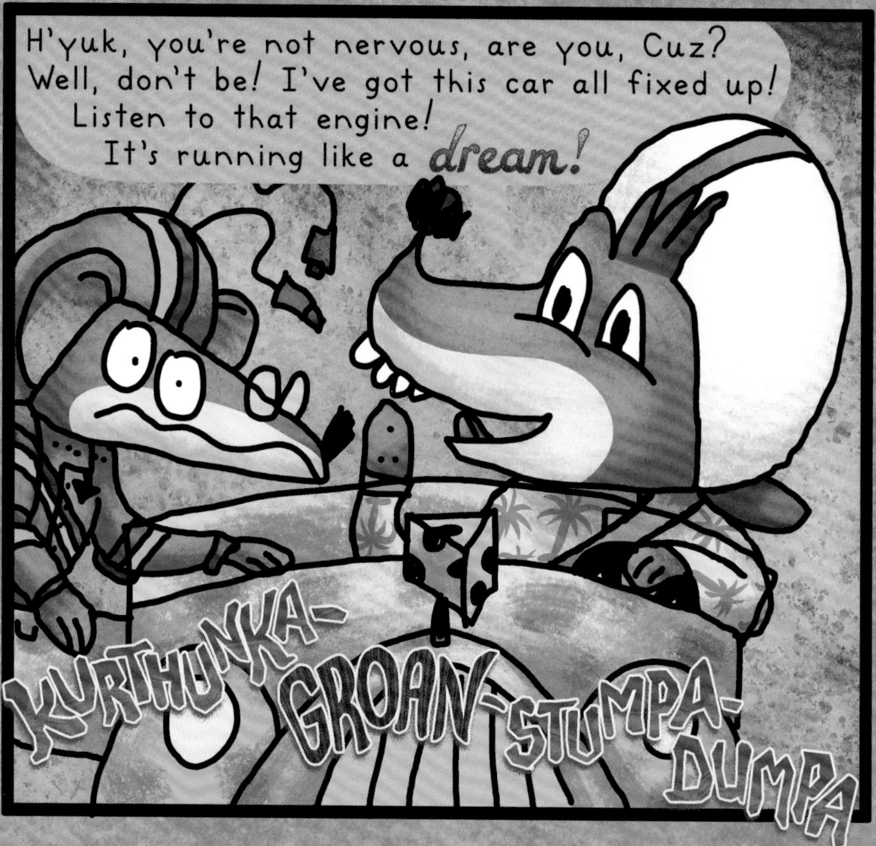
H'yuk, you're not nervous, are you, Cuz? Well, don't be! I've got this car all fixed up! Listen to that engine! It's running like a dream!
KURTHUNKA-GROAN-STUMPA-DUMPA

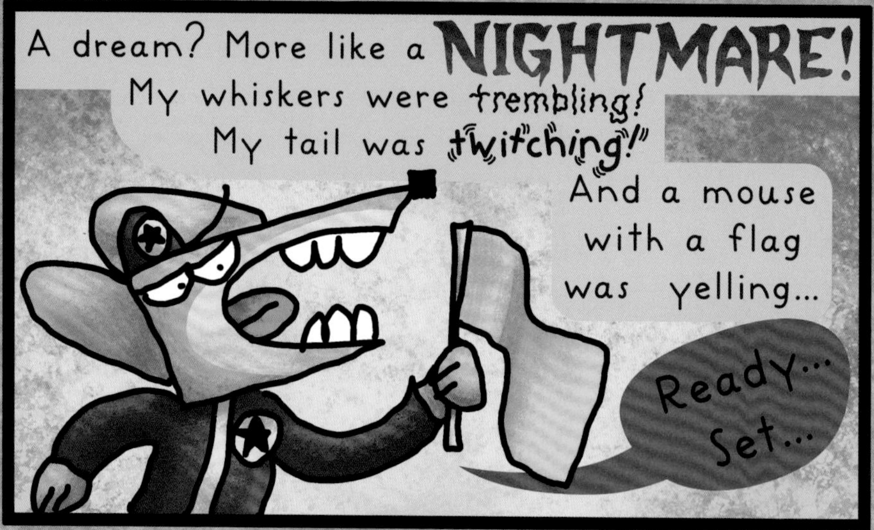
A dream? More like a NIGHTMARE! My whiskers were trembling! My tail was twitching!
And a mouse with a flag was yelling...
Ready... Set...

CHAPTER TWELVE

"GO!"

The mouse with the flag yelled, "Go!"
and all the cars zoomed forward!
Instead of heading straight out of town,
the racecourse went through New Mouse City!

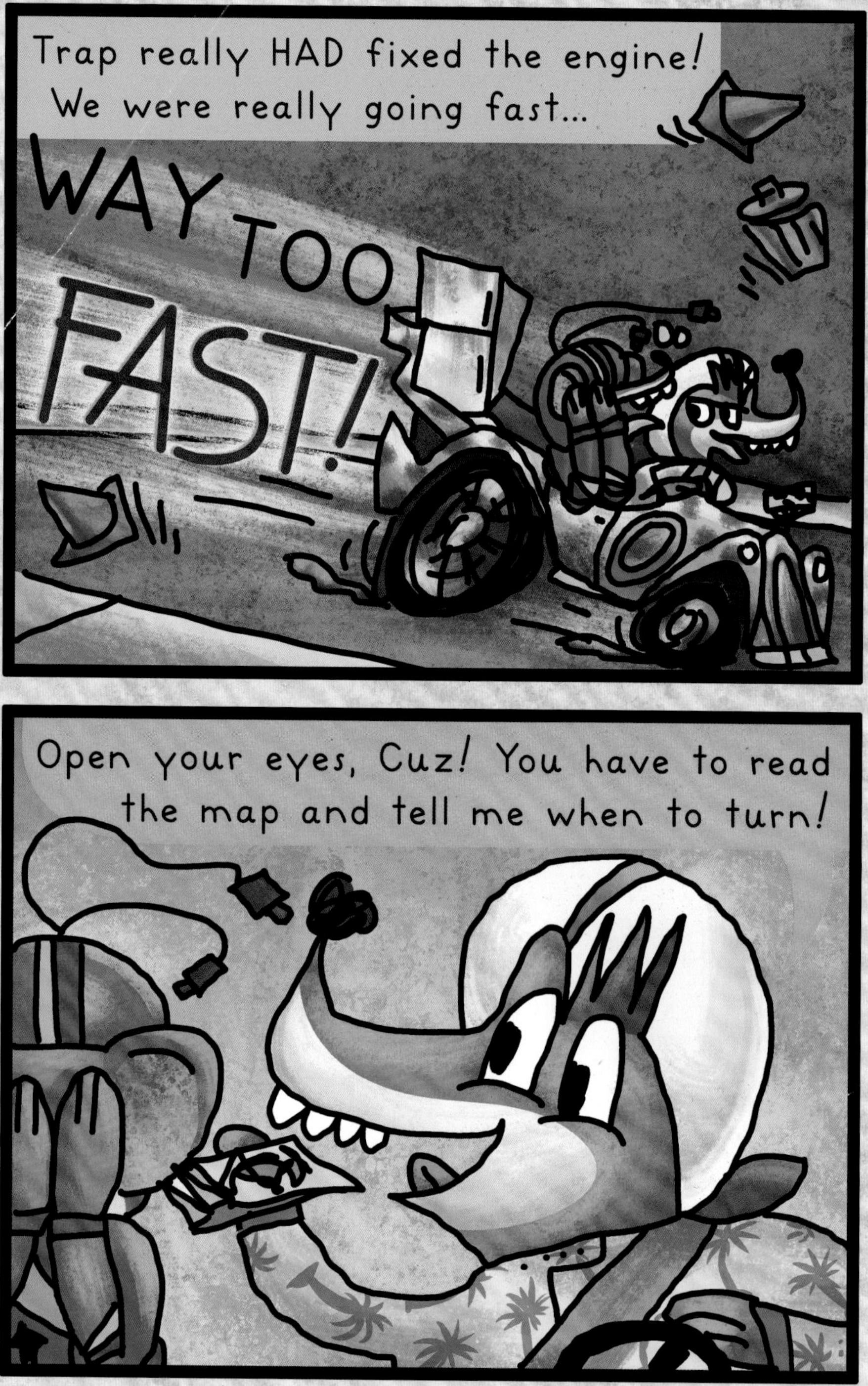
Trap really HAD fixed the engine! We were really going fast...
WAY TOO FAST!
Open your eyes, Cuz! You have to read the map and tell me when to turn!

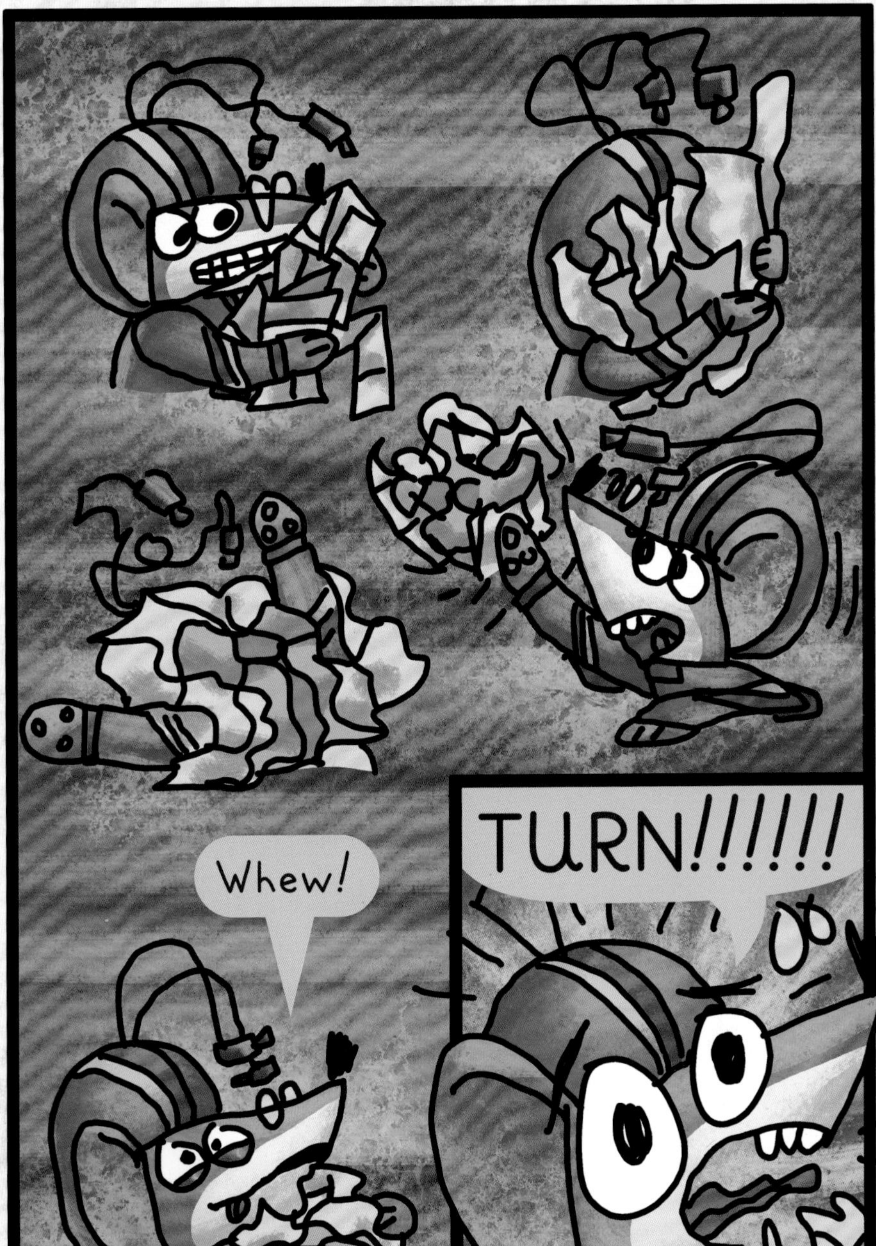
Whew!
TURN!!!!!!

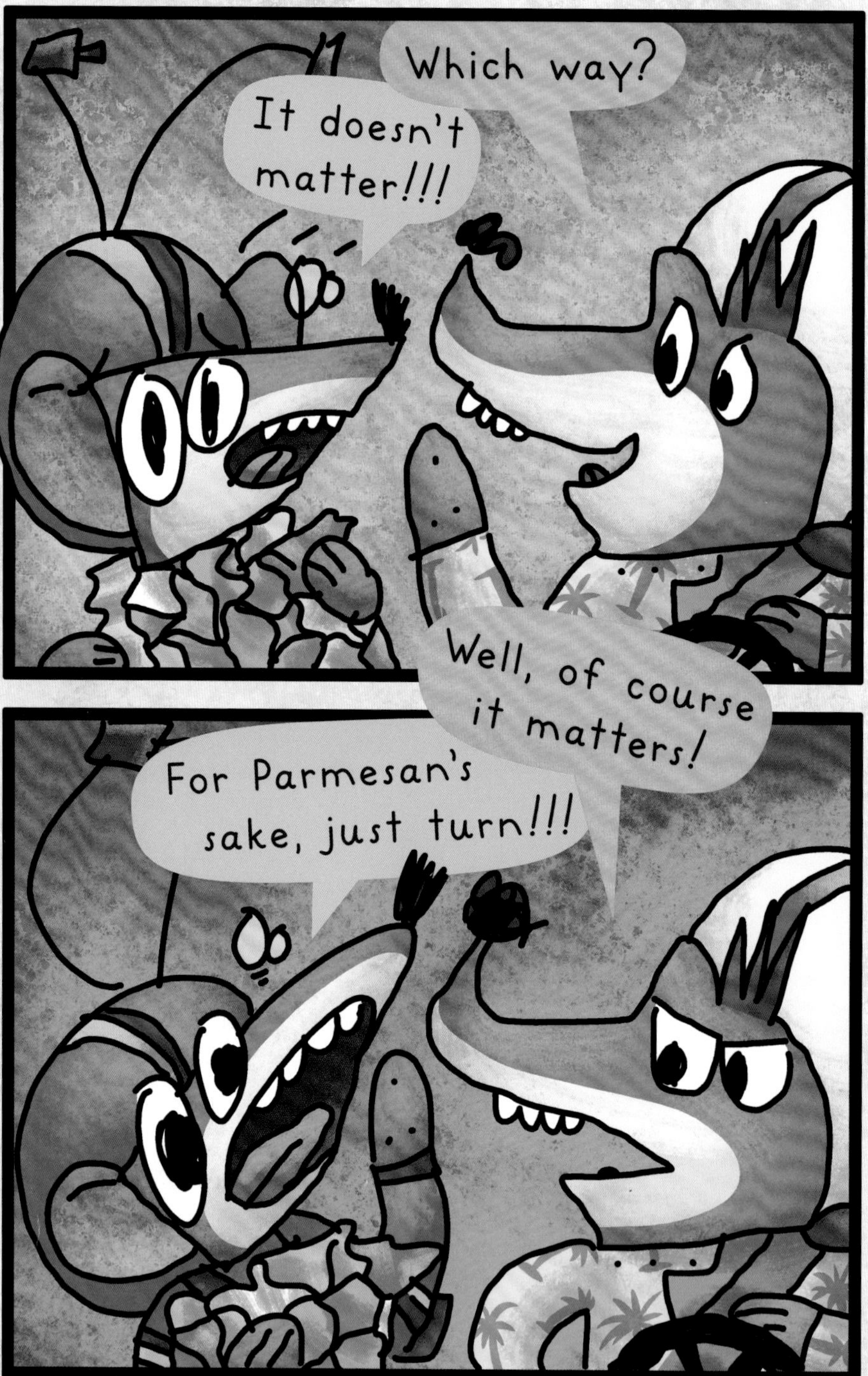
Which way?
It doesn't matter!!!
Well, of course it matters!
For Parmesan's sake, just turn!!!

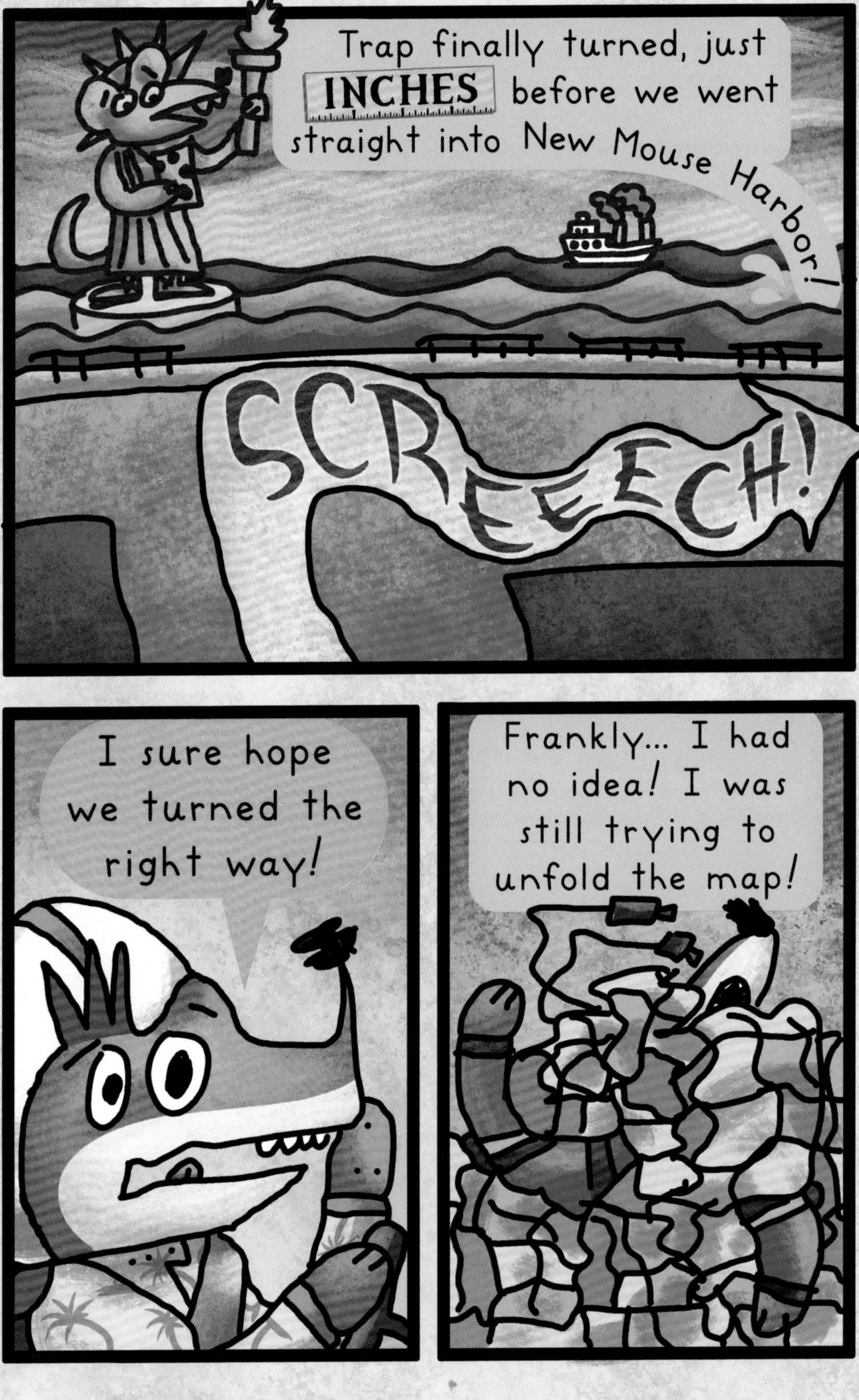

Trap finally turned, just INCHES before we went straight into New Mouse Harbor!
SCREEECH!
I sure hope we turned the right way!
Frankly... I had no idea! I was still trying to unfold the map!

Finally, I was able to flatten out the map enough to find New Mouse Harbor. We had to be somewhere near there!

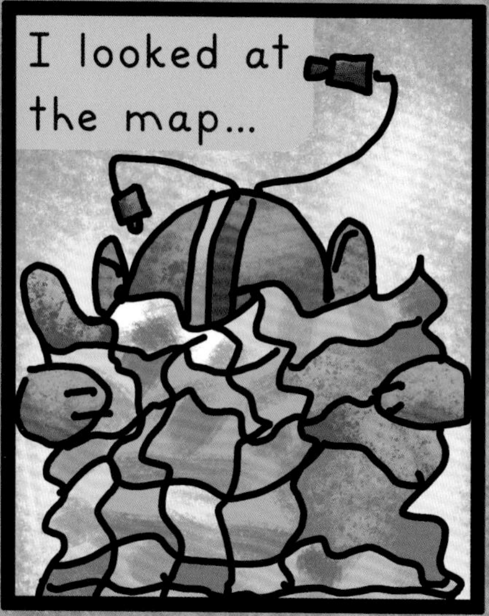
I looked at the map...

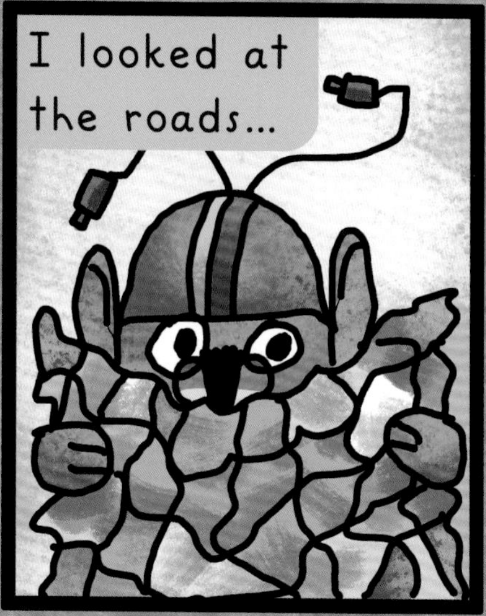
I looked at the roads...

They just didn't match! I had already failed! What would Trap say? What would Thea say? What would Grandfather William **YELL??**

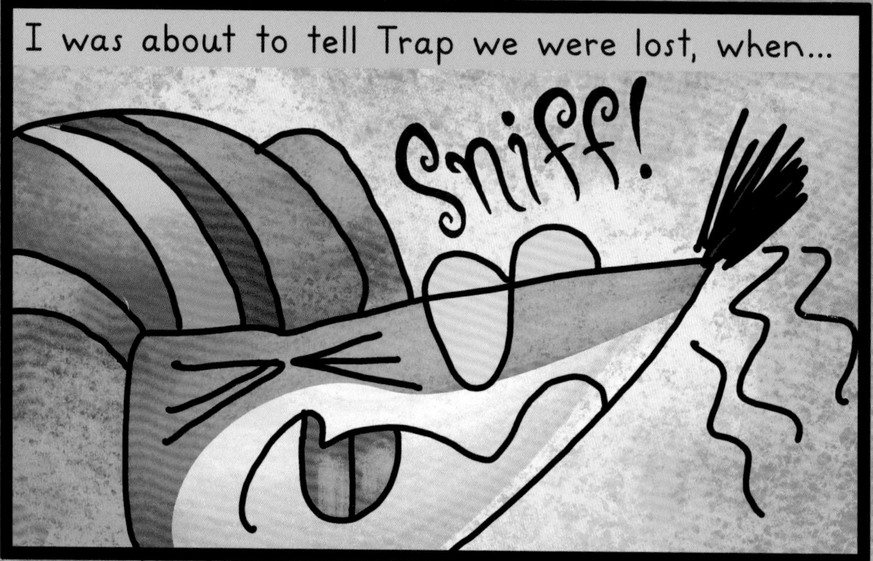
I was about to tell Trap we were lost, when...
Sniff!

CHAPTER THIRTEEN

Welcome to COWPIE Valley!

The **smell** was AWFUL! But it was a **smell** I had smelled before! There was only one place on Mouse Island that smelled like this!

Trap! We're in Cowpie Valley!

Oh, so that's what that is...

What WHAT is?

THAT!

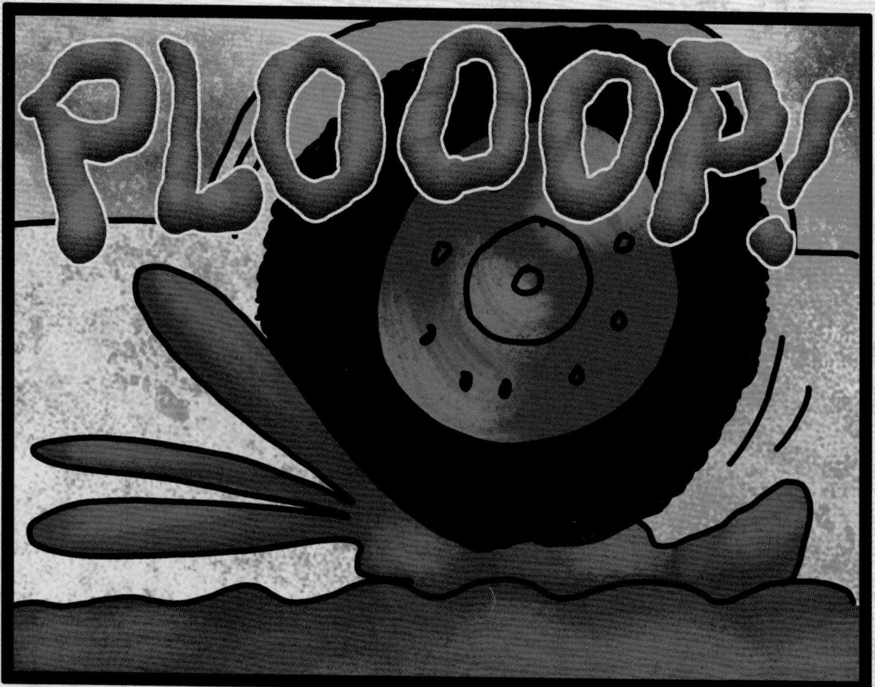
PLOOOP!

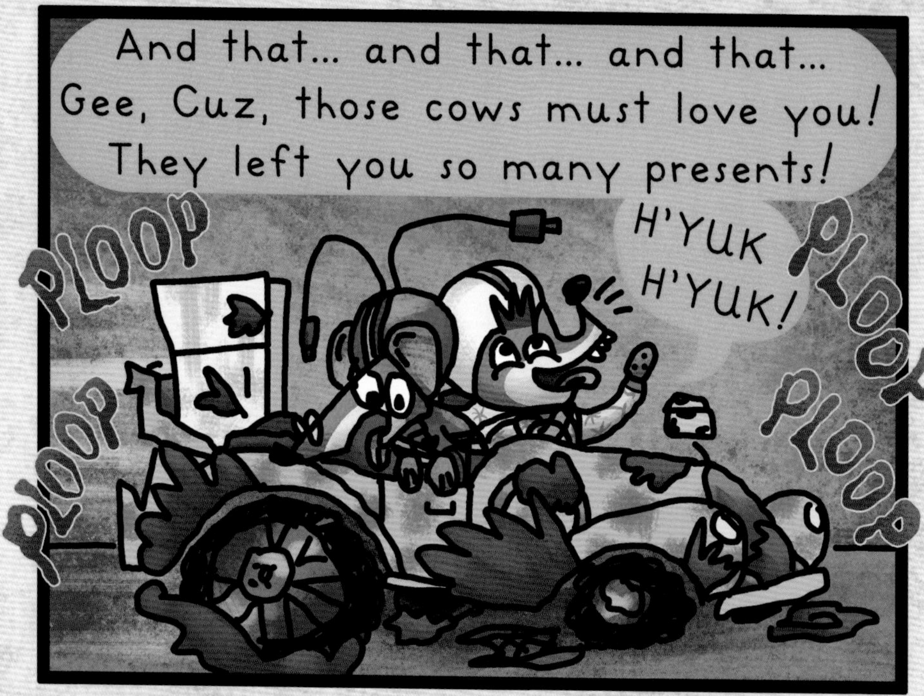
And that... and that... and that...
Gee, Cuz, those cows must love you! They left you so many presents!
H'YUK H'YUK!
PLOOP
PLOOP
PLOOP
PLOOP
PLOOP

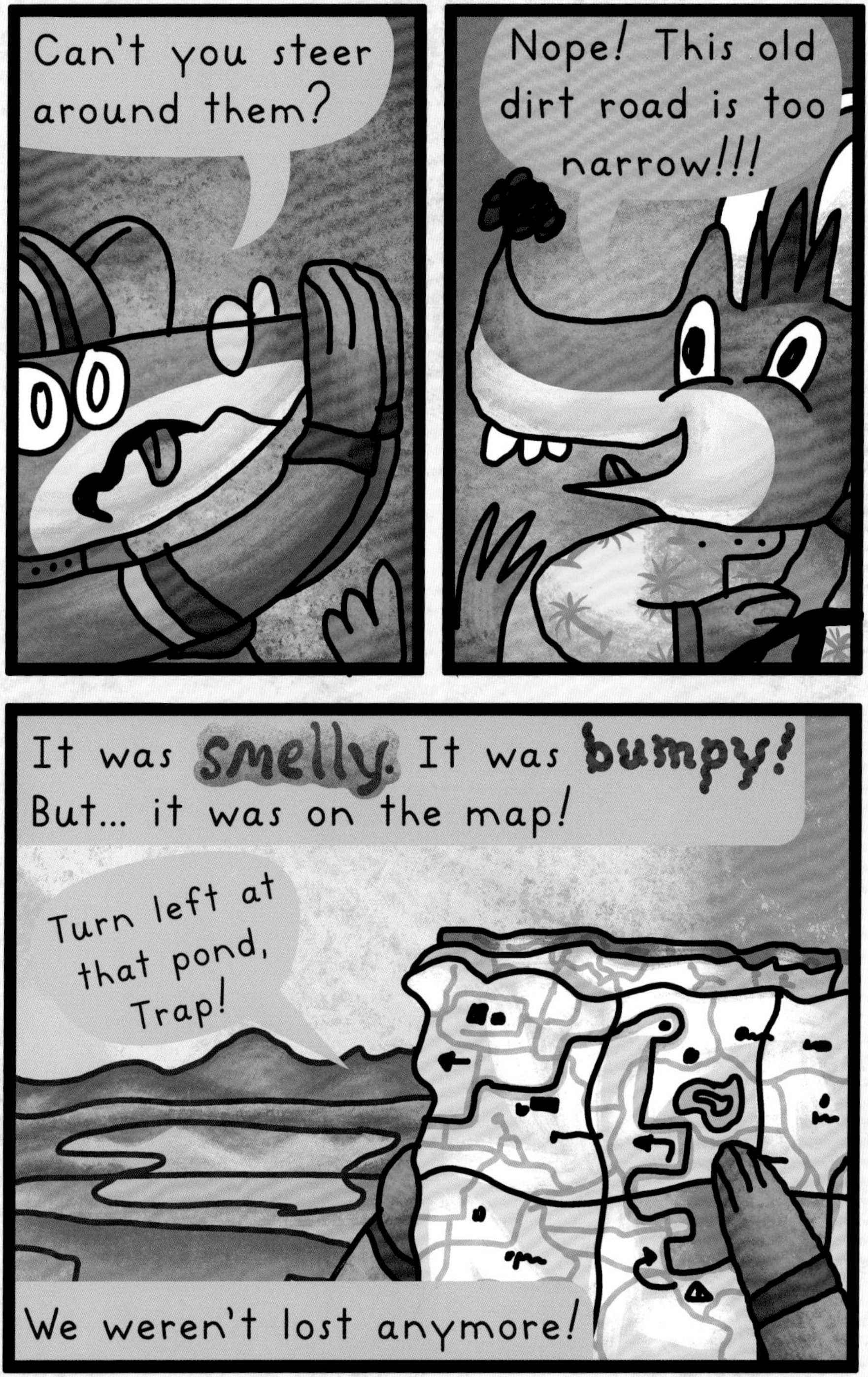
Can't you steer around them?
Nope! This old dirt road is too narrow!!!
It was smelly. It was bumpy! But... it was on the map!
Turn left at that pond, Trap!
We weren't lost anymore!

CHAPTER FOURTEEN
GOOD SPORTS!

Trap did not turn left at the pond.

Trap did not turn right at the pond.

Trap did not turn at all!!!!

CHEDDAR CHUNKS!
UH-OH!
KERSPLOOSH!

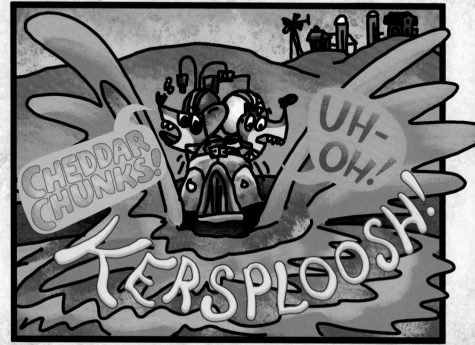

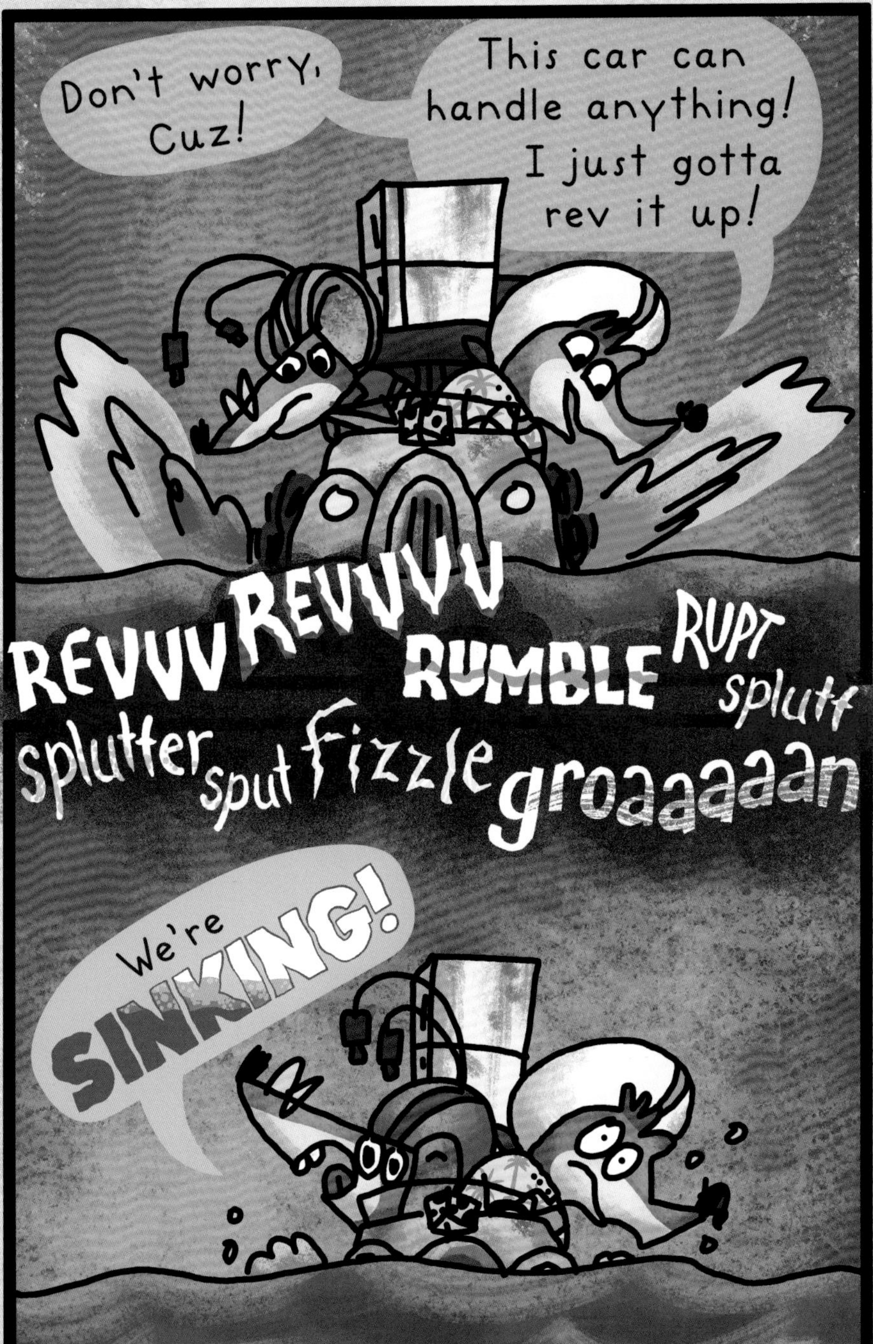
Don't worry, Cuz!
This car can handle anything! I just gotta rev it up!
REVVV REVVVV RUMBLE RUPT
splutf
splutter sput fizzle groaaaaaan
We're SINKING!

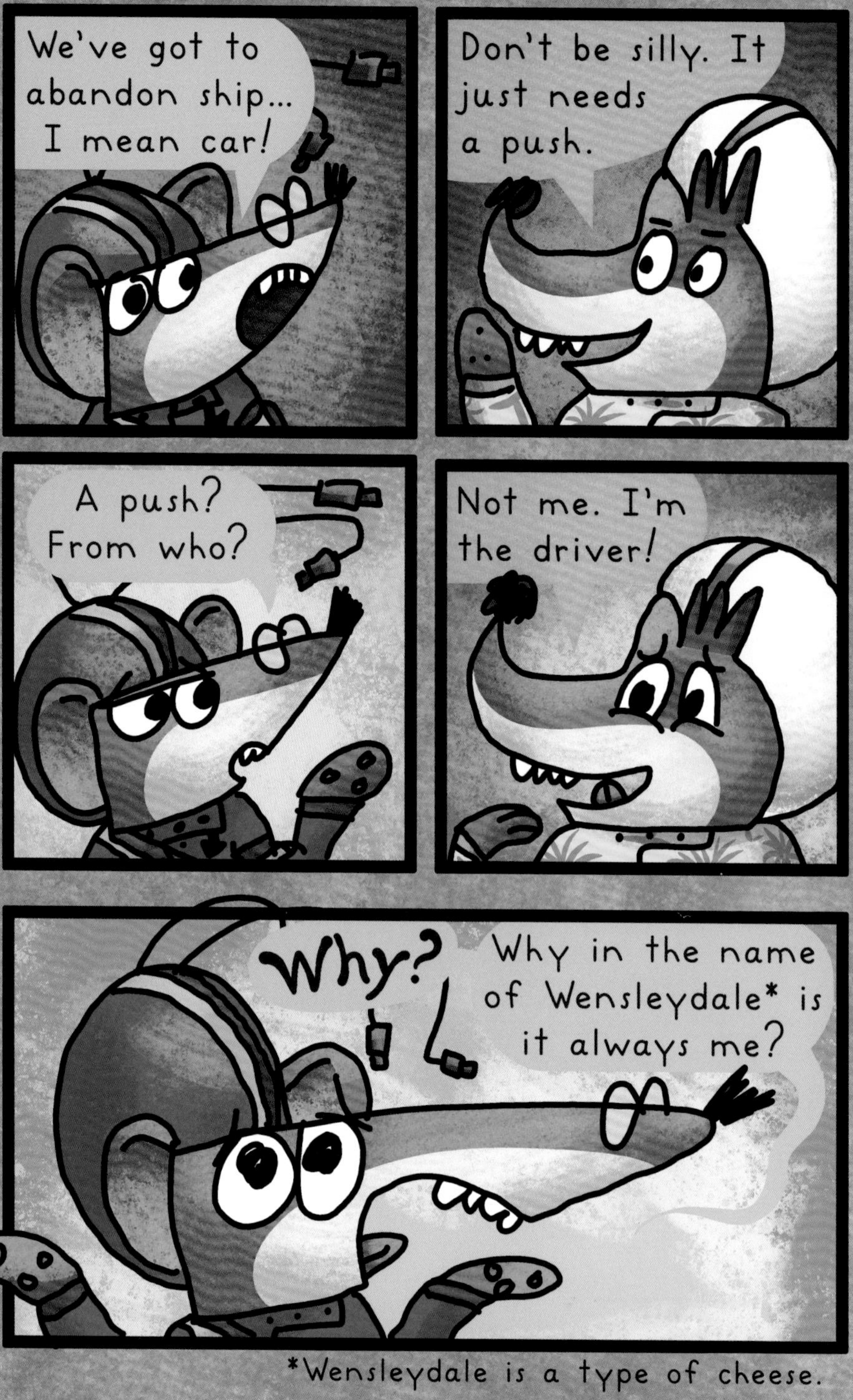
We've got to abandon ship... I mean car!
Don't be silly. It just needs a push.
A push? From who?
Not me. I'm the driver!
Why?
Why in the name of Wensleydale* is it always me?

*Wensleydale is a type of cheese.

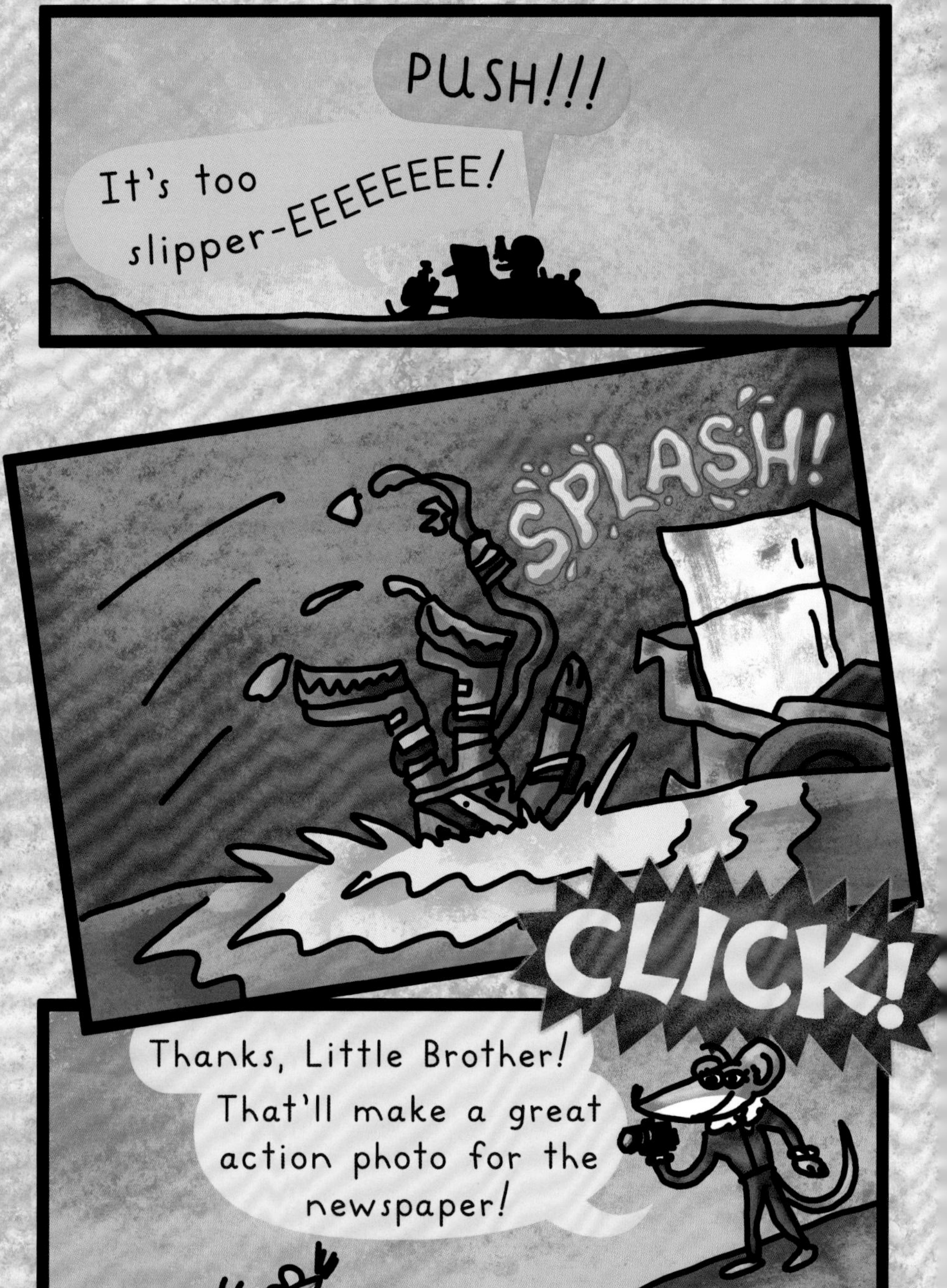
PUSH!!!
It's too slipper-EEEEEEEE!
SPLASH!
CLICK!
Thanks, Little Brother!
That'll make a great action photo for the newspaper!

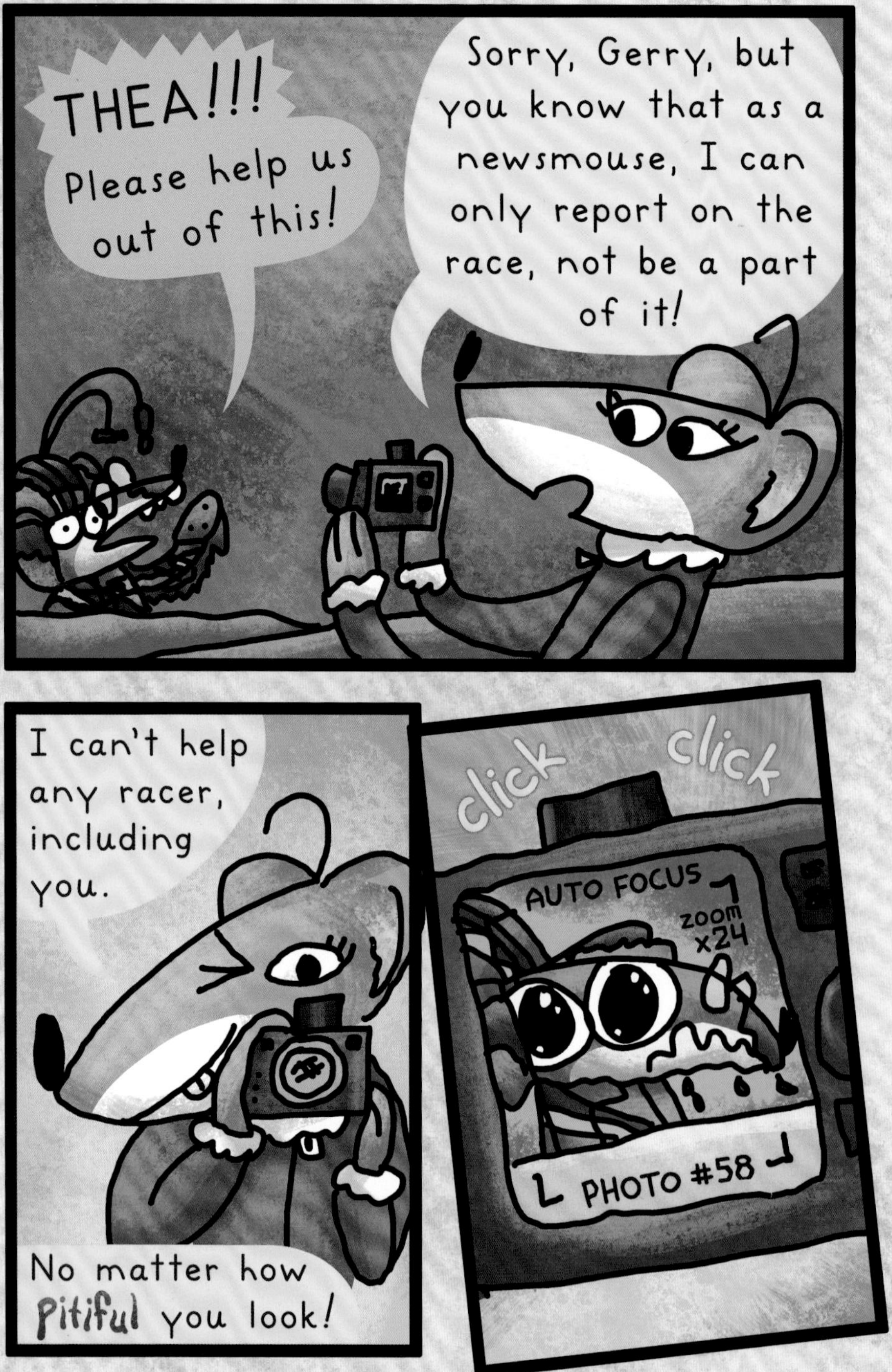
THEA!!!
Please help us out of this!
Sorry, Gerry, but you know that as a newsmouse, I can only report on the race, not be a part of it!
I can't help any racer, including you.
No matter how pitiful you look!
click click
AUTO FOCUS
ZOOM x24
PHOTO #58

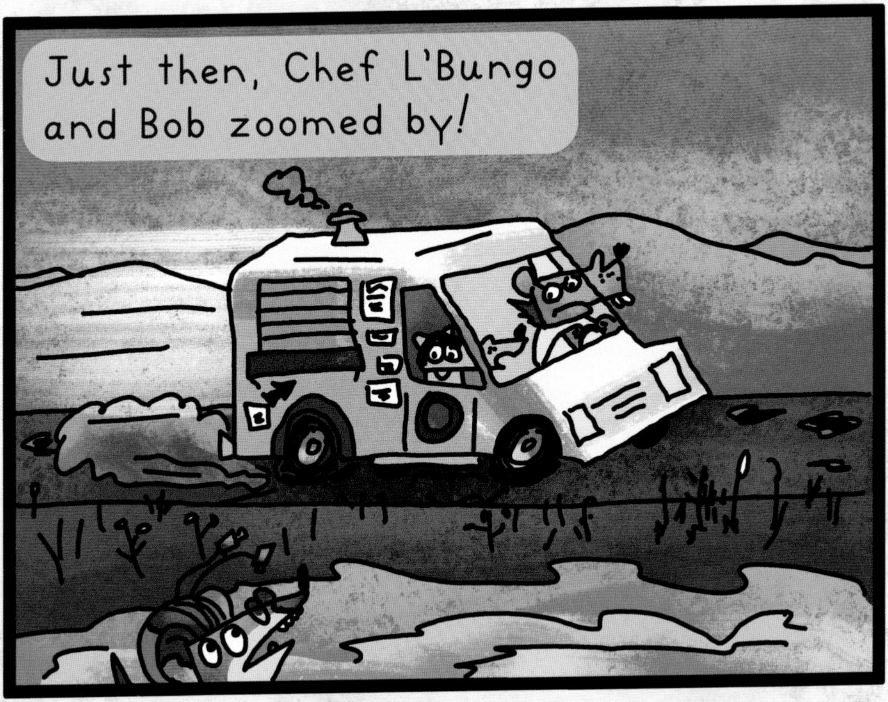
Just then, Chef L'Bungo and Bob zoomed by!

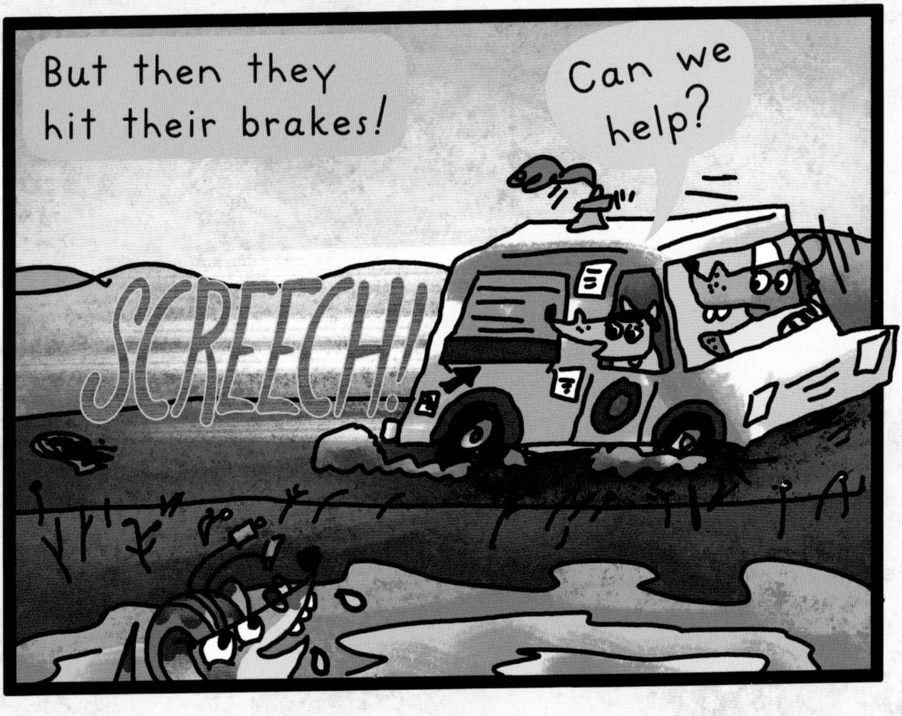
But then they hit their brakes!
Can we help?
SCREECH!

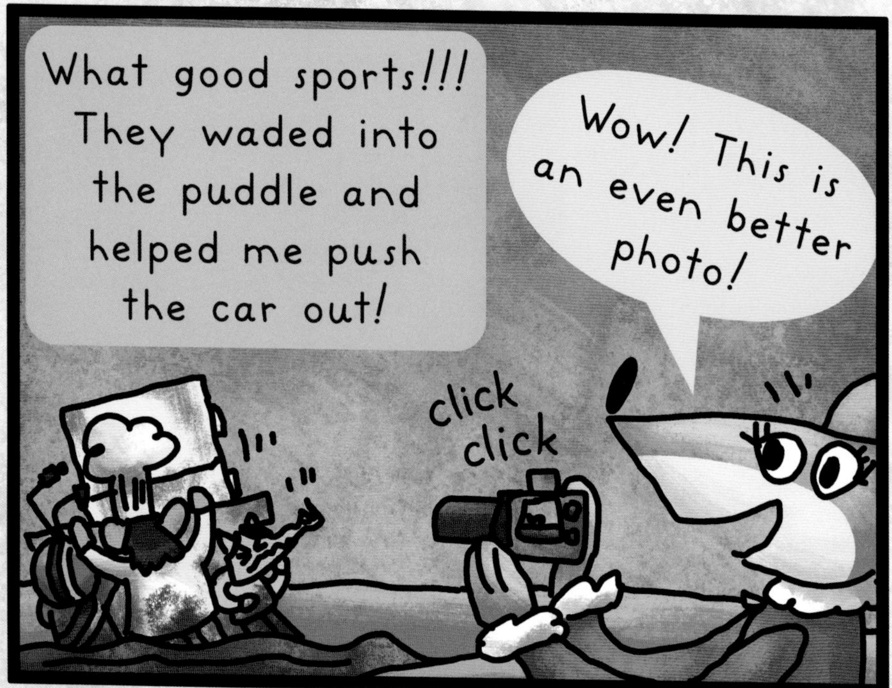
What good sports!!! They waded into the puddle and helped me push the car out!
Wow! This is an even better photo!
click click

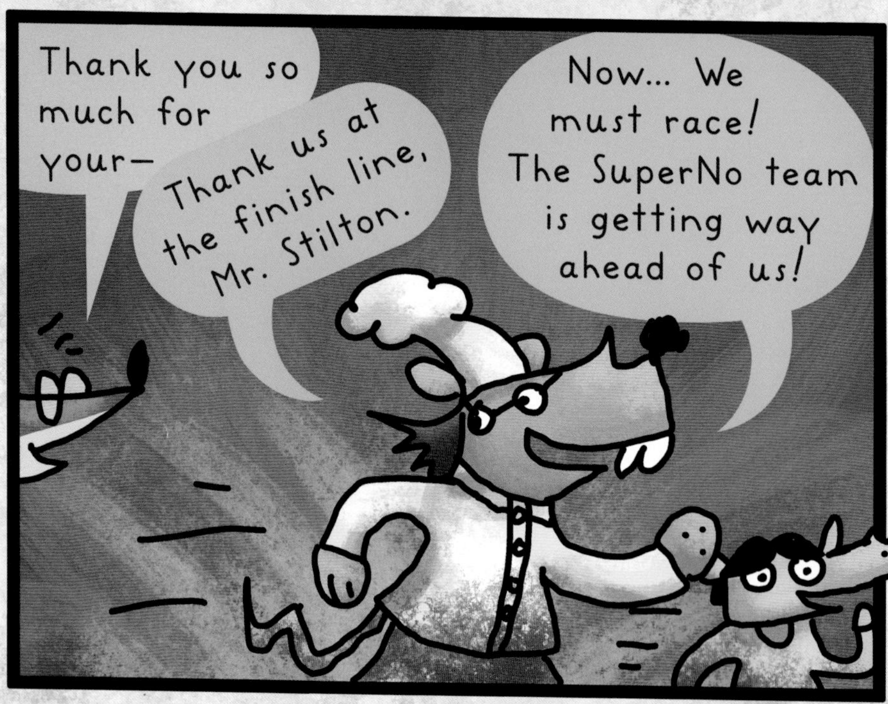
Thank you so much for your—
Thank us at the finish line, Mr. Stilton.
Now... We must race! The SuperNo team is getting way ahead of us!

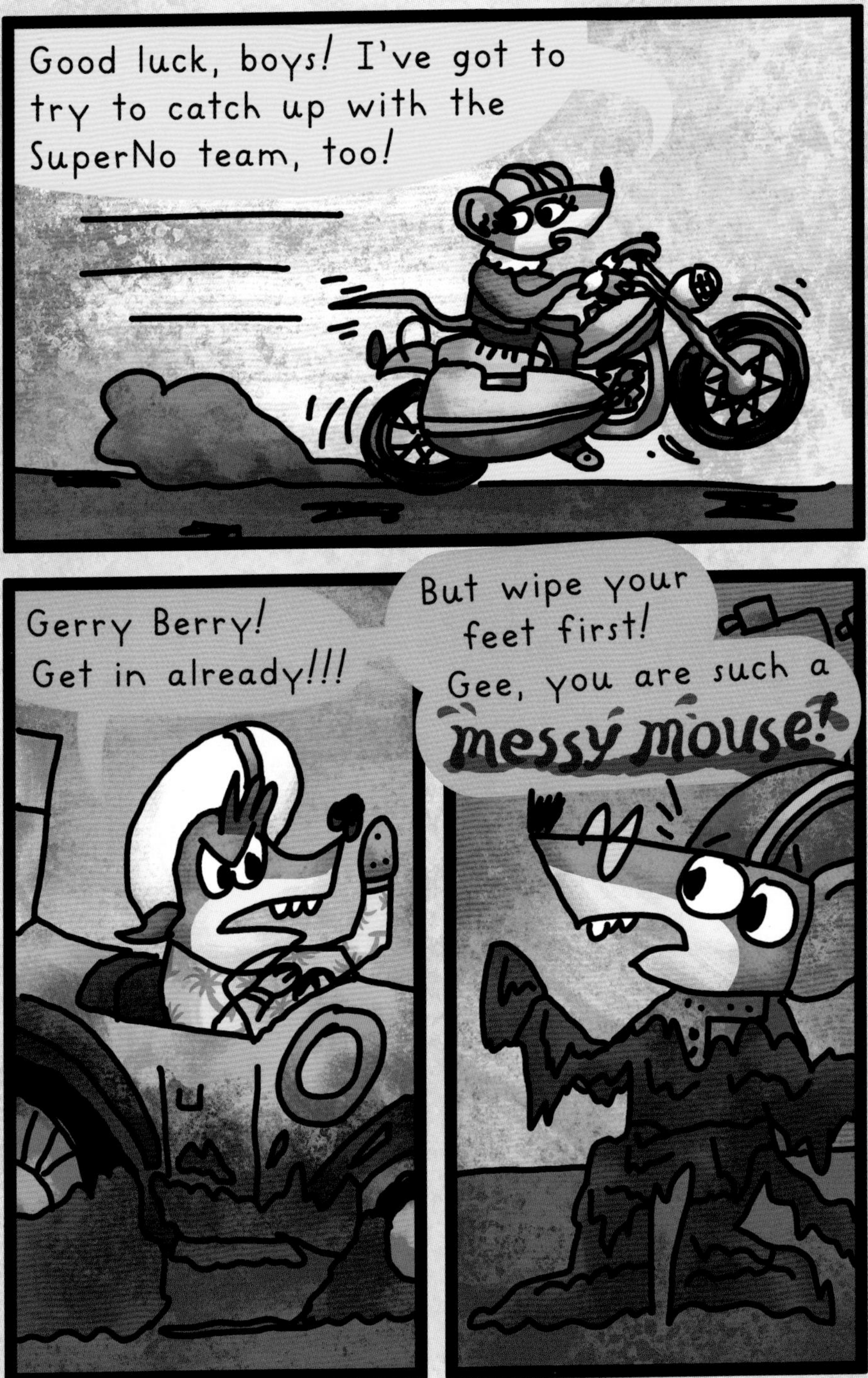
Good luck, boys! I've got to try to catch up with the SuperNo team, too!
Gerry Berry! Get in already!!!
But wipe your feet first!
Gee, you are such a messy mouse!

CHAPTER FIFTEEN

DON'T mess

IT UP THIS TIME!

I scraped most of the **mud** off and climbed back in the car. Trap shoved the map at me and then slammed his foot on the gas! In a second, we were bumping down the road at a
crazy speed!

Don't mess it up this time, Cuz!

BUMP!

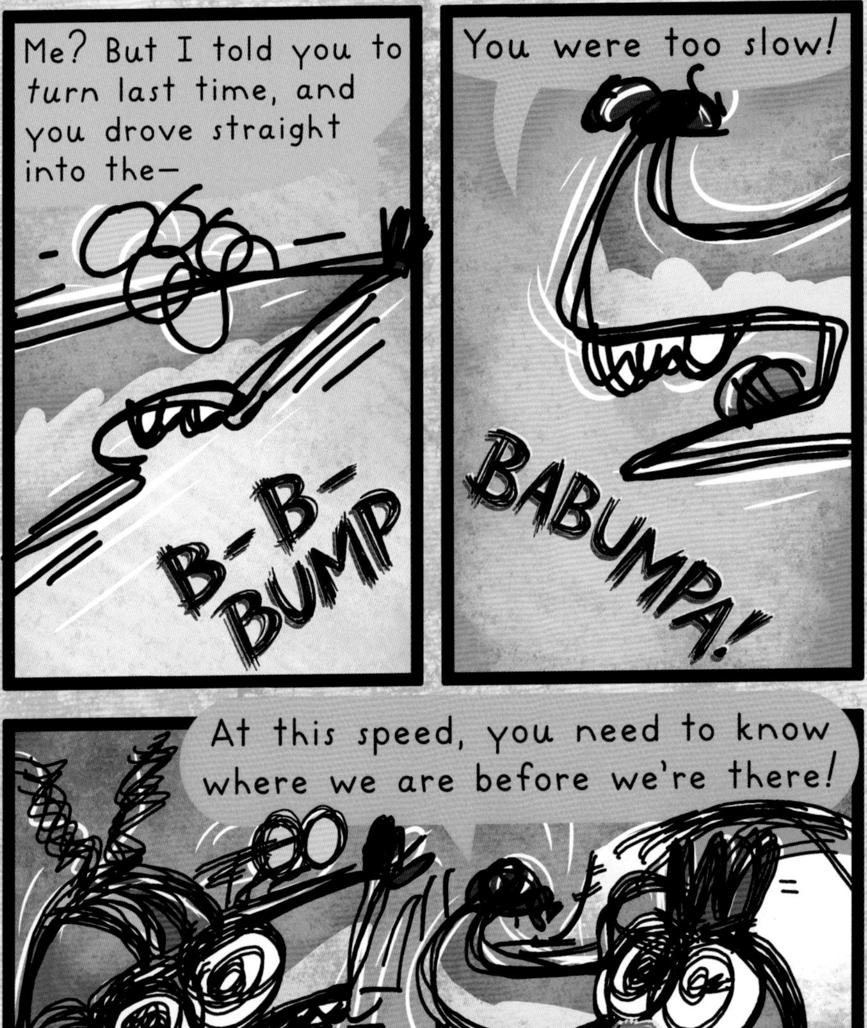
Me? But I told you to *turn* last time, and you drove straight into the—
B-B-BUMP
You were too slow!
BABUMPA!
At this speed, you need to know where we are before we're there!
BUMPA DUMPA BING BANG BUMP!

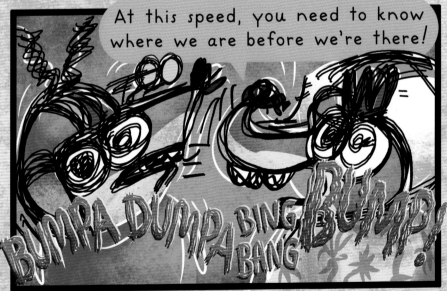

Trap was making less sense than the famouse philosopher Jean-Paul Sartrat! I was so confused, and the road was SO BUMPY, that... I had no idea where we were!!

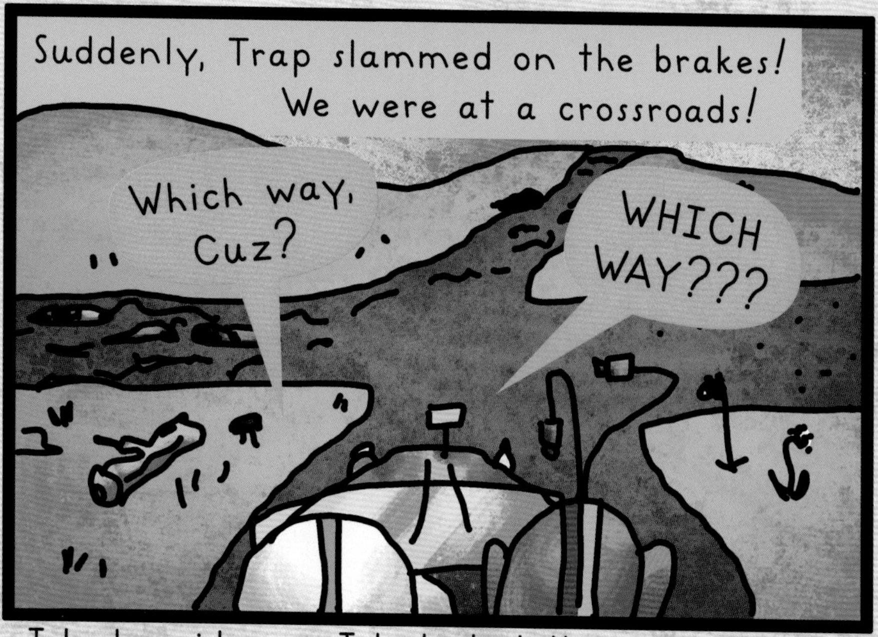
Suddenly, Trap slammed on the brakes! We were at a crossroads!
Which way, Cuz?
WHICH WAY???

I had no idea, so I looked at the roads, and I...
I chose the road that was less bumpy...

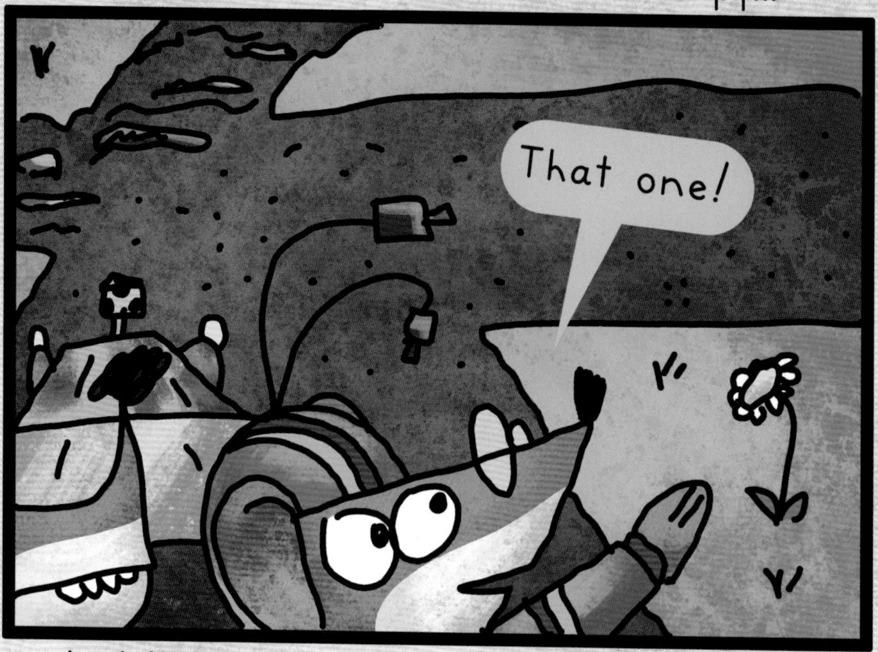
That one!

And that made all the difference, because...

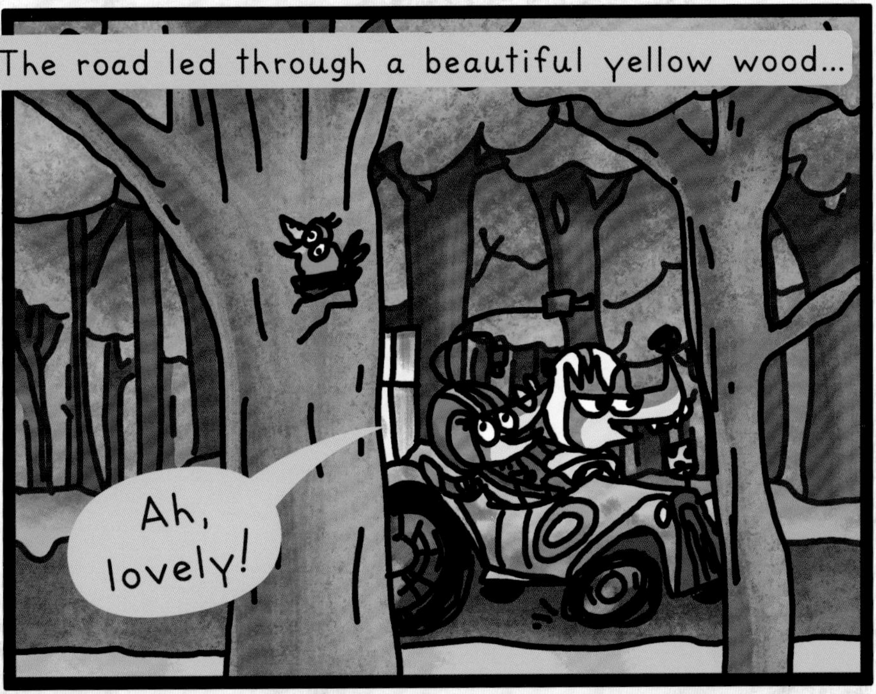
The road led through a beautiful yellow wood...
Ah, lovely!

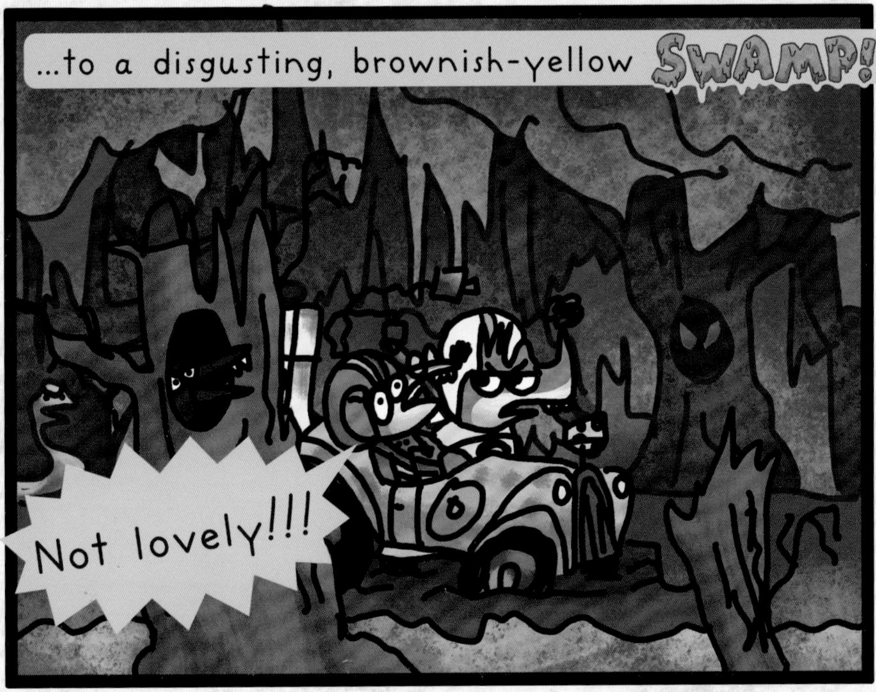
...to a disgusting, brownish-yellow SWAMP!
Not lovely!!!

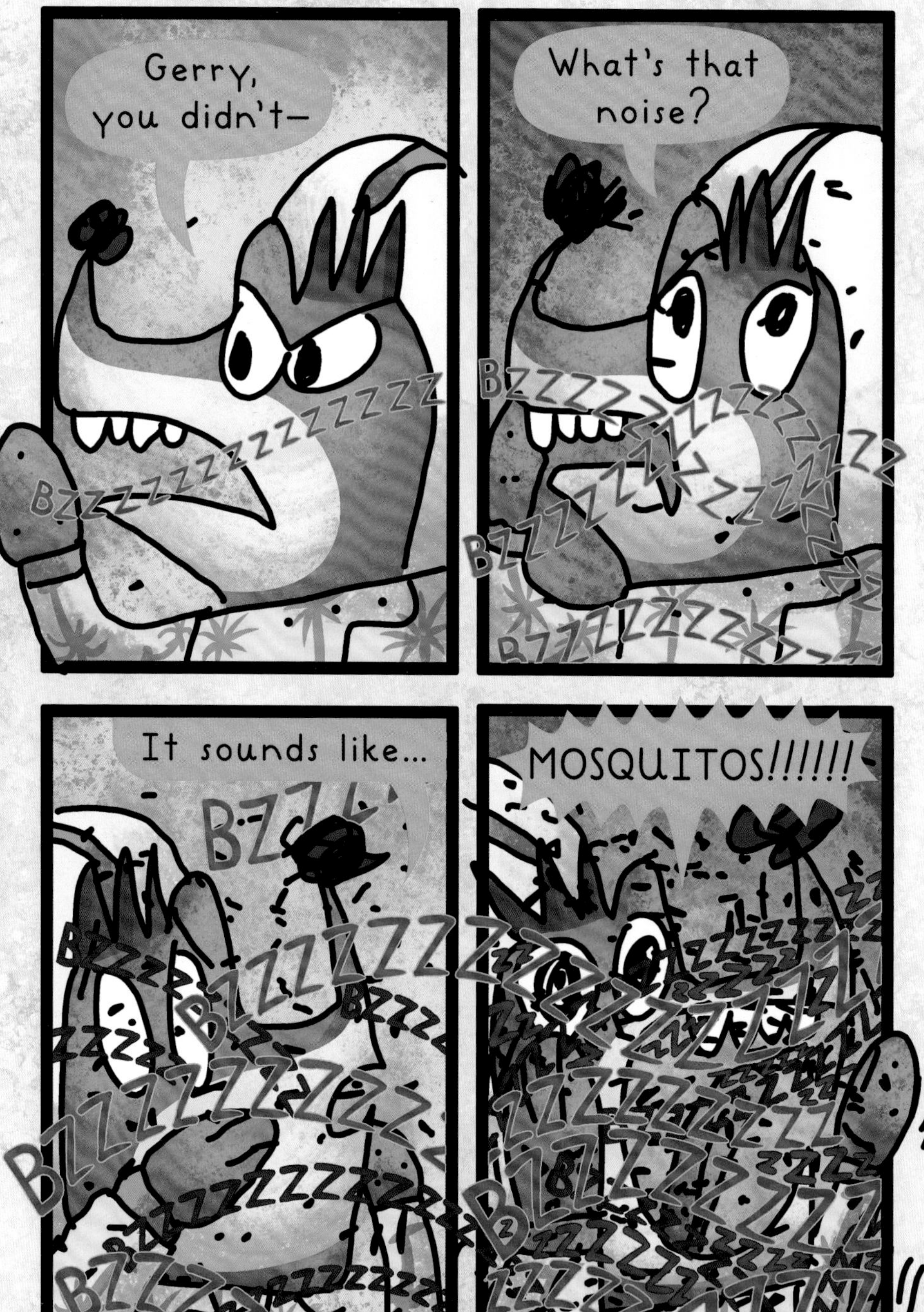
Gerry, you didn't—
BZZZZZZZZZZZZZZZZ
What's that noise?
It sounds like...
MOSQUITOS!!!!!!

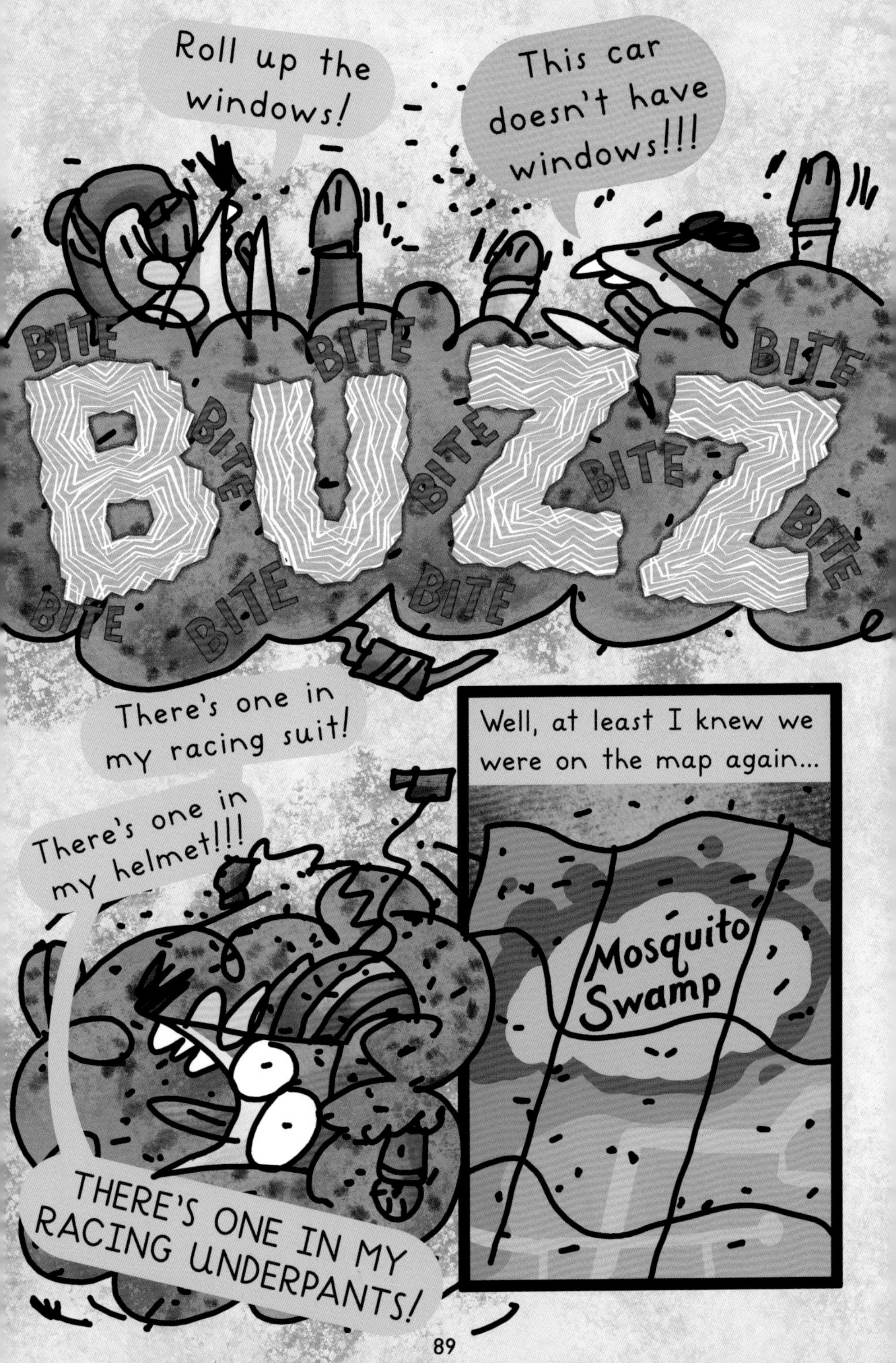
Roll up the windows!
This car doesn't have windows!!!
BITE BITE BITE BITE BITE BITE BITE BITE BITE BITE BITE
BUZZ
There's one in my racing suit!
There's one in my helmet!!!
THERE'S ONE IN MY RACING UNDERPANTS!
Well, at least I knew we were on the map again...
Mosquito Swamp

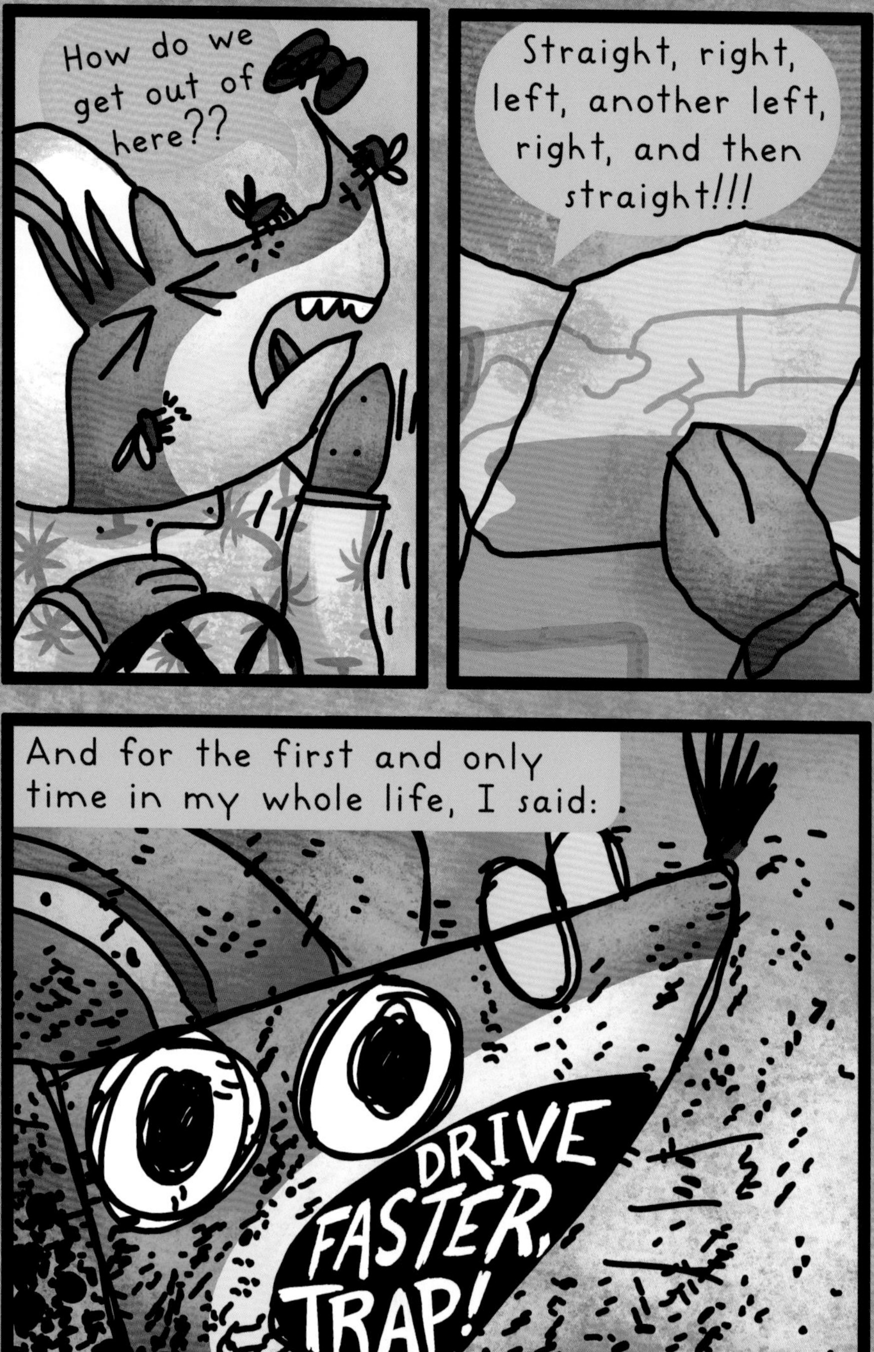
How do we get out of here??
Straight, right, left, another left, right, and then straight!!!
And for the first and only time in my whole life, I said:
DRIVE FASTER, TRAP!

CHAPTER NINETEEN

MEYOWL!

We left the mosquitos behind us...
and soon saw something even scarier
ahead of us...a **SPOOKY CASTLE!**

CRUMBLY CROGLIN!*
What a spooky castle!

*Croglin is a type of cheese.

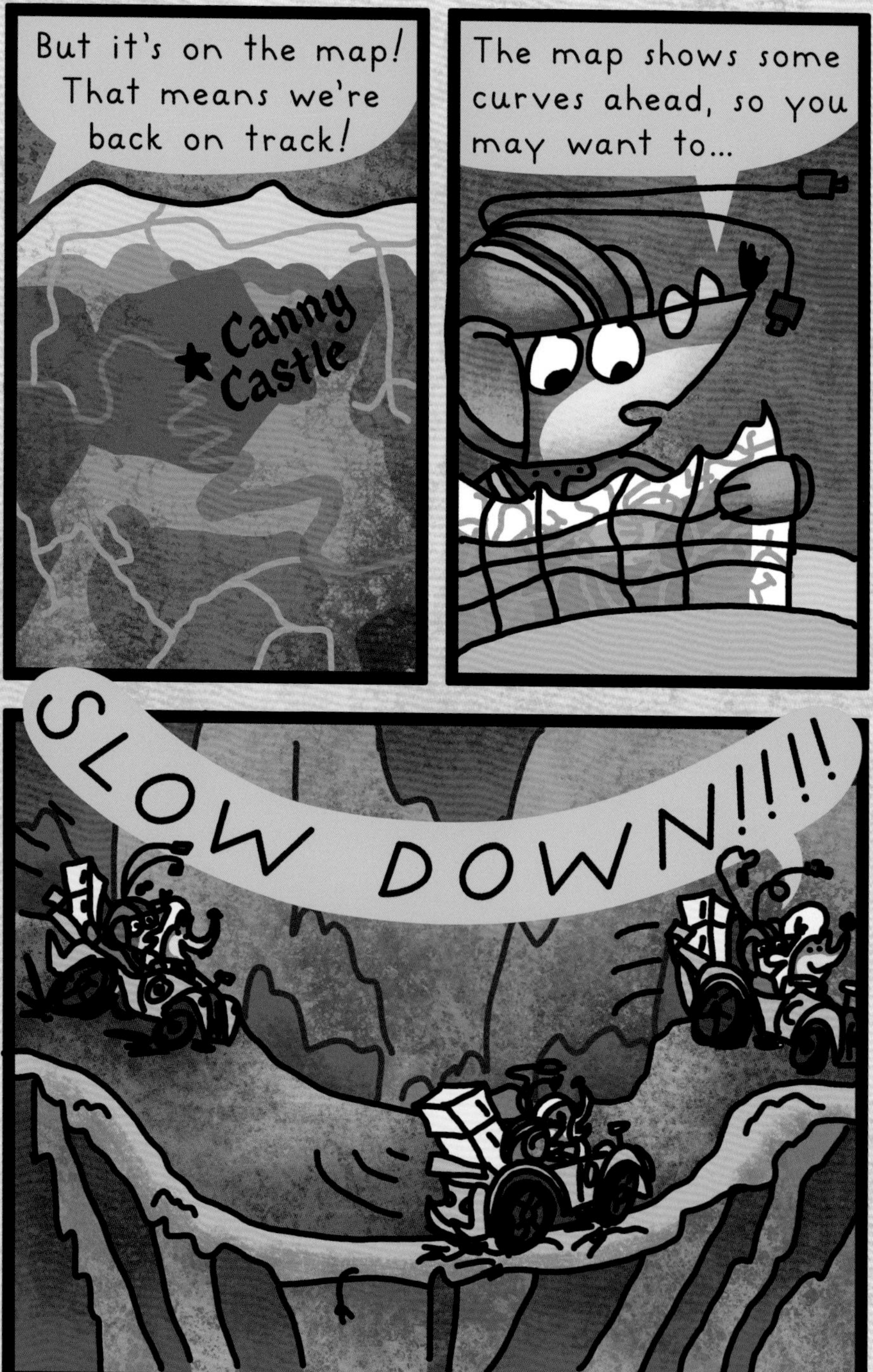
But it's on the map! That means we're back on track!
Canny Castle
The map shows some curves ahead, so you may want to...
SLOW DOWN!!!!

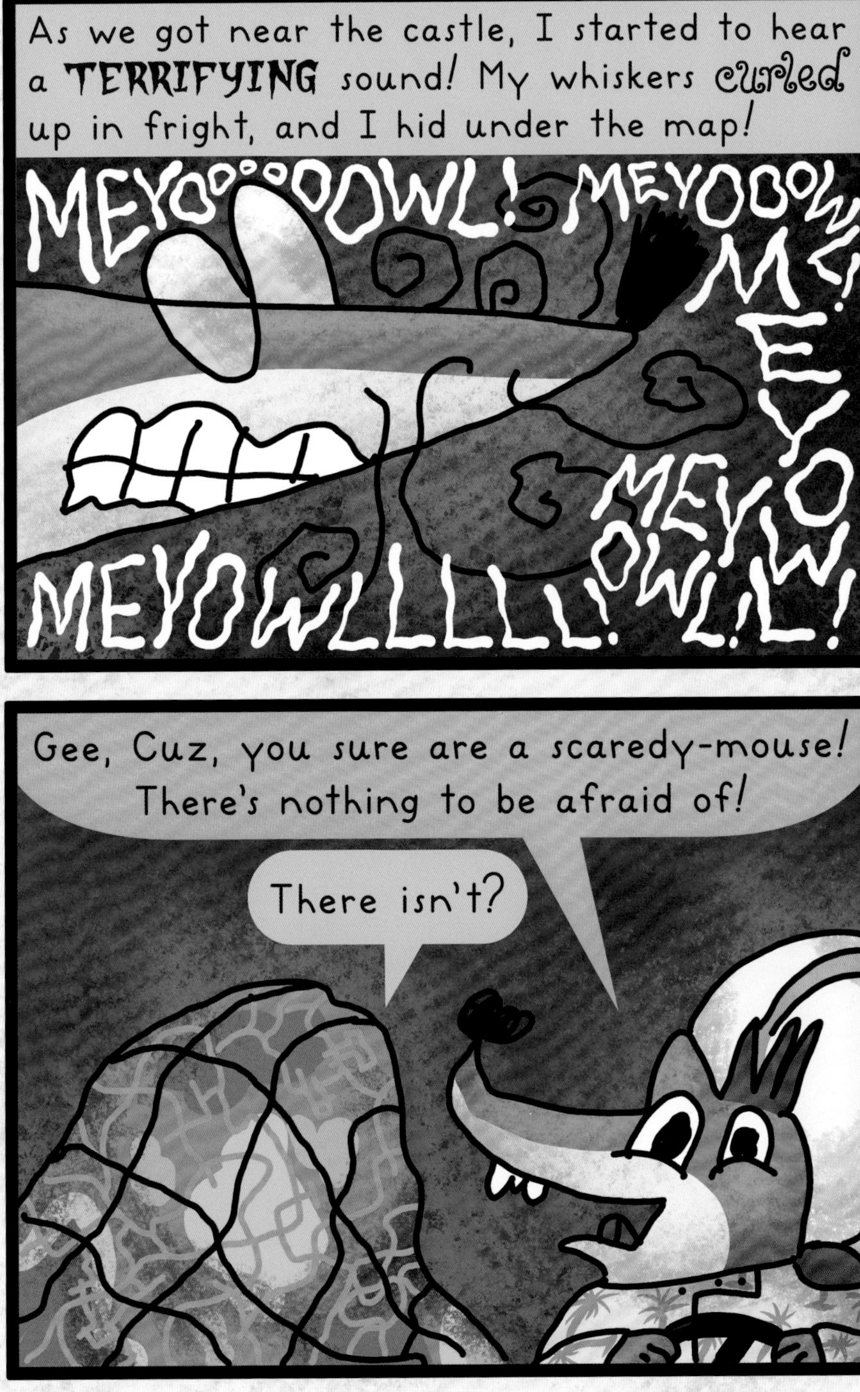
As we got near the castle, I started to hear a TERRIFYING sound! My whiskers curled up in fright, and I hid under the map!
MEYOOOOOWL!
MEYOOOWL!
MEYOWL!
MEYOWL!
MEYOWLLLLL!
Gee, Cuz, you sure are a scaredy-mouse! There's nothing to be afraid of!
There isn't?

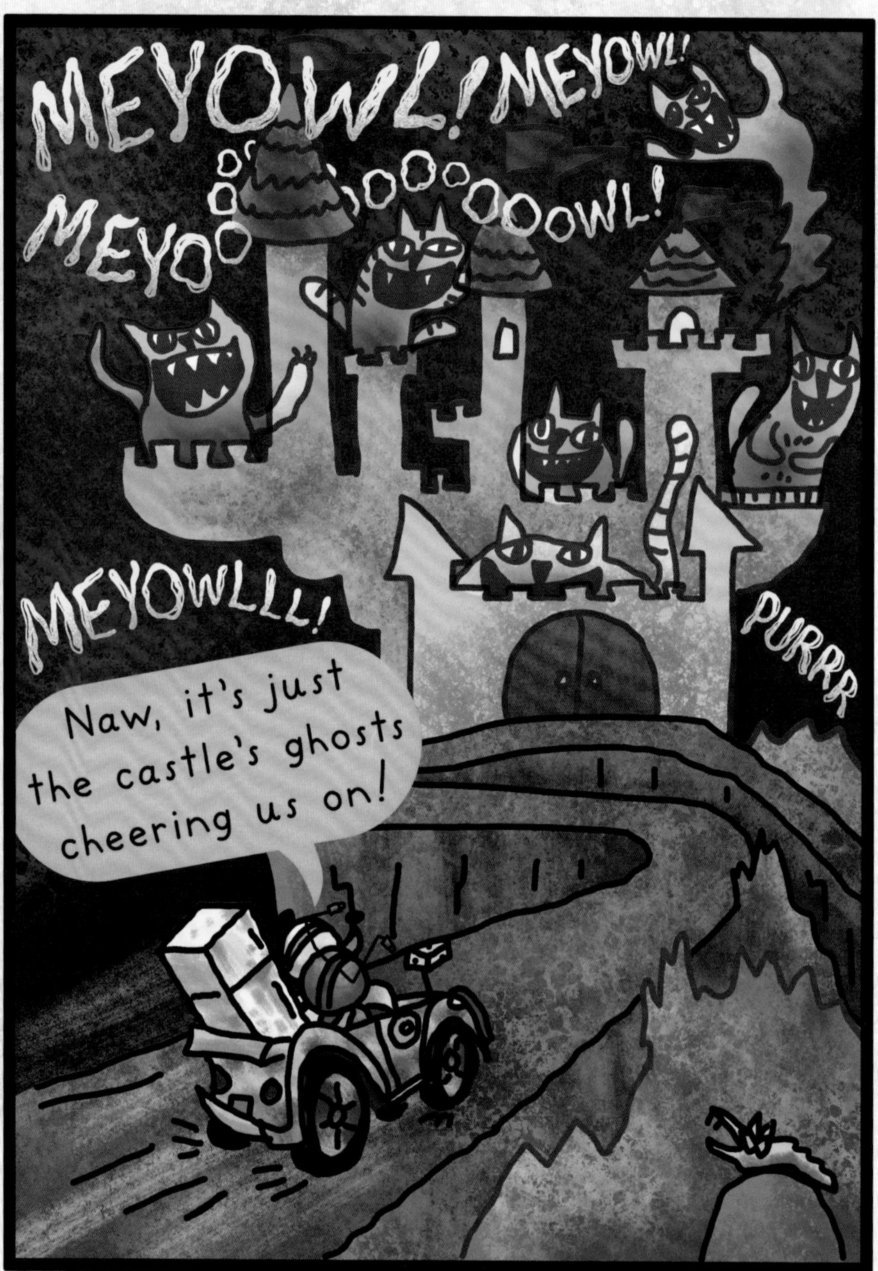
MEYOWL! MEYOWL!
MEYOOOOOOOOOOOWL!
MEYOWLLL!
PURRR
Naw, it's just the castle's ghosts cheering us on!

Of course! The ghost cats of **Canny Castle!** They're old friends of mine. It felt good to hear someone cheering for us at last. For a second, I started to enjoy myself... Then we reached the top and started going down the curvy roads on the other side at *top speed!!*

CHAPTER SEVENTEEN

CAN YOU GIVE US A PAW?

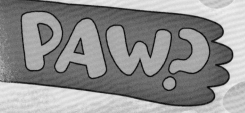

Somehow, Trap got us down that mountain. But right away, the racecourse took us up another one! I was starting to get CARSICK from all the sharp turns and ups and downs!

UGH...
Trap...
Please stop...
Can't stop, Cuz! We've got a race to win! Remember, it's a matter of family—

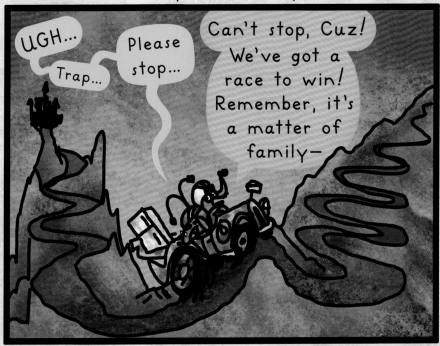

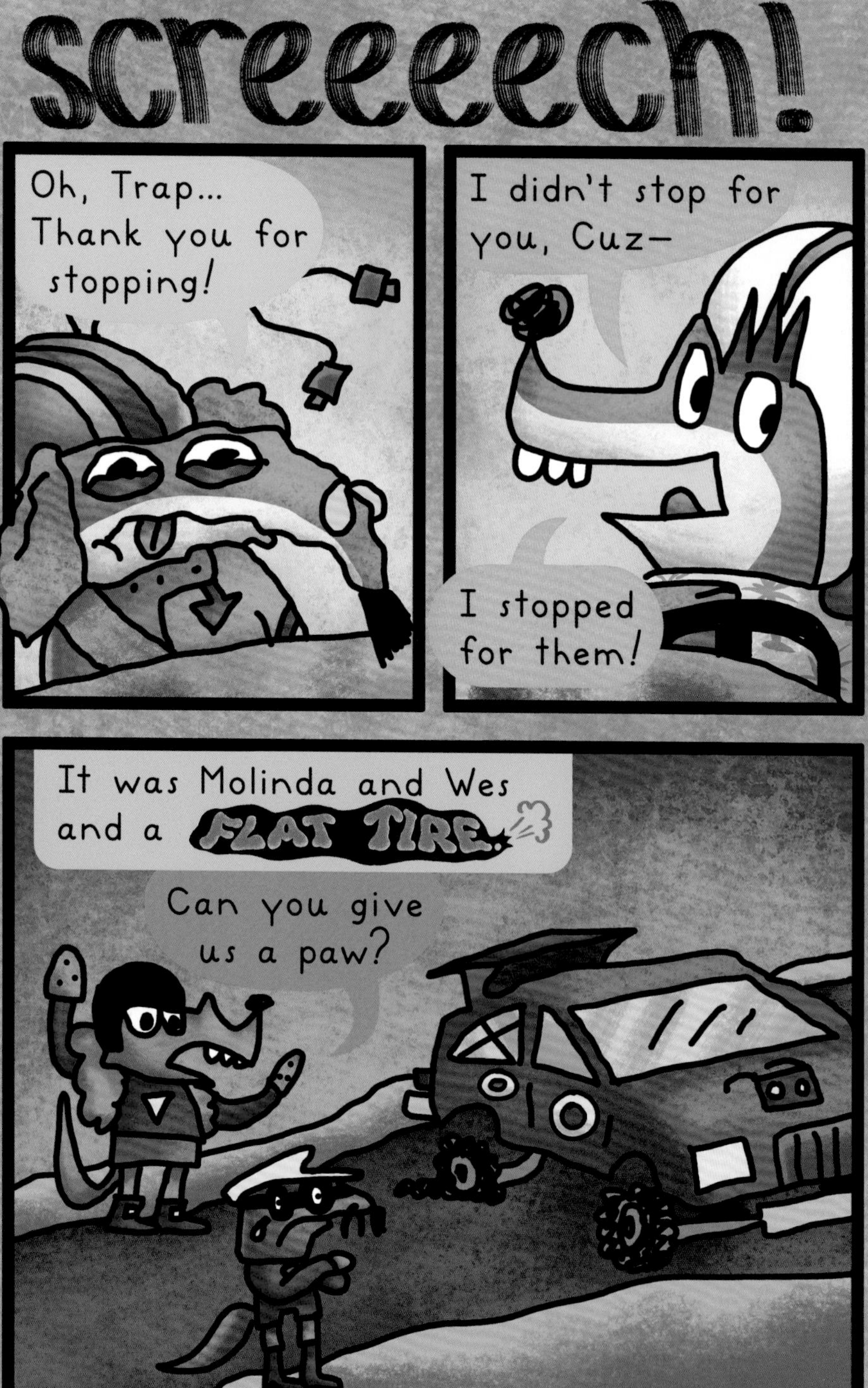
SCREEECH!
Oh, Trap... Thank you for stopping!
I didn't stop for you, Cuz—
I stopped for them!
It was Molinda and Wes and a FLAT TIRE.
Can you give us a paw?

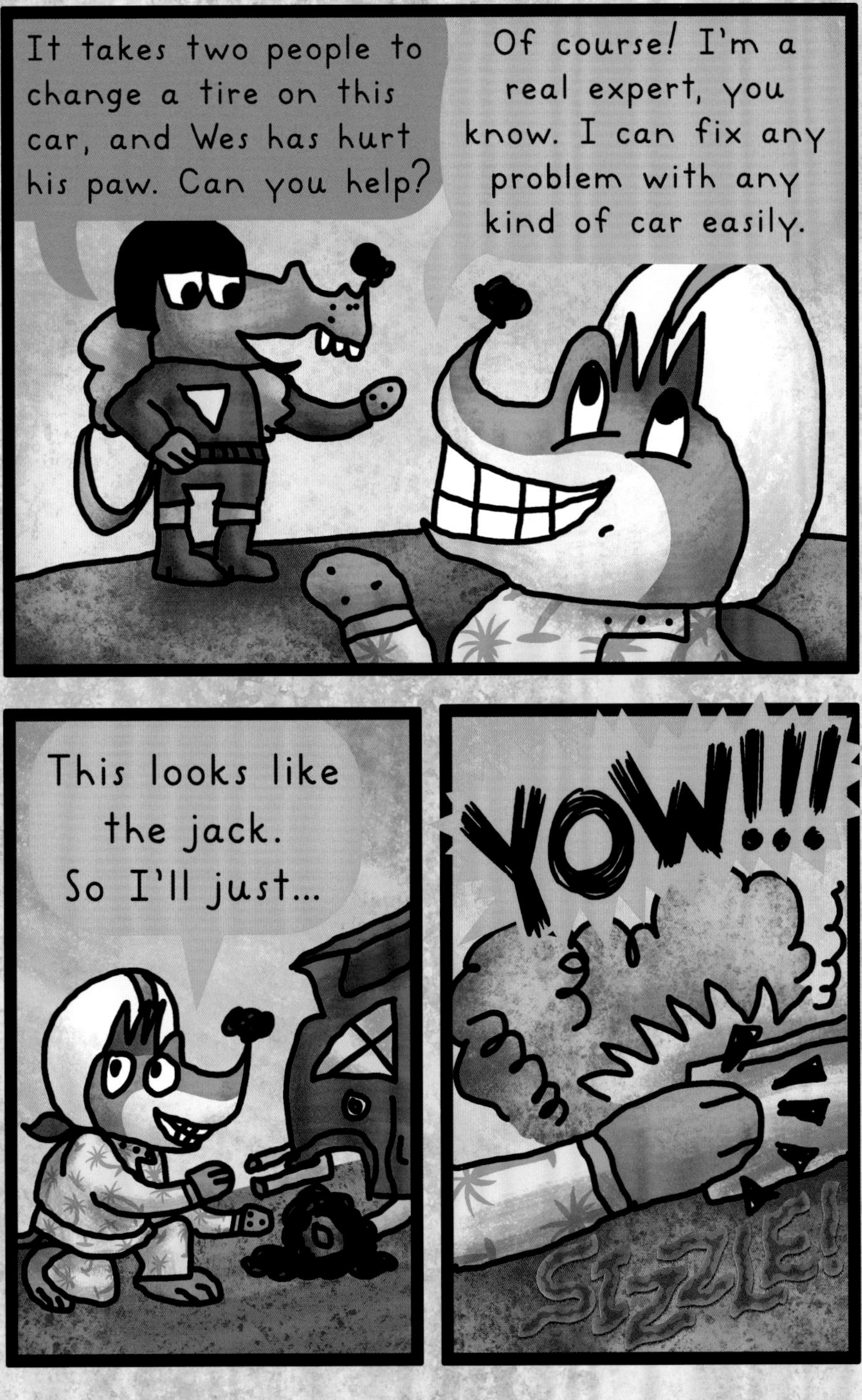
It takes two people to change a tire on this car, and Wes has hurt his paw. Can you help?
Of course! I'm a real expert, you know. I can fix any problem with any kind of car easily.
This looks like the jack. So I'll just...
YOW!!!
SIZZLE!

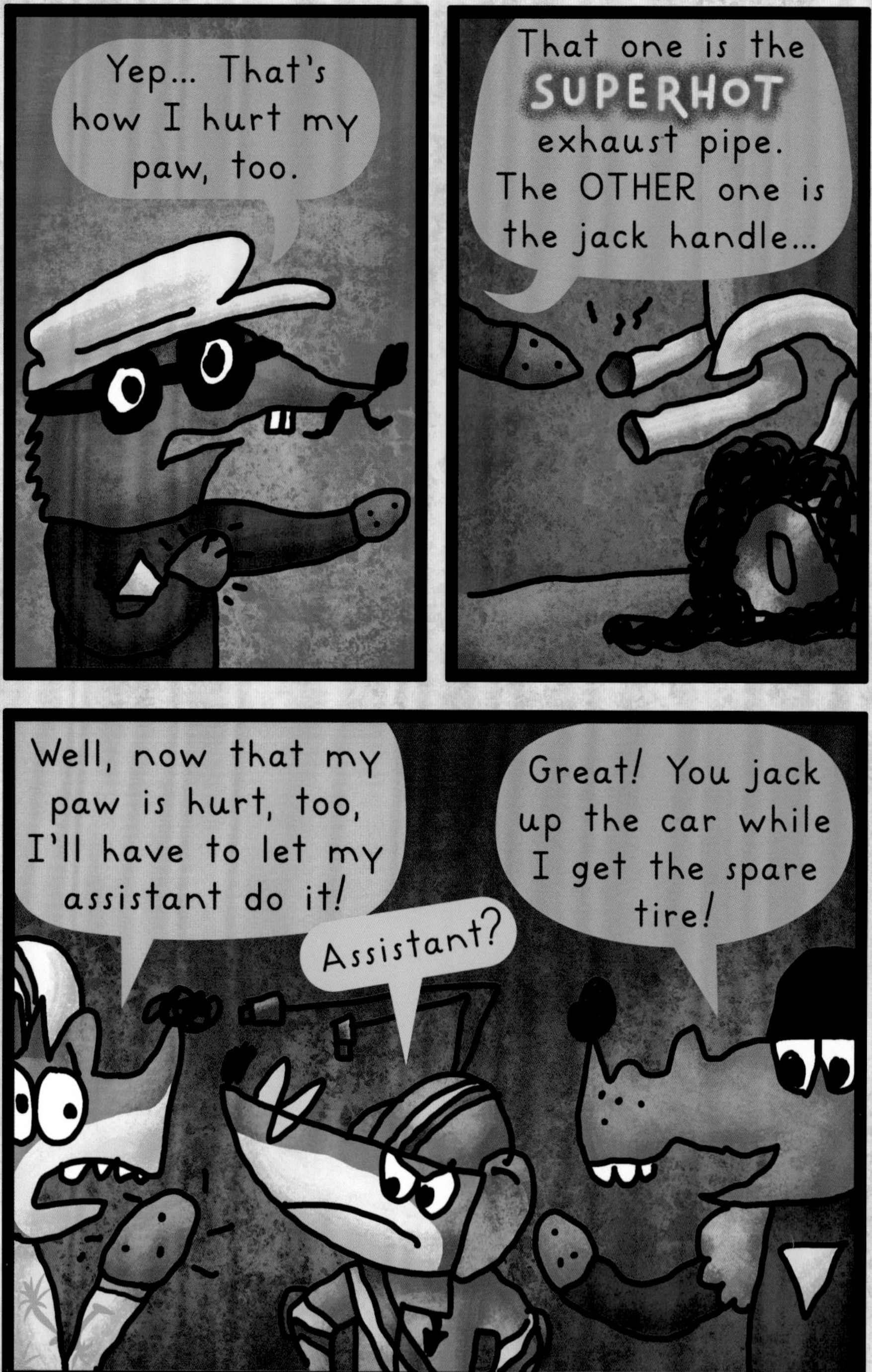
Yep... That's how I hurt my paw, too.
That one is the SUPERHOT exhaust pipe. The OTHER one is the jack handle...
Well, now that my paw is hurt, too, I'll have to let my assistant do it!
Assistant?
Great! You jack up the car while I get the spare tire!

I'm not exactly a strongmouse, but since a jack makes it easier to lift a car, I gave it a try.

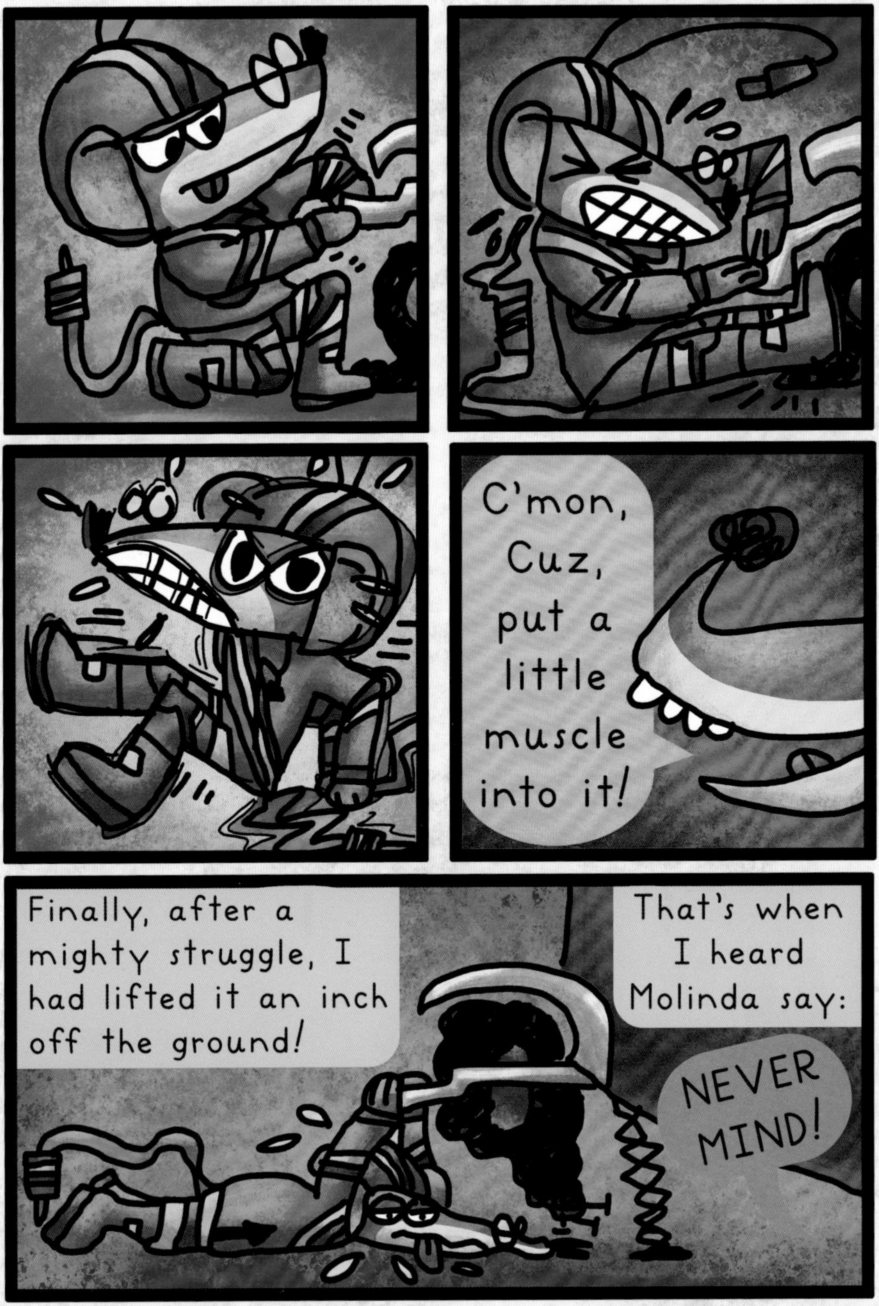
C'mon, Cuz, put a little muscle into it!
Finally, after a mighty struggle, I had lifted it an inch off the ground!
That's when I heard Molinda say:
NEVER MIND!

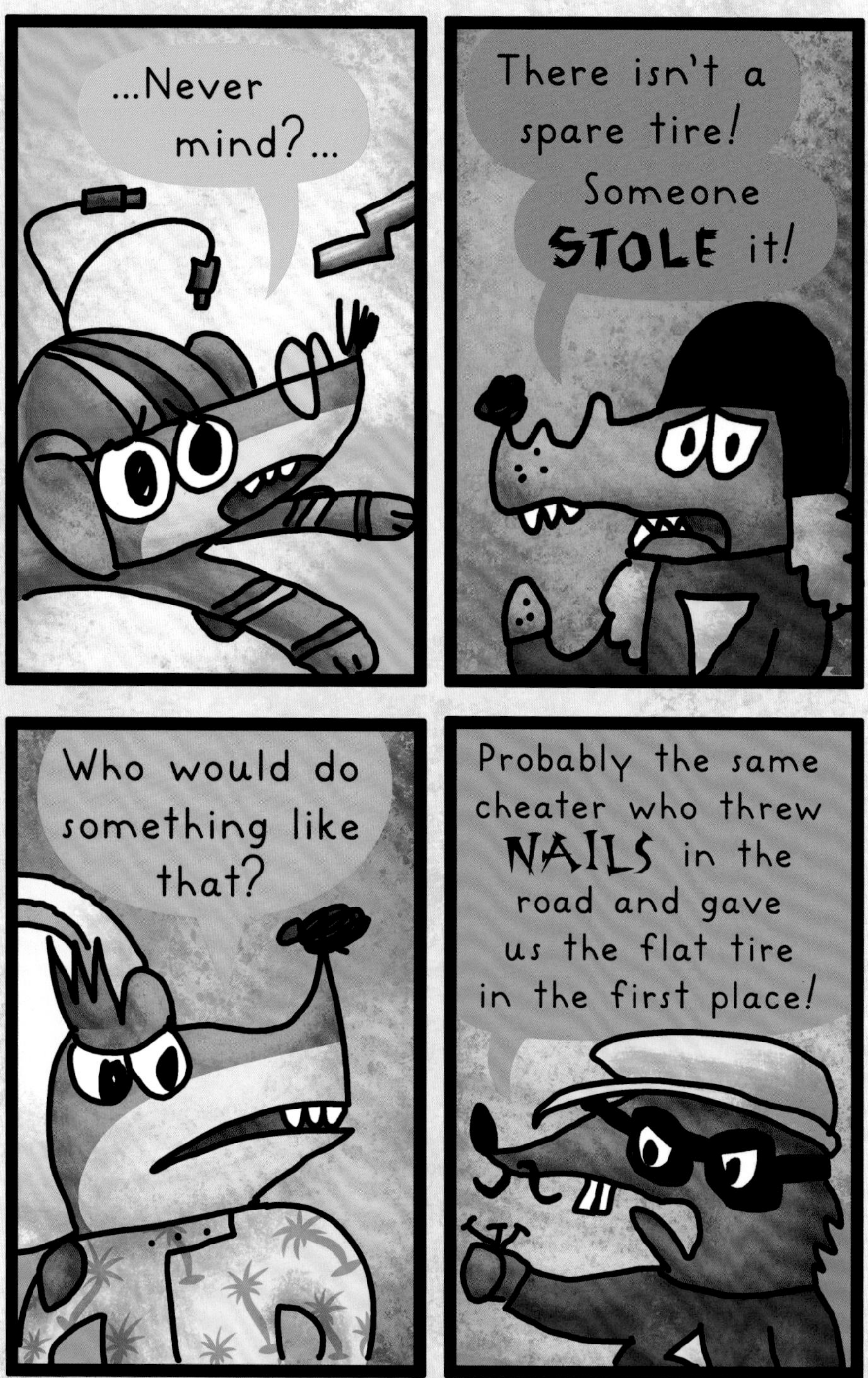
...Never mind?...
There isn't a spare tire! Someone STOLE it!
Who would do something like that?
Probably the same cheater who threw NAILS in the road and gave us the flat tire in the first place!

CLICK!

Whew! Glad I got here in time to get this shot! Racecourse cheating is **BIG NEWS!!** This photo could end up on the front page!

Especially if I can figure out who did it!

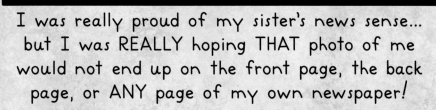

I was really proud of my sister's news sense... but I was REALLY hoping THAT photo of me would not end up on the front page, the back page, or ANY page of my own newspaper!

CHAPTER EIGHTEEN

CLIFF-HANGER!

Thea gave Molinda and Wes a ride into town to find a tow truck. Trap and I headed back to our car to continue the race...

My paw hurts too much to hold the steering wheel! So you're going to have to drive, Cuz!

ME?

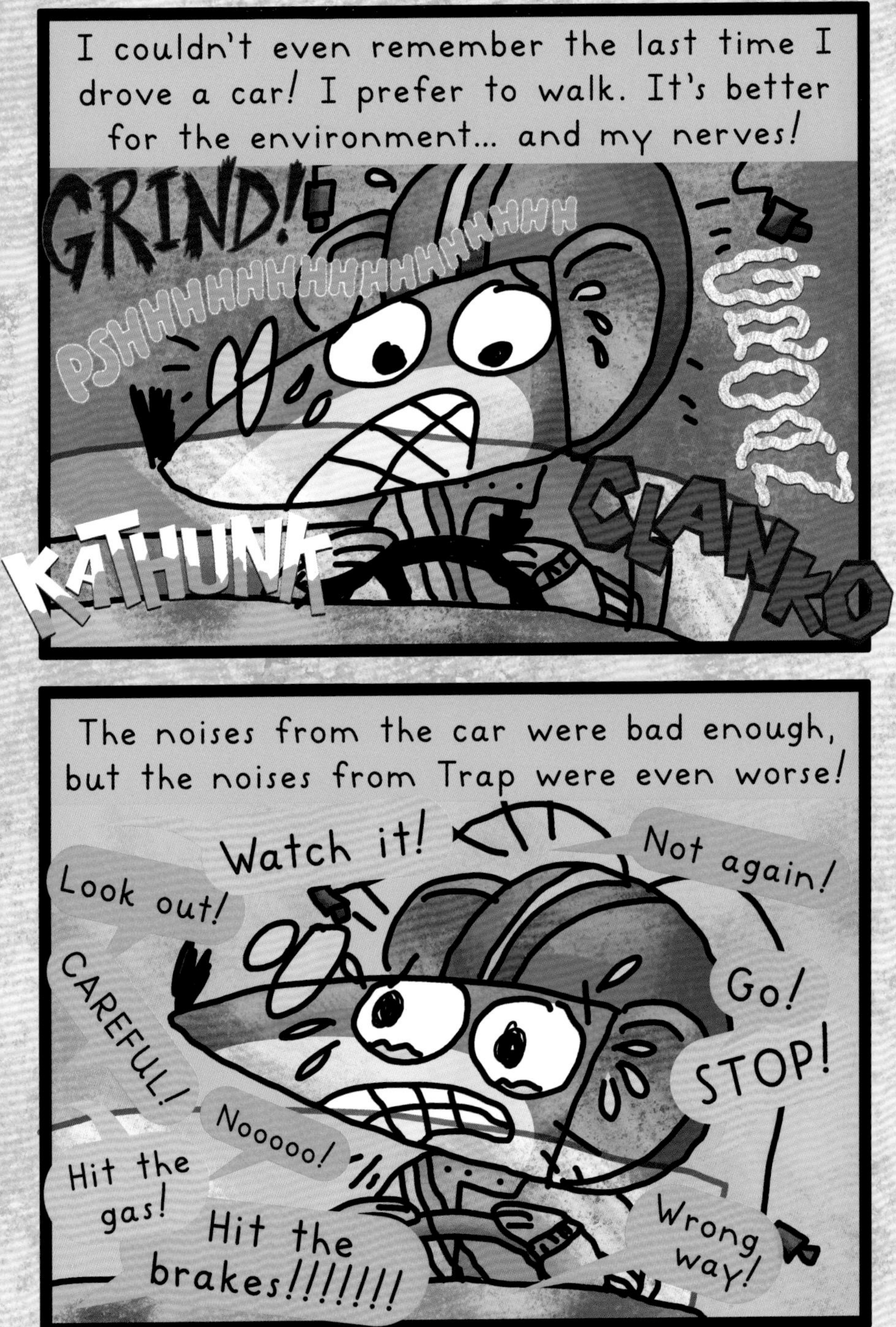
I couldn't even remember the last time I drove a car! I prefer to walk. It's better for the environment... and my nerves!
GRIND!
PSHHHHHHHHHHHHHHHHHHHHH
KATHUNK
CLANKO
The noises from the car were bad enough, but the noises from Trap were even worse!
Watch it!
Not again!
Look out!
CAREFUL!
Go!
STOP!
Nooooo!
Hit the gas!
Hit the brakes!!!!!!!
Wrong way!

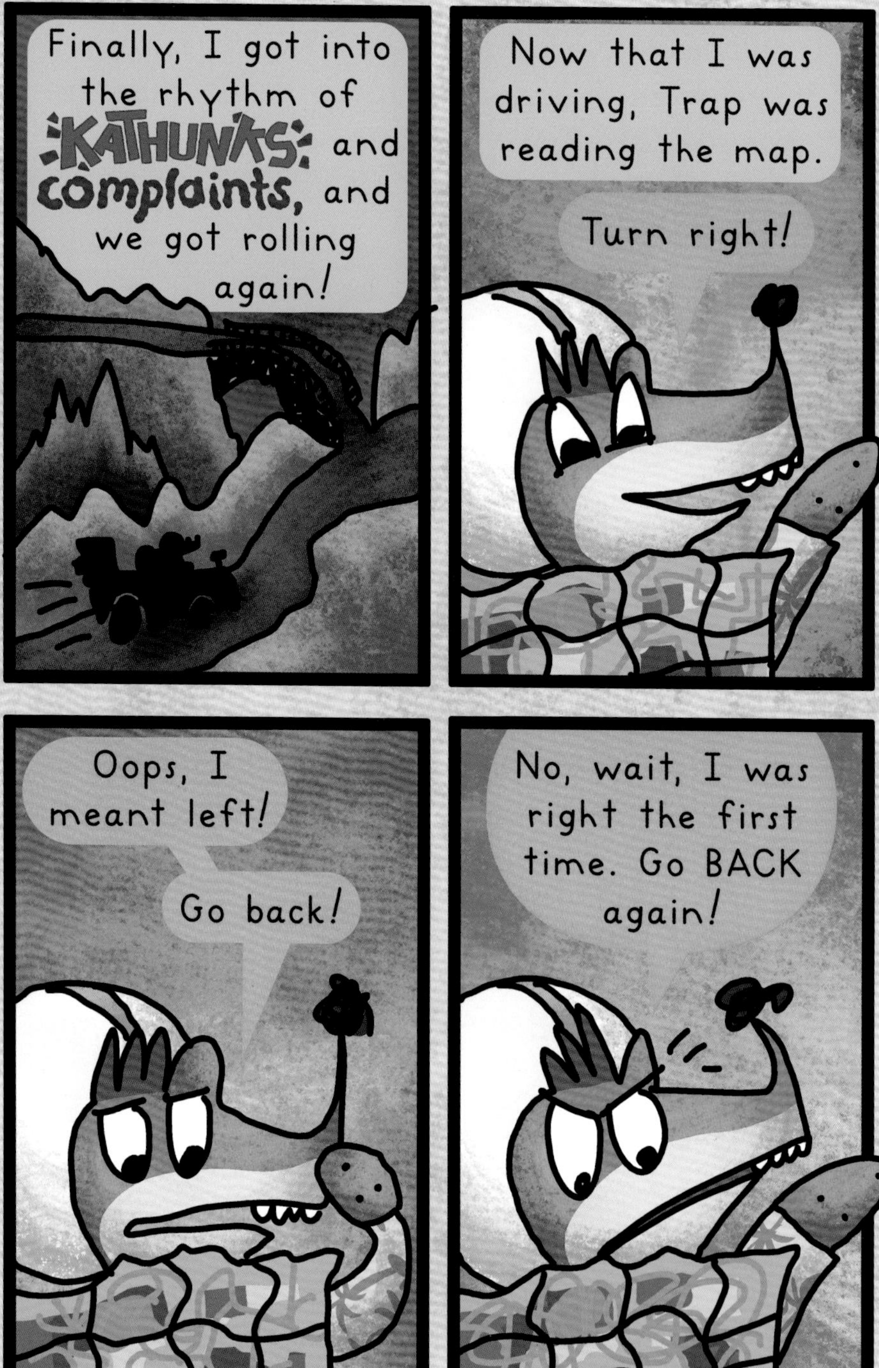
Finally, I got into the rhythm of KATHUNKS and complaints, and we got rolling again!
Now that I was driving, Trap was reading the map.
Turn right!
Oops, I meant left!
Go back!
No, wait, I was right the first time. Go BACK again!

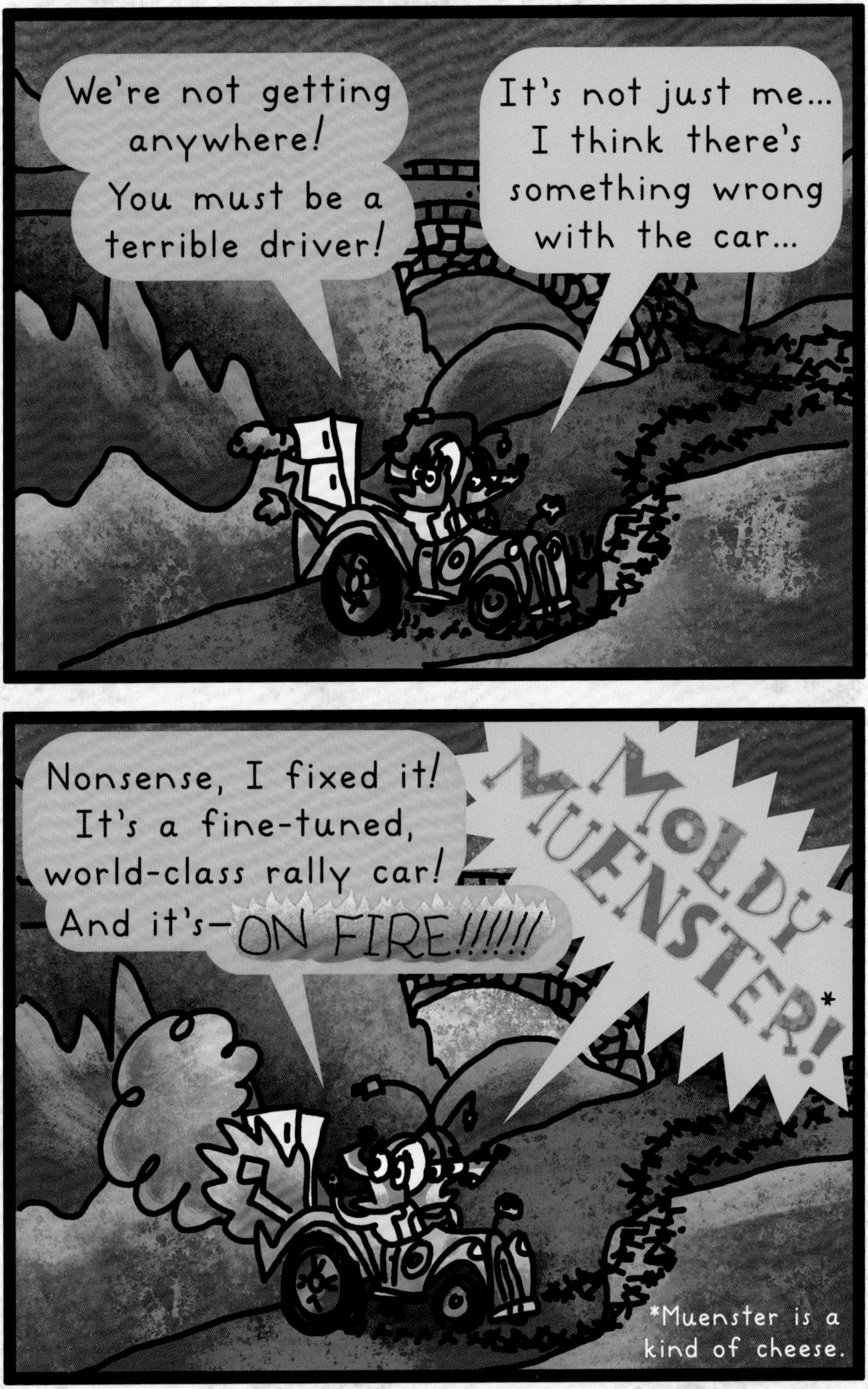
We're not getting anywhere! You must be a terrible driver!
It's not just me... I think there's something wrong with the car...
Nonsense, I fixed it! It's a fine-tuned, world-class rally car! And it's—ON FIRE!!!!!!
MOLDY MUENSTER!*
*Muenster is a kind of cheese.

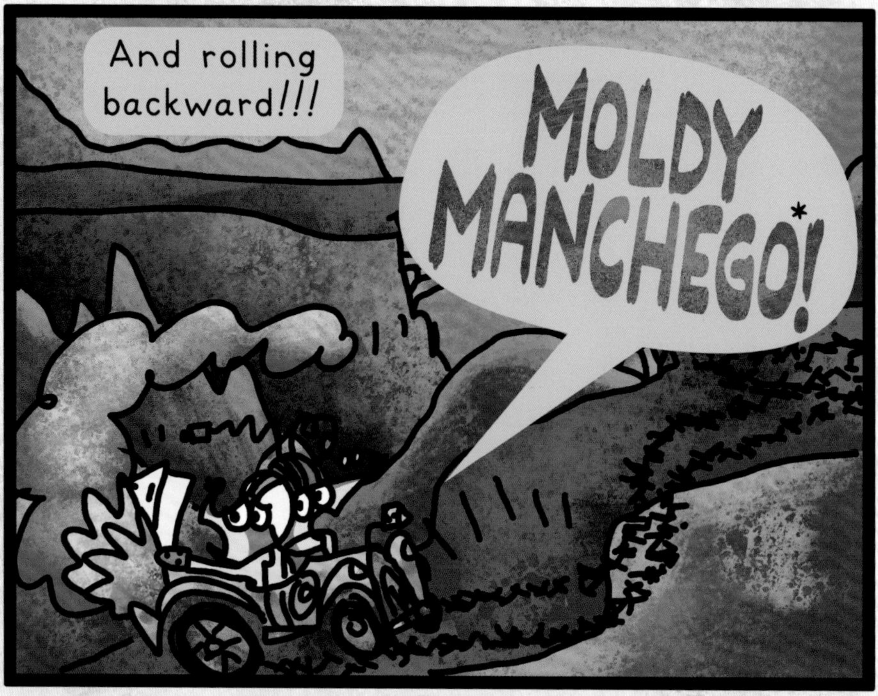
And rolling backward!!!
MOLDY MANCHEGO*!

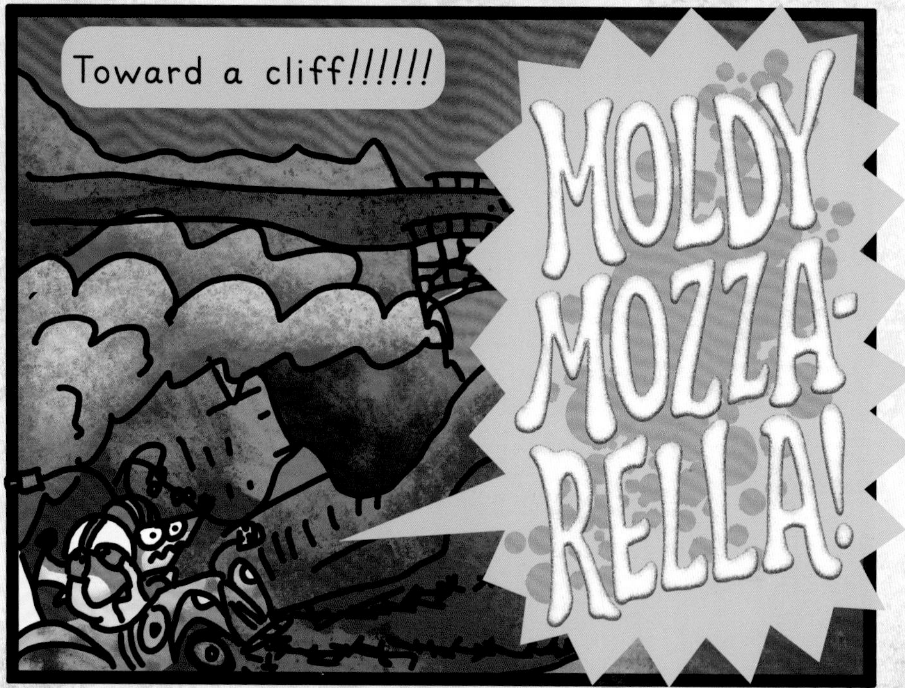
Toward a cliff!!!!!!
MOLDY MOZZA-RELLA!

*Manchego is a kind of cheese.

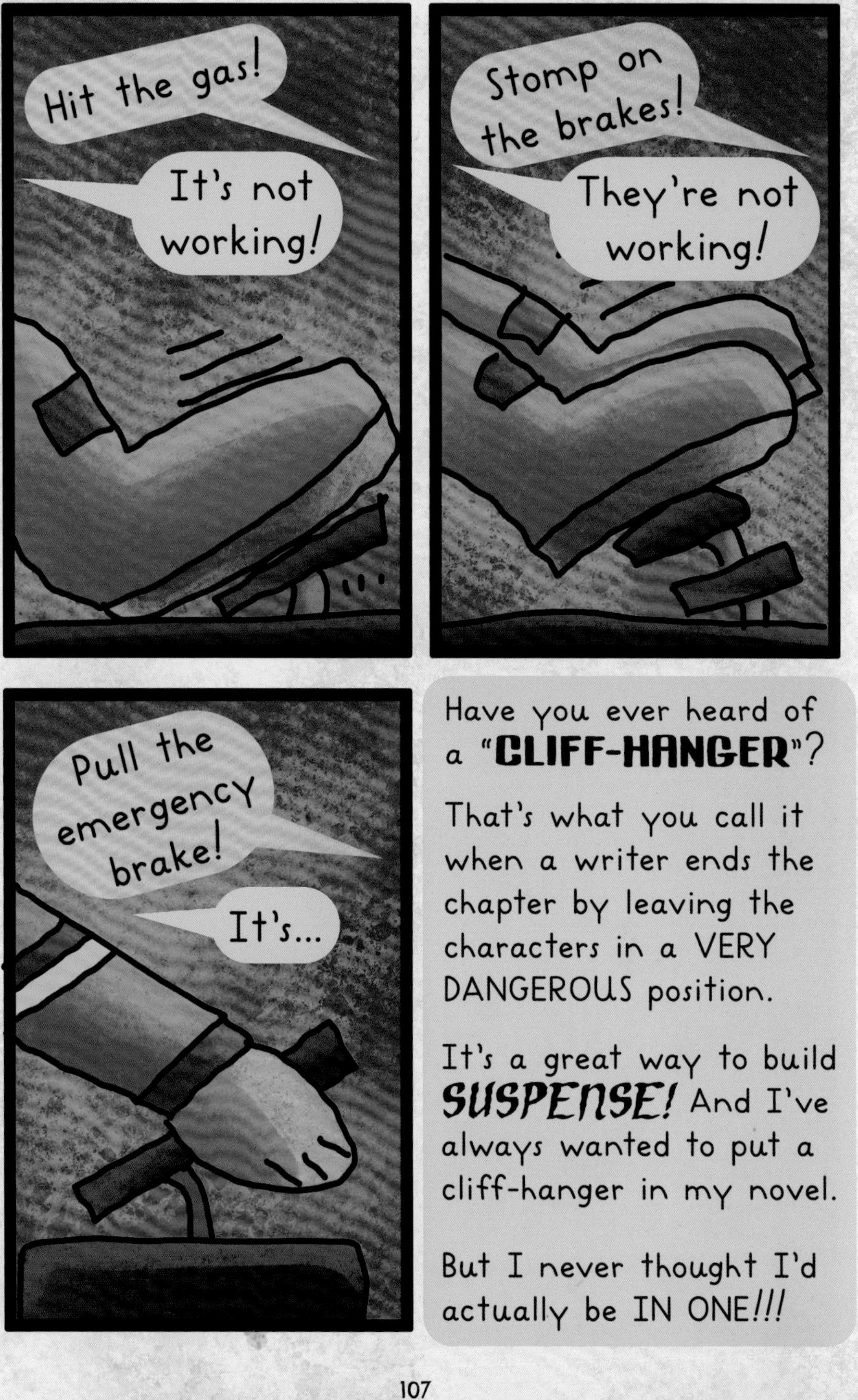
Hit the gas!
It's not working!
Stomp on the brakes!
They're not working!
Pull the emergency brake!
It's...
Have you ever heard of a "CLIFF-HANGER"?
That's what you call it when a writer ends the chapter by leaving the characters in a VERY DANGEROUS position.
It's a great way to build SUSPENSE! And I've always wanted to put a cliff-hanger in my novel.
But I never thought I'd actually be IN ONE!!!

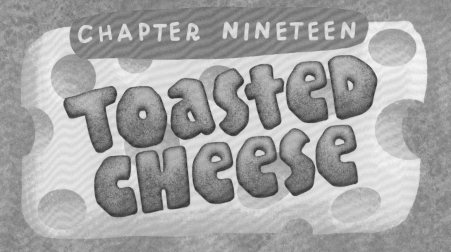

CHAPTER NINETEEN

Toasted Cheese

Well, the emergency brake DID work! And we screeeched to a stop right on the edge of the cliff!

See, Cuz? Just like I said: The car works great!!!
TRAP! The car is teetering on the edge of a cliff AND on fire!

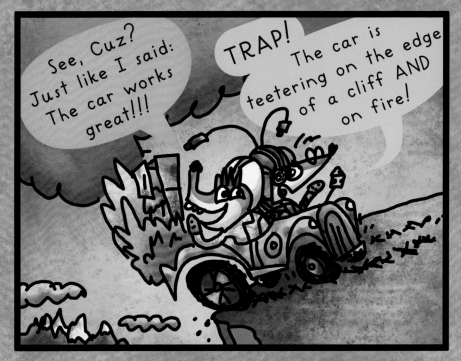

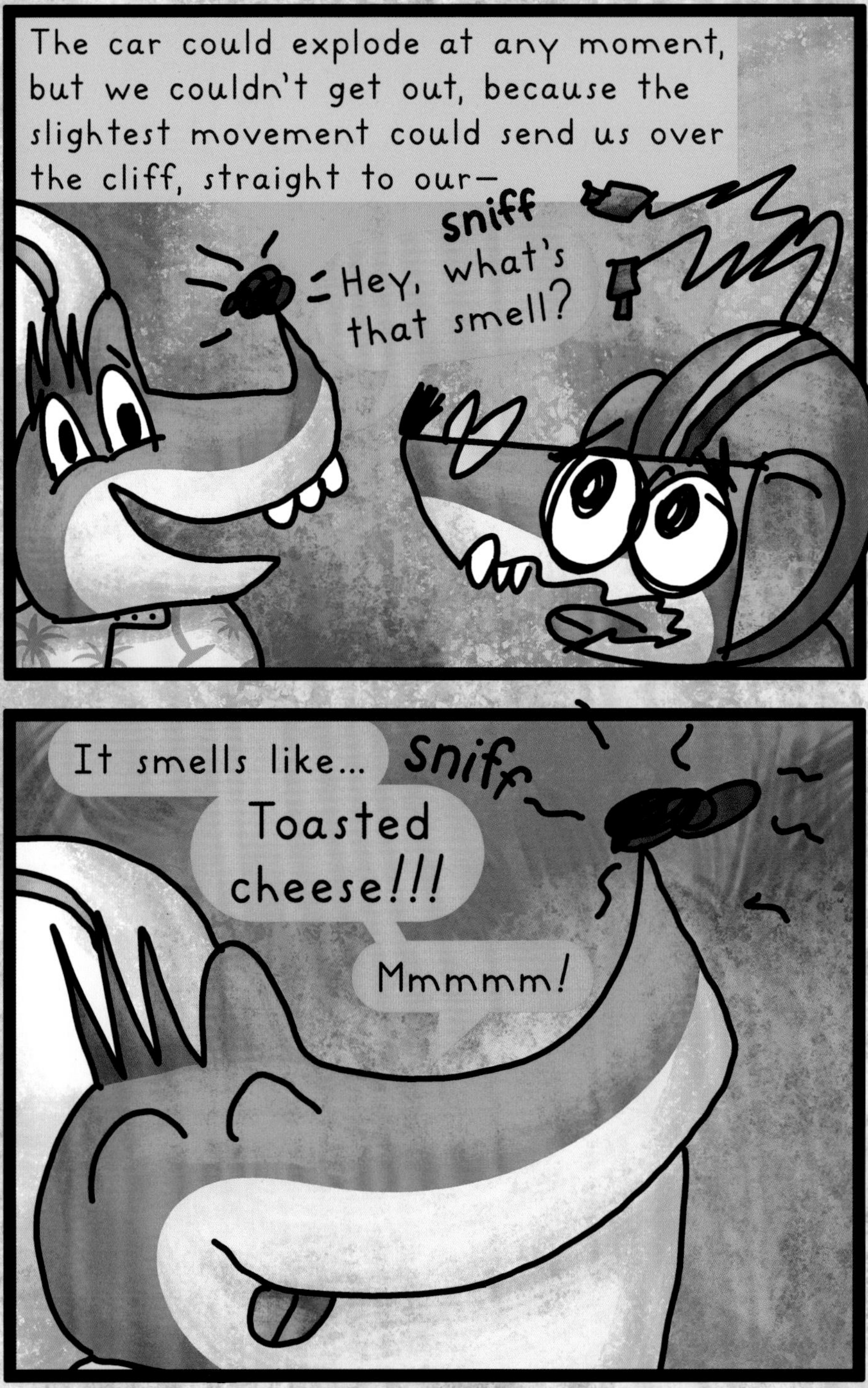
The car could explode at any moment, but we couldn't get out, because the slightest movement could send us over the cliff, straight to our—
sniff
Hey, what's that smell?
It smells like...
Sniff~
Toasted cheese!!!
Mmmmm!

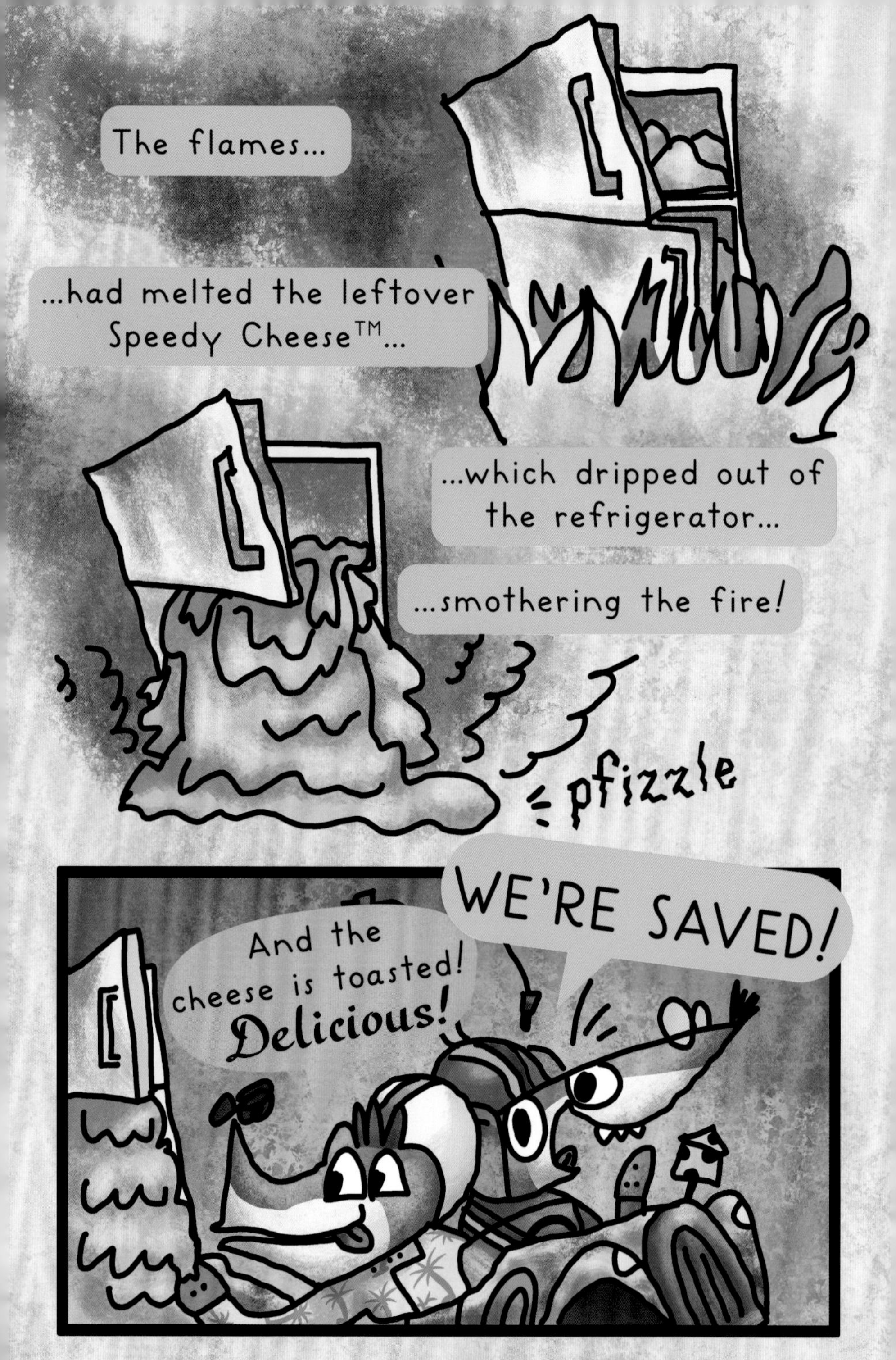
The flames...
...had melted the leftover Speedy Cheese™...
...which dripped out of the refrigerator...
...smothering the fire!
pfizzle
And the cheese is toasted! Delicious!
WE'RE SAVED!

Delicious? It looked more like something my friend Creepella Von Cacklefur would serve at one of her scary parties!

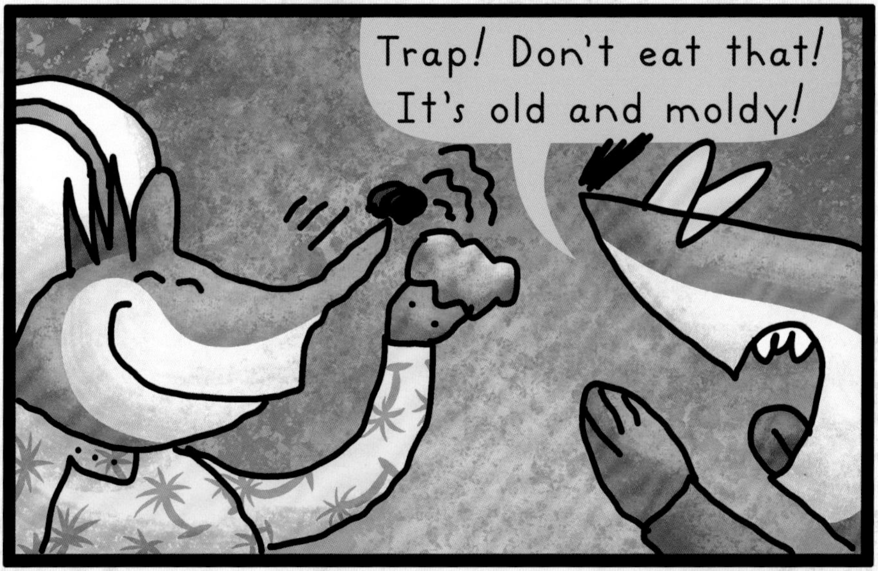
Trap! Don't eat that! It's old and moldy!

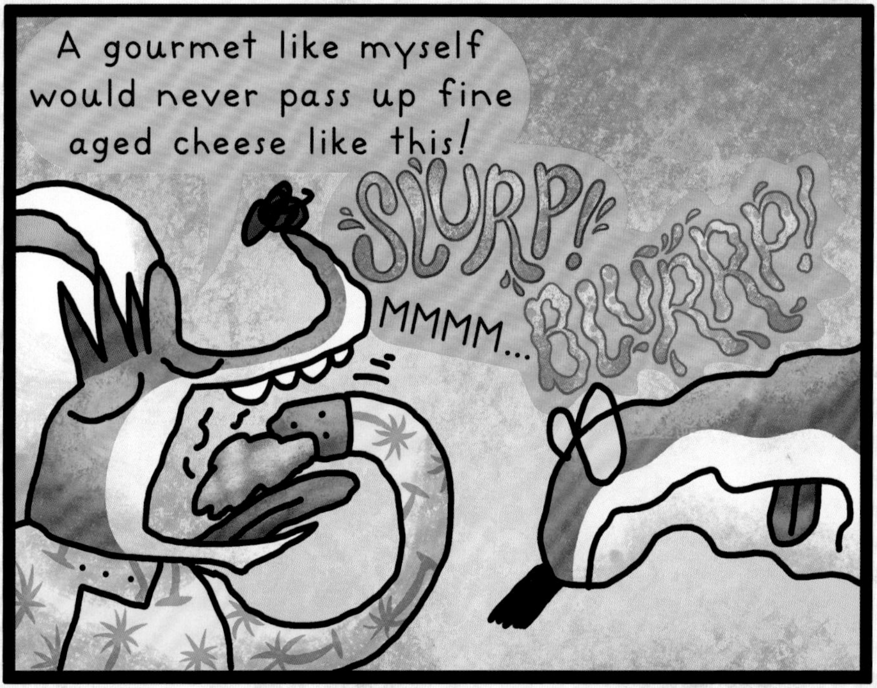
A gourmet like myself would never pass up fine aged cheese like this!
SLURP!
BLURP!
MMMM...

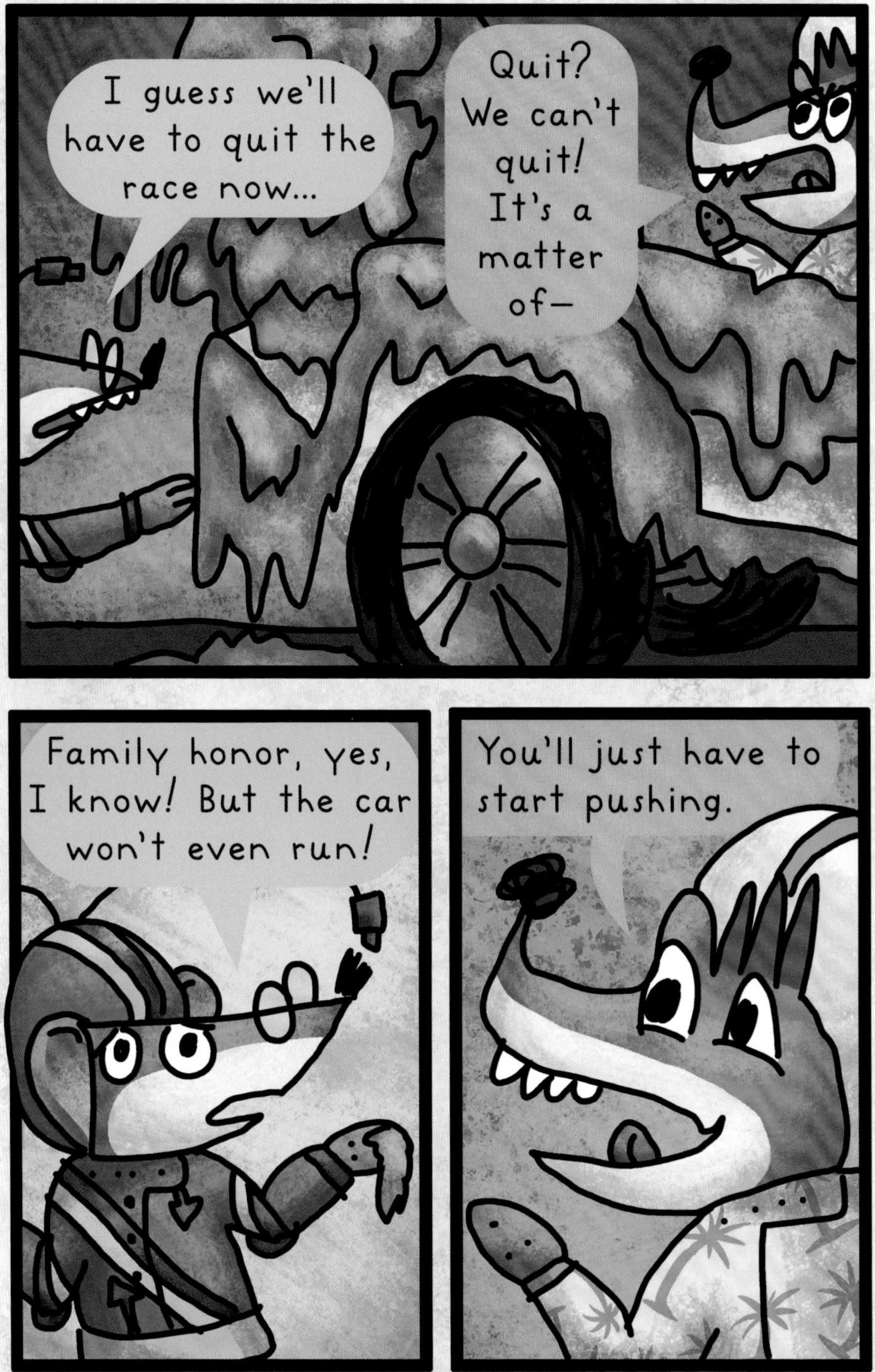
I guess we'll have to quit the race now...
Quit? We can't quit! It's a matter of—
Family honor, yes, I know! But the car won't even run!
You'll just have to start pushing.

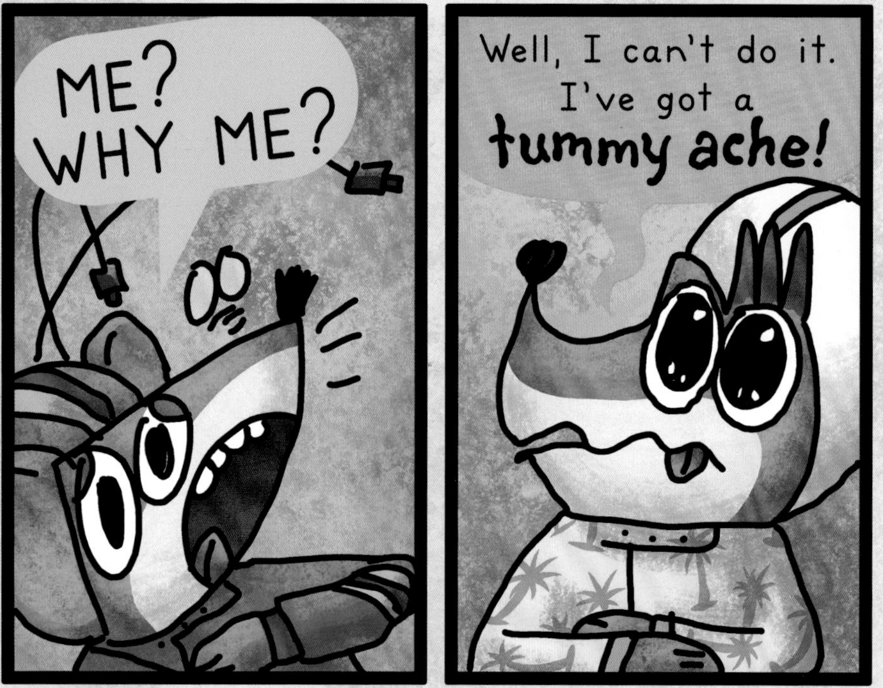
ME? WHY ME?
Well, I can't do it. I've got a **tummy ache!**

I wasn't surprised he had a tummy ache! All that **MOLDY CHEESE** would have put an ordinary rodent in New Mouse City General Hospital!

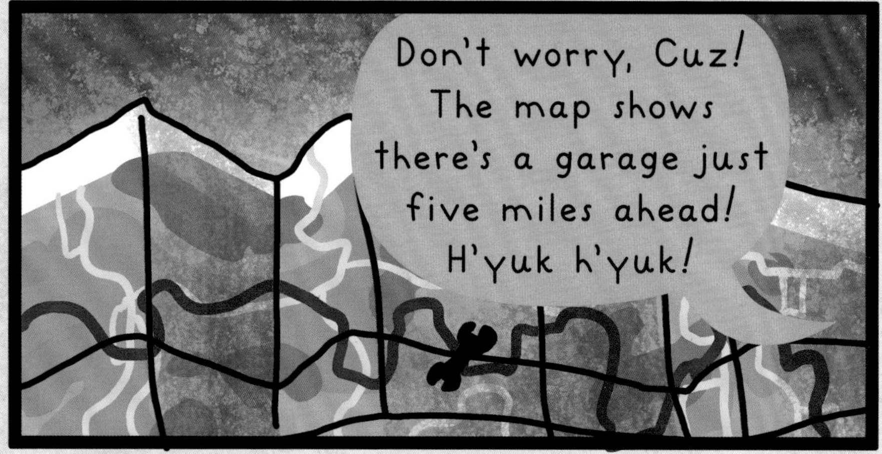
Don't worry, Cuz! The map shows there's a garage just five miles ahead! H'yuk h'yuk!

So I pushed and pushed and pushed...

CHAPTER TWENTY

...AND PUSHED...

...and pushed and pushed and pushed and pushed and fell in a puddle and pushed and pushed and pushed and lost one of my racing boots in some mud and pushed and pushed and pushed and pushed and accidentally pushed the car over my tail and pushed and pushed and pushed...

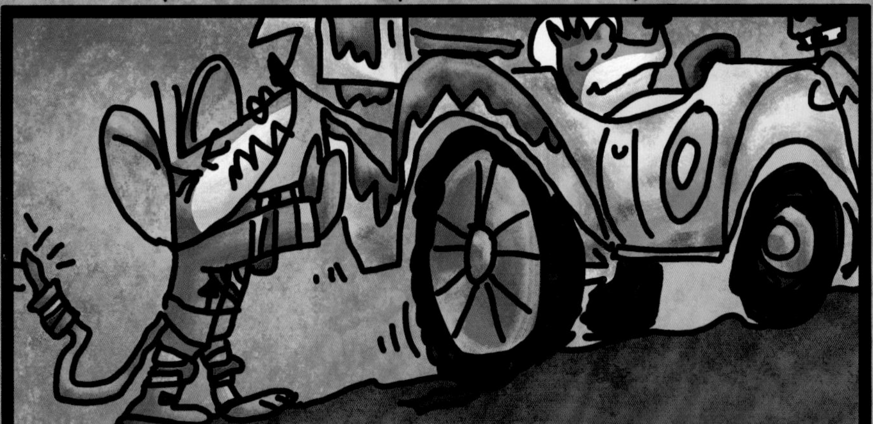

CHAPTER TWENTY-ONE

MAC MOUSENBERRY'S
CHAINSAW
ART GALLERY
AND TRACTOR REPAIR

...and pushed until we came across a weird old mouse revving up a **CHAINSAW**. I didn't want to stop, but I had no choice! I was one tired mouse!

Excuse me, sir, is there a mechanic around here?

Yep! Me! Just let me finish carving this sculpture, and I'll be right with you...

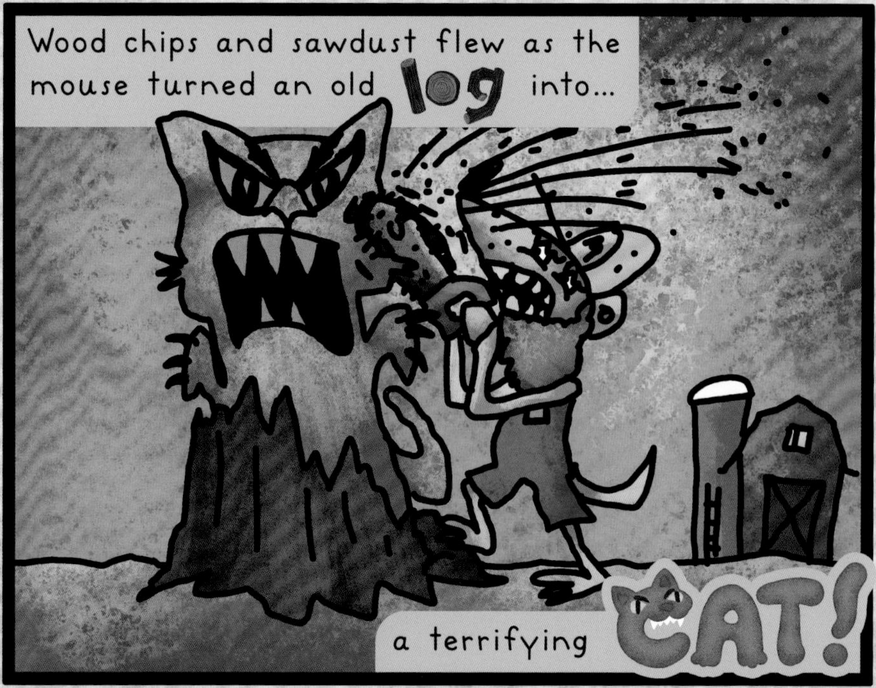
Wood chips and sawdust flew as the mouse turned an old log into...
a terrifying CAT!

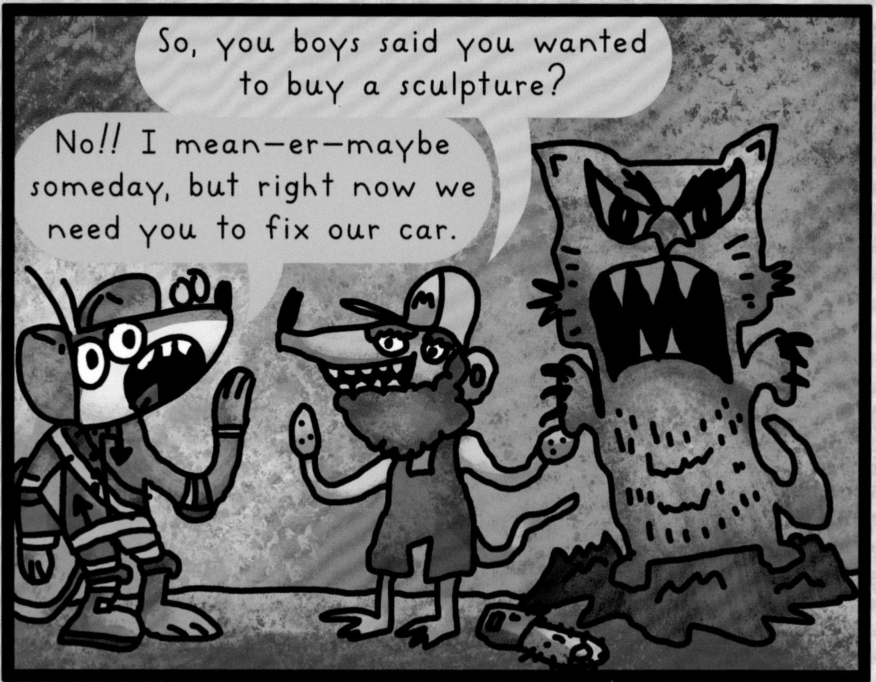
So, you boys said you wanted to buy a sculpture?
No!! I mean—er—maybe someday, but right now we need you to fix our car.

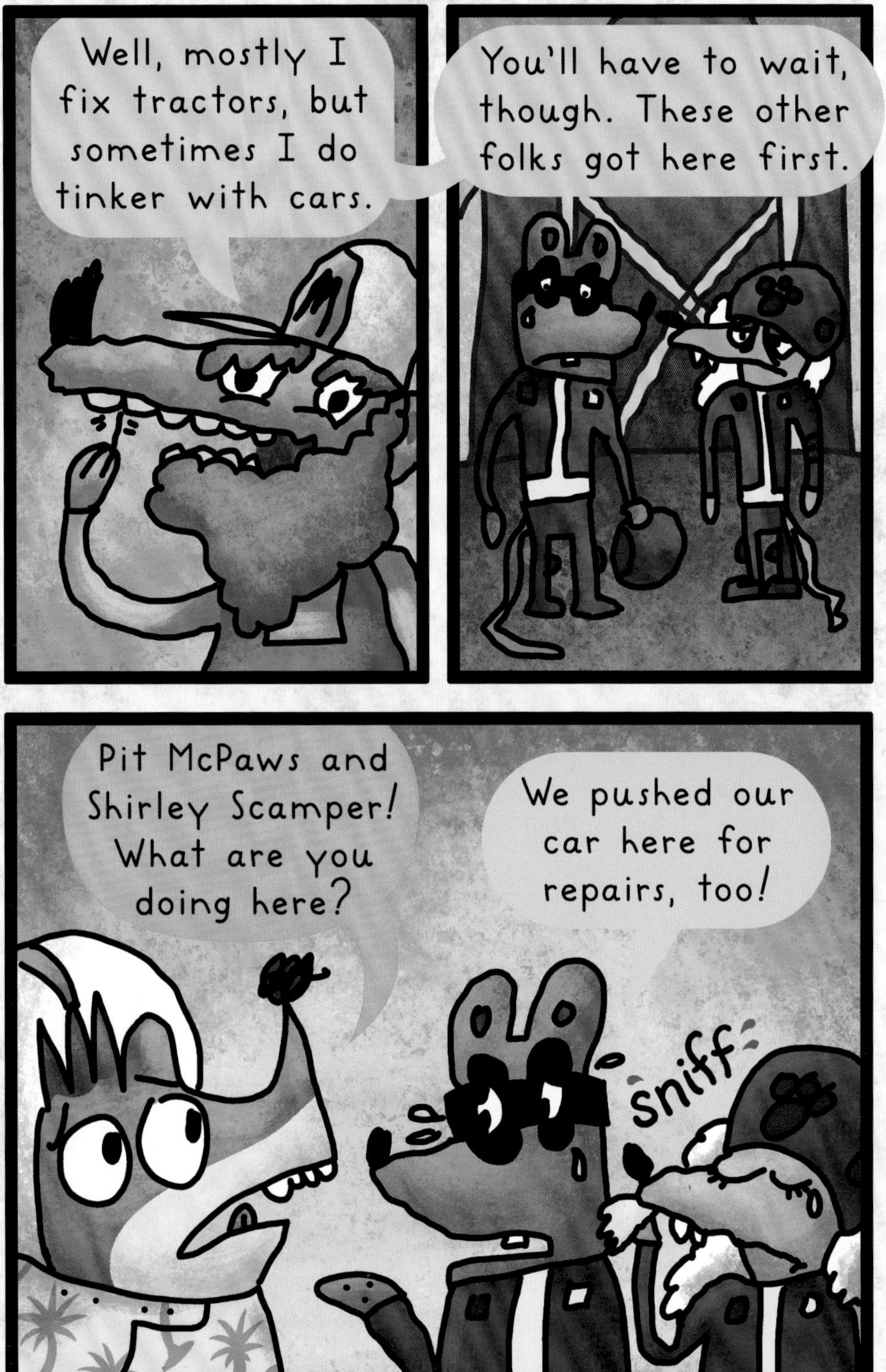
Well, mostly I fix tractors, but sometimes I do tinker with cars.
You'll have to wait, though. These other folks got here first.
Pit McPaws and Shirley Scamper! What are you doing here?
We pushed our car here for repairs, too!
sniff

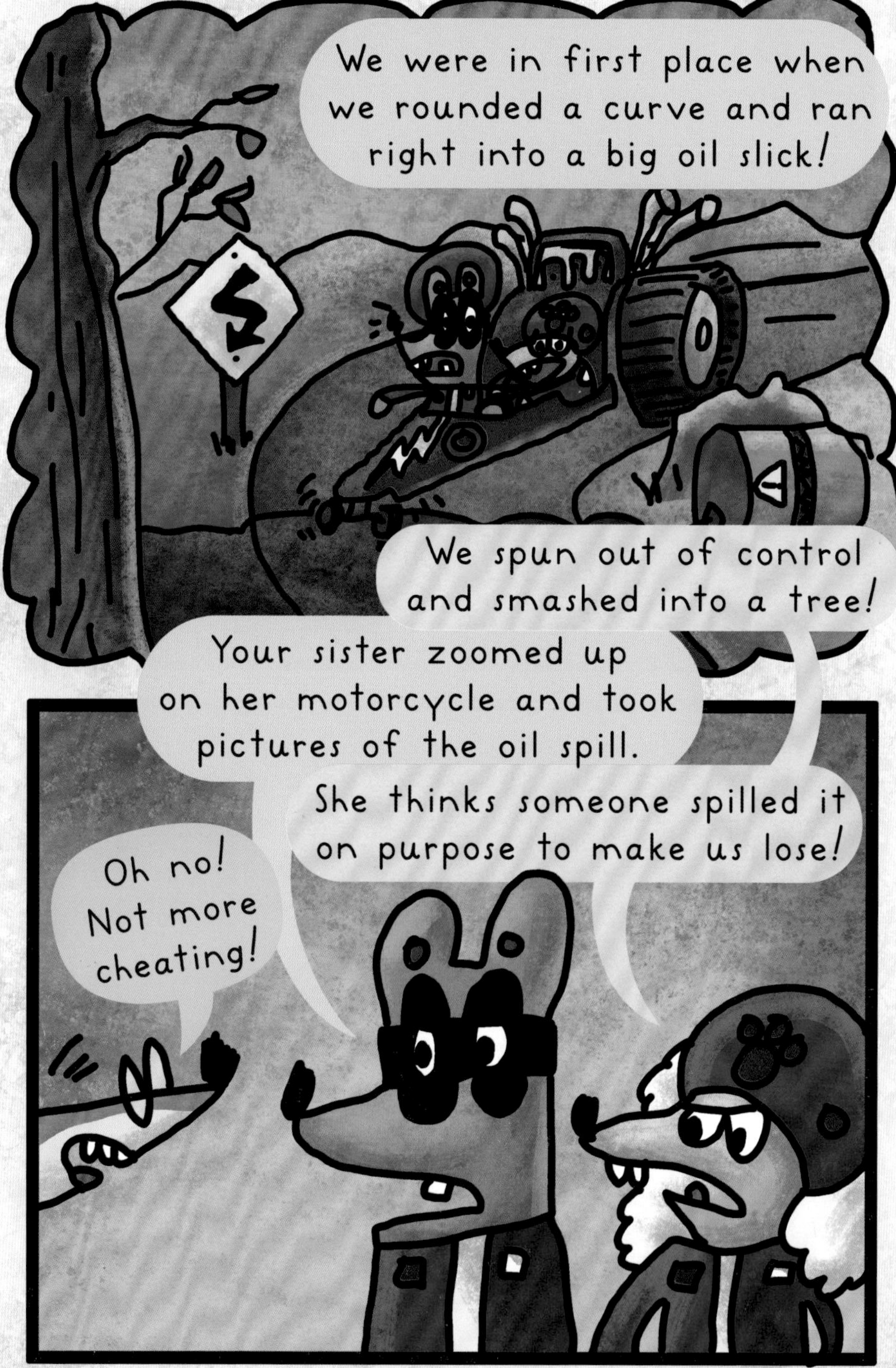

We were in first place when we rounded a curve and ran right into a big oil slick!
We spun out of control and smashed into a tree!
Your sister zoomed up on her motorcycle and took pictures of the oil spill.
She thinks someone spilled it on purpose to make us lose!
Oh no! Not more cheating!

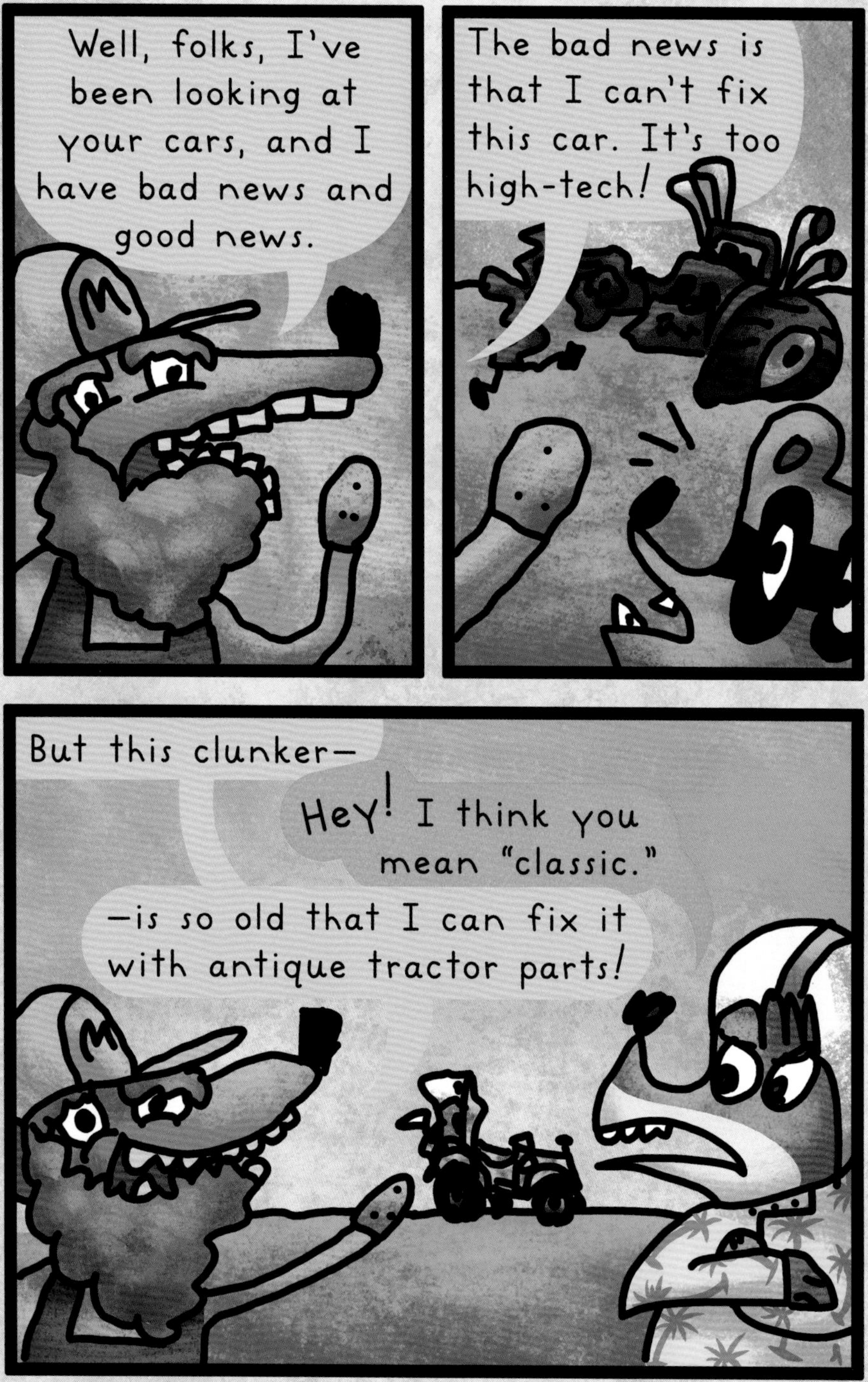
Well, folks, I've been looking at your cars, and I have bad news and good news.
The bad news is that I can't fix this car. It's too high-tech!
But this clunker—
Hey! I think you mean "classic."
—is so old that I can fix it with antique tractor parts!

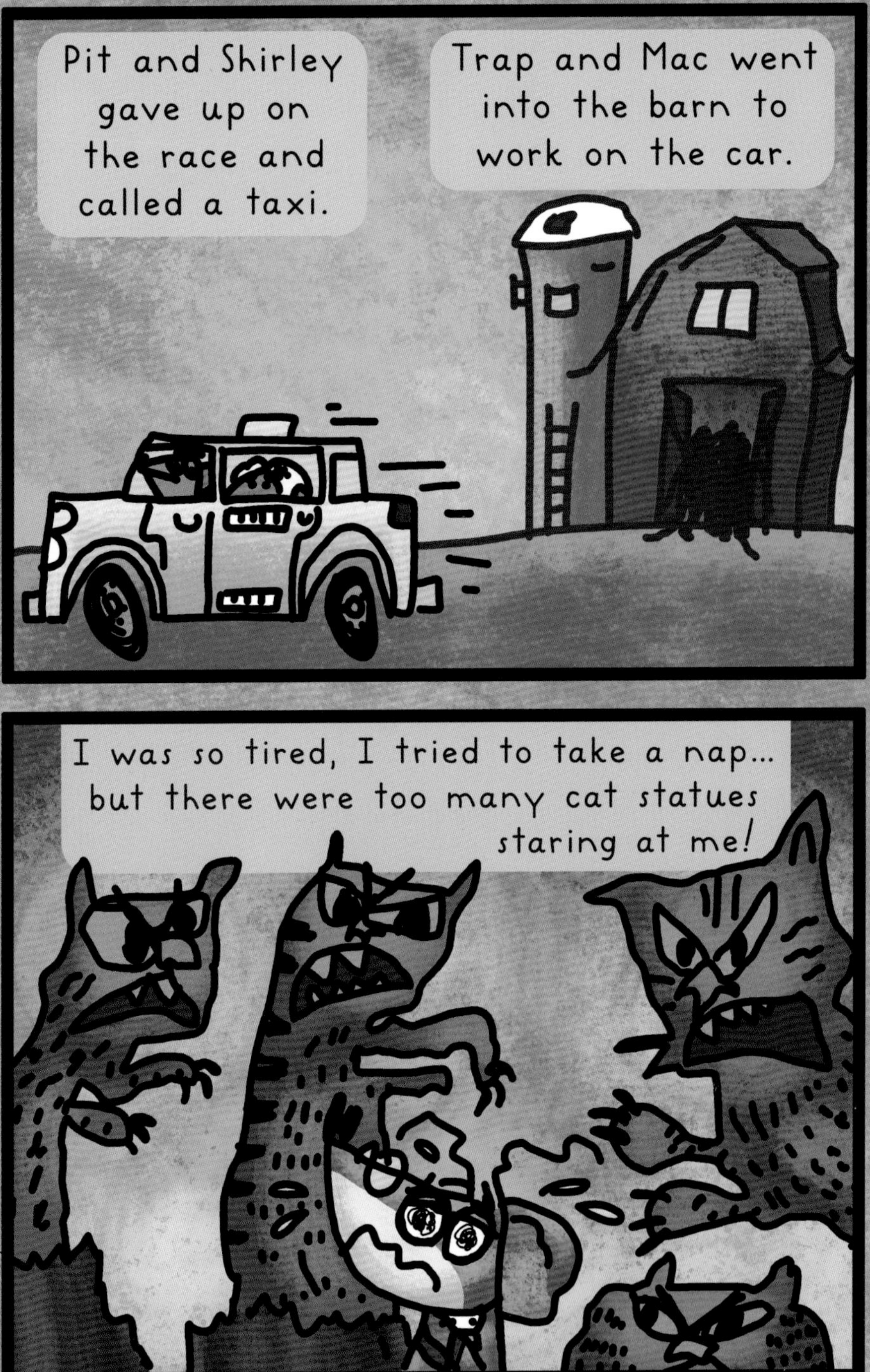
Pit and Shirley gave up on the race and called a taxi.
Trap and Mac went into the barn to work on the car.
I was so tired, I tried to take a nap... but there were too many cat statues staring at me!

CHAPTER TWENTY-TWO

WHY SO MUCH?

Finally, I dozed off and got a few minutes of **uneasy, tail-twitching** sleep before being awoken by Mac waving a **LONG** piece of paper under my nose...

Your cousin said to give this to you...

Wha... What is it?

THE BILL!

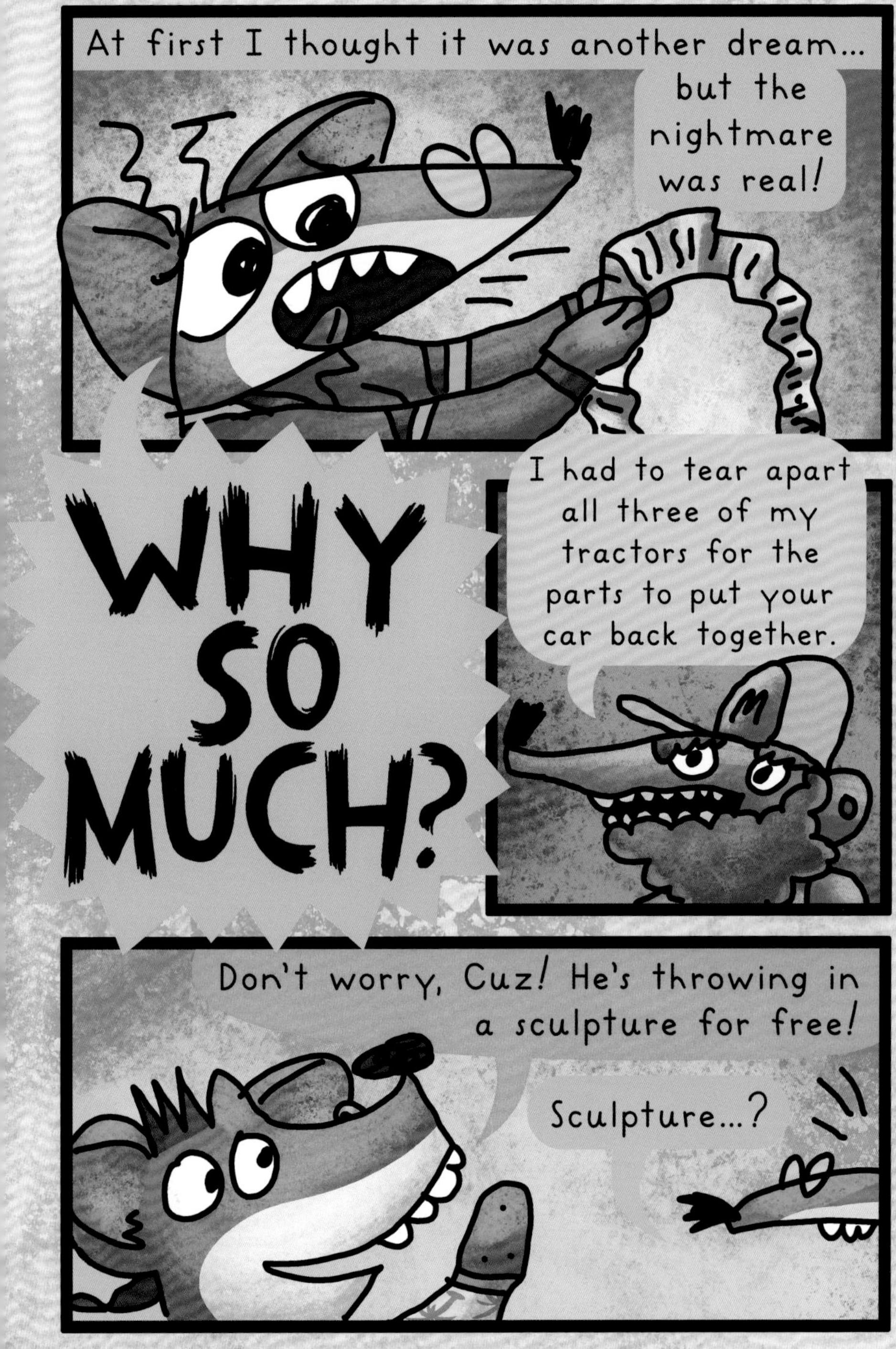
At first I thought it was another dream...
but the nightmare was real!
WHY SO MUCH?
I had to tear apart all three of my tractors for the parts to put your car back together.
Don't worry, Cuz! He's throwing in a sculpture for free!
Sculpture...?

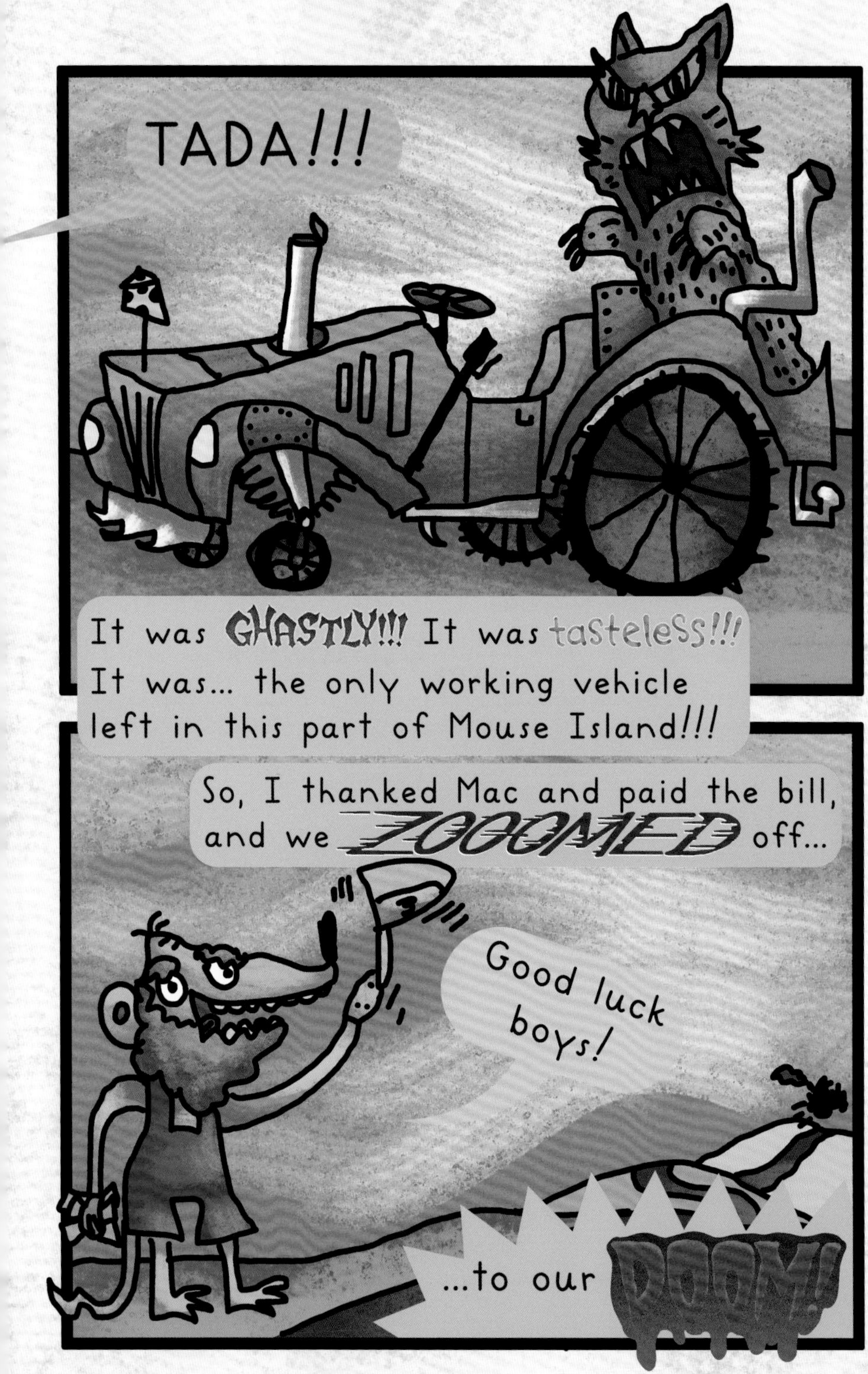
TADA!!!
It was GHASTLY!!! It was tasteless!!!
It was... the only working vehicle left in this part of Mouse Island!!!
So, I thanked Mac and paid the bill, and we ZOOOMED off...
Good luck boys!
...to our DOOM!

CHAPTER TWENTY-THREE

HELP! I'M *RALLY-* SICK!

Somehow, the tractor parts made the car go ═══*faster!* But they also made all the **bumps** worse! And the **bumps** kept getting bigger as we headed through Havarti Hills...

Slow down!!!

H'yuk, no way!!! We're catching big air now, Cuz!

WELCOME TO: Havarti Hills (*HAVARTI IS A KIND OF CHEESE)

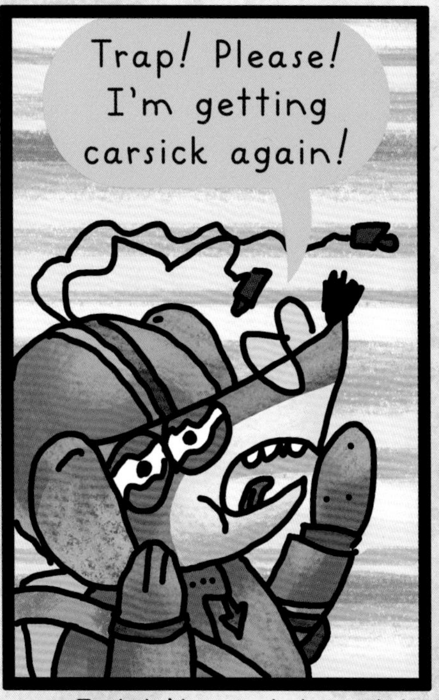
Trap! Please! I'm getting carsick again!

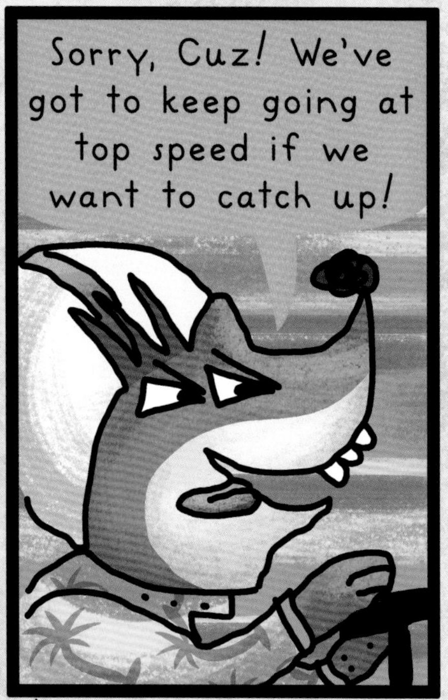
Sorry, Cuz! We've got to keep going at top speed if we want to catch up!

I didn't want to catch up! I didn't want to go top speed! I didn't even want to keep going! I wasn't just carsick, I was **RALLY-SICK!**

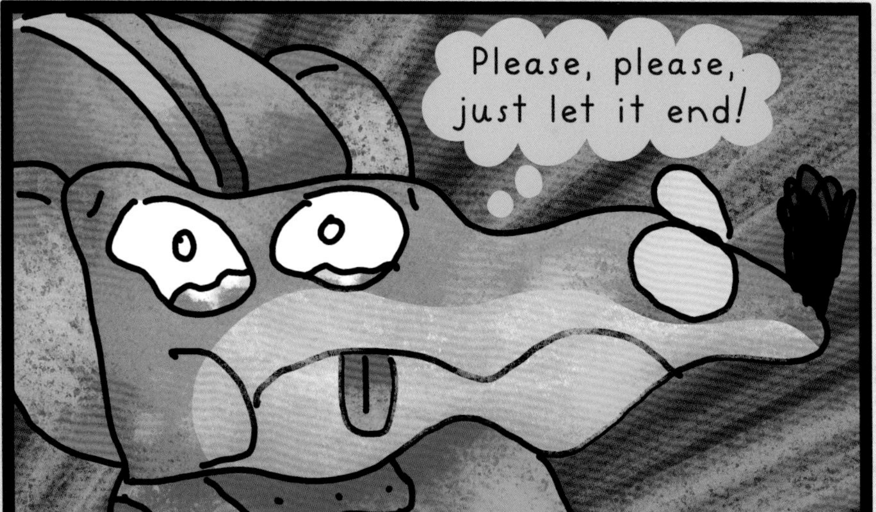
Please, please, just let it end!

CHAPTER TWENTY-FOUR

The End!

Do you know the famouse saying:

Be careful what you wish for?

Well...

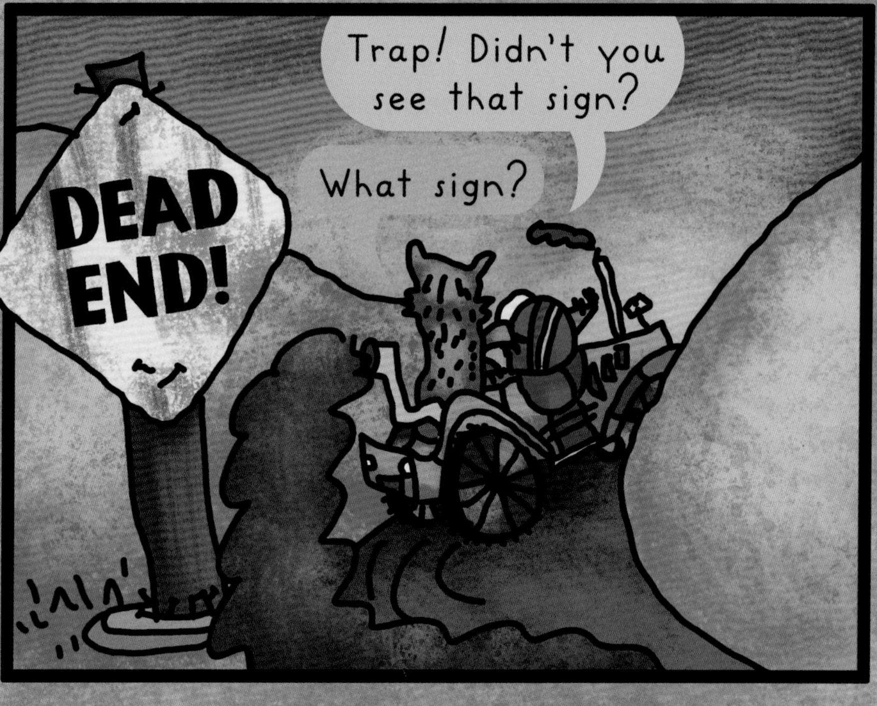

Trap! Didn't you see that sign?
What sign?
DEAD END!

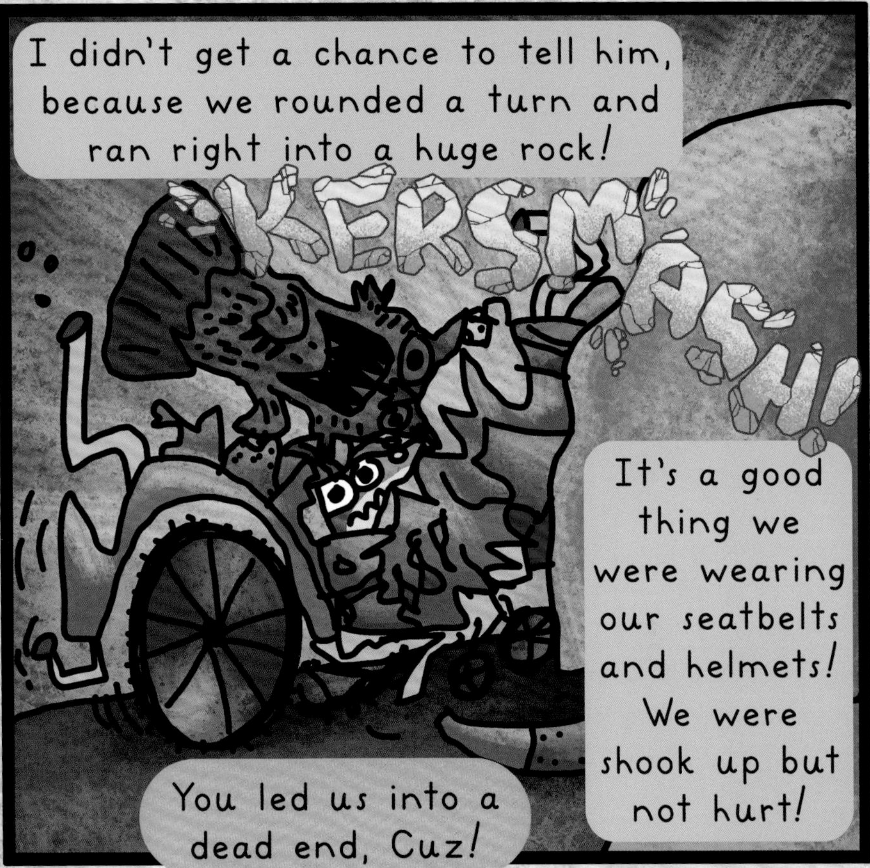
I didn't get a chance to tell him, because we rounded a turn and ran right into a huge rock!
KERSMASH!
It's a good thing we were wearing our seatbelts and helmets! We were shook up but not hurt!
You led us into a dead end, Cuz!

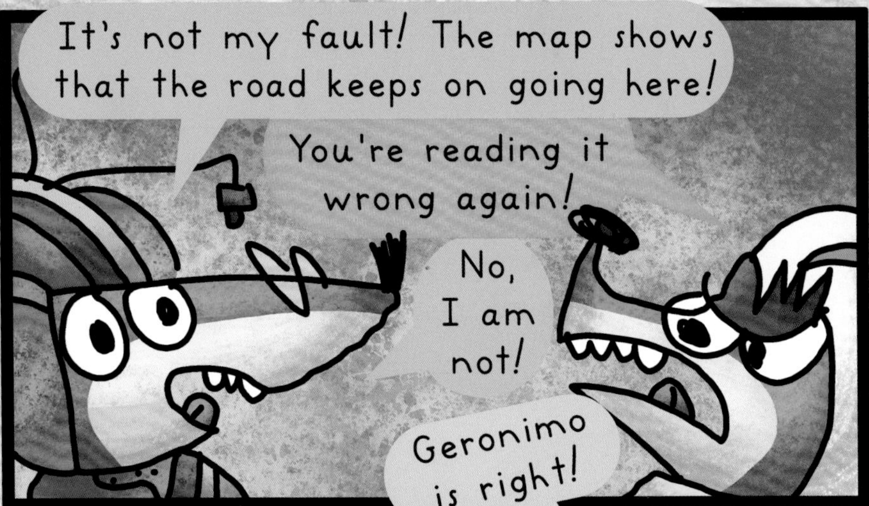
It's not my fault! The map shows that the road keeps on going here!
You're reading it wrong again!
No, I am not!
Geronimo is right!

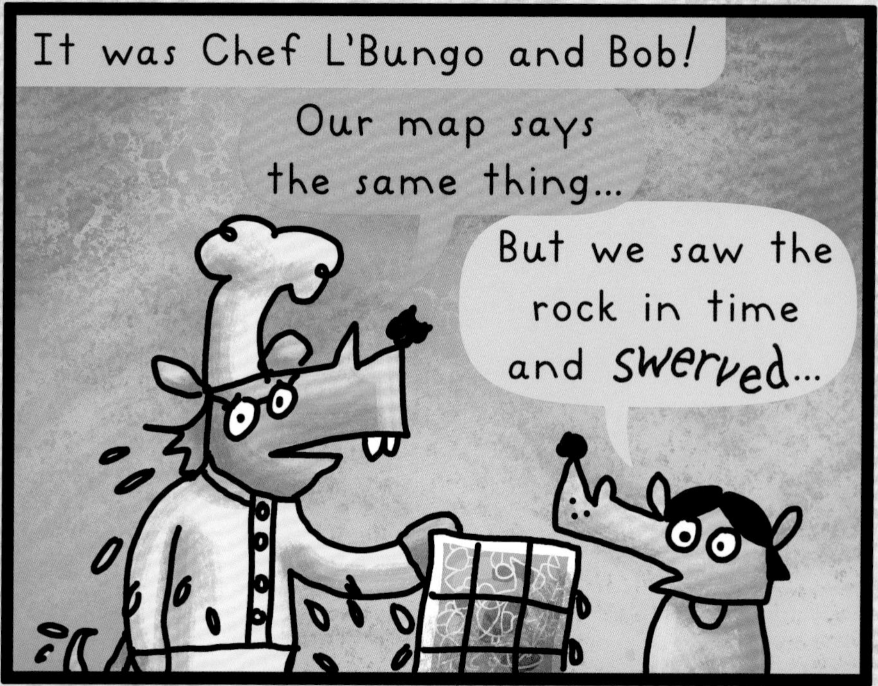
It was Chef L'Bungo and Bob!
Our map says the same thing...
But we saw the rock in time and swerved...

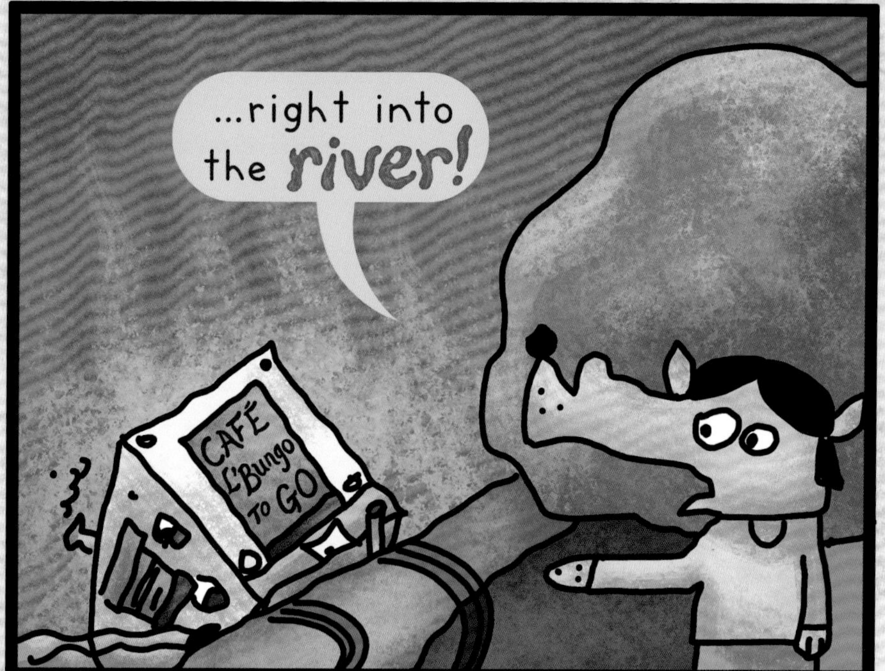
...right into the river!
CAFÉ L'Bungo TO GO

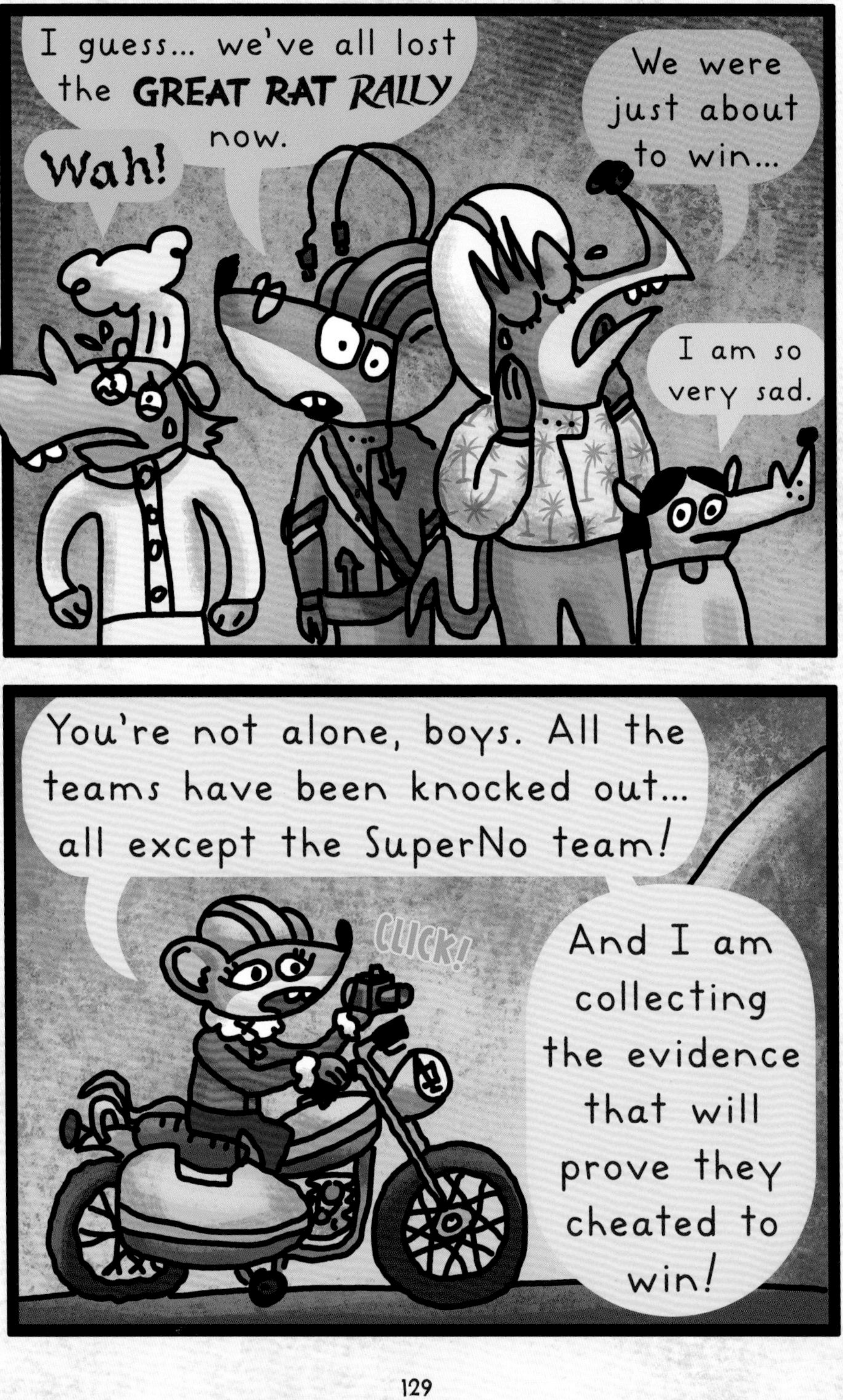
I guess... we've all lost the GREAT RAT RALLY now.
Wah!
We were just about to win...
I am so very sad.
You're not alone, boys. All the teams have been knocked out... all except the SuperNo team!
CLICK!
And I am collecting the evidence that will prove they cheated to win!

CHAPTER TWENTY-FIVE

SABOTAGE!

We had all been so upset, we had not heard Thea roll up on her motorcycle. Chef L'Bungo and Bob were shocked to hear about the cheating, and we all wanted Thea to explain.

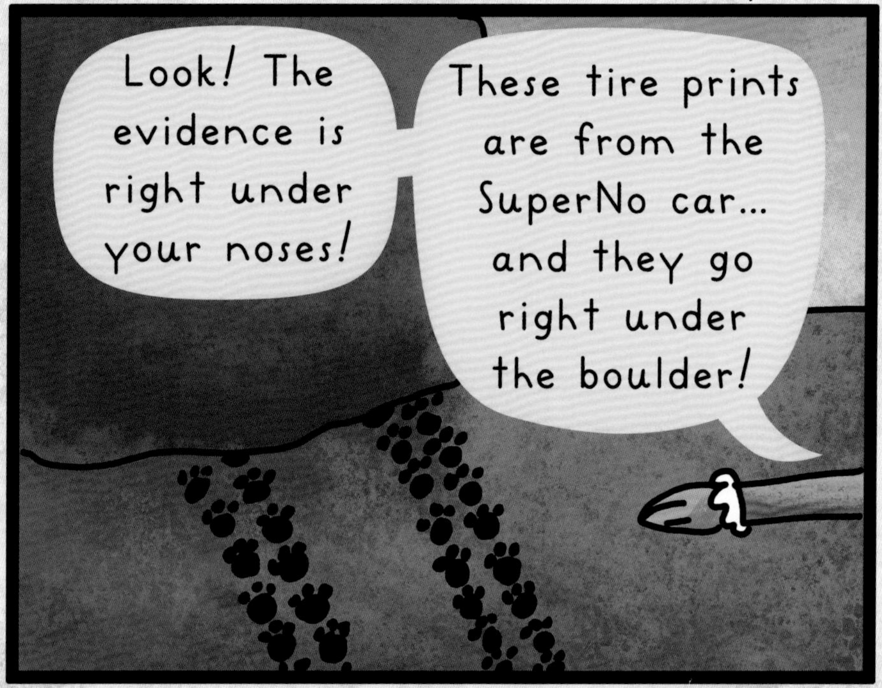
Look! The evidence is right under your noses!
These tire prints are from the SuperNo car... and they go right under the boulder!

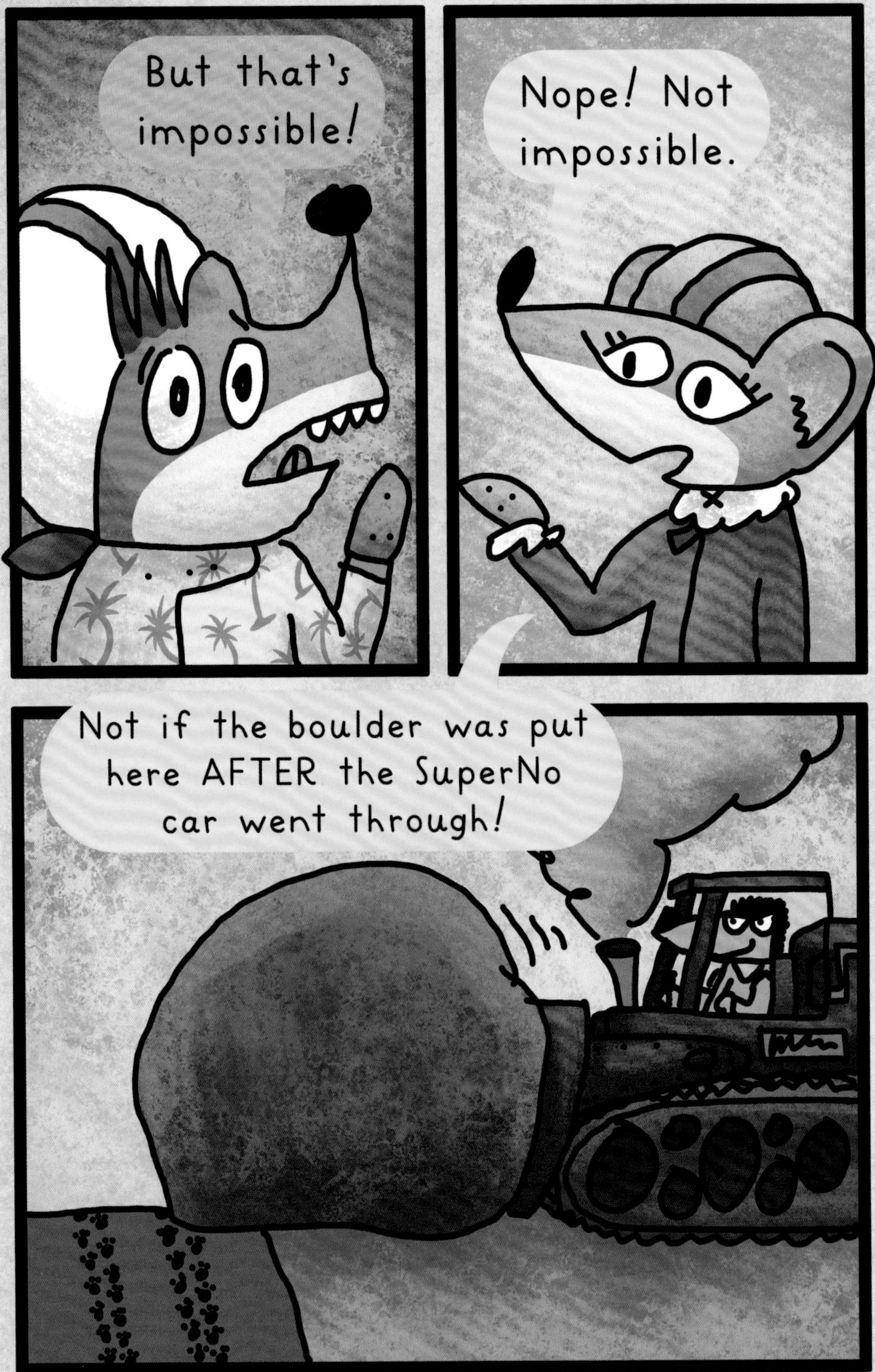
But that's impossible!
Nope! Not impossible.
Not if the boulder was put here AFTER the SuperNo car went through!

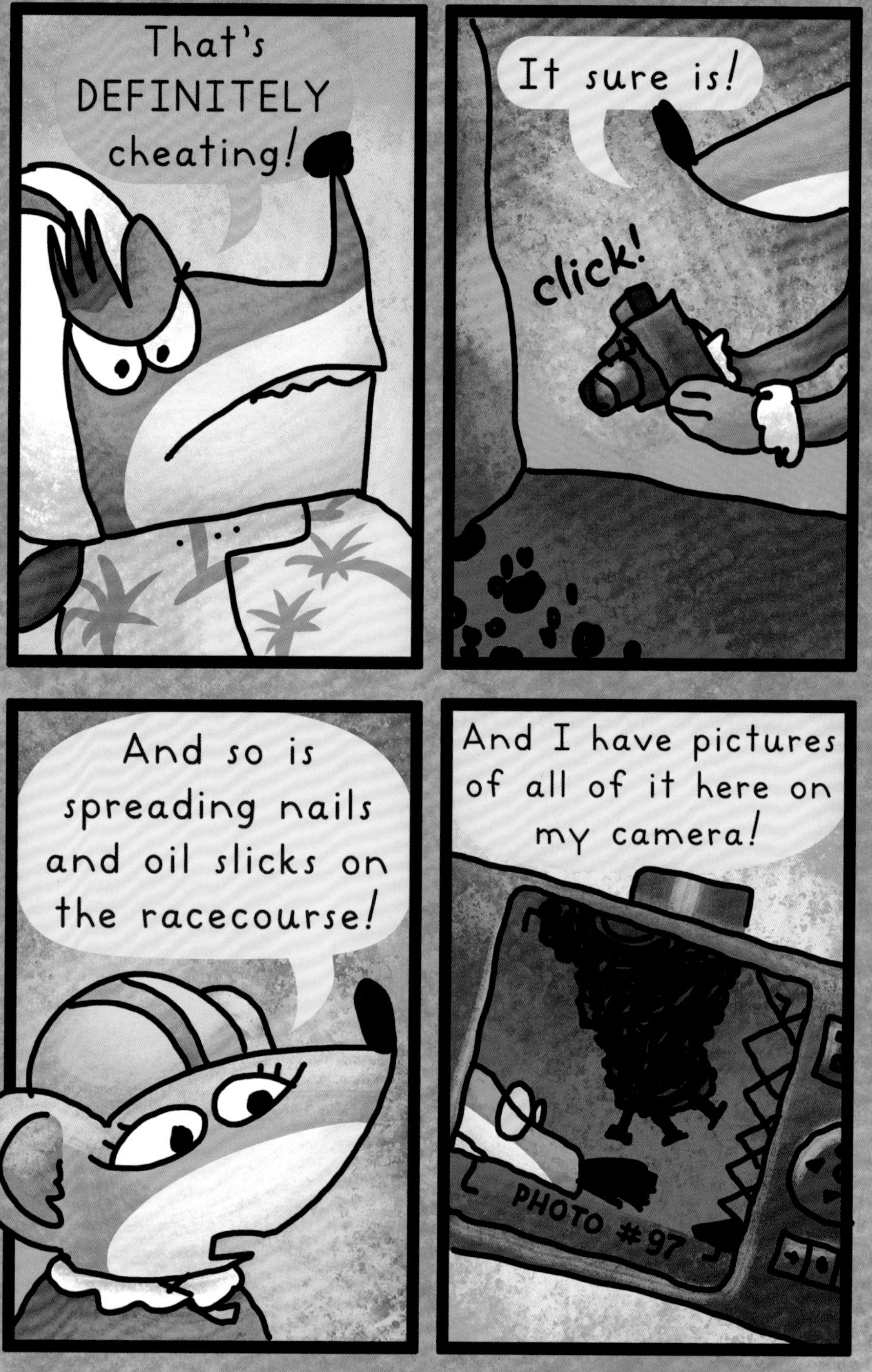
That's DEFINITELY cheating!
It sure is!
click!
And so is spreading nails and oil slicks on the racecourse!
And I have pictures of all of it here on my camera!
PHOTO #97

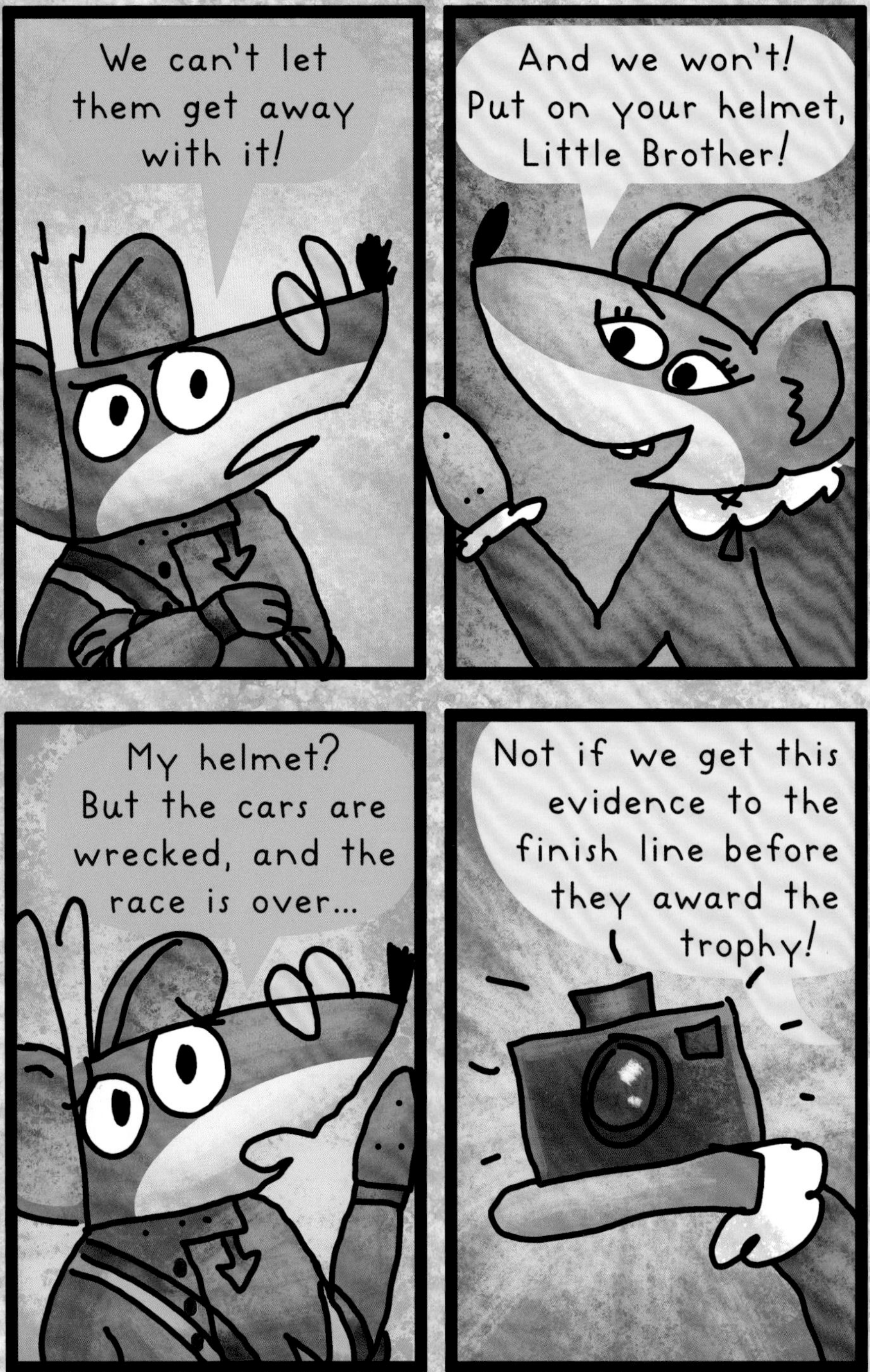
We can't let them get away with it!
And we won't! Put on your helmet, Little Brother!
My helmet? But the cars are wrecked, and the race is over...
Not if we get this evidence to the finish line before they award the trophy!

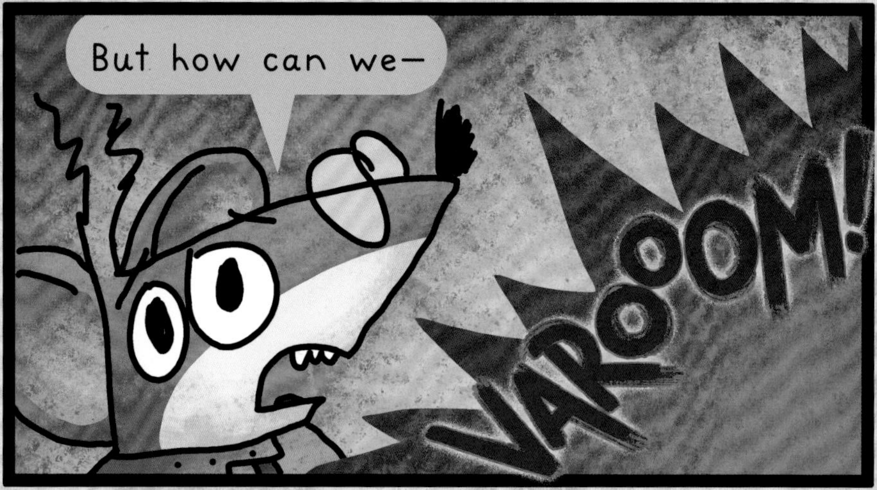
But how can we—
VAROOOM!

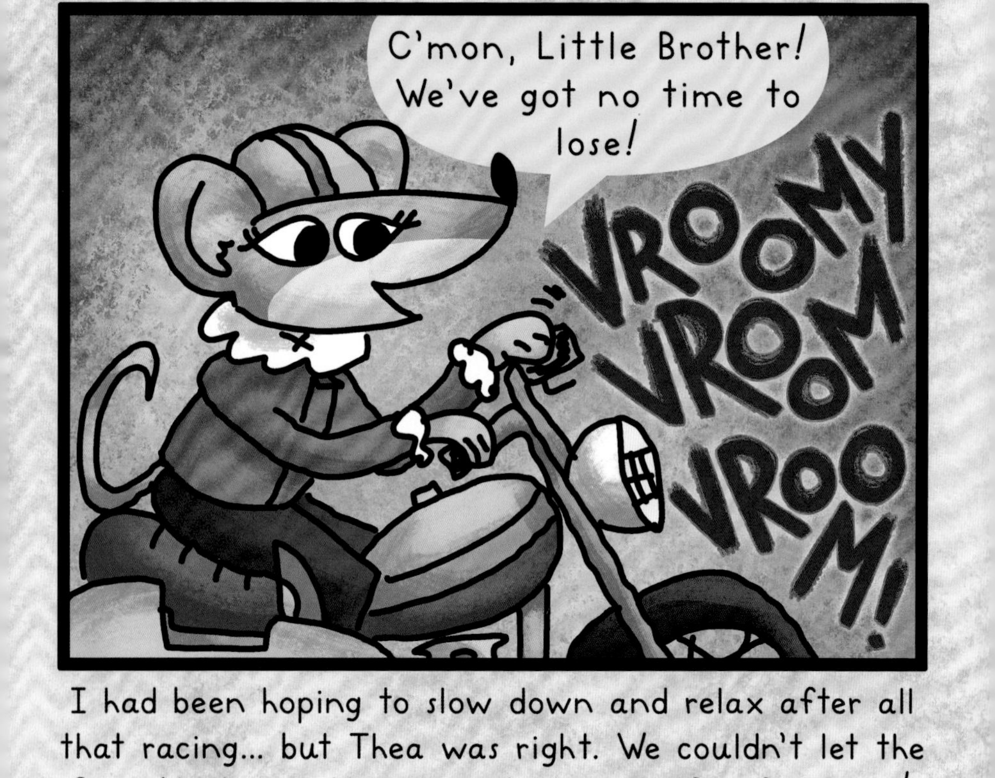
C'mon, Little Brother! We've got no time to lose!
VROOMVROOMVROOOM!

I had been hoping to slow down and relax after all that racing... but Thea was right. We couldn't let the SuperNo team cheat everybody out of a fair race! So I put on my helmet and got in...the sidecar.

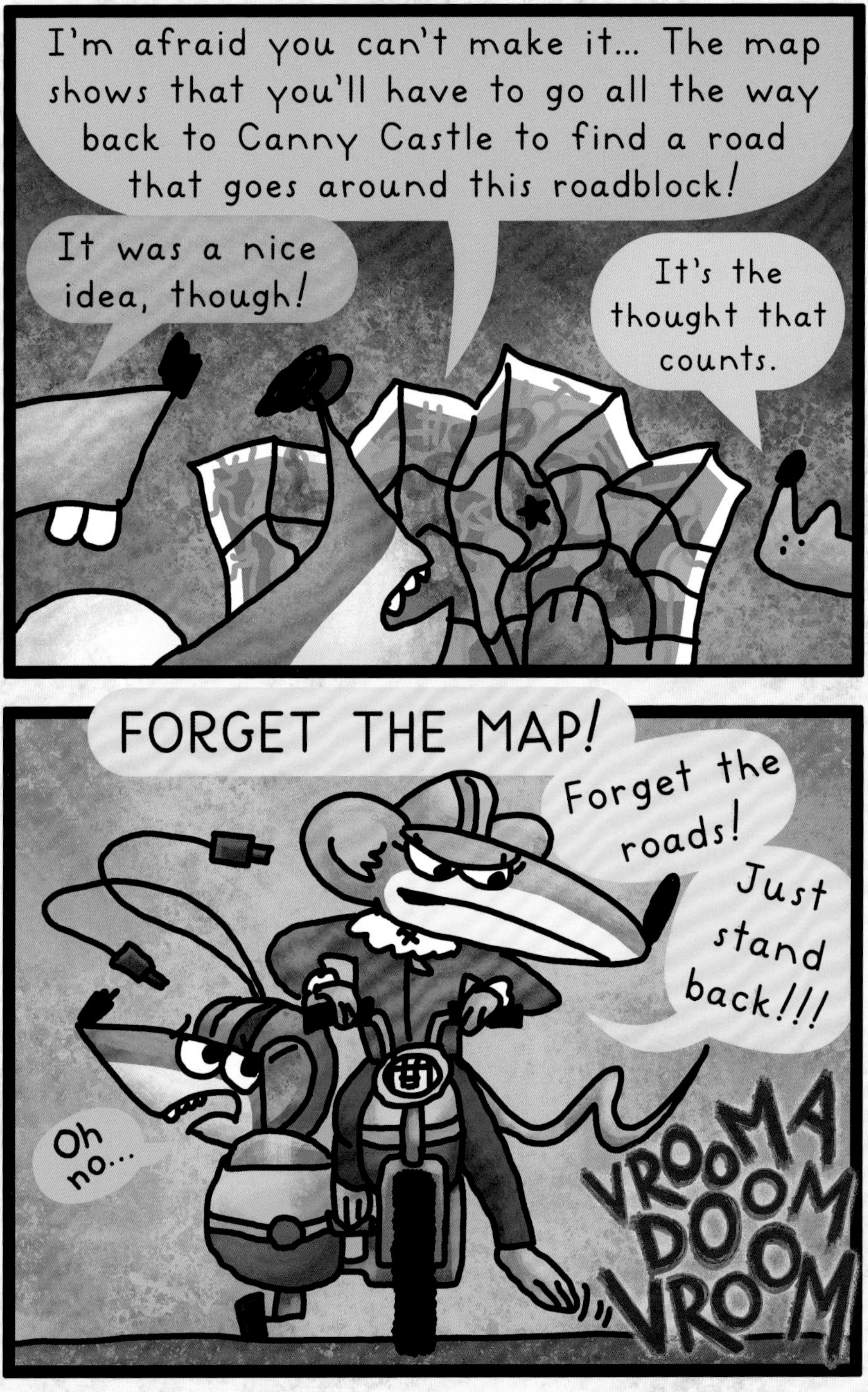
I'm afraid you can't make it... The map shows that you'll have to go all the way back to Canny Castle to find a road that goes around this roadblock!
It was a nice idea, though!
It's the thought that counts.
FORGET THE MAP!
Forget the roads!
Just stand back!!!
Oh no...
VROOMA VROOM DOOOM VROOM

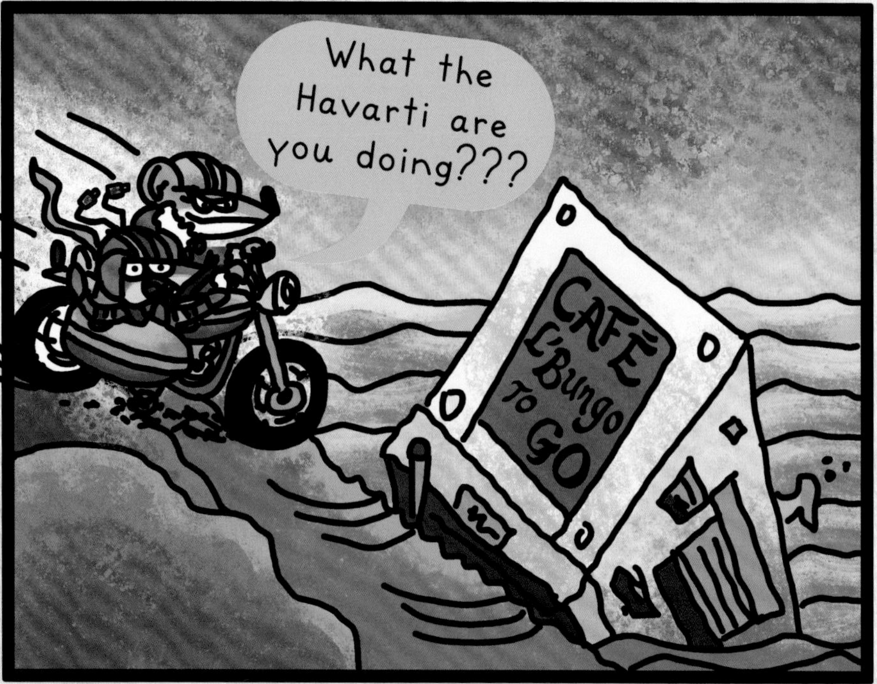
What the Havarti are you doing???
CAFÉ L'Bungo TO GO

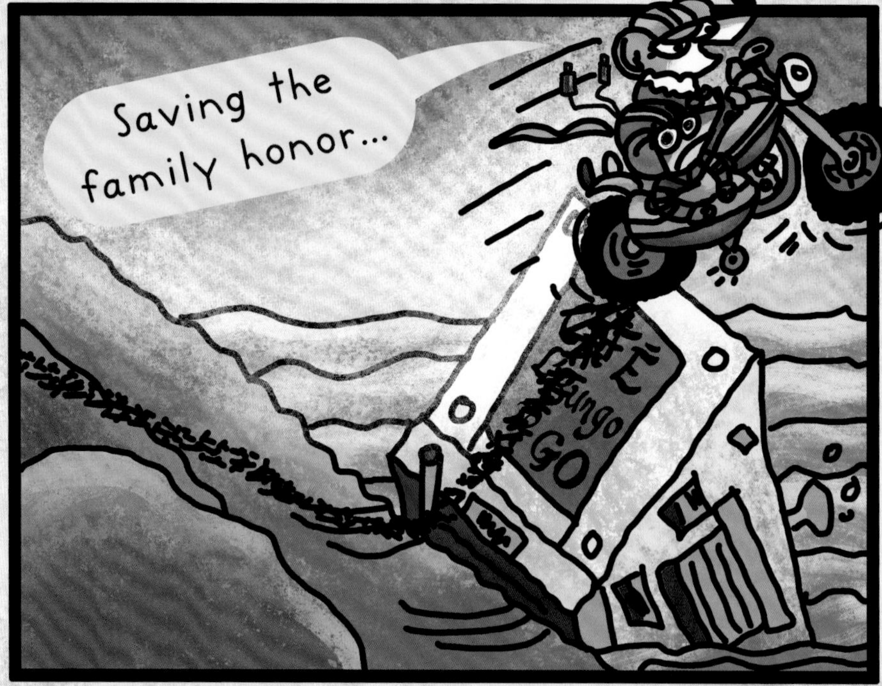
Saving the family honor...
CAFÉ L'Bungo GO

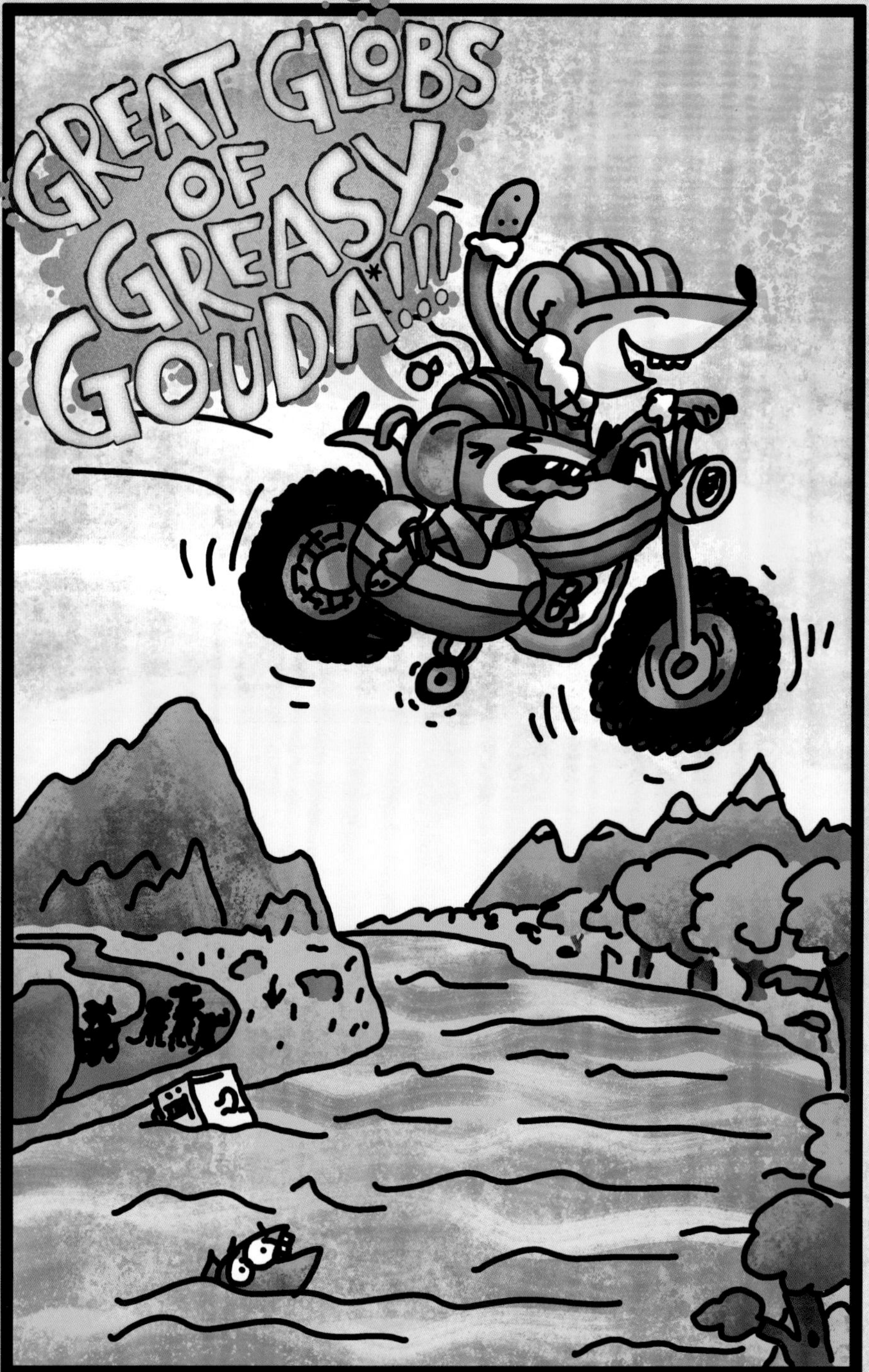
GREAT GLOBS OF GREASY GOUDA*!!!

*Gouda is a type of... Oh dear! I'm feeling faint!
I think I might—

CHAPTER TWENTY-SIX

WELCOME TO
(cough cough)
Fossil Forest

All I could remember was shutting my eyes as we flew across the river. When I opened them, I was surrounded by **puffy clouds!**

Did we miss the jump?

Did we crash in the river?

Is this THE END???

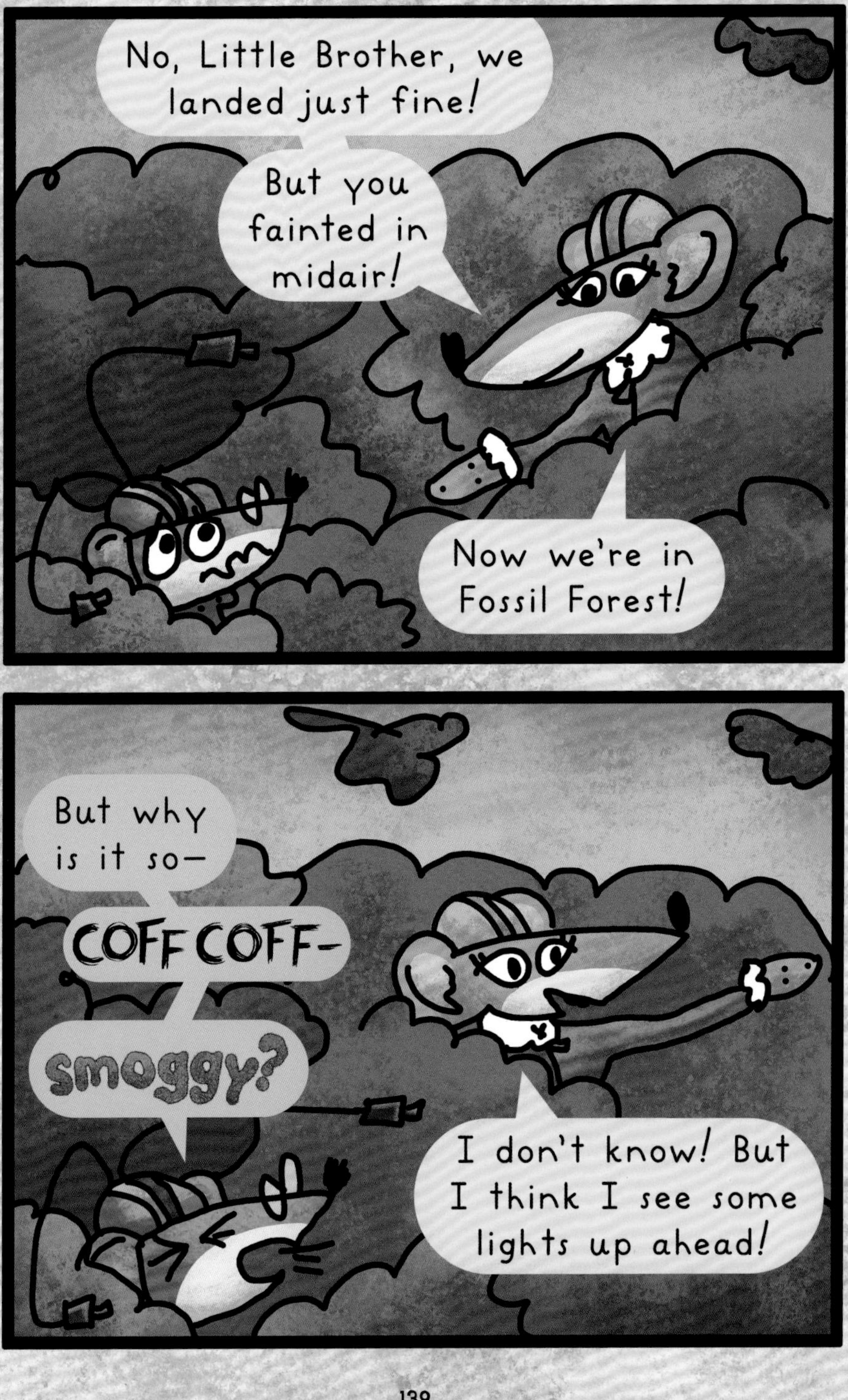
No, Little Brother, we landed just fine!
But you fainted in midair!
Now we're in Fossil Forest!
But why is it so—
COFF COFF—
smoggy?
I don't know! But I think I see some lights up ahead!

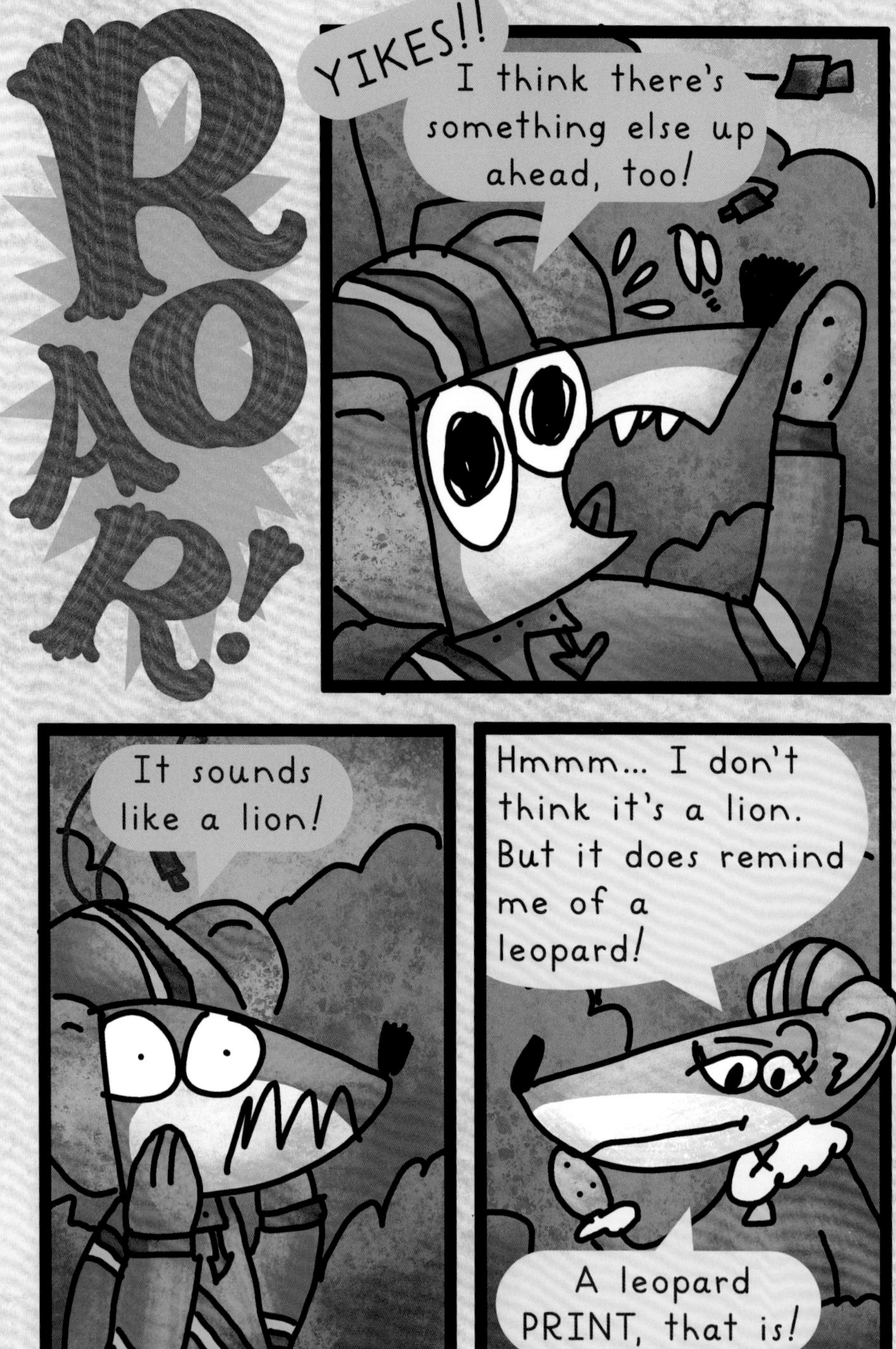
ROAR!
YIKES!!
I think there's something else up ahead, too!
It sounds like a lion!
Hmmm... I don't think it's a lion. But it does remind me of a leopard!
A leopard PRINT, that is!

CHAPTER TWENTY-SEVEN

The Mysterious ROAR!!

Thea reminded me that the engine of a SuperNo car sounds a lot like a **ROARING** lion. I was glad that there wasn't a real lion in the forest, but I couldn't figure out why there would be a race car here, either.

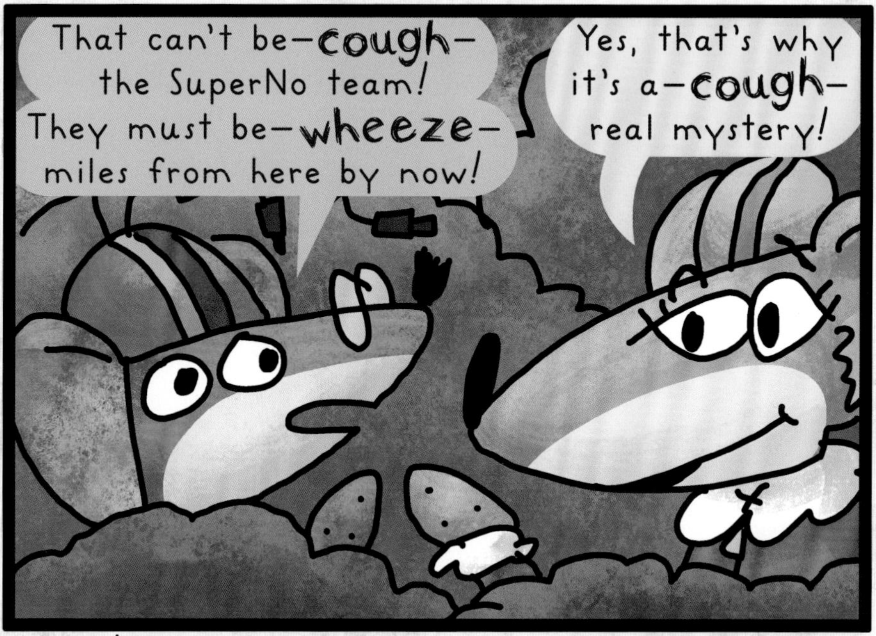

That can't be—cough—the SuperNo team! They must be—wheeze—miles from here by now!
Yes, that's why it's a—cough—real mystery!

Oh no! If you know my sister, you know she can NEVER resist trying to solve a Mystery!

Let's list our clues...

1. Lots of SMOKE!

cough! HACK! cough!

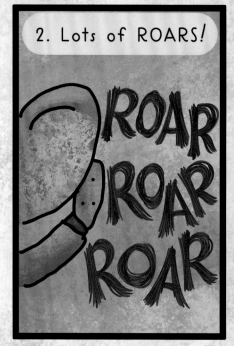

2. Lots of ROARS!

ROAR ROAR ROAR

3. Lots of GUARDS!

Wait! What?

SHHHHHHH!

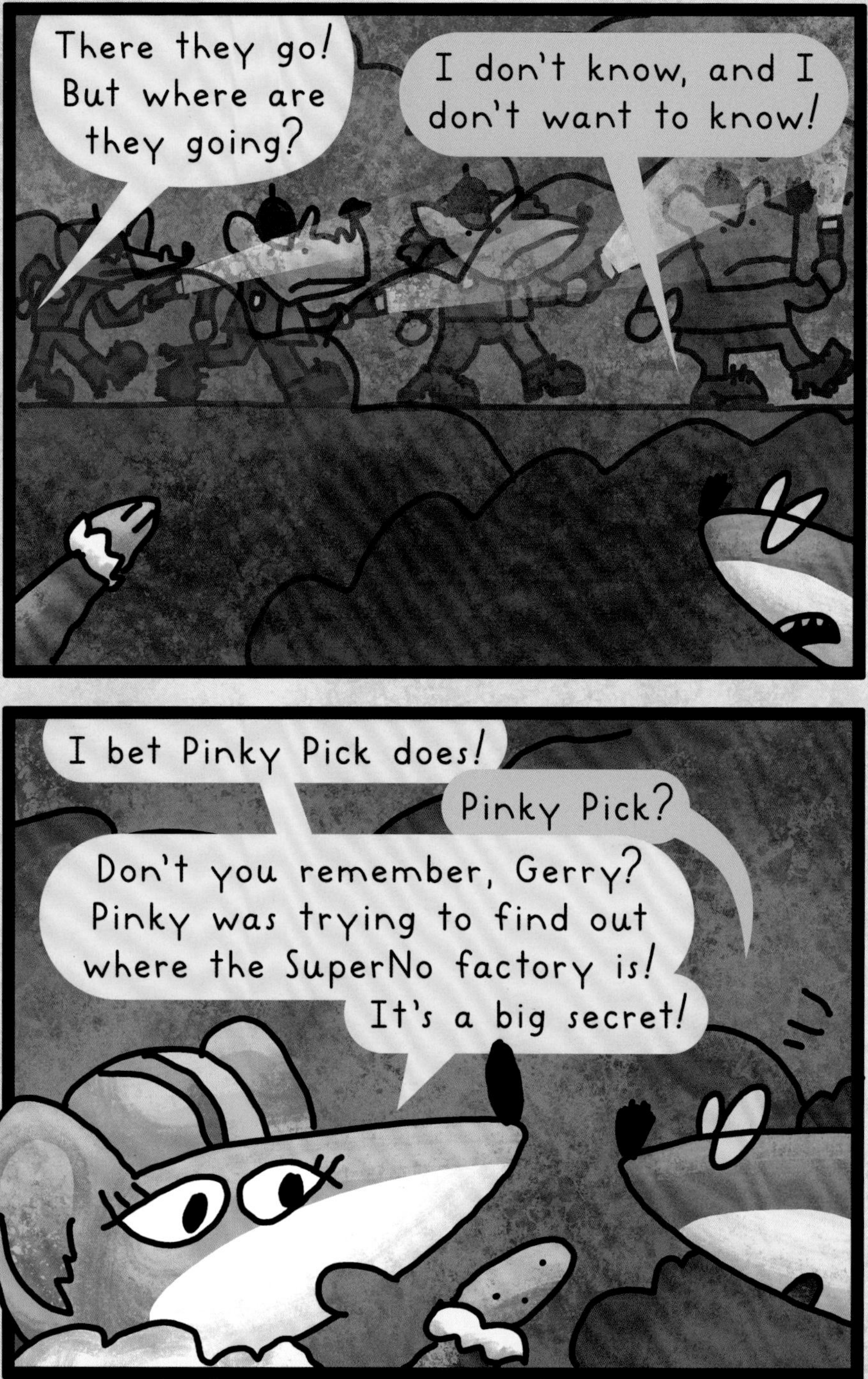
There they go! But where are they going?
I don't know, and I don't want to know!
I bet Pinky Pick does!
Pinky Pick?
Don't you remember, Gerry? Pinky was trying to find out where the SuperNo factory is!
It's a big secret!

C'mon! If we follow those guards, we might get a huge scoop for **THE RODENT'S GAZETTE!**

Follow them? But they look mean and grumpy and likely to stomp on anyone they find! Plus, it's so smoky we can barely see where WE'RE going, and this forest is creepy, and maybe those guys roar like the lions, and—

Do you want to be a scaredy-mouse, or do you want to get the scoop?

Well, I can never resist the chance to get a good story for the newspaper!

Plus, I **HATE** being called a scaredy-mouse!

So I agreed...

But I sure wished I could have seen where I was going, because a few minutes later...

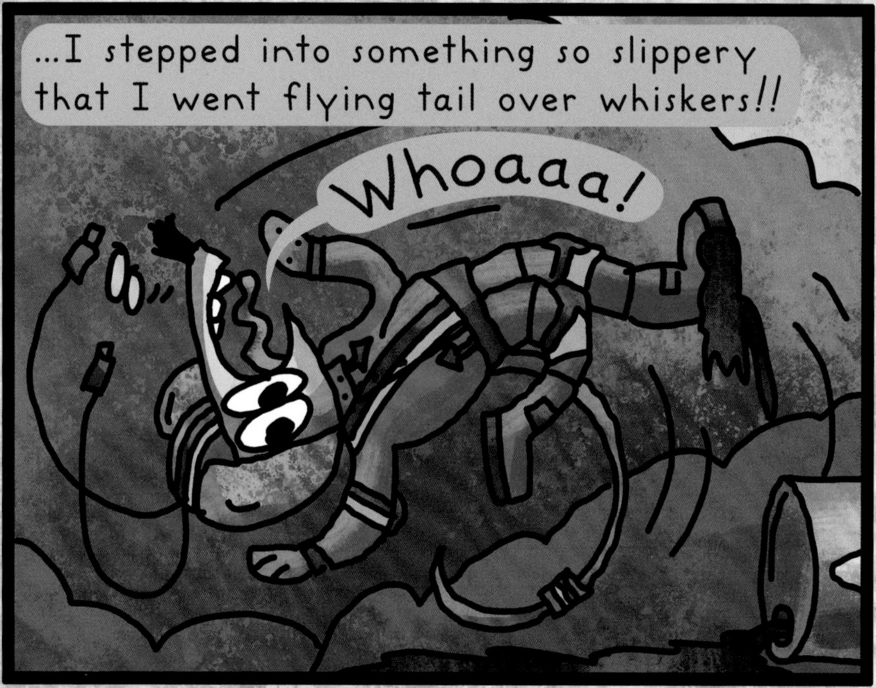
...I stepped into something so slippery that I went flying tail over whiskers!!
Whoaaa!

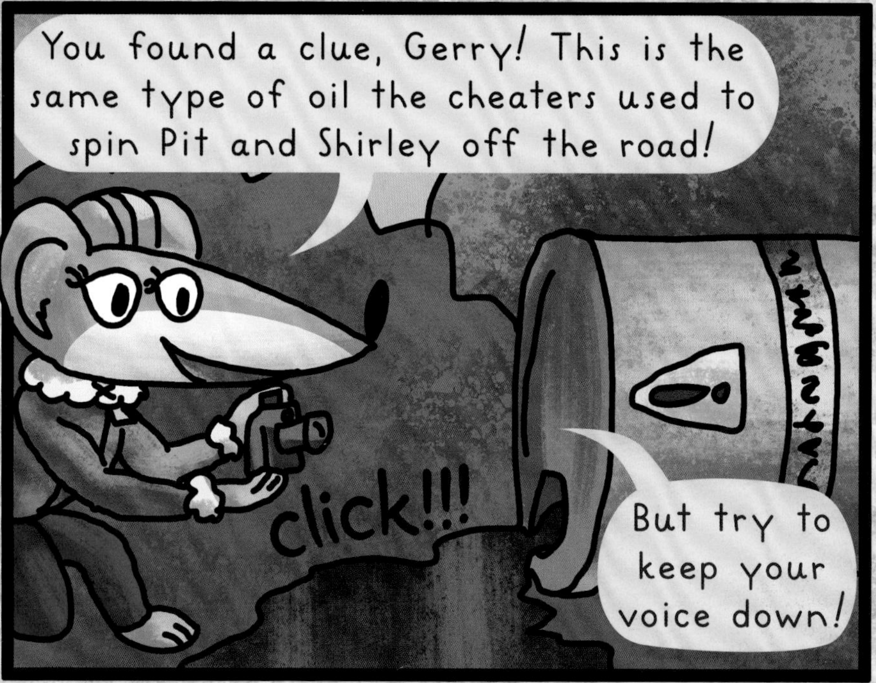
You found a clue, Gerry! This is the same type of oil the cheaters used to spin Pit and Shirley off the road!
click!!!
But try to keep your voice down!

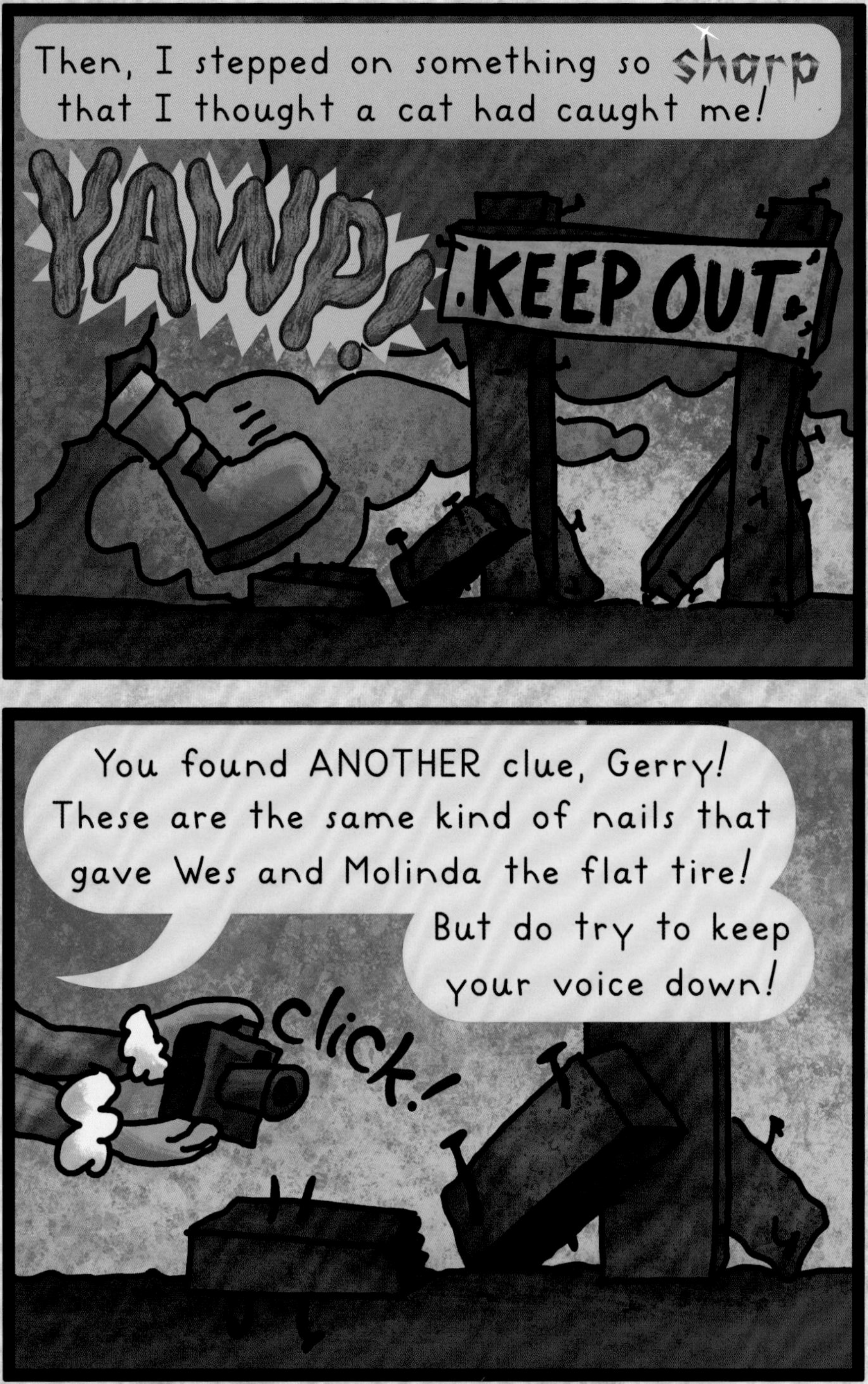
Then, I stepped on something so sharp that I thought a cat had caught me!
YAWP!
KEEP OUT
You found ANOTHER clue, Gerry! These are the same kind of nails that gave Wes and Molinda the flat tire!
But do try to keep your voice down!
click!

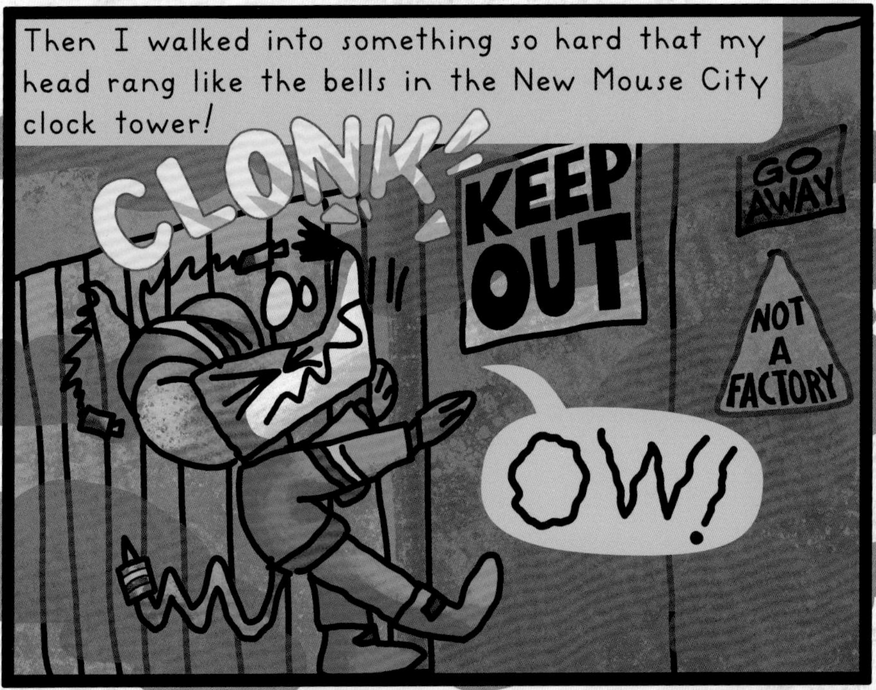
Then I walked into something so hard that my head rang like the bells in the New Mouse City clock tower!
CLONK!
KEEP OUT
GO AWAY
NOT A FACTORY
OW!

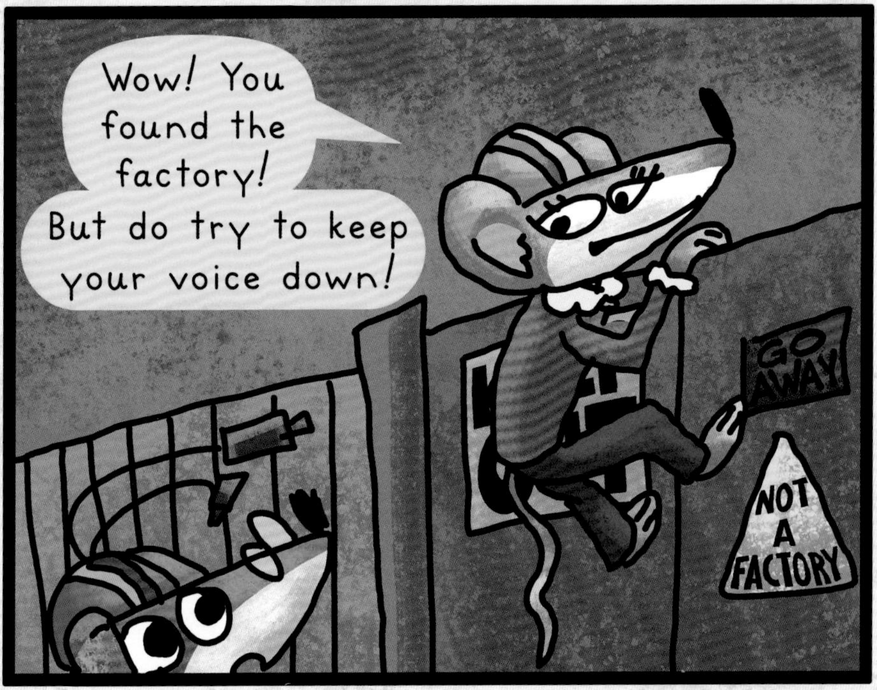
Wow! You found the factory!
But do try to keep your voice down!
GO AWAY
NOT A FACTORY

CHAPTER TWENTY-EIGHT

THE FACTORY

I did NOT want to climb over that gate! But Thea said we had to make sure it was the SuperNo factory. Then her photos would prove that the SuperNo team was cheating.

But what we saw on the other side was proof of something else, too...

The SuperNo company was **POLLUTING!**

The factory was causing so many kinds of POLLUTION!
AIR pollution!
click!
LIGHT pollution!
click!
GROUND pollution!
click!
WATER pollution!
click!
And, of course, NOISE pollution!
ROAR!!

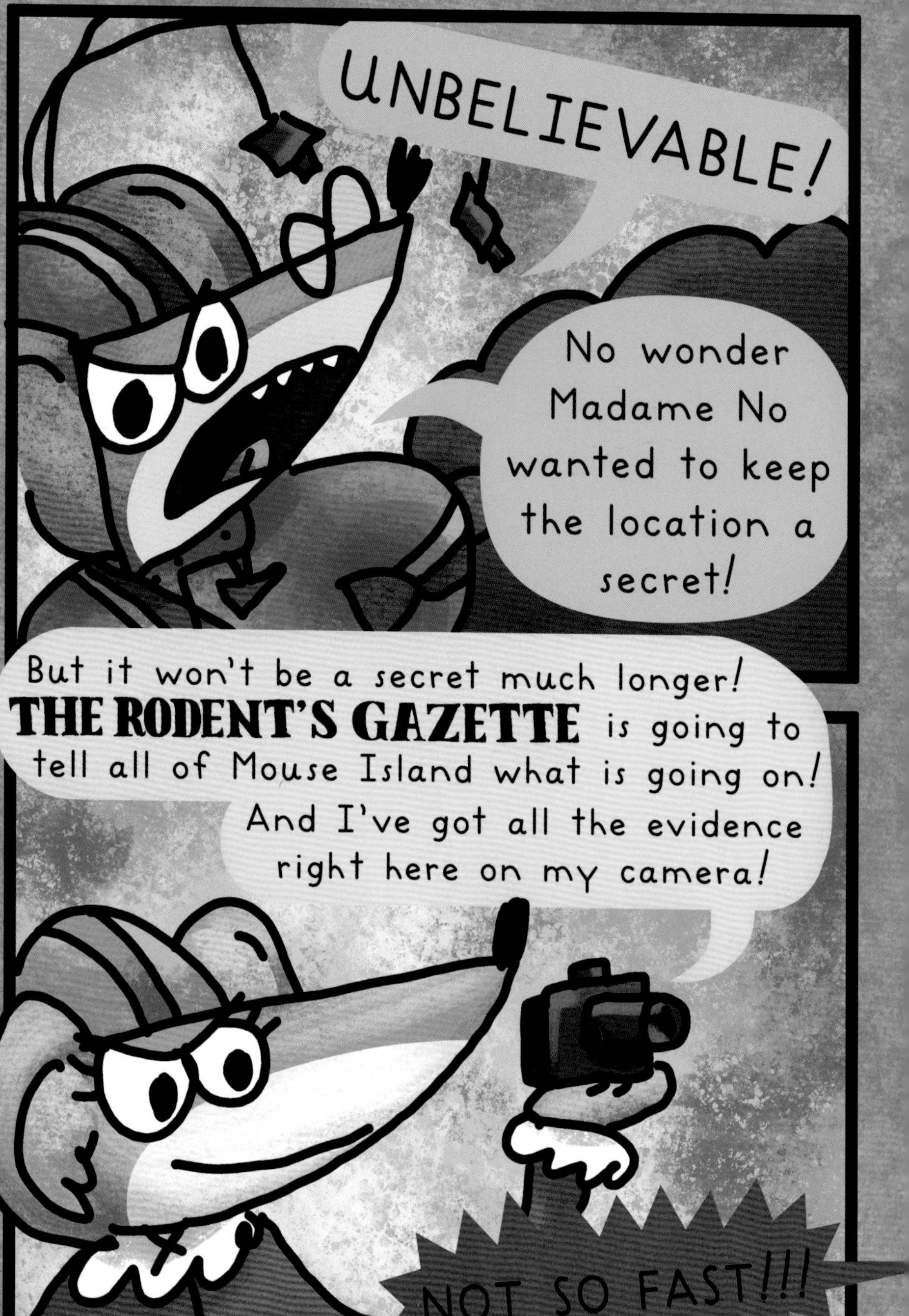
UNBELIEVABLE!
No wonder Madame No wanted to keep the location a secret!
But it won't be a secret much longer! THE RODENT'S GAZETTE is going to tell all of Mouse Island what is going on! And I've got all the evidence right here on my camera!
NOT SO FAST!!!

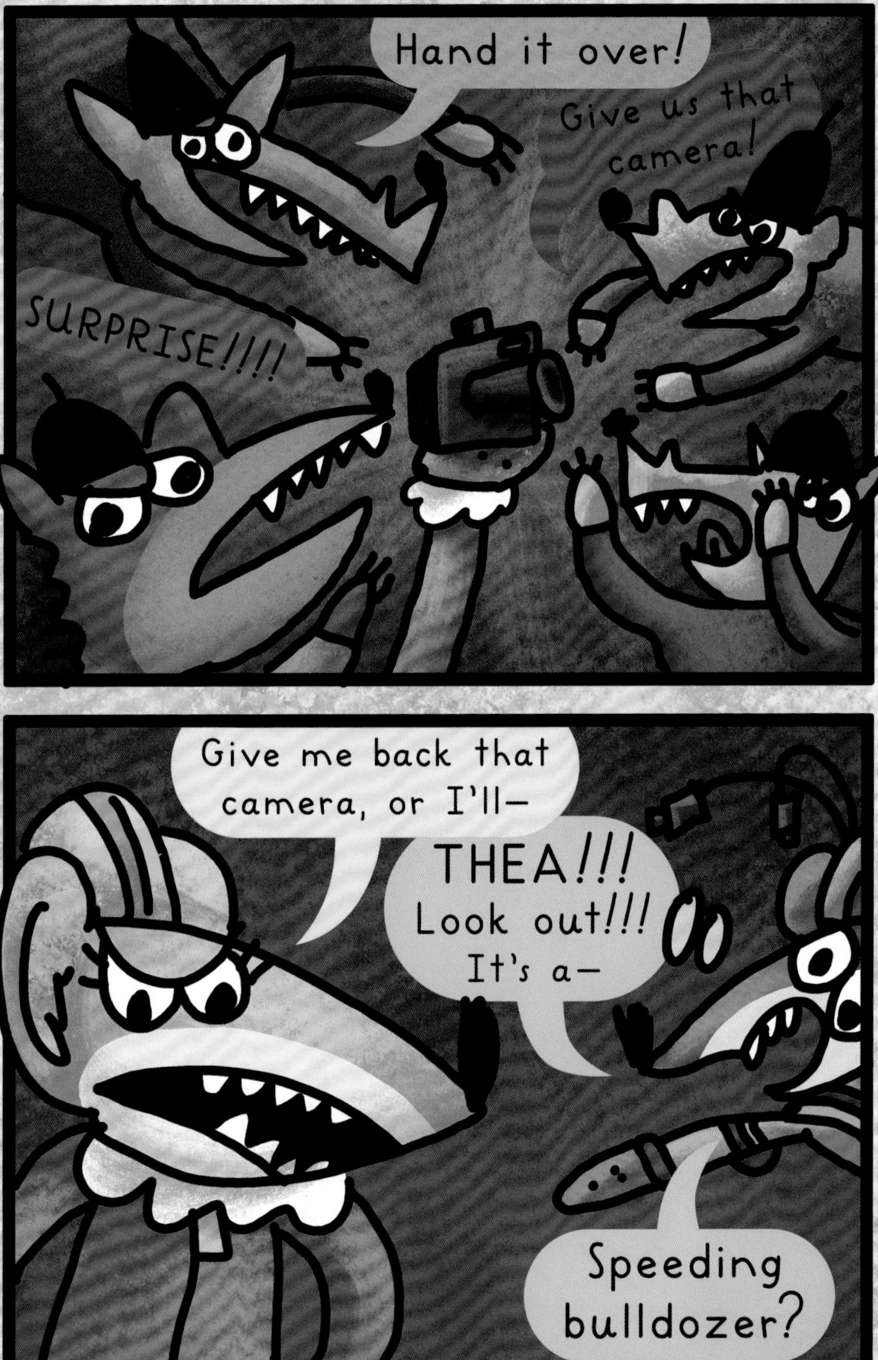
Hand it over!
Give us that camera!
SURPRISE!!!!
Give me back that camera, or I'll—
THEA!!! Look out!!! It's a—
Speeding bulldozer?

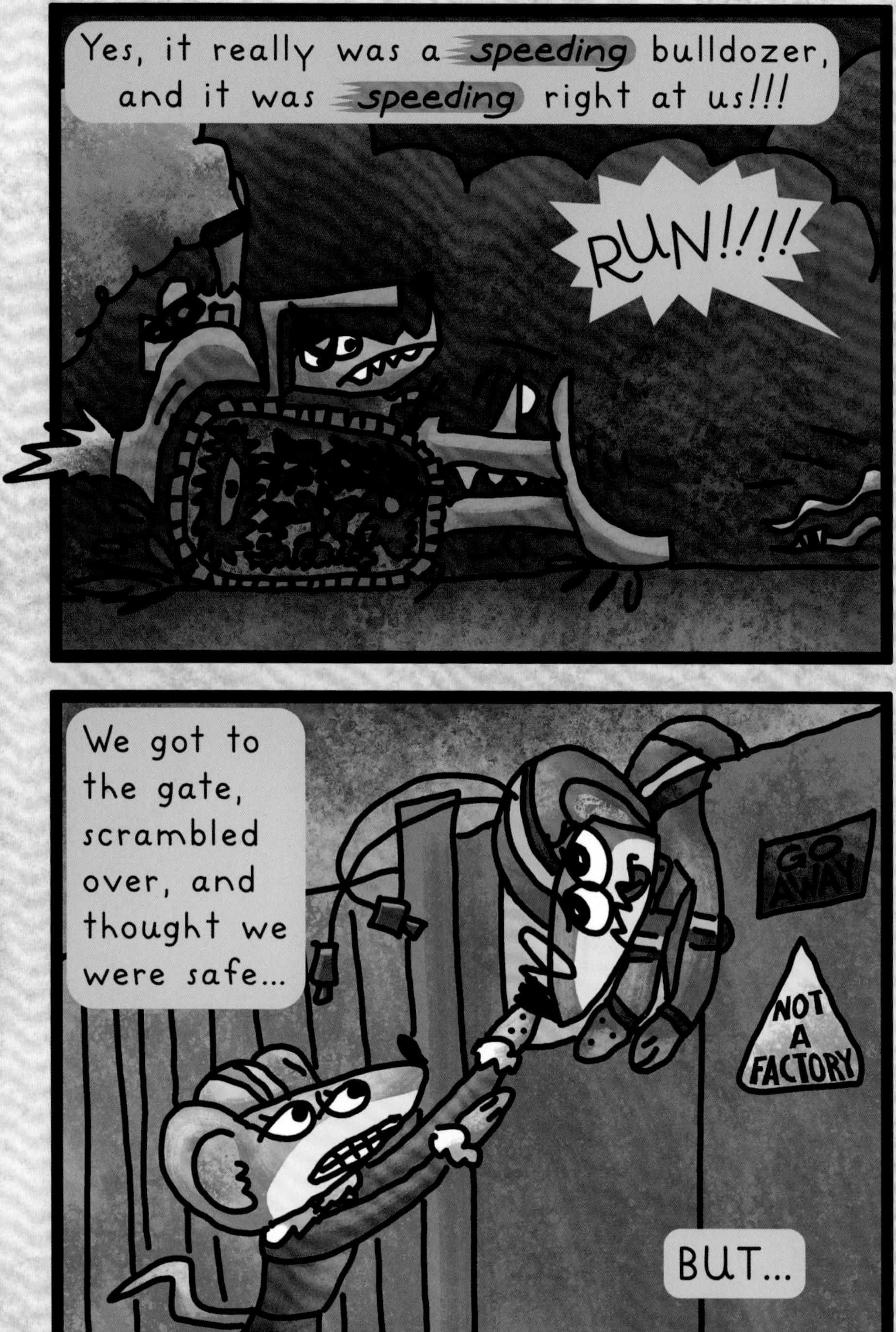

Yes, it really was a speeding bulldozer, and it was speeding right at us!!!
RUN!!!!
We got to the gate, scrambled over, and thought we were safe...
GO AWAY
NOT A FACTORY
BUT...

CHAPTER TWENTY-NINE

HIGH-SPEED (BULLDOZER) CHASE!

The bulldozer **BUSTED** the gate open and kept on coming! I have to admit, SuperNo makes a really strong and really fast bulldozer. But I sure wish they didn't!

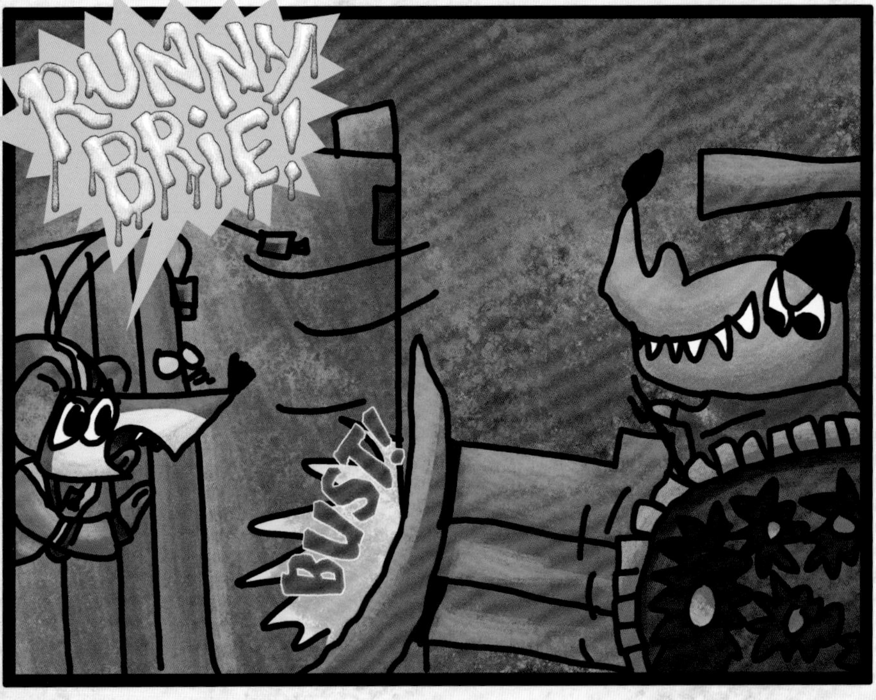
RUNNY BRIE!
BUST!

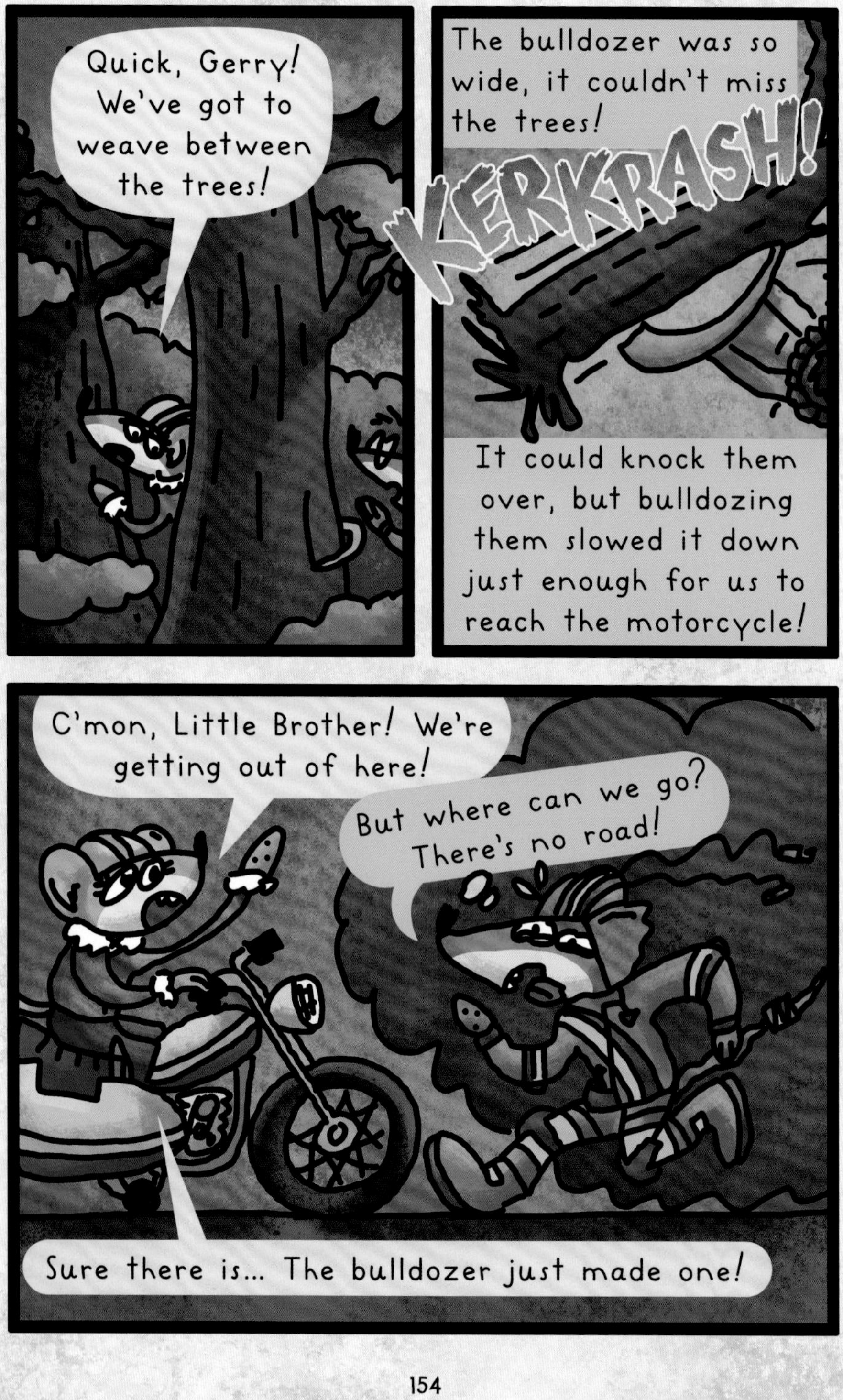

Quick, Gerry! We've got to weave between the trees!
The bulldozer was so wide, it couldn't miss the trees!
KERKRASH!
It could knock them over, but bulldozing them slowed it down just enough for us to reach the motorcycle!
C'mon, Little Brother! We're getting out of here!
But where can we go? There's no road!
Sure there is... The bulldozer just made one!

CHAPTER THIRTY

TO THE FINISH LINE!

Thea **REVVED** the engine and spun the tires, and we took off... not AWAY from the bulldozer and angry guards, but TOWARD the bulldozer and angry guards! And then... OVER them!

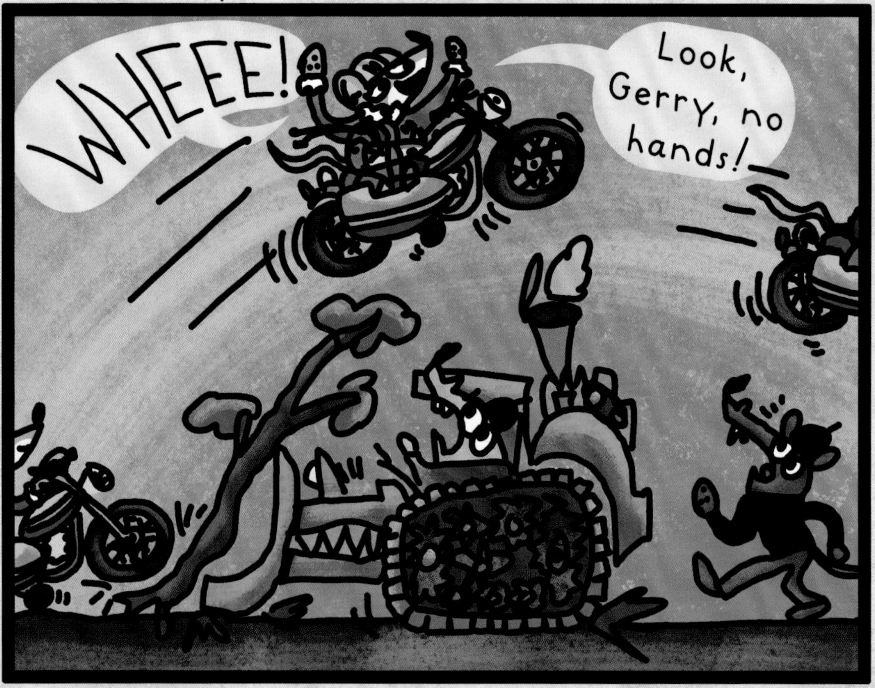
WHEEEE!
Look, Gerry, no hands!

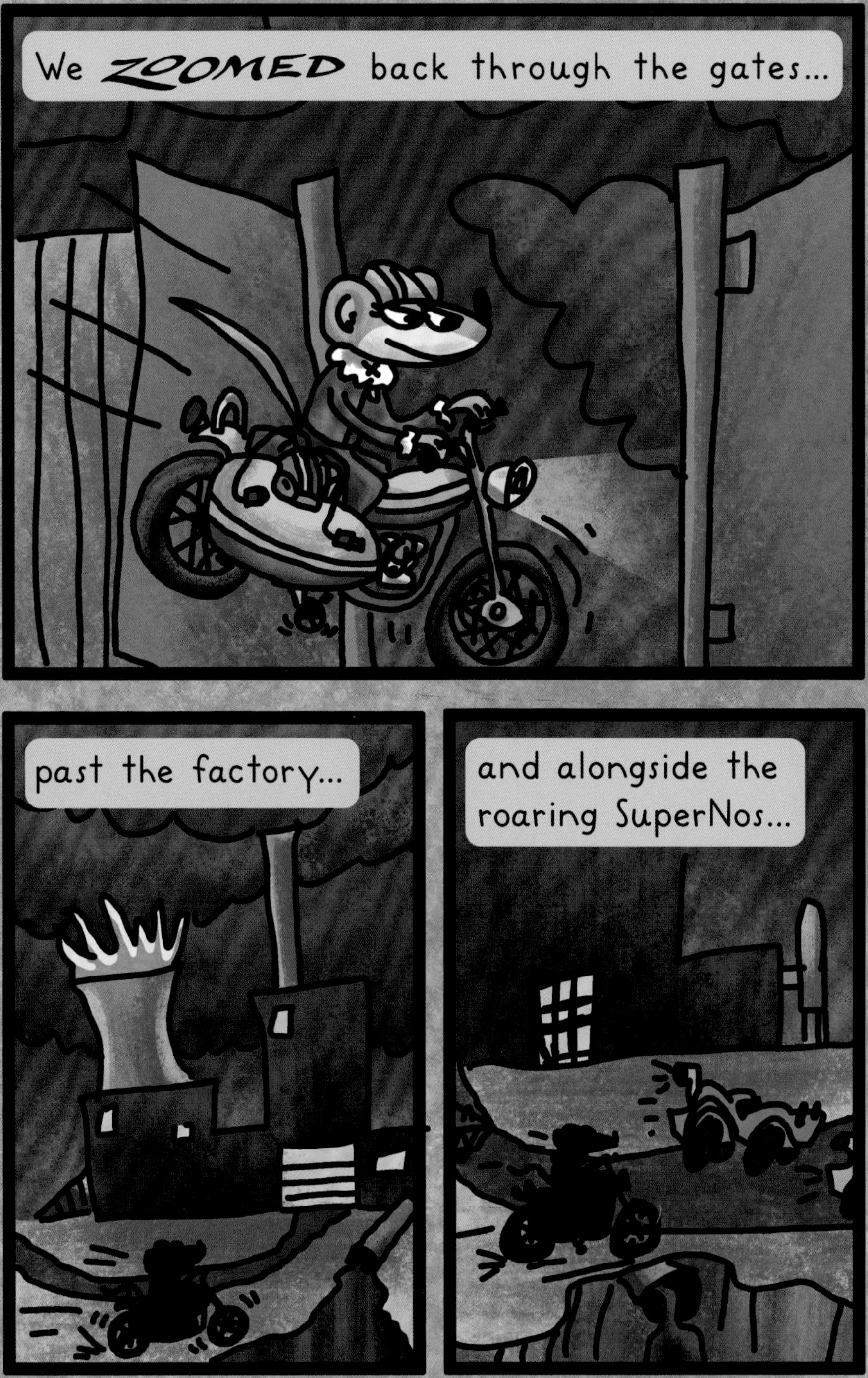
We ZOOMED back through the gates...
past the factory...
and alongside the roaring SuperNos...

I could hardly believe it... We'd actually made it out of there without getting caught, clobbered, or bulldozed!!!

I have to admit, that was great driving, Thea!

But... where exactly are we going?

To the **finish line!**

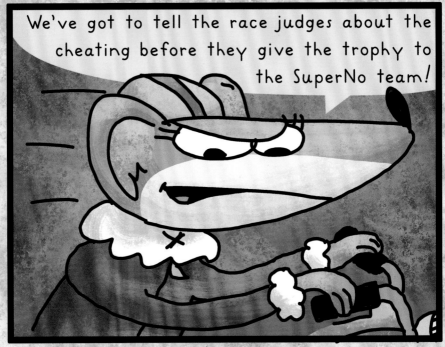

We've got to tell the race judges about the cheating before they give the trophy to the SuperNo team!

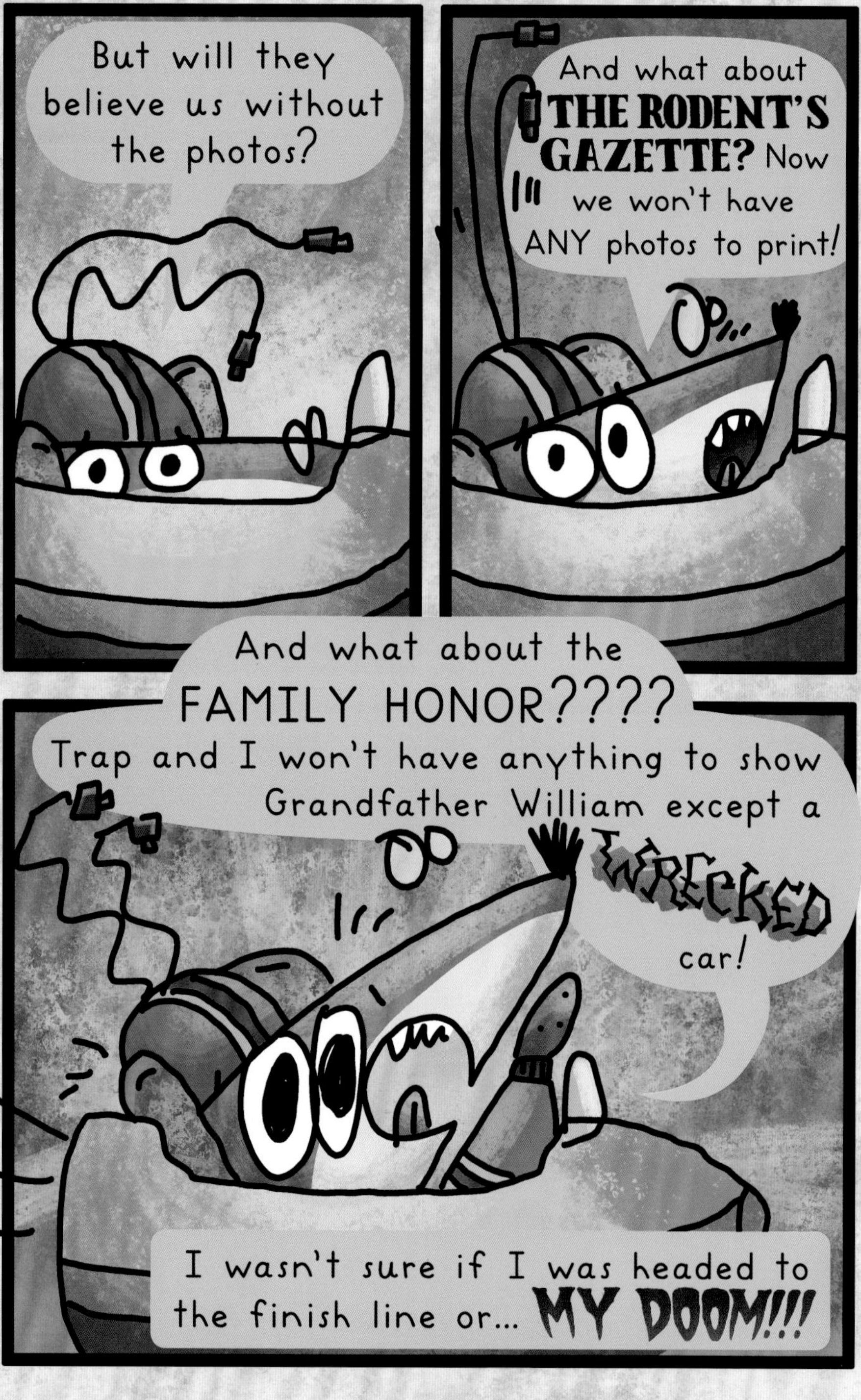

But will they believe us without the photos?
And what about THE RODENT'S GAZETTE? Now we won't have ANY photos to print!
And what about the FAMILY HONOR???? Trap and I won't have anything to show Grandfather William except a WRECKED car!
I wasn't sure if I was headed to the finish line or... MY DOOM!!!

CHAPTER THIRTY-ONE

HOW DID YOU GET TO MOUSEPORT?

As Thea zoomed down the highway toward the Rally's finish line in Mouseport, I thought of one thing that made me feel better...

This LONG, LOUD, bumpy, muddy day was almost over...

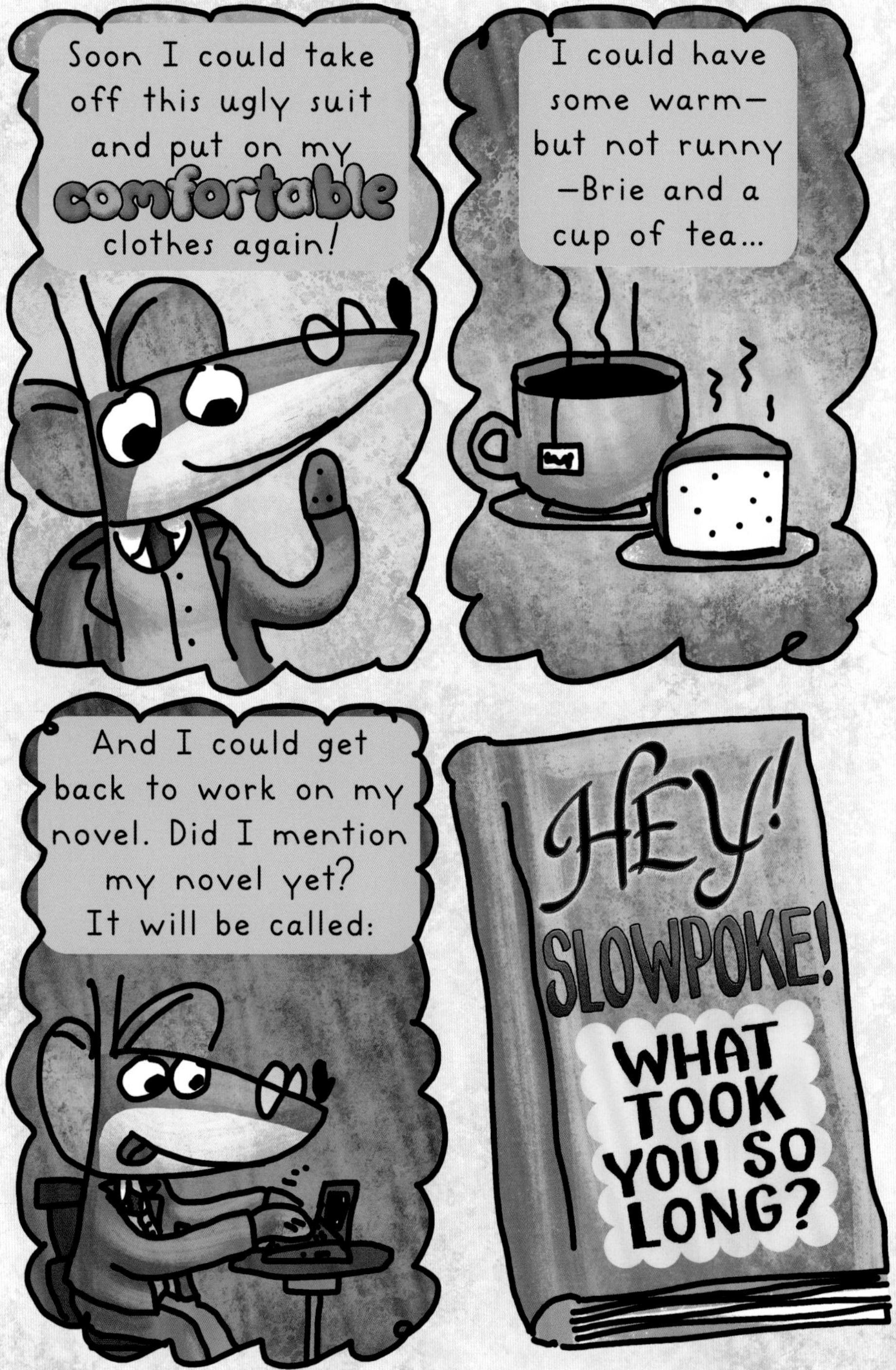

Soon I could take off this ugly suit and put on my comfortable clothes again!
I could have some warm—but not runny—Brie and a cup of tea...
And I could get back to work on my novel. Did I mention my novel yet? It will be called:
HEY! SLOWPOKE!
WHAT TOOK YOU SO LONG?

No! That's **NOT** the name of my novel! It's what someone was yelling at me as soon as we pulled into town!

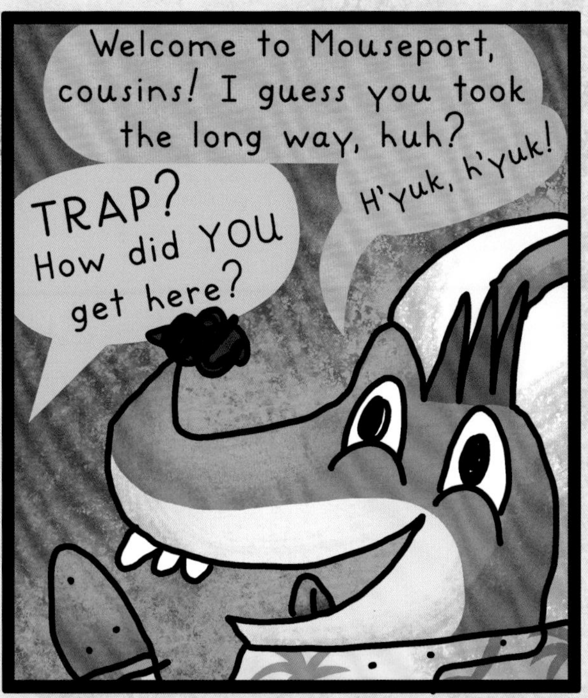
Welcome to Mouseport, cousins! I guess you took the long way, huh?
H'yuk, h'yuk!
TRAP? How did YOU get here?

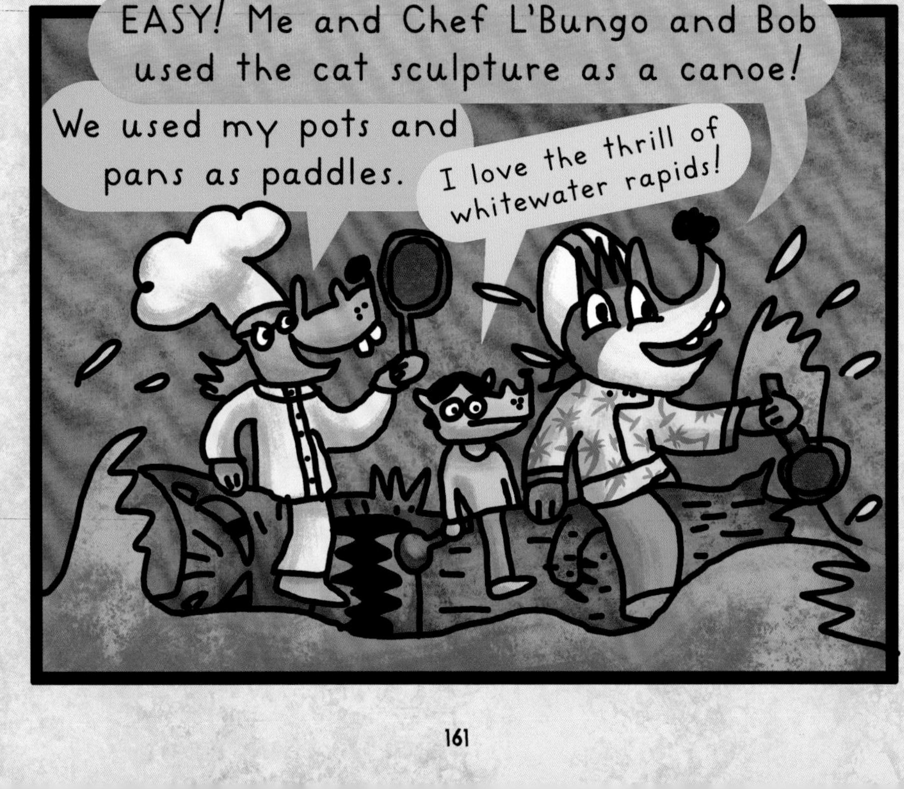
EASY! Me and Chef L'Bungo and Bob used the cat sculpture as a canoe!
We used my pots and pans as paddles.
I love the thrill of whitewater rapids!

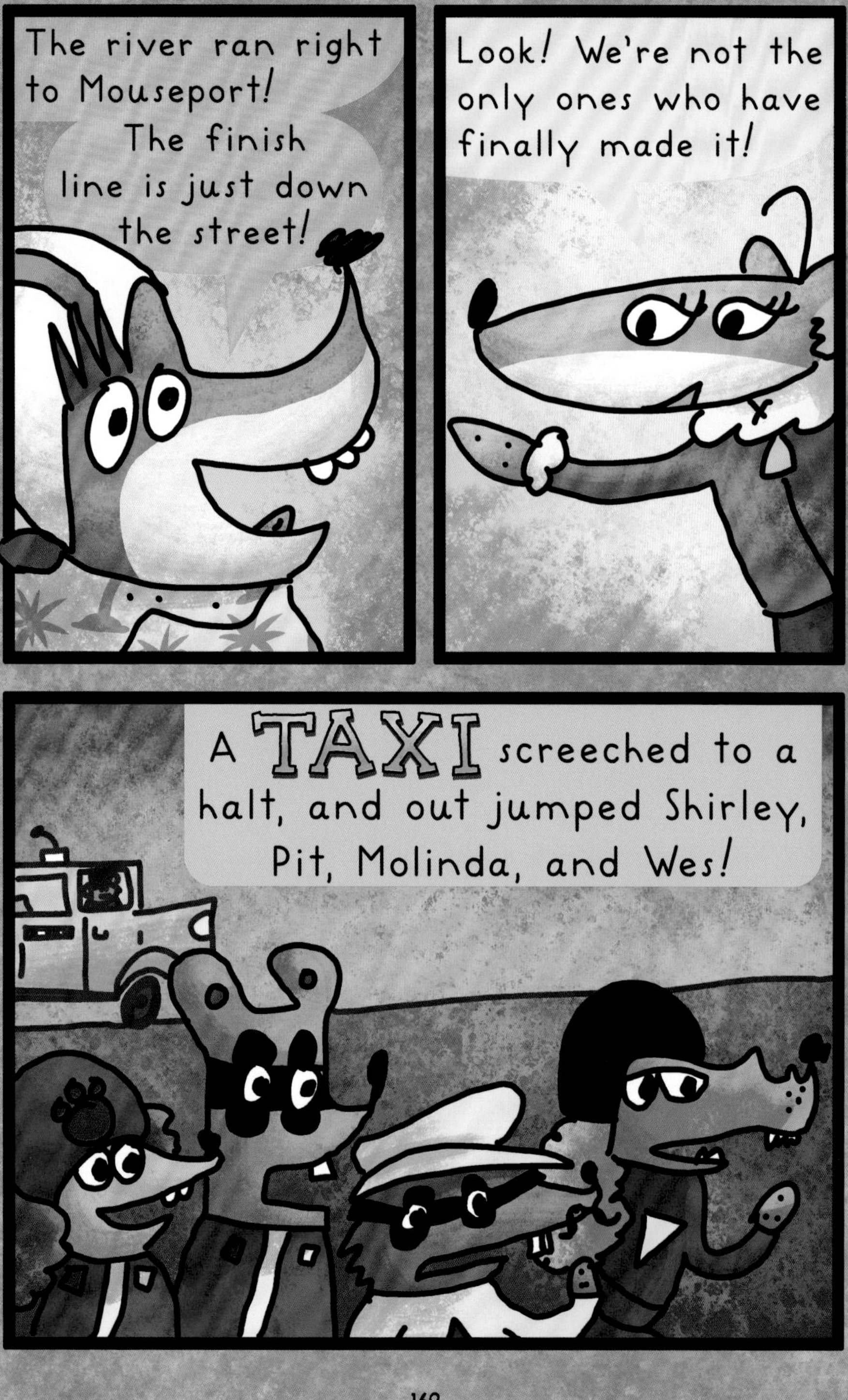
The river ran right to Mouseport!
The finish line is just down the street!
Look! We're not the only ones who have finally made it!
A TAXI screeched to a halt, and out jumped Shirley, Pit, Molinda, and Wes!

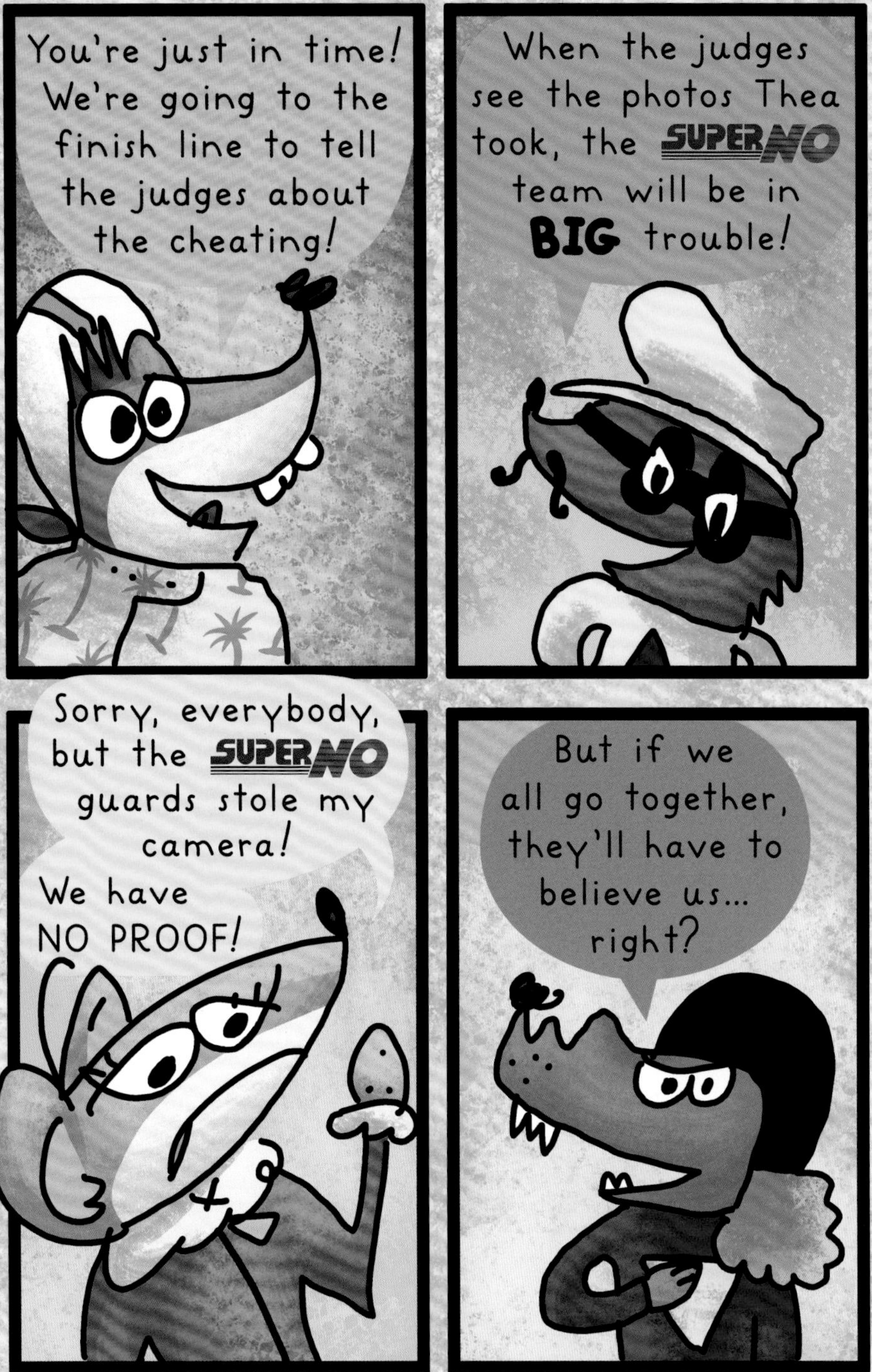

You're just in time! We're going to the finish line to tell the judges about the cheating!
When the judges see the photos Thea took, the SUPER NO team will be in BIG trouble!
Sorry, everybody, but the SUPER NO guards stole my camera!
We have NO PROOF!
But if we all go together, they'll have to believe us... right?

CHAPTER THIRTY-TWO

NO!

When we got to the finish line, there was a huge crowd there. They were all cheering for the SuperNo team!

YAY!
Wow! The SuperNo cars are even faster than I thought!
I was going to buy one...but now I'm going to buy TWO!
Best car EVER!
I'm buying stock in the SuperNo company! They're going to make millions!
FINISH

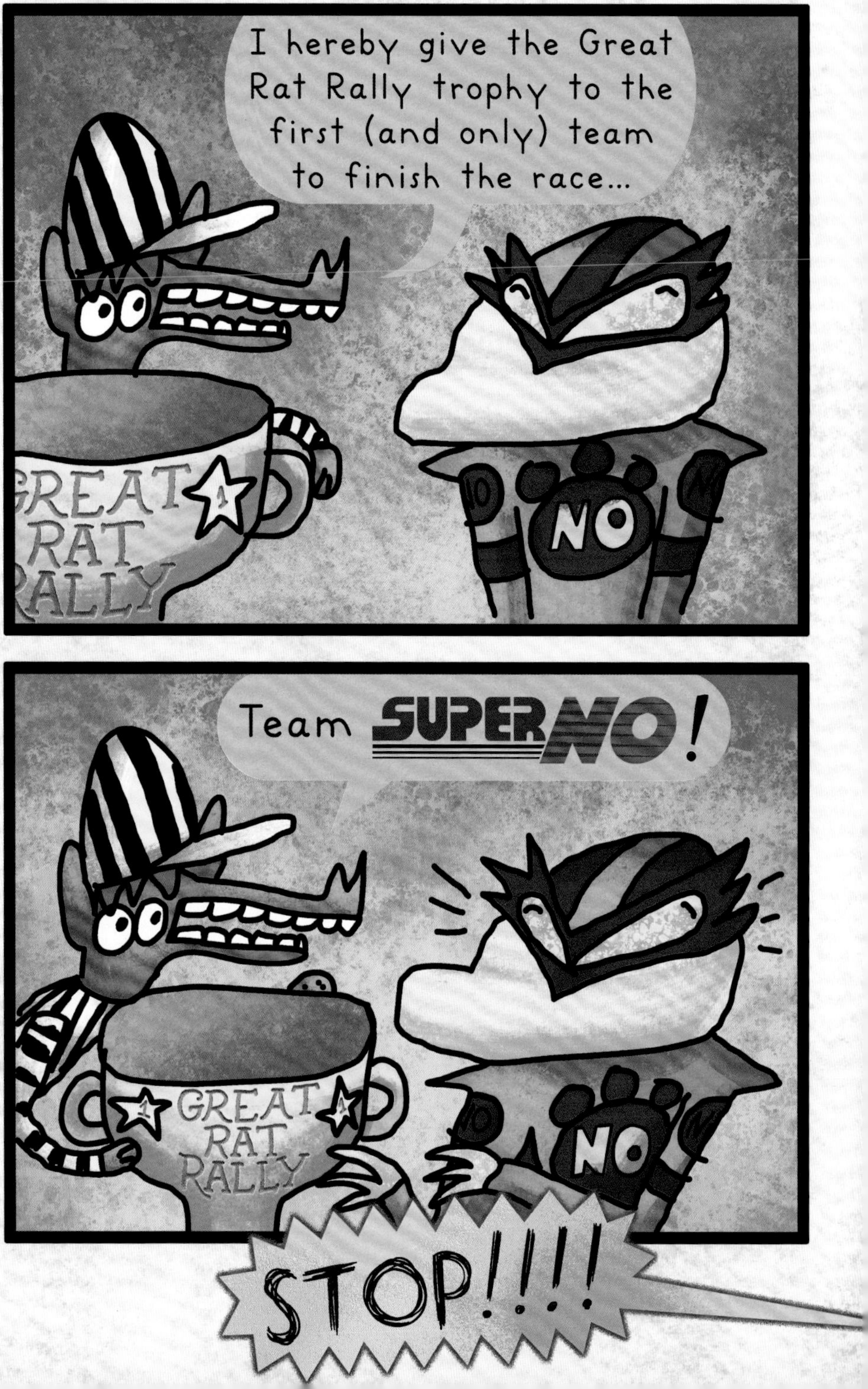
I hereby give the Great Rat Rally trophy to the first (and only) team to finish the race...
GREAT RAT RALLY
NO
Team SUPERNO!
GREAT RAT RALLY
NO
STOP!!!!

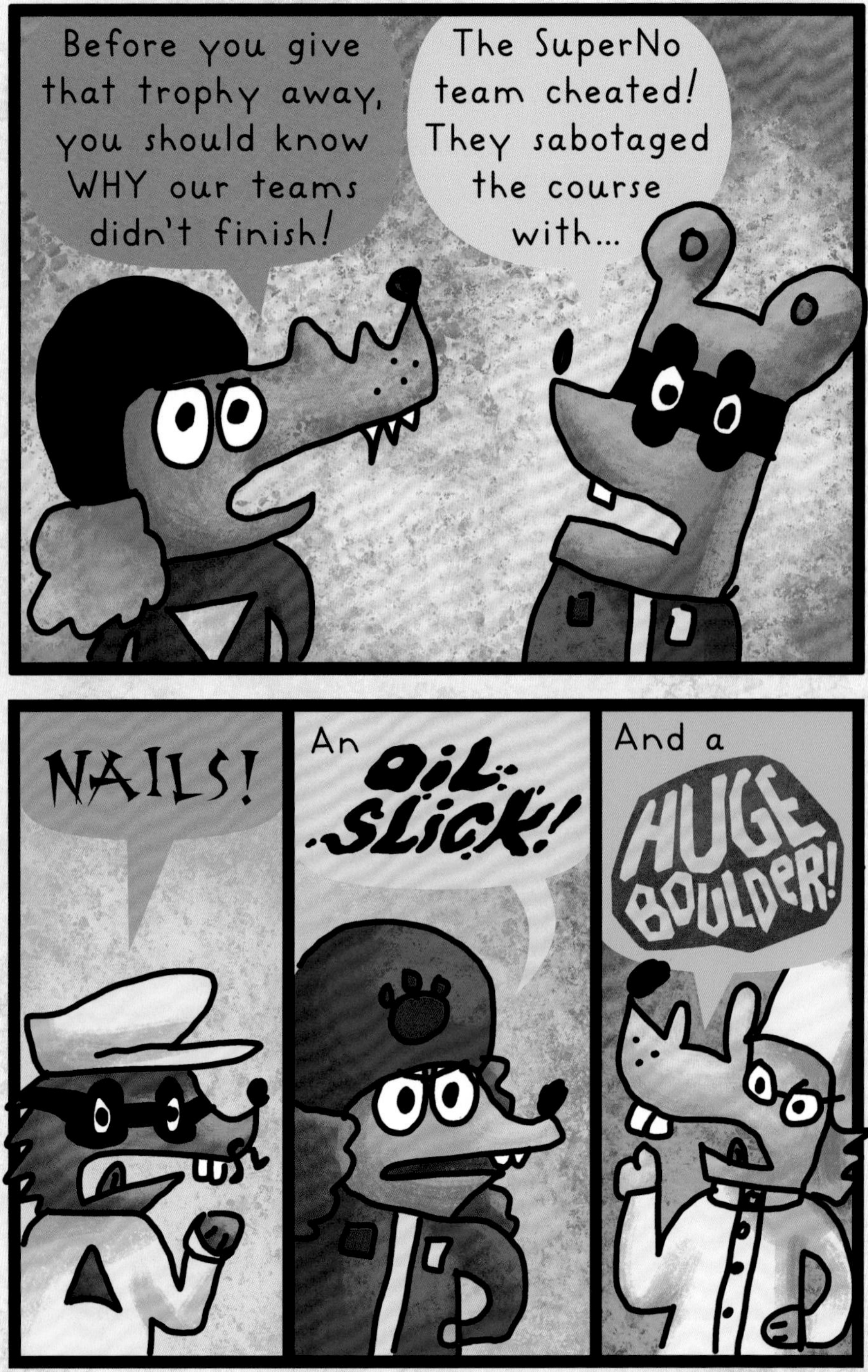
Before you give that trophy away, you should know WHY our teams didn't finish!
The SuperNo team cheated! They sabotaged the course with...
NAILS!
An
OIL SLICK!
And a
HUGE BOULDER!

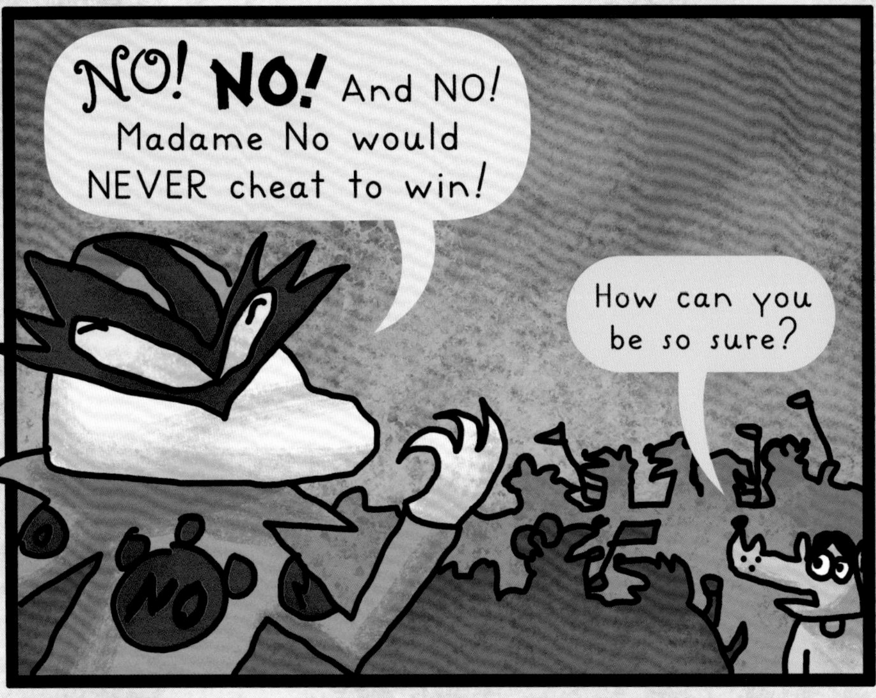
NO! NO! And NO! Madame No would NEVER cheat to win!
How can you be so sure?
NO

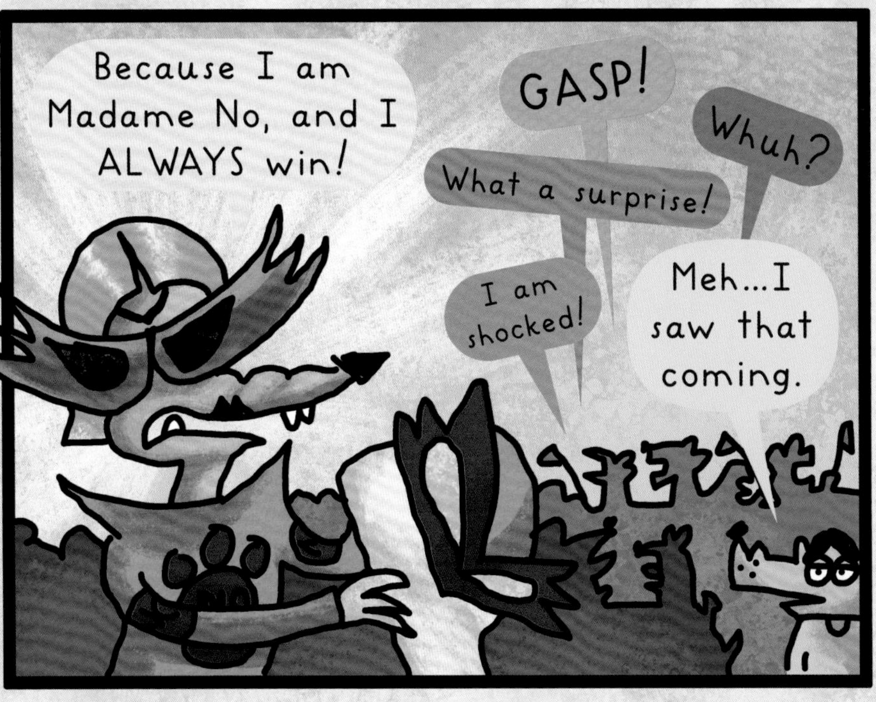
Because I am Madame No, and I ALWAYS win!
GASP!
Whuh?
What a surprise!
I am shocked!
Meh...I saw that coming.

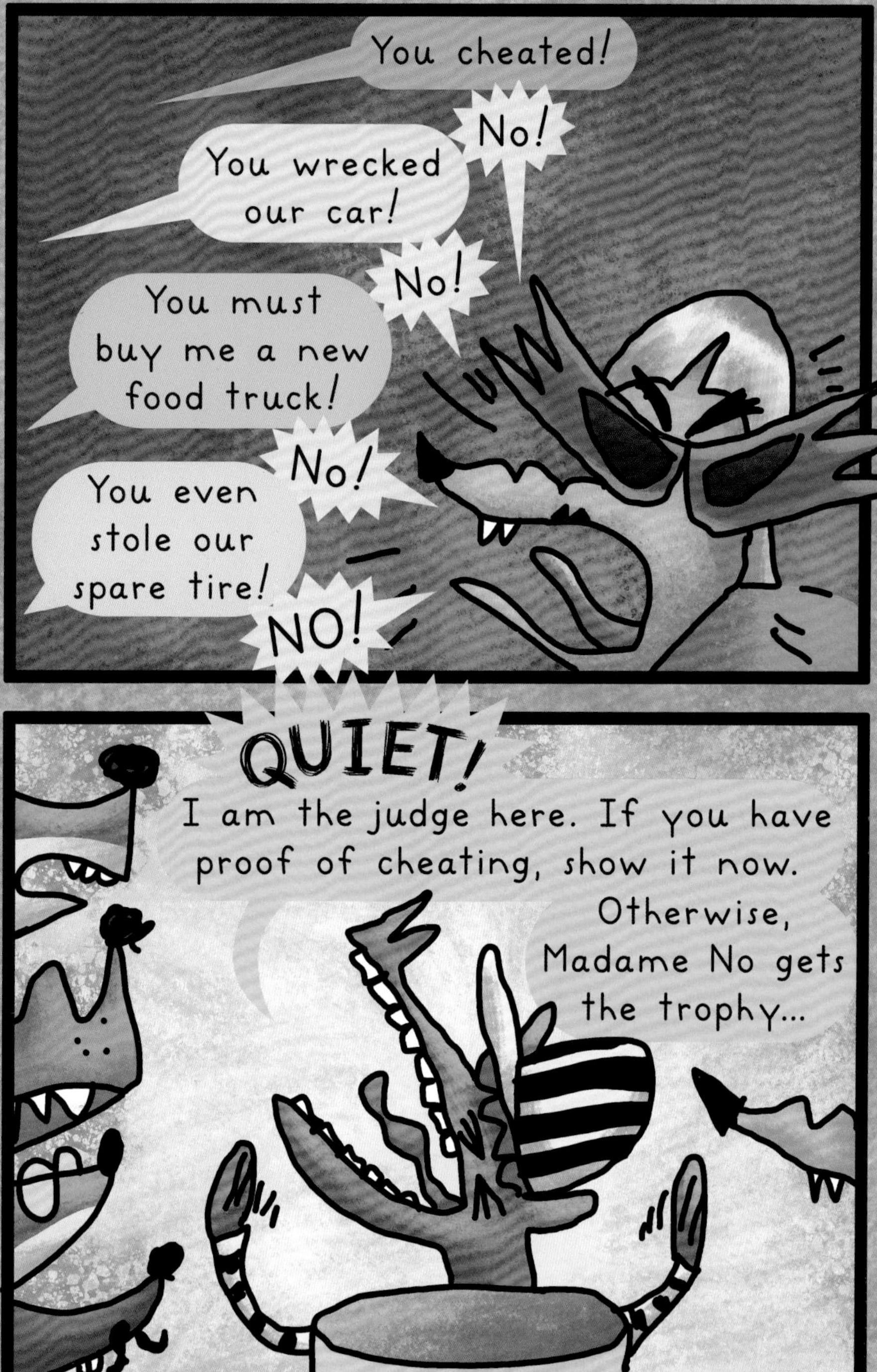
You cheated!
No!
You wrecked our car!
No!
You must buy me a new food truck!
No!
You even stole our spare tire!
NO!
QUIET!
I am the judge here. If you have proof of cheating, show it now.
Otherwise, Madame No gets the trophy...

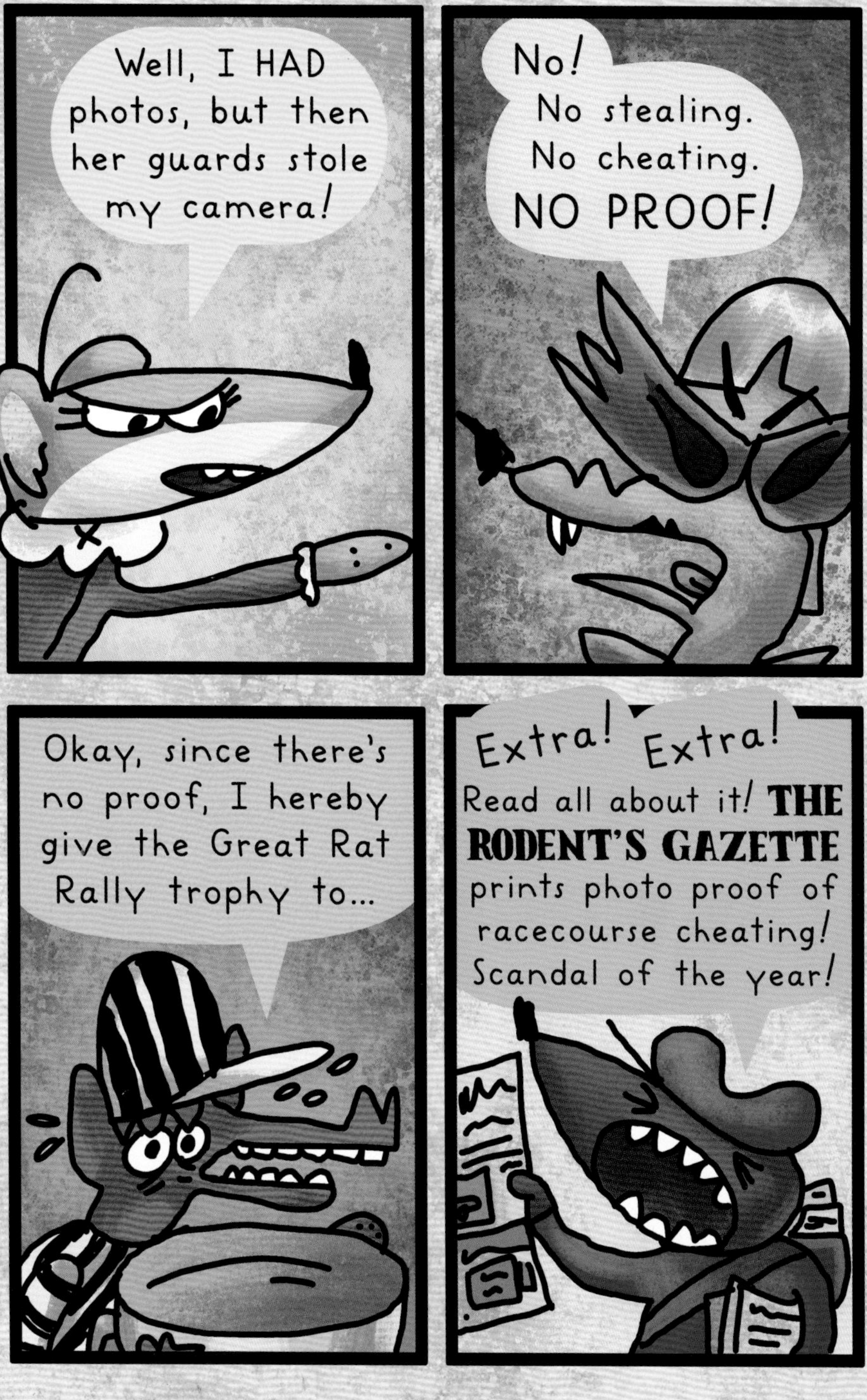
Well, I HAD photos, but then her guards stole my camera!
No! No stealing. No cheating. NO PROOF!
Okay, since there's no proof, I hereby give the Great Rat Rally trophy to...
Extra! Extra!
Read all about it! THE RODENT'S GAZETTE prints photo proof of racecourse cheating! Scandal of the year!

CHAPTER THIRTY-THREE

FRONT PAGE NEWS!

Photographic proof? In my own newspaper? It was impossible! How could we have photos without Thea's camera? I had to find out...fast!

Quick, give me one of those papers!
That'll be 2 bucks!
But it's my newspaper! I am the publisher!
In that case, it's 2 bucks AND I want a raise!

UNBELIEVABLE! But I paid!

THE RODENT'S GAZETTE

SPECIAL GREAT RAT RALLY EDITION - $2

RALLY RUINED BY CHEATERS!

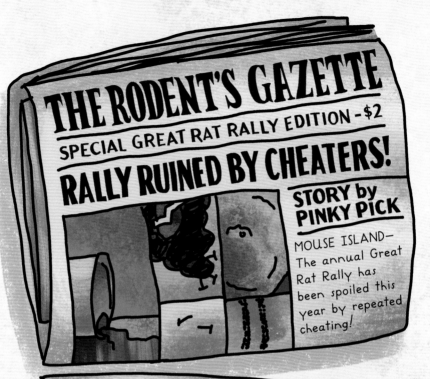

STORY by PINKY PICK

MOUSE ISLAND— The annual Great Rat Rally has been spoiled this year by repeated cheating!

Most racing teams were knocked out of the race by sabotage of the racecourse, including an oil slick, scattered nails, and even a giant boulder blocking the course. All clues point to Madame No's SuperNo team as the cheaters.

Oil drums, nails, and even a bulldozer big enough to move a boulder were found at a SuperNo factory less than a mile from the course.

MORE on pages 2-56.

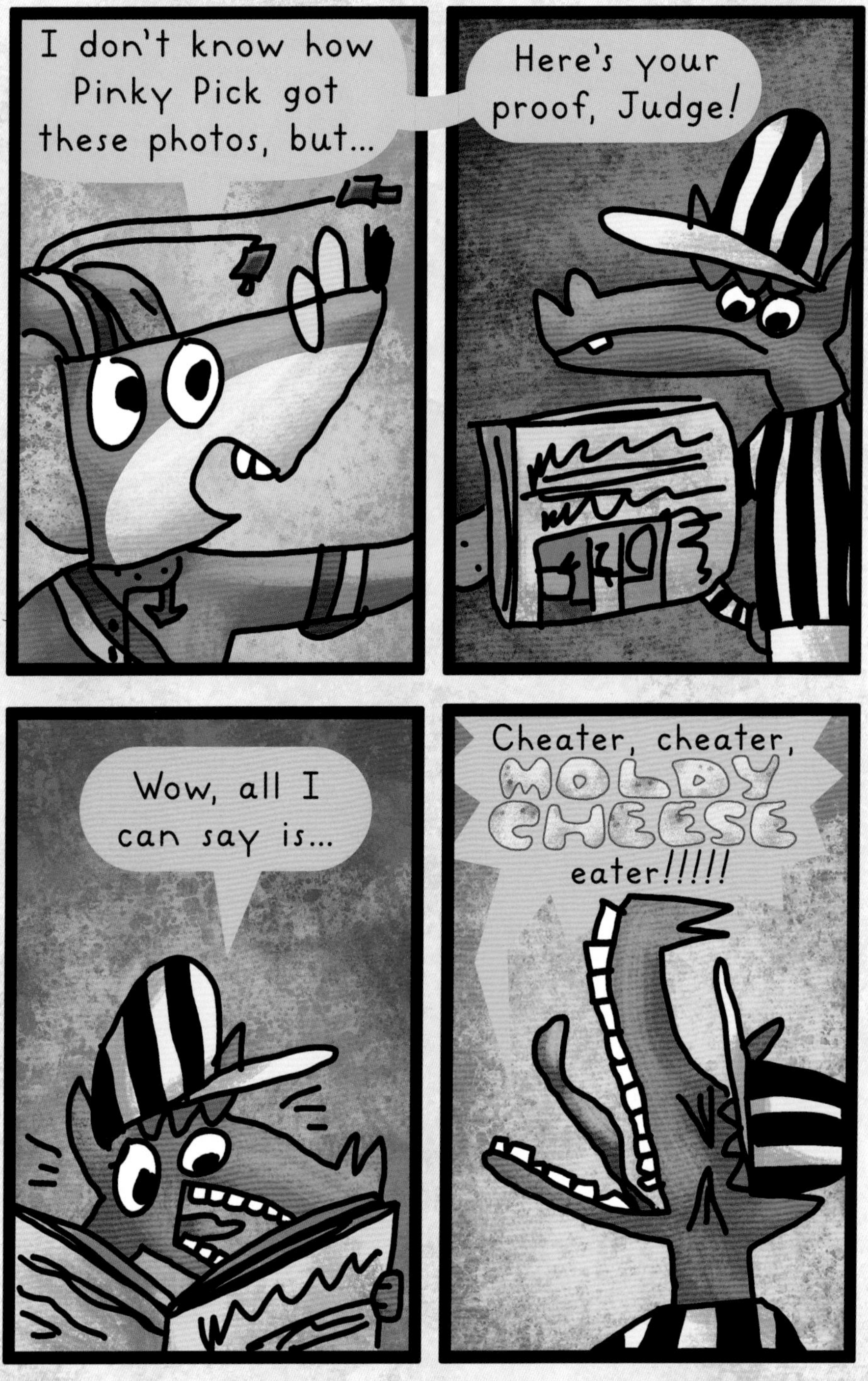
I don't know how Pinky Pick got these photos, but...
Here's your proof, Judge!
Wow, all I can say is...
Cheater, cheater, MOLDY CHEESE eater!!!!!

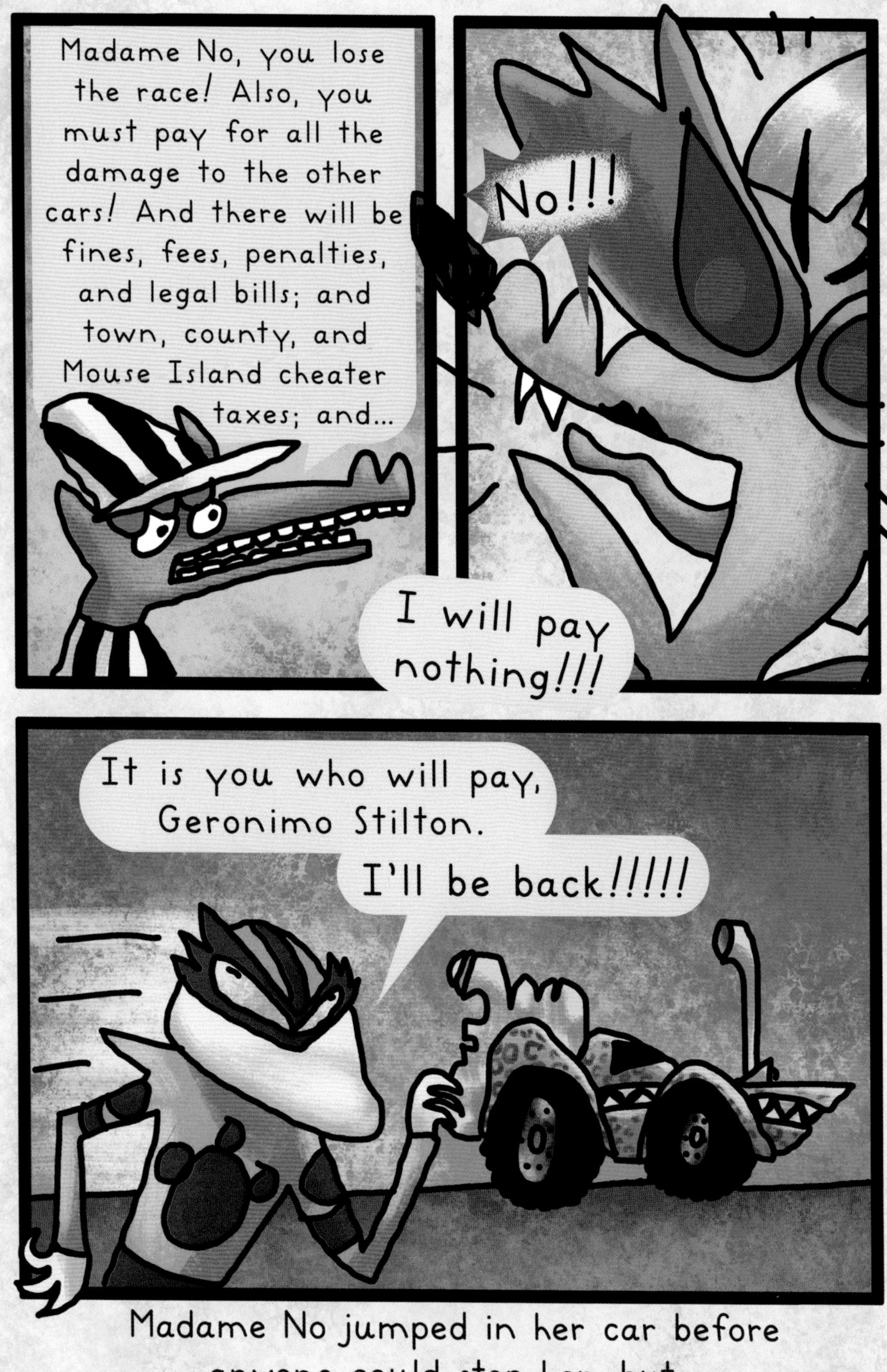
Madame No, you lose the race! Also, you must pay for all the damage to the other cars! And there will be fines, fees, penalties, and legal bills; and town, county, and Mouse Island cheater taxes; and...
No!!!
I will pay nothing!!!
It is you who will pay, Geronimo Stilton.
I'll be back!!!!!

Madame No jumped in her car before anyone could stop her, but...

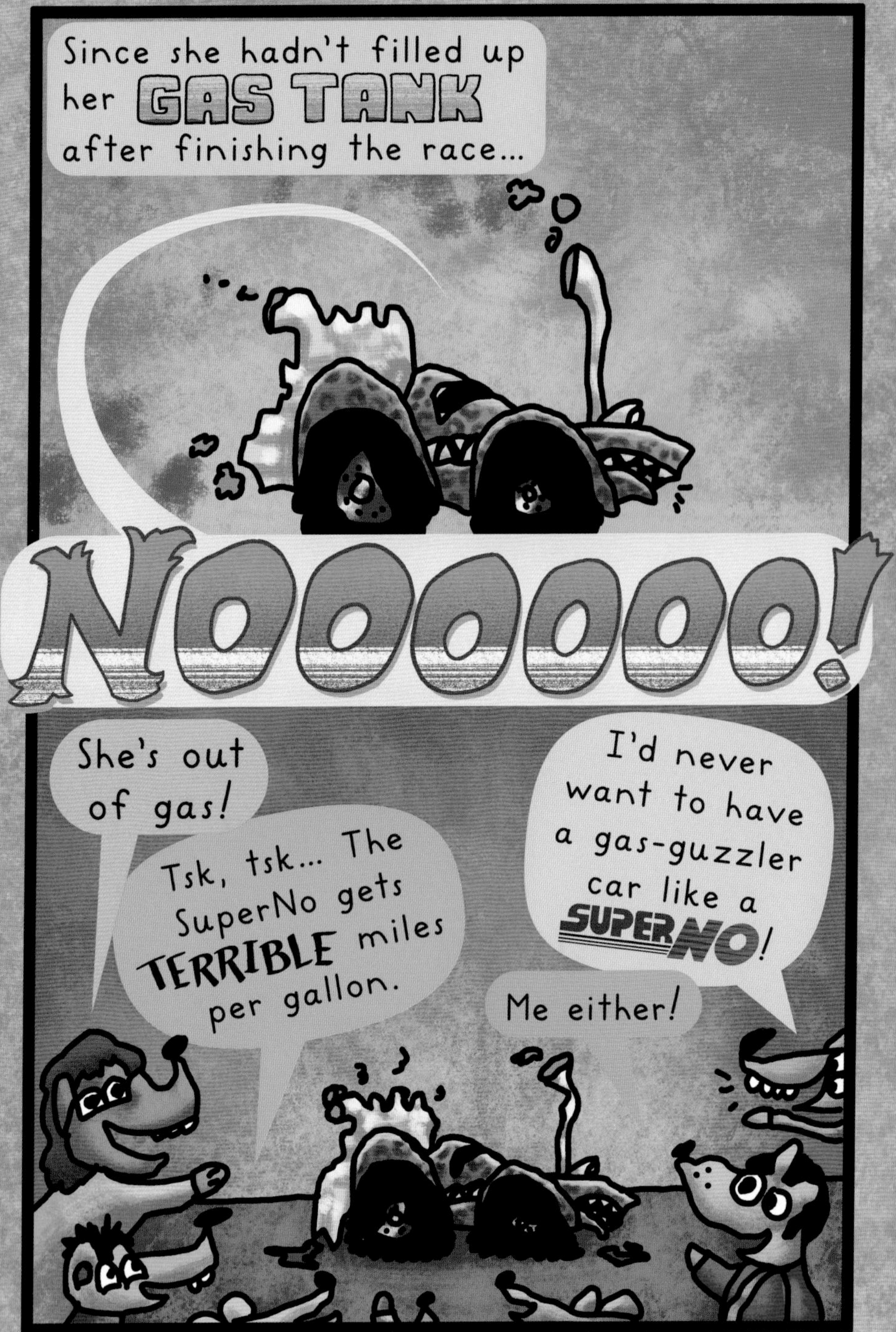
Since she hadn't filled up her GAS TANK after finishing the race...
NOOOOOO!
She's out of gas!
Tsk, tsk... The SuperNo gets TERRIBLE miles per gallon.
I'd never want to have a gas-guzzler car like a SUPERNO!
Me either!

CHAPTER THIRTY-FOUR

HOW?????

While the rest of the mice were busy laughing at Madame No, I was calling the office. I had to find out how Pinky Pick got the story!

Hey, Boss! Did you see the paper? I thought we did a good job, considering that you were on vacation!

CALLING....
PINKY PICK
RODENT'S GAZE

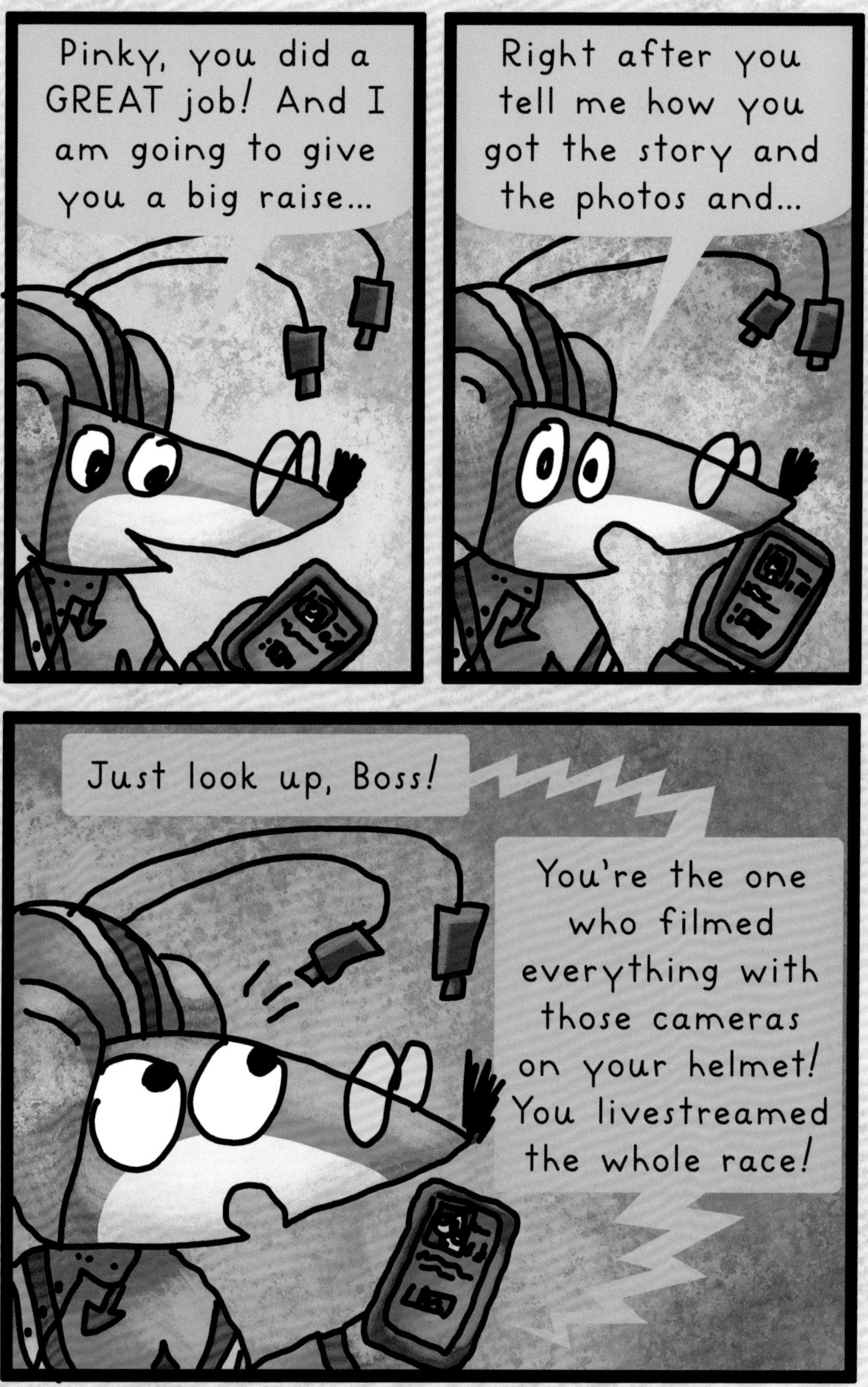
Pinky, you did a GREAT job! And I am going to give you a big raise...
Right after you tell me how you got the story and the photos and...
Just look up, Boss!
You're the one who filmed everything with those cameras on your helmet! You livestreamed the whole race!

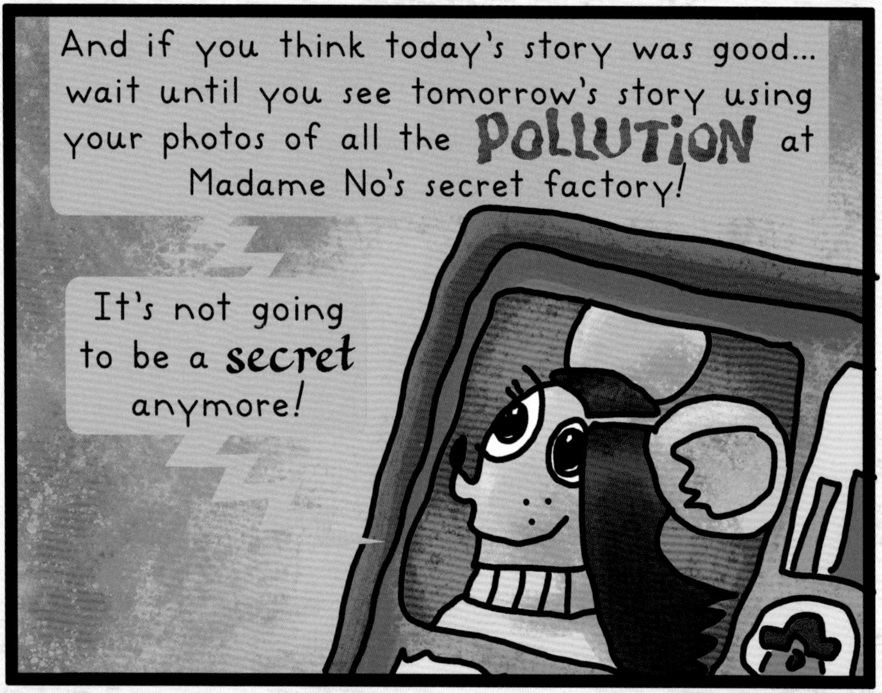
And if you think today's story was good... wait until you see tomorrow's story using your photos of all the POLLUTION at Madame No's secret factory!
It's not going to be a secret anymore!

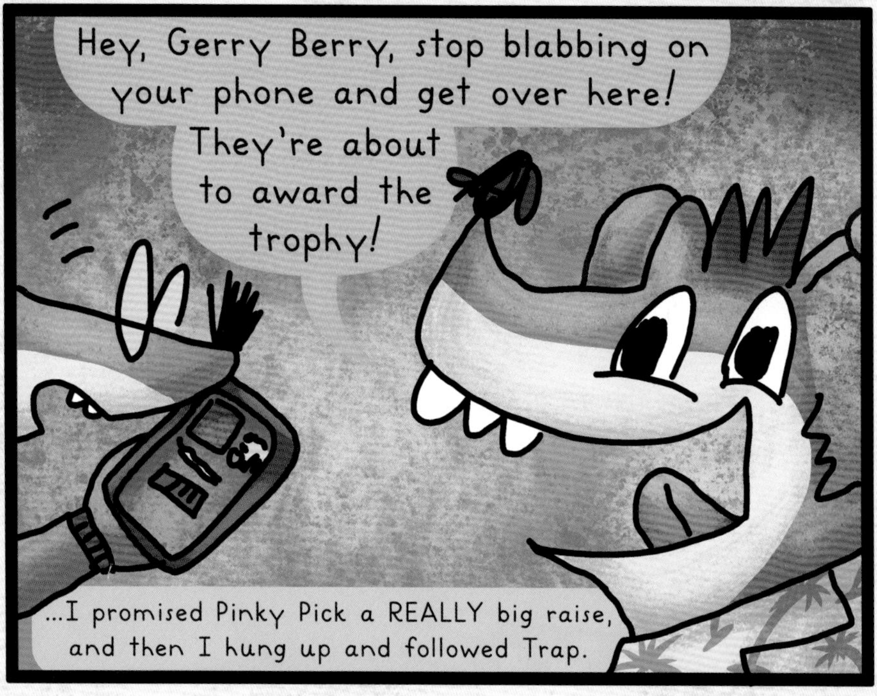
Hey, Gerry Berry, stop blabbing on your phone and get over here! They're about to award the trophy!
...I promised Pinky Pick a REALLY big raise, and then I hung up and followed Trap.

CHAPTER THIRTY-FIVE

THE WINNERS ARE...

I wondered how they could pick a winner when only Madame No's car actually finished the race. The judge must have wondered, too, because he had been reading a huge rule book.

Since none of the cars finished, the prize should go to the first racers to arrive. But you all got here at the same time!

So... the winners are...

RALLY RULES

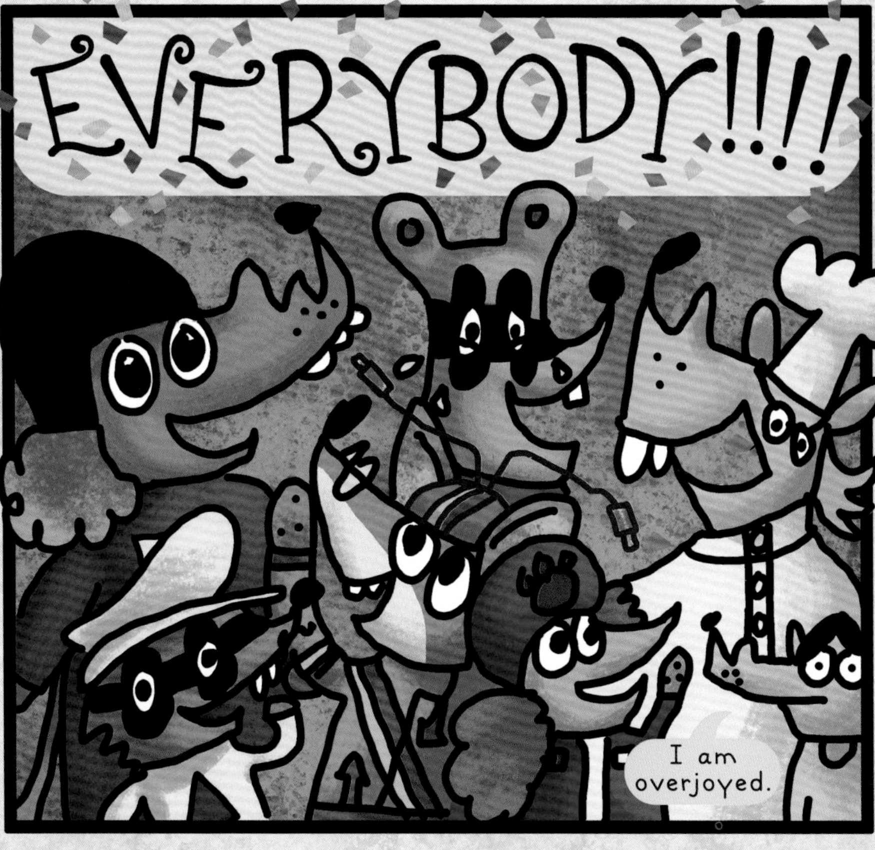
EVERYBODY!!!!
I am overjoyed.

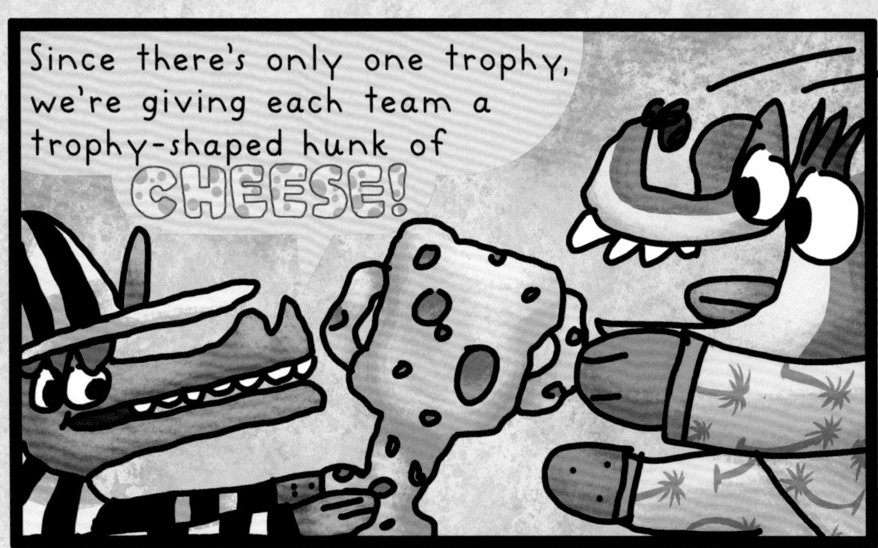
Since there's only one trophy, we're giving each team a trophy-shaped hunk of
CHEESE!

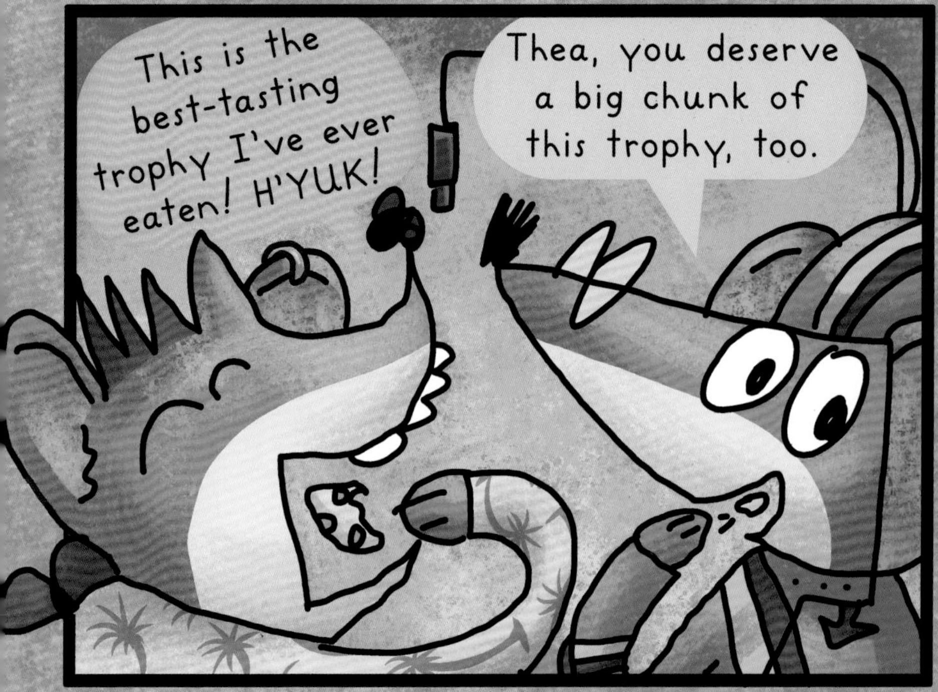
This is the best-tasting trophy I've ever eaten! H'YUK!
Thea, you deserve a big chunk of this trophy, too.

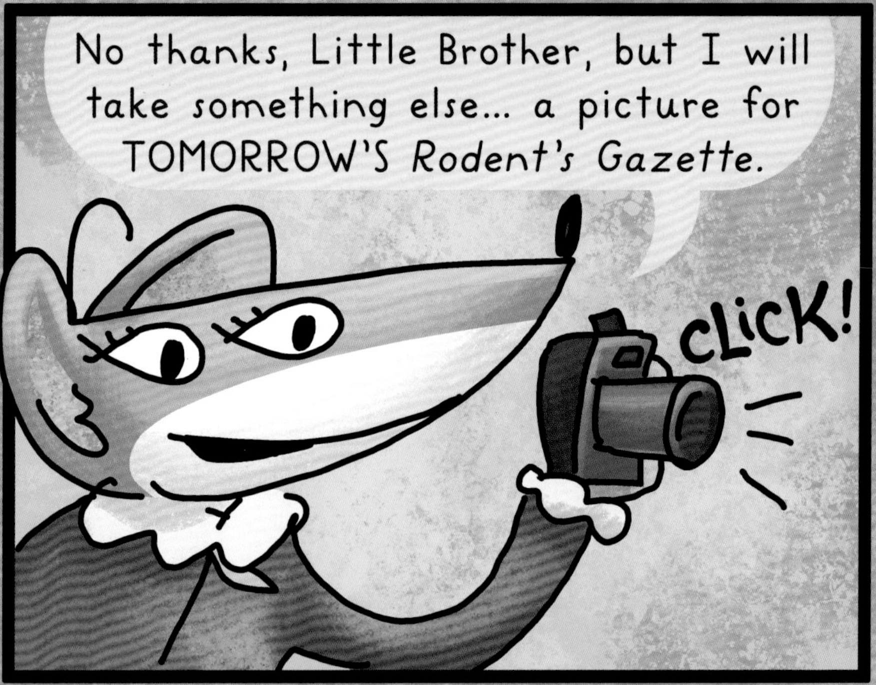
No thanks, Little Brother, but I will take something else... a picture for TOMORROW'S *Rodent's Gazette*.
CLICK!

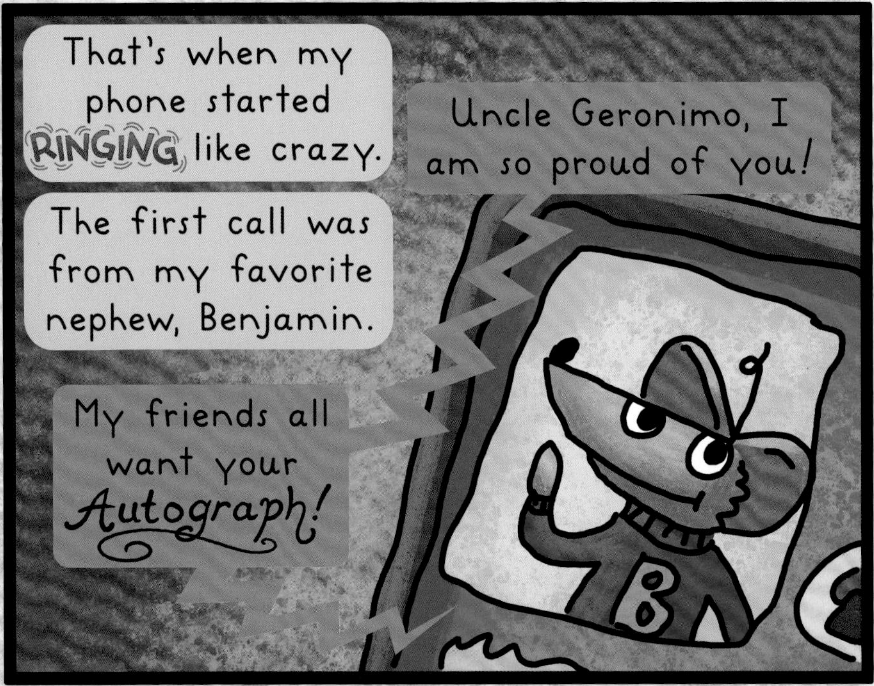
That's when my phone started RINGING like crazy.
Uncle Geronimo, I am so proud of you!
The first call was from my favorite nephew, Benjamin.
My friends all want your Autograph!
B

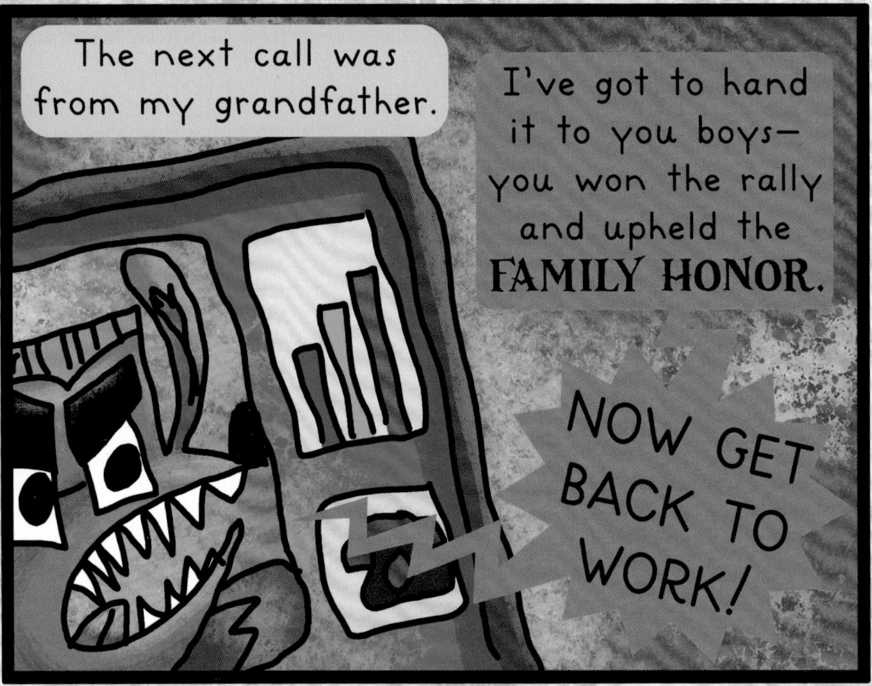
The next call was from my grandfather.
I've got to hand it to you boys—you won the rally and upheld the FAMILY HONOR.
NOW GET BACK TO WORK!

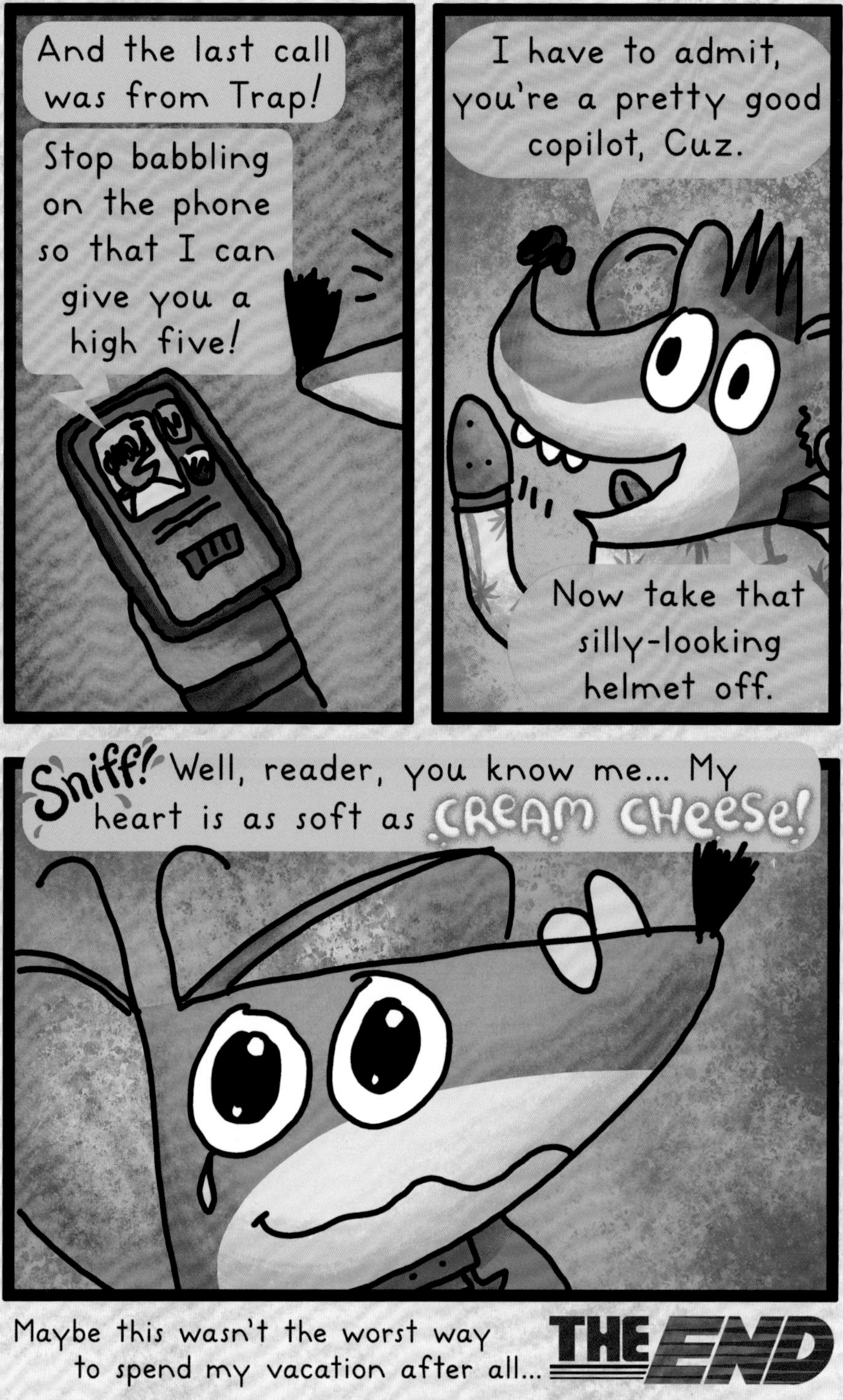
And the last call was from Trap!
Stop babbling on the phone so that I can give you a high five!
I have to admit, you're a pretty good copilot, Cuz.
Now take that silly-looking helmet off.
Sniff! Well, reader, you know me... My heart is as soft as CREAM CHEESE!
Maybe this wasn't the worst way to spend my vacation after all...
THE END

EPILOGUE

EXTRA! EXTRA! DON'T READ ALL ABOUT IT!

A few days later I was back at work in my office... (Well, actually I was taking my ten o'clock cheese-and-book break.)

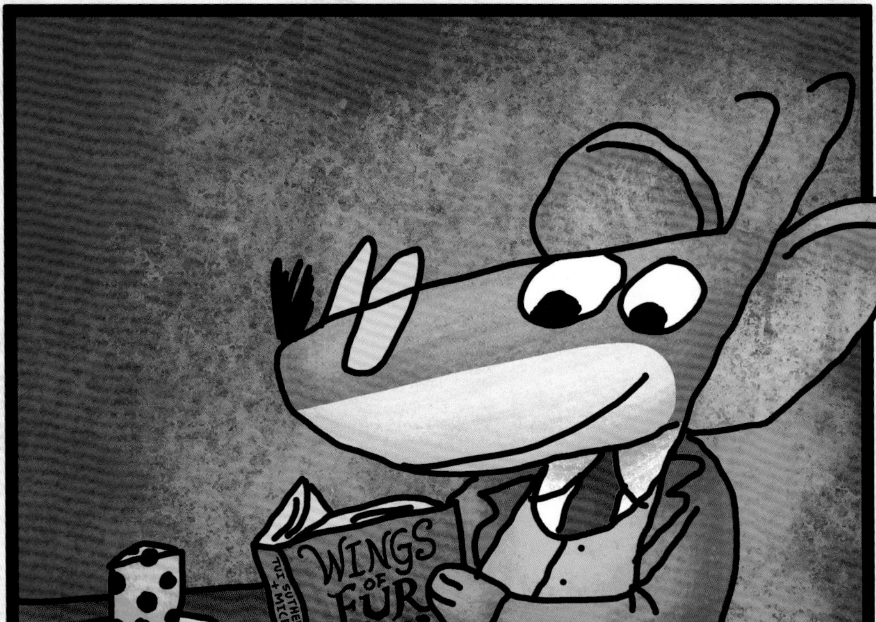
WINGS OF FUR
TUI SUTHERRAT

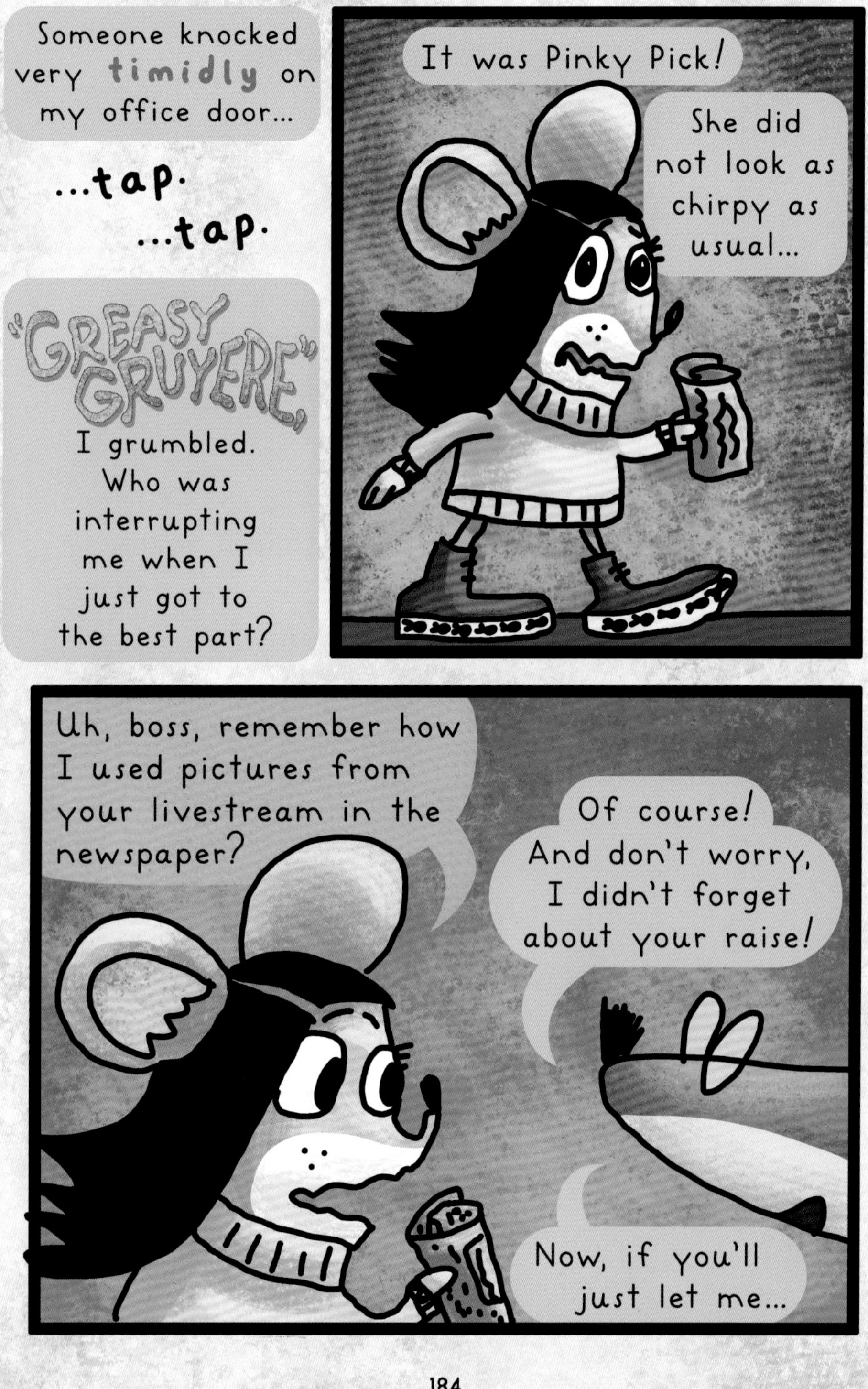
Someone knocked very timidly on my office door...
...tap.
...tap.
"GREASY GRUYERE,"
I grumbled. Who was interrupting me when I just got to the best part?
It was Pinky Pick!
She did not look as chirpy as usual...
Uh, boss, remember how I used pictures from your livestream in the newspaper?
Of course! And don't worry, I didn't forget about your raise!
Now, if you'll just let me...

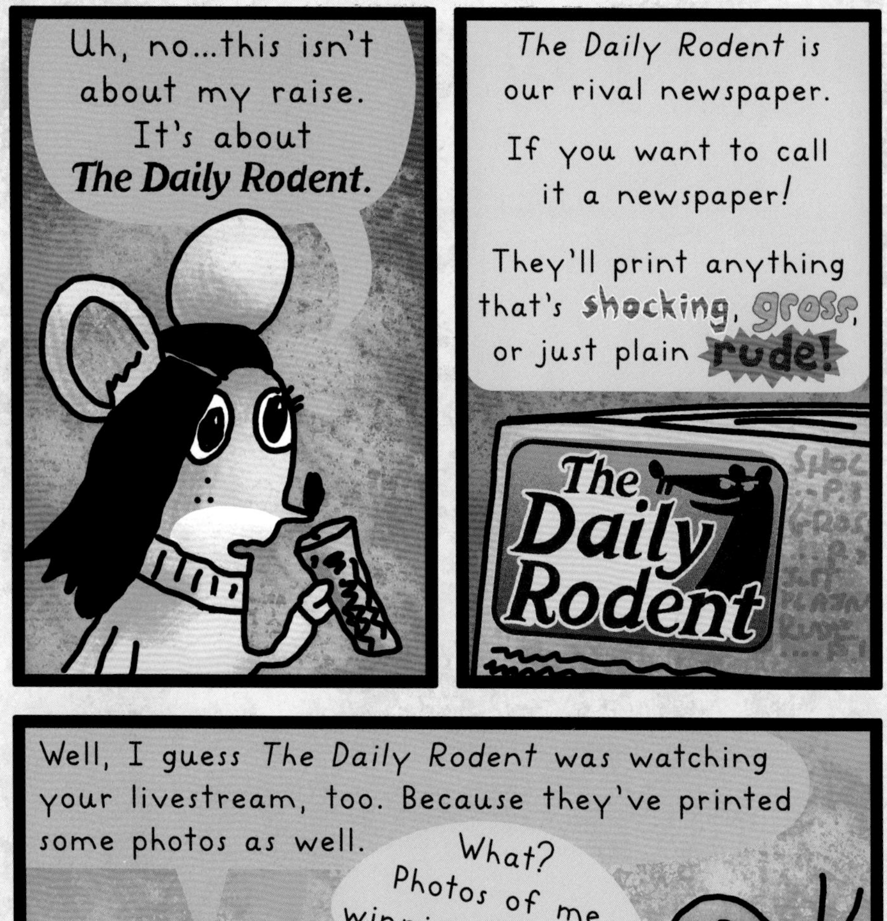
Uh, no...this isn't about my raise. It's about **The Daily Rodent.**
The Daily Rodent is our rival newspaper.
If you want to call it a newspaper!
They'll print anything that's shocking, gross, or just plain rude!
The Daily Rodent
Well, I guess *The Daily Rodent* was watching your livestream, too. Because they've printed some photos as well.
What? Photos of me winning the race?

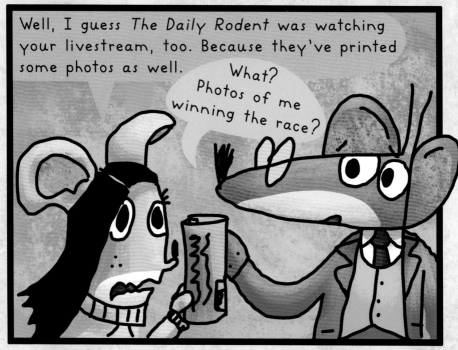

GREAT RAT... *REALLY?*

New Mouse City's own GerWRONGimo STINKton makes a FUEL of himself on and off—
WAY off—the race course!

SHOCKING video footage shows local "newsmouse" screaming, crying, whining, and sending his race car way, WAY off the race course!

As bad as he was at reading a map, when Ger—HONK—imo sat behind the wheel, things went from bad to even WORSE! He almost backed the car over a cliff! Luckily it caught fire before he got that far! This mouse shouldn't be allowed to drive a golf ball, much less a race car in Mouse Island's once-glamorous race!

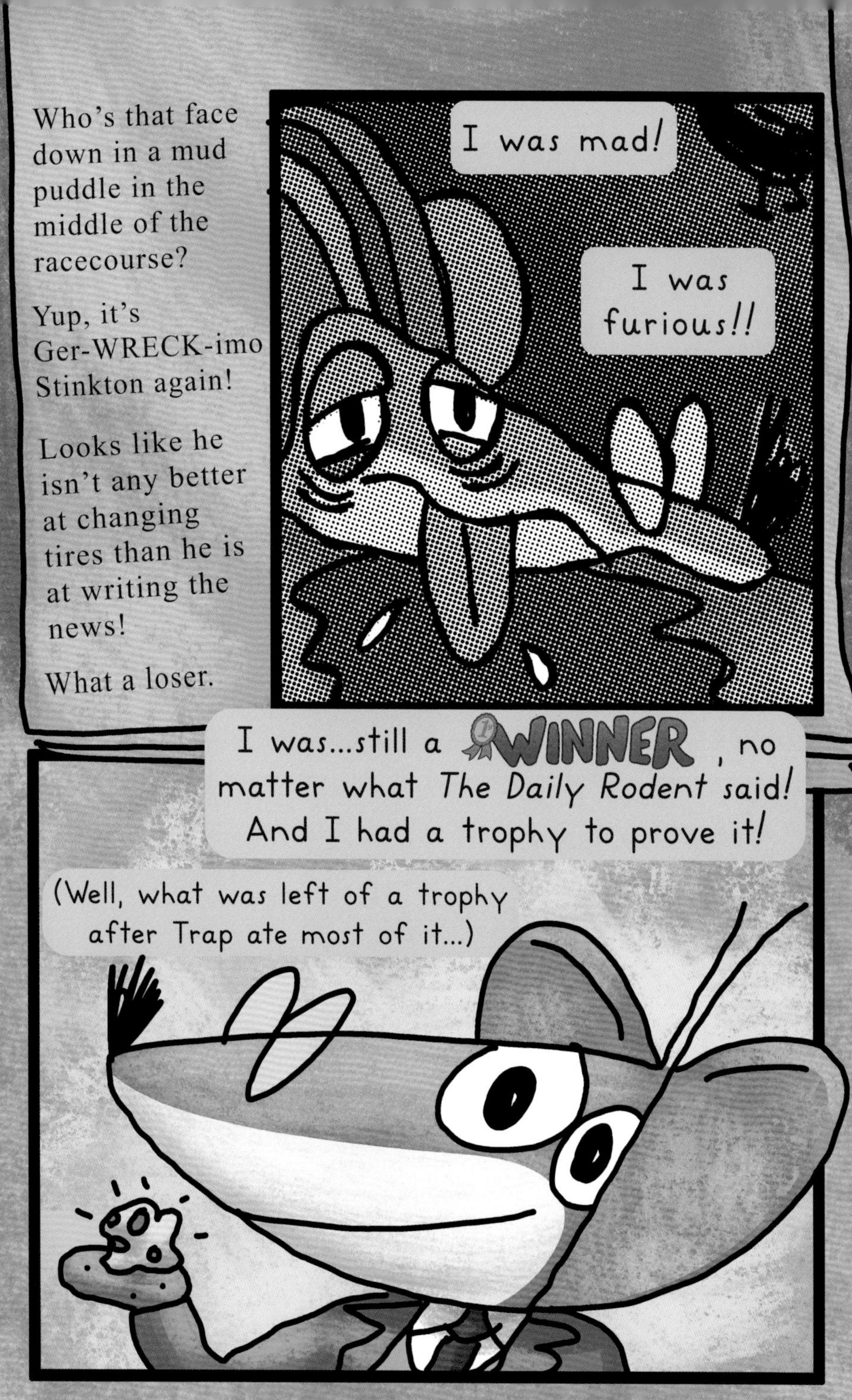
Who's that face down in a mud puddle in the middle of the racecourse?
Yup, it's Ger-WRECK-imo Stinkton again!
Looks like he isn't any better at changing tires than he is at writing the news!
What a loser.
I was mad!
I was furious!!
I was...still a WINNER, no matter what The Daily Rodent said! And I had a trophy to prove it!
(Well, what was left of a trophy after Trap ate most of it...)

Meanwhile...

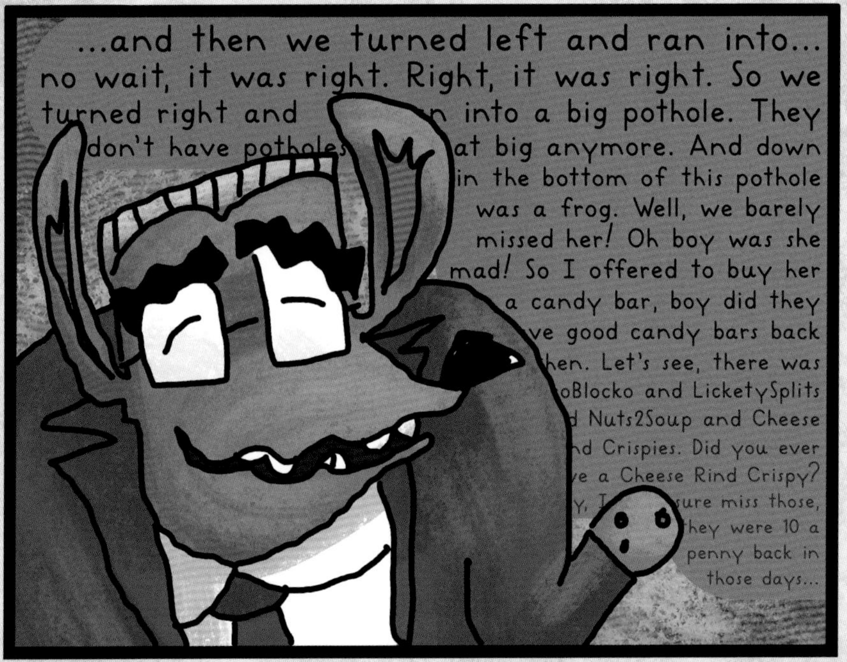
...and then we turned left and ran into...
no wait, it was right. Right, it was right. So we
turned right and into a big pothole. They
don't have potholes at big anymore. And down
in the bottom of this pothole
was a frog. Well, we barely
missed her! Oh boy was she
mad! So I offered to buy her
a candy bar, boy did they
ve good candy bars back
hen. Let's see, there was
oBlocko and LicketySplits
d Nuts2Soup and Cheese
nd Crispies. Did you ever
e a Cheese Rind Crispy?
sure miss those,
they were 10 a
penny back in
those days...

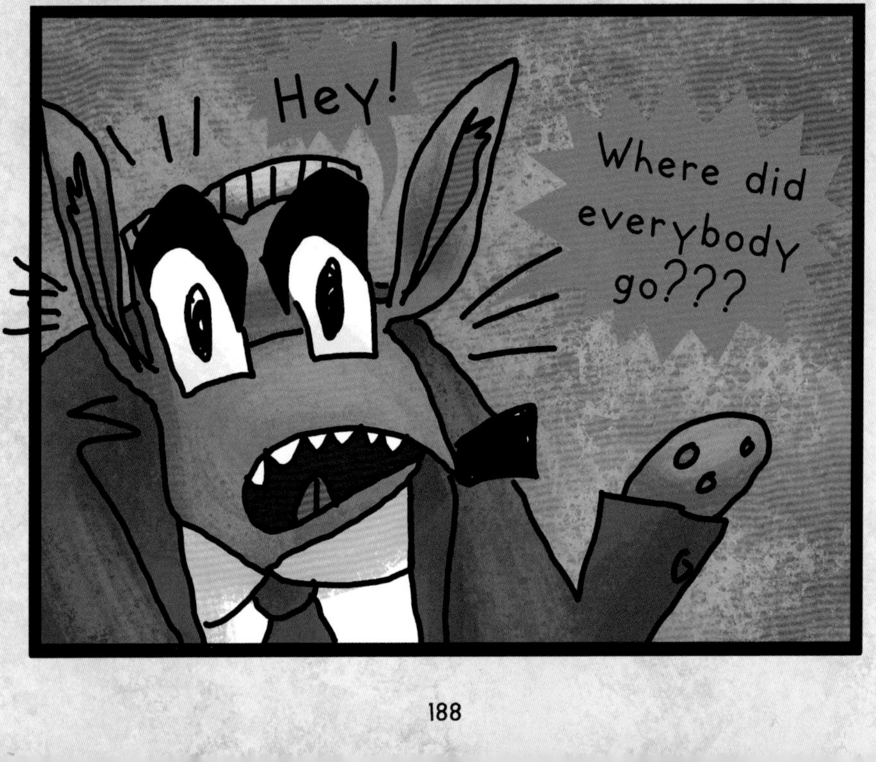
Hey!
Where did everybody go???

The Music of Mac Mousenberry

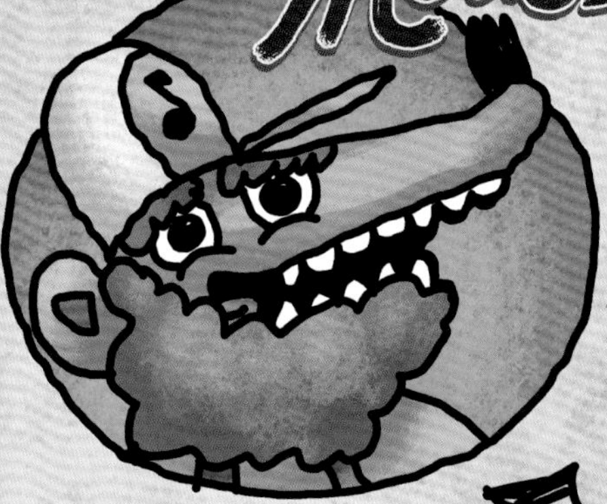

The **MASTER** of the musical chainsaw has chosen his most *touching* songs for this ***EXCLUSIVE*** collection!

INCLUDES THESE BELOVED MELODIES:

- ♪ *Rhapsody in Blue Cheese*
- ♪ *Uptown Logger*
- ♪ *You Are the Cracker Beneath My Croglin*
- ♪ *Summer Bries*
- ♪ *Don't Go Cuttin' My Cheese! (Duet with Bob)*
- ♪ *Mouse Island Polka*
- ♪ *Colby Maybe*

...and *many more!*

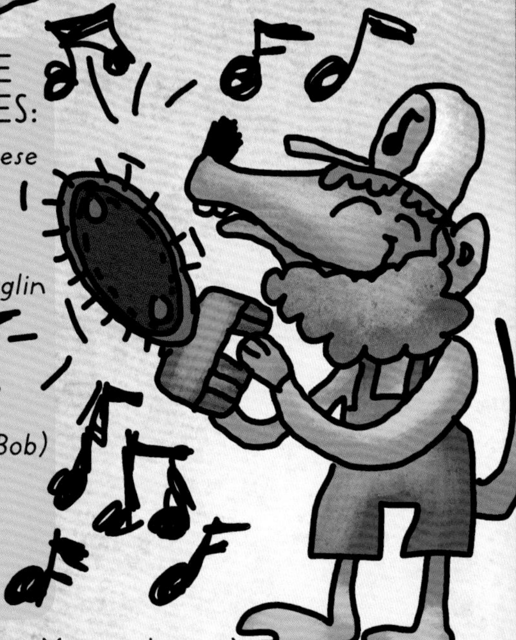

Available ONLY at Mac Mousenberry's Chainsaw Art Gallery and Tractor Repair! Stop by and ask about our special oil change and a song package! Or buy a **BIG WOODEN CAT!**

♬ ♪ YOU CAN'T GO WRONG ♪ ♬
WITH A MAC MOUSENBERRY SONG!

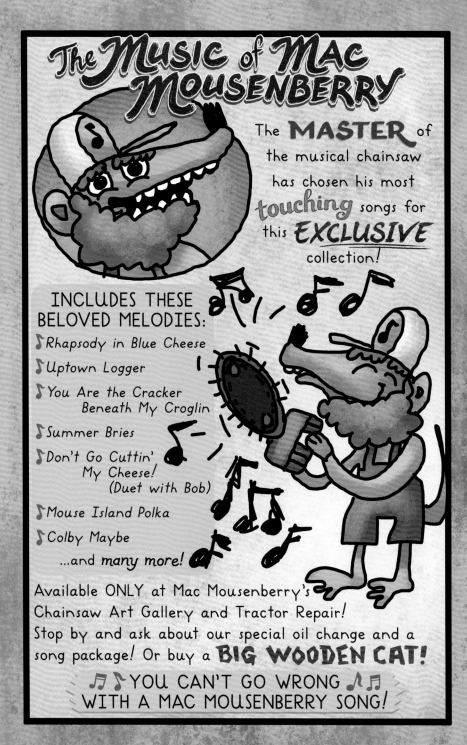

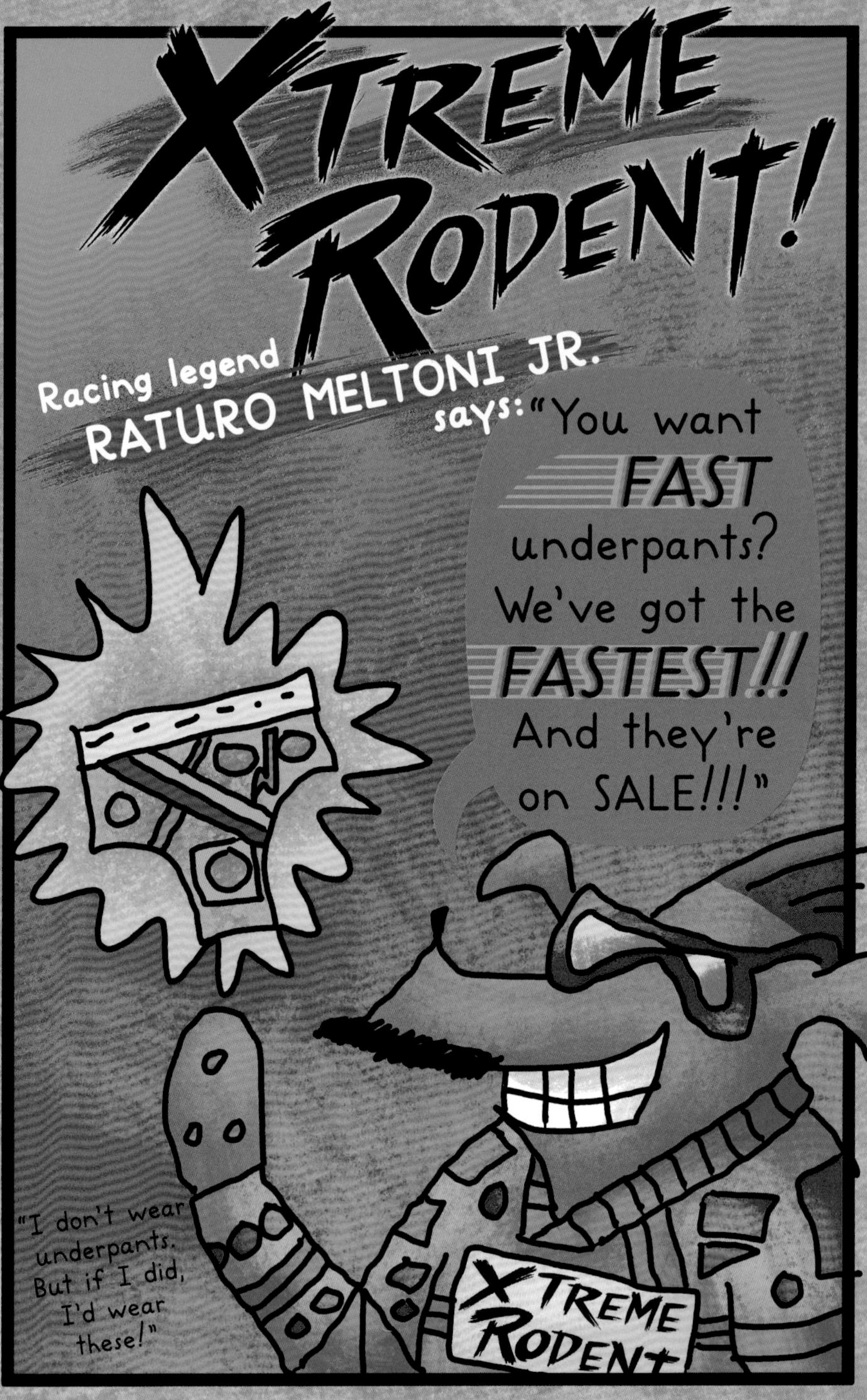
XTREME RODENT!
Racing legend RATURO MELTONI JR. says: "You want FAST underpants? We've got the FASTEST!!! And they're on SALE!!!"
"I don't wear underpants. But if I did, I'd wear these!"
XTREME RODENT

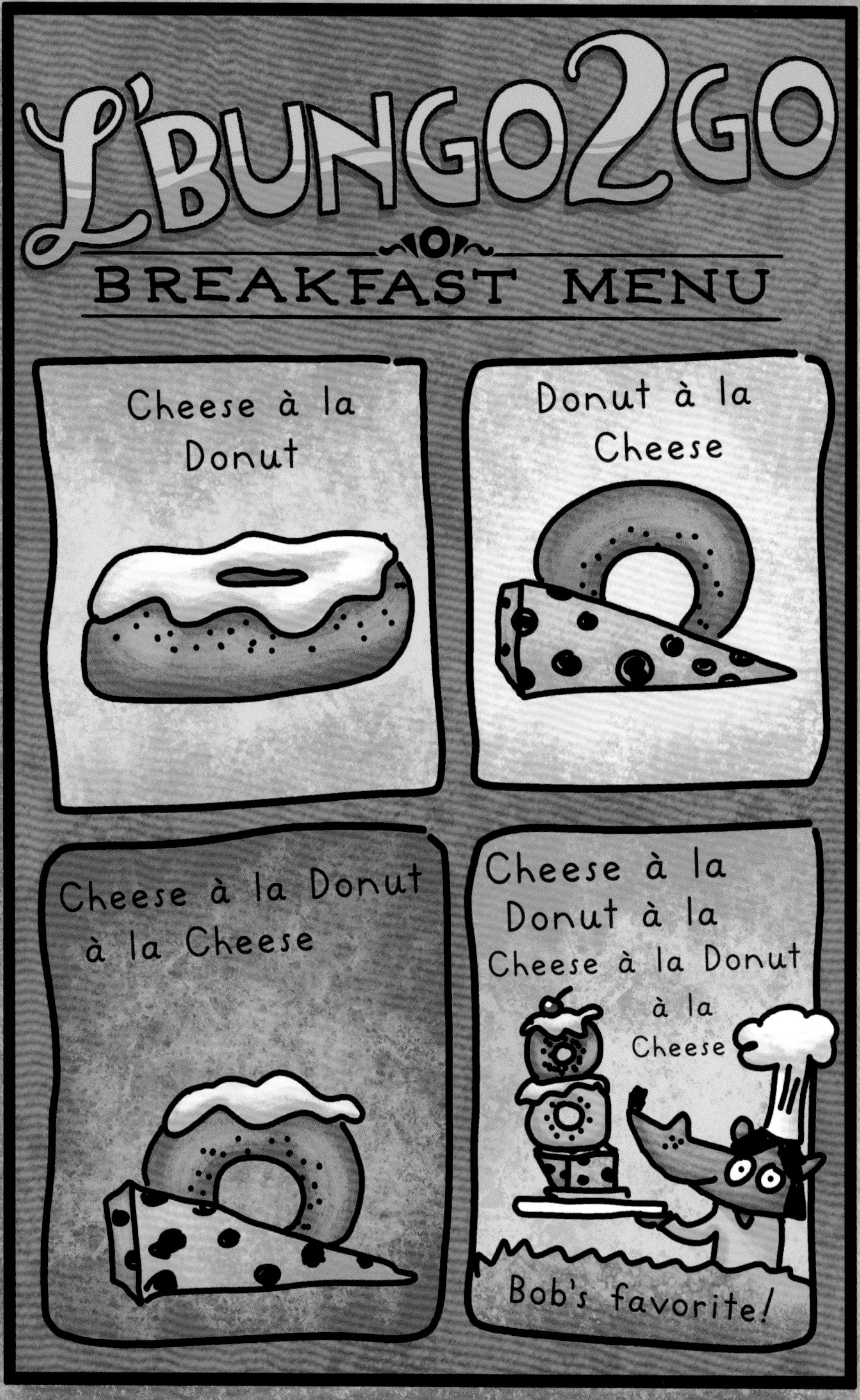
L'BUNGO2GO
BREAKFAST MENU
Cheese à la Donut
Donut à la Cheese
Cheese à la Donut à la Cheese
Cheese à la Donut à la Cheese à la Donut à la Cheese
Bob's favorite!

¢HEAP JUNK FOR LE$$

=YOUR PRANK SUPERSTORE=

OUR PROMISE: We test every prank on our cousin before we will sell it! Guaranteed yuks!

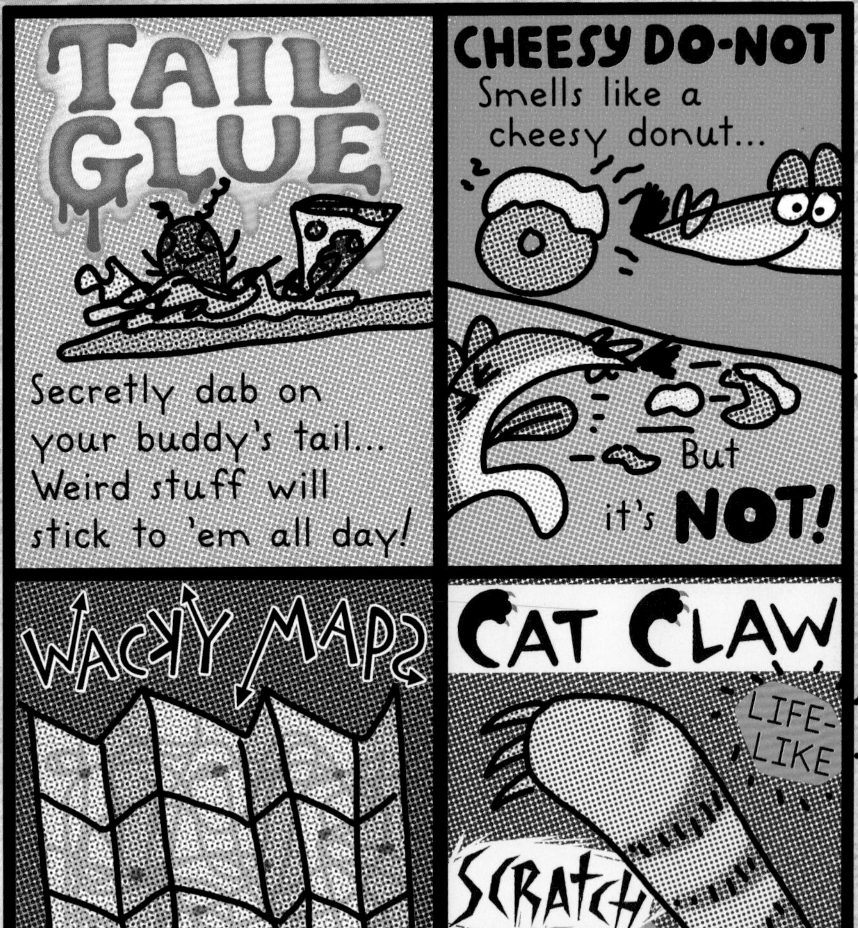

TAIL GLUE
Secretly dab on your buddy's tail... Weird stuff will stick to 'em all day!
CHEESY DO-NOT
Smells like a cheesy donut...
But it's NOT!
WACKY MAPS
Looks real... But every turn is a wrong one!
CAT CLAW
LIFE-LIKE
SCRATCH
your pal's window and listen to 'em
SQUEAL!

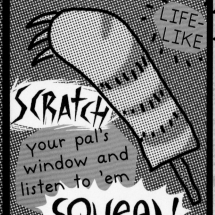

You've never seen
Geronimo Stilton like this before!

Get your paws on the all-new

Geronimo Stilton

graphic novels. You've gouda* have them!

*Gouda is
a type
of cheese.

DON'T MISS ANY ORIGINAL

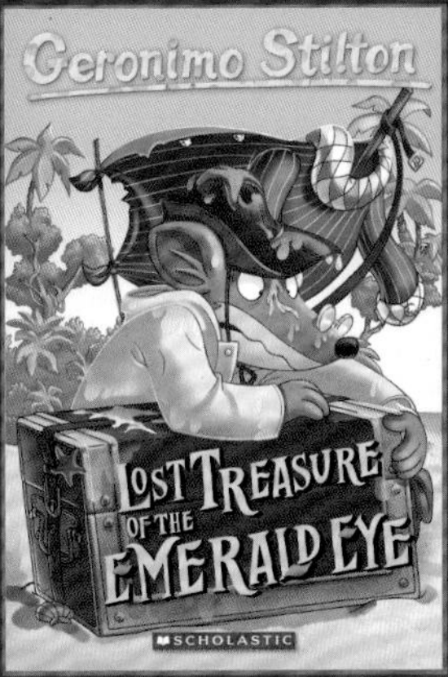
Geronimo Stilton
LOST TREASURE OF THE EMERALD EYE
SCHOLASTIC

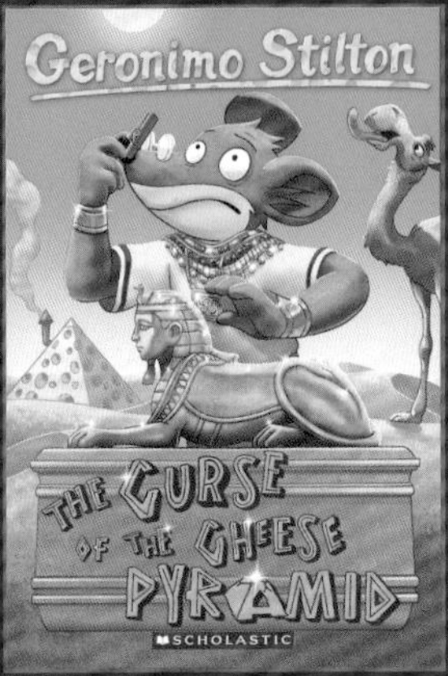
Geronimo Stilton
THE CURSE OF THE CHEESE PYRAMID
SCHOLASTIC

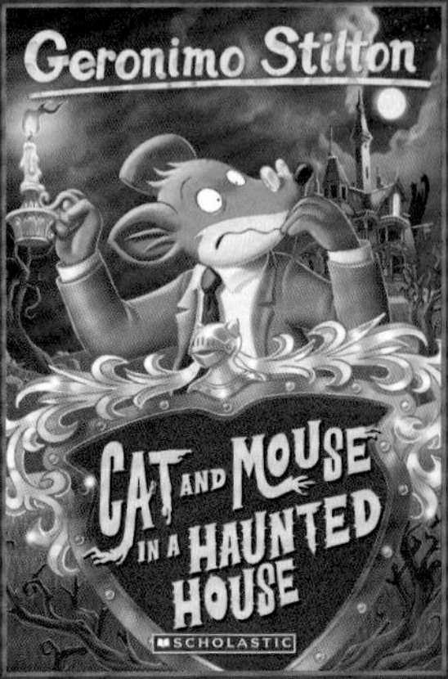
Geronimo Stilton
CAT AND MOUSE IN A HAUNTED HOUSE
SCHOLASTIC

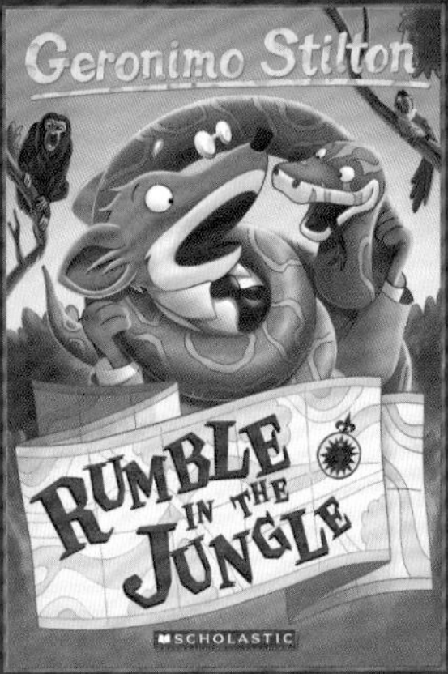
Geronimo Stilton
RUMBLE IN THE JUNGLE
SCHOLASTIC

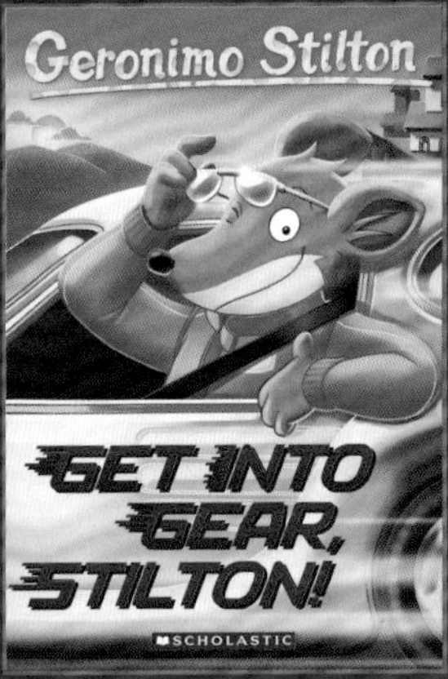
Geronimo Stilton
GET INTO GEAR, STILTON!
SCHOLASTIC

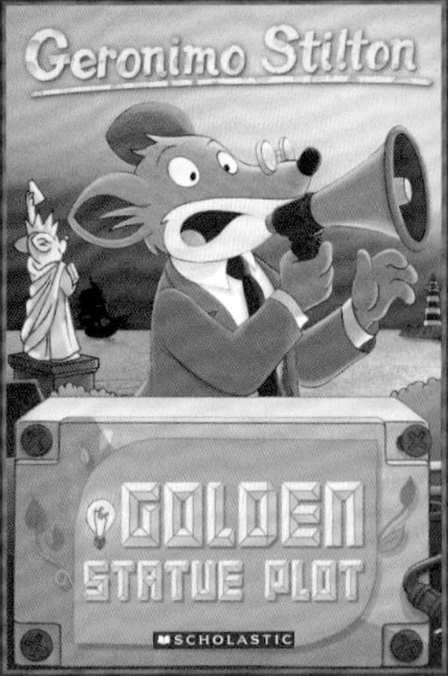
Geronimo Stilton
GOLDEN STATUE PLOT
SCHOLASTIC

OF GERONIMO'S ADVENTURES!

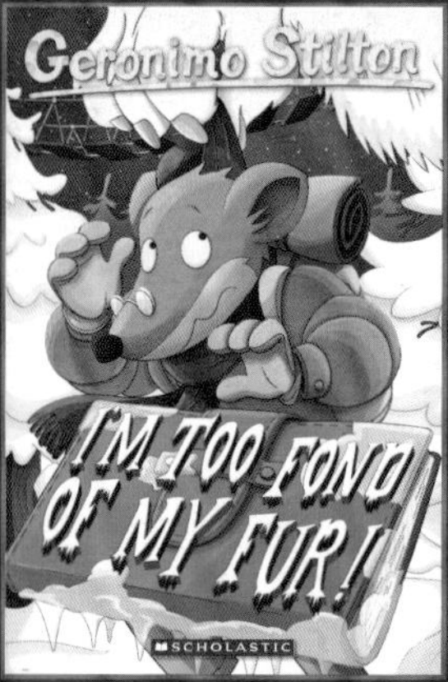
Geronimo Stilton
I'M TOO FOND OF MY FUR!
SCHOLASTIC

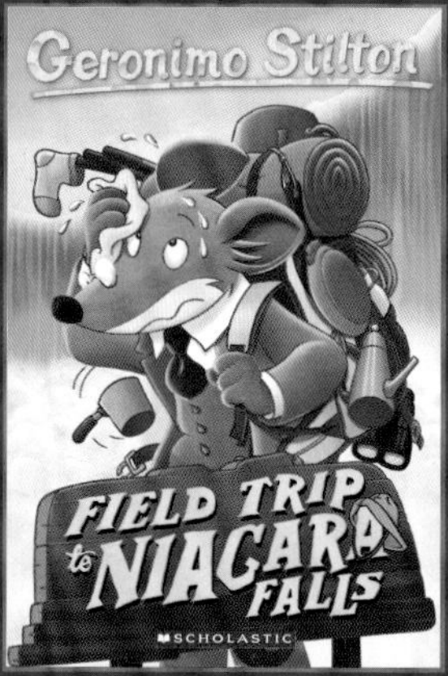
Geronimo Stilton
FIELD TRIP to NIAGARA FALLS
SCHOLASTIC

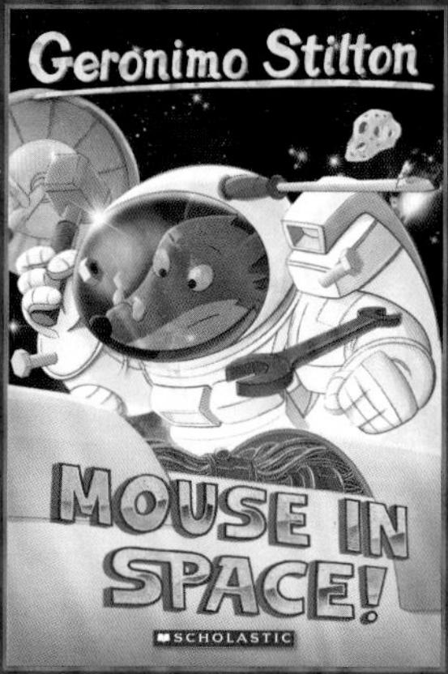
Geronimo Stilton
MOUSE IN SPACE!
SCHOLASTIC

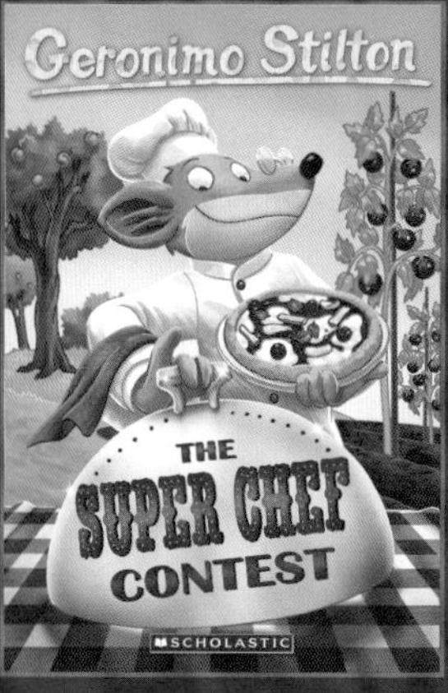
Geronimo Stilton
THE SUPER CHEF CONTEST
SCHOLASTIC

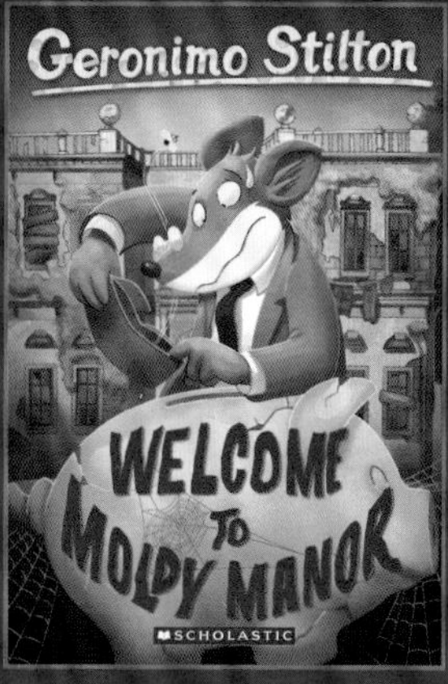
Geronimo Stilton
WELCOME TO MOLDY MANOR
SCHOLASTIC

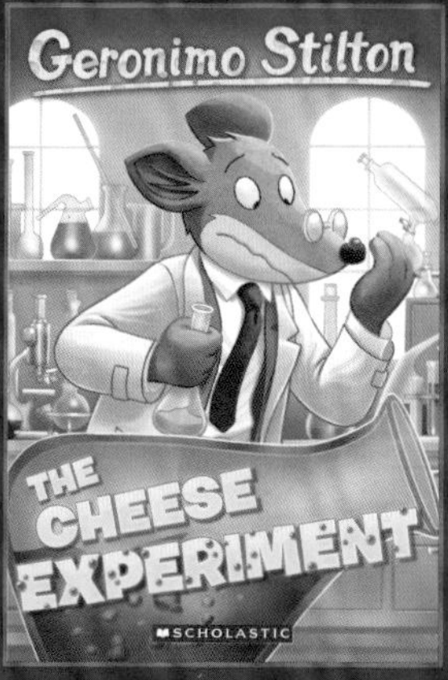
Geronimo Stilton
THE CHEESE EXPERIMENT
SCHOLASTIC

Geronimo Stilton

is an author and the editor-in-chief of *The Rodent's Gazette*, New Mouse City's most popular newspaper. He was awarded the Ratitzer Prize for his investigative journalism and the Anderson 2000 Prize for Personality of the Year. His books have been published all over the world. He loves to spend all his spare time with his family and friends.

Elisabetta Dami was born in Milan, Italy, and is the daughter of a book publisher. She loves adventures of all kinds, all over the world: She has piloted small planes and parachuted, climbed Mount Kilimanjaro, trekked in Nepal, run the New York City Marathon three times, and visited wildlife reservations in Africa where she had close encounters with elephants and gorillas . . . But she believes books are the greatest adventure, and this is why she created Geronimo Stilton!

Tom Angleberger is the author of lots of books about talking animals, talking plants, and even a piece of talking paper, namely Origami Yoda. Since middle school, he has drawn countless comics and cartoons but this is the first time he has drawn a whole graphic novel. He lives in the mountains of Virginia with his wife, Cece Bell, who has also drawn a graphic novel, *El Deafo*.

Corey Barba is a Los Angeles-based cartoonist, writer, and musician. As a kid, he loved monsters, cartoons, puppets, and mad scientists. As an adult, he combines all those things in his work every day. In addition to coloring books for Scholastic, he has worked for DreamWorks Animation, SpongeBob Comics, *MAD* magazine, and lots of other fun stuff!

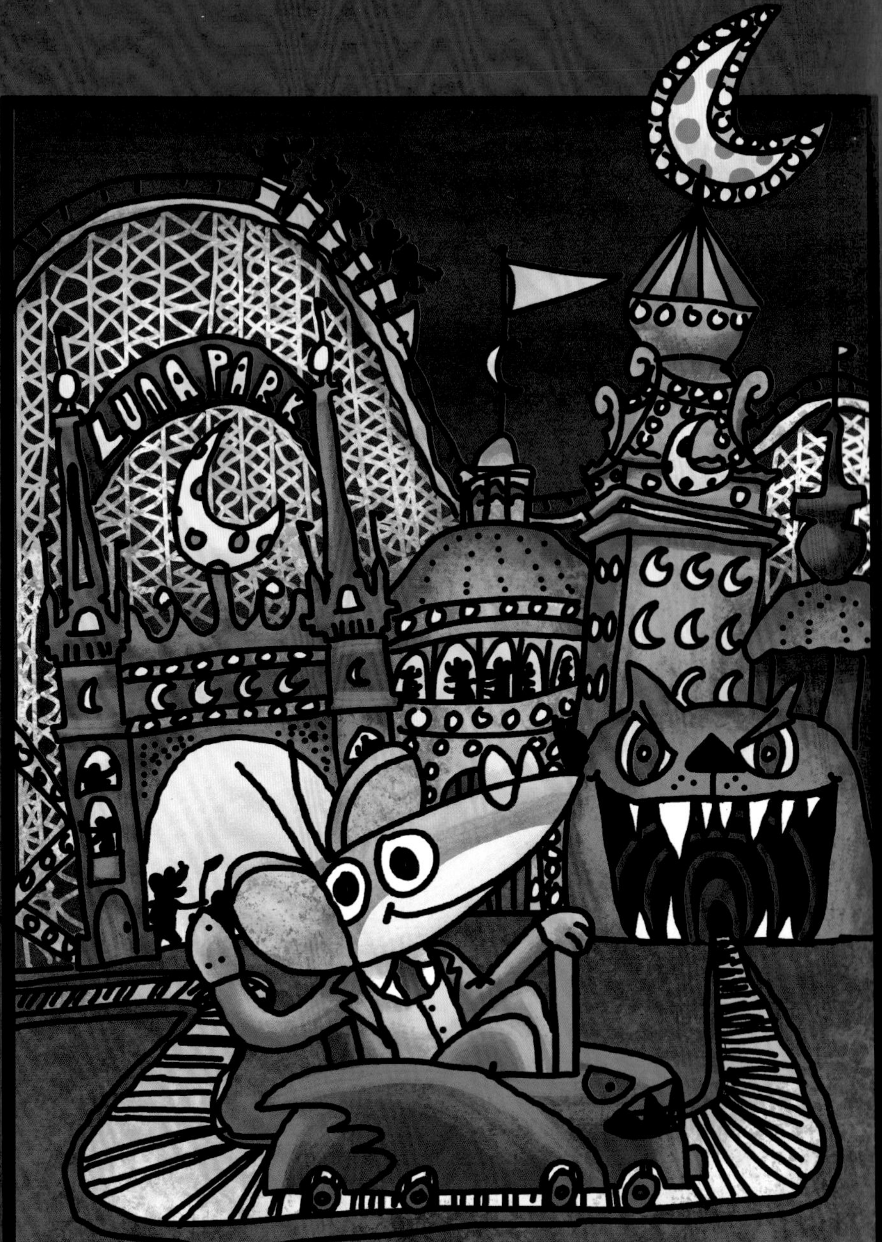
LUNA PARK

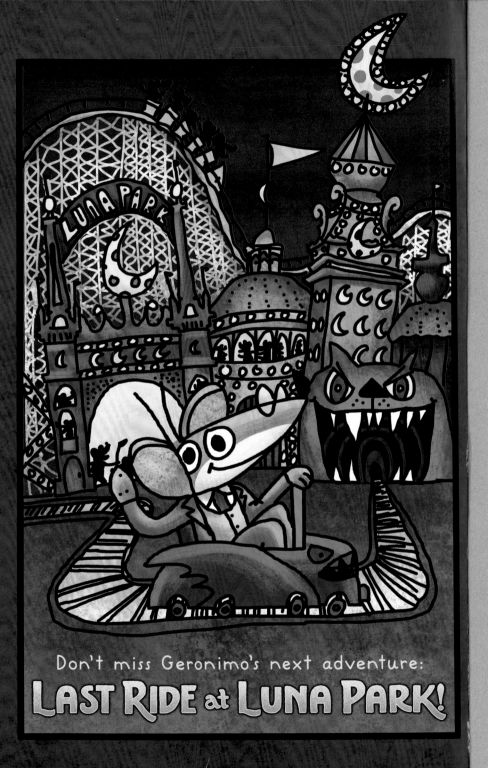

Don't miss Geronimo's next adventure:

LAST RIDE at LUNA PARK!